THE PENGUIN CLASSICS

FOUNDER EDITOR (1944–64): E. V. RIEU

HONORÉ DE BALZAC was born at Tours in 1799, the son of a civil servant. He spent nearly six years as a boarder in a Ven-dôme school, then went to live in Paris, working as a lawyer's clerk, then as a hack writer. Between 1820 and 1824 he wrote a number of novels under various pseudonyms, many of them in collaboration, after which he unsuccessfully tried his luck at publishing, printing and type-founding. At the age of thirty, heavily in debt, he returned to literature with a dedicated fury and wrote the first novel to appear under his own name, *The Chouans*. During the next twenty years he wrote about ninety novels and shorter stories, among them many masterpieces, to which he gave the comprehensive title the *Human Comedy*. He died in 1850, a few months after his marriage to Evelina Hanska, the Polish countess with whom he had maintained amorous relations for eighteen years.

SYLVIA RAPHAEL was educated at George Watson's Ladies' College, Edinburgh, and at the Universities of Edinburgh and Oxford. She has taught French language and literature at the Universities of Glasgow and London, specializing in the field of nineteenth-century French literature.

Honoré de Balzac

SELECTED SHORT STORIES

SELECTED AND TRANSLATED
WITH AN INTRODUCTION BY
SYLVIA RAPHAEL

PENGUIN BOOKS

Penguin Books Ltd, Harmondsworth, Middlesex, England
Penguin Books, 625 Madison Avenue, New York, New York 10022, U.S.A.
Penguin Books Australia Ltd, Ringwood, Victoria, Australia
Penguin Books Canada Ltd, 2801 John Street, Markham, Ontario, Canada
Penguin Books (N.Z.) Ltd, 182–190 Wairau Road, Auckland 10, New Zealand

—

This translation first published 1977

—

Made and printed in Great Britain by
Hazell Watson & Viney Ltd, Aylesbury, Bucks
Set in Monotype Garamond

Contents

Introduction

MANY people are surprised when they first learn that Balzac wrote short stories. He is so well known as the author of often very long novels that it is not always realized that there are nearly fifty short stories of varying length in the *Comédie humaine* (the name he gave to his collected fictional writings) and that he wrote many of these before he started on what were to become his longer and better-known works. Short stories were popular in the early 1830s in France and by the end of 1832 Balzac had written nearly thirty. One critic remarked with some surprise that 'M. de Balzac has tried to write something other than short stories', when *The Country Doctor* (a full-length novel) was published in 1833. But though, after 1833, Balzac turned most of his attention to longer works he continued to write short stories throughout his life, the last being published in 1845, five years before his death in 1850.

It is natural that in so prolific a writer the quality of his work should be uneven, and among the many short stories that Balzac wrote some appear to us today to be trivial, others too melodramatic or sentimental and others again preoccupied with mystical or philosophical thoughts which can only be fully understood in connection with some of the full-length novels. But most of the stories have the great merit of any good tale, namely, they arouse the reader's curiosity and keep him in suspense so that he wants to know what happens. Very often the story starts with a mysterious situation. An unknown man is following a terrified old lady through deserted streets in the snow; later a stranger penetrates the hiding place of nuns and a priest. The reader wants to know who is this man

7

and is kept in suspense till the end, when the answer is revealed ('An Incident in the Reign of Terror'). In 'The Conscript', Madame de Dey suddenly refuses to receive visitors. The reader finds out why later on in the story, but receives a shock of surprise when, at the end, it is revealed that the man who arrives at Madame de Dey's house is not her son. Sometimes there is a little delay in introducing the problem which will puzzle the reader, as in 'The Atheist's Mass', when it is only after the great surgeon's atheism has been amply demonstrated that we discover he goes regularly to Mass. The description of the deserted house and garden in 'La Grande Bretèche' prepares the way for the mystery which surrounds the desolate mansion, and the dreary salt-marshes of Brittany are a necessary part of the tragic atmosphere which surrounds the mysterious figure on the rock in 'A Tragedy by the Sea'. But whether the mystery is introduced right at the start, or only after some preliminary descriptive or explanatory pages, the tension is heightened as the story proceeds and the reader is left in suspense till the unexpected, often ironic, sometimes tragic dénouement. It is not for nothing that Balzac has been called the father of the detective story.

Balzac's short stories have, however, more to offer than just a good, melodramatic yarn. Balzac combined with his lively imagination a minute observation of the details of everyday life, acute social and psychological insight and a keen sense of the irony of the human condition. In fact, the short stories contain many of the same qualities which have made his great reputation as a novelist. Balzac was born in 1799, which meant that although he was too young to experience the grim days of the Revolution and the Reign of Terror he knew people who had, and he himself lived through the turbulent years of the Napoleonic wars, the fall of Napoleon, the Restoration and the 1830 Revolution. His stories thus contain an interest which is often incidental to the tale they tell. We are perhaps, today, not so interested in Balzac's theories of telepathy which inspired the theme of 'The Conscript', but if we want to know what it felt like to be an aristocrat in a small French provincial town during the Reign of Terror, the description of Madame de Dey's life at Carentan tells us eloquently. Similarly the atmosphere of panic in 'An Incident in the Reign of Terror' brings vividly home to us the experiences many royalists must have had at that time as well as adding to the tension of the story. 'Facino Cane' may seem a rather far-fetched and romanticized tale, but the background setting, which Balzac himself says has nothing to do with the story, gives a picture of working-class life which has an interest of its own. The plot of 'The Purse' verges perhaps on the insipid and sentimental, that of 'Domestic Peace' on the trivial, but the former gives a touching picture of some of the victims of France's political vicissitudes and the latter shows us an aspect of the Napoleonic era in all its splendour and glory. The violence of the past may be no consolation for that of our own time, but 'El Verdugo' reminds us that the cruelty and heroism of war were as tragic in the days of the Peninsular War as they are now. In 'The Red Inn' we have both a vivid picture of a Rhineland inn in 1799 and an indication of a young German's reactions to the French occupation of that area during the Revolutionary wars. Balzac gives us a fascinating insight into the life of a past age and the short stories, like the novels, are full of interest to anyone who wants to know what it felt like to be alive during one of the most violent and disturbed periods of French history.

But human nature does not change as fundamentally or as fast as social and economic conditions, and many of its aspects portrayed by Balzac are just as relevant today as they were over a century ago. We see human greed, for instance, not only in the crude form of murder for the sake of money in 'The Red Inn', but more subtly when the young men at the end of the story all vote in favour of the narrator's *not* marrying the heiress of the guilty businessman, so that they may have a chance of marrying her themselves. In 'La Grande Bretèche', where three different narrators contribute to the tension of the story, it gradually becomes apparent that the garrulous lawyer, the chatty landlady and the buxom servant-girl are less affected by the tragedy than concerned for their own financial interest. Self-interest may be mixed with more generous motives in the behaviour of Madame de Dey's suitors in 'The Conscript', though Balzac certainly suggests that the latter are merely a cover for the former. Another side of human nature is movingly demonstrated in 'The Atheist's Mass', where the unselfish devotion of the humble water-carrier is matched only by the profound gratitude and deep religious feeling (in the broadest sense of those words) of the irascible, often selfish, eminent atheistic surgeon. Balzac's awareness of the complexity of human beings, of the coexistence within them of conflicting traits, comes out clearly in the story of Desplein who, self-centred and ambitious, forms a bond with the water-carrier which survives even the latter's death. The water-carrier himself is sufficient evidence that Balzac, despite his royalist and anti-democratic opinions, had a profound sympathy with the poor and under-privileged. Similarly the poor fisherman in 'A Tragedy by the Sea' and the workers and the charwoman in 'Facino Cane' are depicted with compassion and a deep appreciation both of their problems and of their worth.

The contradictory feelings of human beings give ample scope for the irony which is never long absent from Balzac's work. Sometimes this is expressed frivolously, as in Madame de Listomère of 'A Study in Feminine Psychology', sometimes tragically, as in Pierre Cambremer of 'A Tragedy by the Sea', or surprisingly, as in the executioner of 'An Incident in the Reign of Terror'. There is a humorous touch in the ironic comment on the Marquis de Listomère, who reads the newspaper 'to acquire, with the journalist's help, a personal opinion on the state of France', and humour of a more sustained kind in 'Pierre Grassou', which contains amusing caricature of the bourgeois attitude to art, a good-natured portrait of the mediocre but financially successful painter, and a dig at the crafty trickery of the art dealer who trades on the vanity of the bourgeois and the financial need of the artist.

Balzac is constantly aware too of the irony provided by chance in human affairs. With his melodramatic imagination and love of extremes he sometimes overdoes the ironic endings of his tales; yet the contrast between the grandiose longings of Facino Cane and his death from a chill, recorded in a brief, final sentence, is tellingly effective. The death of Madame de Vaudremont, the rich, aristocratic coquette of 'Domestic Peace', in a fire at a society ball appears more artificially contrived in the interests of dramatic irony. Other examples of ironic turns of fate are the arrival of the conscript instead of Madame de Dey's son, and the execution of Prosper Magnan in 'The Red Inn' for a murder he has dreamed of but not committed. The short stories thus frequently illustrate the conflicts and contradictions inherent in human life and personality.

Those already familiar with some of the novels of the *Comédie humaine* will find again in the short stories many of the characters they have met elsewhere and sometimes they will learn more about an old acquaintance by seeing him in a different situation. Eugène de Rastignac, for instance, who in *Old Goriot* is a struggling student living in a seedy Parisian boarding-house, is presented at a happier stage of his career in 'A Study in Feminine Psychology'. It is almost with the pleasure of meeting an old friend that we find him sipping tea in his dressing-gown with his feet up on the fire-dogs. Bianchon, the medical student who comes in to dinner in the boarding-house of *Old Goriot*, figures in several of the short stories as a narrator, particularly in 'The Atheist's Mass', where we see how his career is furthered by his association with Desplein. That distinguished surgeon attends to many of the characters in the *Comédie humaine* and the account of his early life and career becomes all the more interesting when we are already acquainted with the personality. 'A Tragedy by the Sea' adds to our knowledge of the philosophic genius, Louis Lambert, whose madness and subsequent death are related in the novel of that name. Readers of *César Birotteau* will be interested to note the reference to César's employer and predecessor, Monsieur Ragon, in his perfumier's shop, the Reine des Fleurs, at the end of 'An Incident in the Reign of Terror'. Such readers, as well as those familiar with *Eugénie Grandet* and *La Rabouilleuse*, will know all about the unfortunate results of Maître Roguin's bankruptcy referred to by Monsieur Regnault in 'La Grande Bretèche'. And if you have

read *Lost Illusions* you will have met d'Arthez who, like Desplein, struggled with poverty in the Rue des Quatre-Vents.
The short stories are, in fact, intimately related to the rest of
the *Comedie humaine*, and to those who may be at first a little
daunted by the length of the novels, these tales can perhaps
provide an accessible introduction to it. On the other hand,
those who have already read some of the novels will often
find that themes and characters reappear in the short stories
in a way that can help in the understanding and appreciation of
the longer works.

The more we know about the life and personality of Balzac
the more we find him in his work, and a further interest of his
short stories lies in the glimpses they afford of the personality
and experiences of their author. There are references to his
own life at the beginning of 'Facino Cane' when he talks of
his time in the Rue de Lesdiguières where he lived in a garret,
struggling to make his way as an author, subsisting on a diet
like that of Desplein or Pierre Grassou in the days of their
poverty. When in 'The Atheist's Mass' Balzac writes of
'creditors being today the most real shape assumed by the
ancient Furies', it is clearly his own debts he is thinking of,
and similarly, when Desplein describes his poverty-stricken
youth and inveighs against the 'obstacles which hatred, envy,
jealousy and calumny have placed between me and success',
Balzac is describing his own frustrations. A quite different
aspect of his personality is revealed in Rastignac's morning
reveries in 'A Study in Feminine Psychology'. The most
interesting aspects of Balzac, however, are those which relate
to his work as an imaginative writer, and here again the short
stories have something to offer. In 'Facino Cane', for instance, he gives us an account of his remarkable ability to
imagine himself into the minds and hearts of others by what
he calls 'a power of intuitive observation' which enables him
'to live their lives'. In the same story he shows the quality of
his imagination when he prefers his own dream-picture of
Venice, unsullied by reality. 'I gazed . . . at all those wonders
which the scholar appreciates all the more, in that he can
colour them as he pleases and does not deprive his dreams of

their poetry by the sight of reality.' The narrator of 'La Grande Bretèche', who enjoys composing 'delightful stories' about the ruined house, 'intoxicates' himself with 'unpublished fictions', and uses the legal information given by Monsieur Regnault as the basis for an absorbing 'Radcliffe-like novel', obviously bears a strong resemblance to Balzac himself. And we get a vivid picture of Balzac's literary ambitions in this description of Louis Lambert: 'I was standing, compass in hand, on a rock a hundred fathoms above the ocean where white horses were riding on the breakers, and I was mapping out my future, filling it with literary works, like a surveyor who plans fortresses and palaces on a piece of wasteland.' These words were written in 1834; till his death in 1850 Balzac was incessantly occupied in producing those literary works which have proved more durable than many fortresses and palaces built at the same period.

S. D. R.

The translation follows the text given by Pierre Citron in the Intégrale edition of *La Comédie humaine* (Editions du Seuil, 1965). This is based on the copy of the Furne edition of *La Comédie humaine* which belonged to Balzac and which contains his own corrections.

El Verdugo

THE clock in the belfry of the little town of Menda had just struck midnight. At that moment a young French officer, leaning on the parapet of a long terrace which bordered the gardens of the castle at Menda, seemed more deeply lost in thought than was consistent with the carefree life of a soldier. But one must add that never were time, place and night more suited to meditation. The beautiful Spanish sky described an azure dome above his head. The gleam of the stars and the gentle moonlight illuminated a charming valley which spread out prettily at his feet. Leaning against an orange tree in bloom, the battalion commander could see, a hundred feet below him, the town of Menda, which seemed to be sheltering from the north winds at the foot of the rock on which the castle was built. When he turned his head he could see the sea, whose gleaming waters framed the landscape with a broad band of silver. The castle was lit up. The happy commotion of a ball, the sound of the orchestra, the laughter of officers and their partners, could be heard mingled with the distant murmur of the waves. The coolness of the night gave a kind of energy to his body, wearied by the heat of the day. And the gardens were planted with scented trees and sweet-smelling flowers, so that the young man felt as if steeped in a bath of perfume.

Menda castle belonged to a Spanish grandee, who at that time was living in it with his family. Throughout the evening the older daughter had looked at the officer with an interest marked with such sadness that the compassionate feeling expressed by the Spanish girl might well have been the cause of the Frenchman's reverie. Clara was beautiful and although she had three brothers and a sister, the Marquis de Léganès' possessions seemed substantial enough to lead Victor Marchand to believe that the young lady would have a rich dowry.

But how could he presume to believe that the daughter of the old man – of all the noblemen in Spain the most infatuated with his grandeeship – might be given to the son of a Parisian grocer? Besides, the French were hated. The battalion commanded by Victor Marchand had been quartered in the little town of Menda in order to control the surrounding countryside, which was under the sway of the Marquis de Léganès, because the marquis had been suspected by General G–t–r, who governed the province, of organizing a rising in favour of Ferdinand VII. A recent dispatch from Marshal Ney gave grounds for fearing that the English would soon land on the coast, and mentioned the marquis as a man who maintained intelligence links with the London Cabinet. So in spite of the fact that the Spaniard had received Victor Marchand and his soldiers well, the young officer was continually on his guard. As he made his way to the terrace where he was going to study the state of the town and countryside entrusted to his care, he was wondering how he should interpret the friendship which the marquis had never ceased to show him, and how the calm of the district could be reconciled with his general's anxieties. But for the last moment or two these thoughts had been banished from the young commander's mind by a feeling of prudence and by a very legitimate curiosity. He had just noticed quite a large number of lights in the town. Although it was the Saint Jacques festival, he had that very morning ordered lights to be put out at the hour prescribed by his regulations. Only the castle had been exempted from this ruling. He could see his soldiers' bayonets gleaming here and there at their usual stations, but there was a solemn silence and nothing suggested that the Spaniards were a prey to the excitement of a festival. After trying to explain to himself the townspeople's infringement of the regulations, he thought this breach of the curfew contained a mystery which was all the more inexplicable since he had left officers in charge of the night-watch. With youthful impetuosity he was about to dart through a breach in the wall so as to hurry down the rocky slope and thus reach a little sentry-post at the entrance to the town on the castle side more quickly than by the usual road, when a faint sound stopped him in his course. He thought he could hear the sound of a woman's light step on the sanded path. He turned round and saw nothing, but he was struck by the extraordinary brilliance of the ocean. Suddenly he noticed a sight so disastrous that he remained motionless with surprise, thinking that his eyes deceived him. By the growing light of the moon he could make out sails some considerable distance away. He started and tried to convince himself that this sight was an optical illusion caused by the fantastic effects of the waves and the moon. Just then, a hoarse voice pronounced the officer's name; he looked towards the breach and saw slowly rising above it the head of the soldier whom he had ordered to accompany him to the castle.

'Is that you, Major?'

'Yes, well what is it?' the young man said in a low voice. A kind of presentiment warned him to act cautiously.

'Those rascals over there are moving about like worms and I have come quickly to tell you about the little things I have noticed.'

'Speak,' replied Victor Marchand.

'I have just been following a man from the castle who came in this direction with a lantern in his hand. A lantern is a terribly suspicious object! I don't think *that* Christian needs to light candles at this hour. They want to destroy us, I said to myself, and I began to follow close on his heels. So, Major, I have discovered an interesting bundle of wood on a block of stone three paces from here.'

A terrible shout, which suddenly rang out in the town, interrupted the soldier. A sharp flash lit up the major. The poor grenadier received a bullet in his head and fell. A fire of burning straw and dry wood made a brilliant conflagration, ten paces from the young man. The musical instruments and the laughter could no longer be heard coming from the ball-room. A deathly silence, interrupted by groans, had suddenly taken the place of the noise and music of the party. The cannon shot rang out over the white expanse of the ocean. A cold sweat broke out on the young officer's brow. He had no sword. He realized that his soldiers had perished and that the

English were about to land. He saw himself dishonoured if he lived; he saw himself brought before a court-martial. He then estimated with a glance the depth of the valley and was about to rush down into it when Clara's hand seized his.

'Fly,' she said, 'my brothers are following me in order to kill you. At the foot of the cliff over there you will find Juanito's Andalusian horse. Go!'

She pushed him. The young man, amazed, looked at her for a moment. But presently, in obedience to the instinct of self-preservation which never deserts even the strongest of men, he dashed forward into the castle grounds, going in the direction that she had indicated, and ran over rocks which, until then, had been a path only for goats. He heard Clara shouting to her brothers to pursue him. He heard his murderers' steps. He heard several bullets whistle past his ears, but he reached the valley, found the horse, mounted it and disappeared with the speed of lightning.

In a few hours the young officer reached the headquarters of General G–t–r, whom he found at dinner with his staff.

'I bring you my head!' cried the battalion commander as he arrived looking pale and distraught. He sat down and recounted the horrible incident. His tale was received with a terrifying silence.

'I consider you as more unfortunate than criminal,' the terrible general replied at last. 'You are not responsible for the Spaniards' crime and unless the marshal decides otherwise, I absolve you from blame.' These words gave only slight consolation to the unhappy officer.

'When the Emperor knows about it!' he exclaimed.

'He will want to have you shot,' said the general, 'but we shall see. Now let's say no more about this,' he added severely, 'except to avenge it in a way that will impress a healthy terror on this country where they make war like savages.'

An hour later, a whole regiment, a cavalry detachment and an artillery convoy were on their way. The general and Victor marched at the head of the column. The soldiers, who had been told of the massacre of their comrades, were possessed by an unparalleled rage. The distance between the town of

Menda and their headquarters was covered with miraculous speed. On the way, the general found whole villages under arms. Each one of these miserable, straggling townships was surrounded and its inhabitants decimated.

By an inexplicable chance, the English ships had stopped and advanced no further. But it was learned later that these ships were carrying only artillery and that they were in advance of the other transport vessels. Thus the town of Menda, deprived of its expected defenders whose arrival appeared to be heralded by the appearance of the English sails, was surrounded by French troops who hardly needed to fire a shot. The terror-stricken inhabitants offered to surrender unconditionally. With a self-sacrificing devotion which was not unusual in the Peninsula, the Frenchmen's murderers, judging from the general's reputation for cruelty that Menda would perhaps be set on fire and the whole population put to the sword, offered to give themselves up to him. He accepted the offer, stipulating as a condition that the inhabitants of the castle, from the lowest servant to the marquis, should be delivered into his hands. These terms being agreed, the general promised to spare the rest of the population and to prevent his soldiers from pillaging the town or setting fire to it. A huge indemnity was demanded and the richest inhabitants gave themselves up as hostages in order to guarantee the payment which had to be made within twenty-four hours.

The general took all the precautions necessary for the safety of his troops, provided for the defence of the district and refused to billet his soldiers in the houses. After organizing their camp he went up to the castle and took possession of it in a military manner. The members of the Léganès family and the servants were carefully watched, bound and confined in the room where the ball had taken place. From the windows of that room the terrace which dominated the town could easily be seen. The headquarters were set up in an adjoining gallery, where the general first of all held a council about the steps to be taken to oppose the English landing. After dispatching an aide-de-camp to Marshal Ney and giving orders to establish coastal batteries, the general and his staff dealt with the prisoners. Two hundred Spaniards, who had been surrendered by the inhabitants of the town, were immediately shot on the terrace. After this military execution the general ordered as many gallows to be erected on the terrace as there were people in the hall of the castle, and the town executioner to be summoned. Victor Marchand took advantage of the time which remained before dinner to go and see the prisoners. He soon returned to the general.

'I come to ask you to exercise mercy,' he said in a voice filled with emotion.

'You!' exclaimed the general in a tone of bitter irony.

'Alas,' replied Victor, 'the acts of mercy I ask for are sad ones. The marquis, seeing the gallows erected, expressed the hope that you would change the method of execution for his family and begs you to have those of noble birth beheaded.'

'So be it,' said the general.

'They also ask to be given the consolations of religion and to be freed from their bonds. They promise not to try to escape.'

'I agree,' said the general, 'but you will answer for them.'

'Furthermore the old man offers you his whole fortune if you will spare his young son.'

'Indeed!' replied the general. 'His property already belongs to King Joseph.' He stopped. A contemptuous thought wrinkled his brow and he added, 'I will give them more than they want. I appreciate the importance of his last request. Well, let him buy immortality for his name but let Spain remember for ever his treason and his punishment. I shall give life and fortune to that one of his sons who will fulfil the task of executioner. Go, and say no more about it.'

Dinner was served. The officers sat down to dinner and satisfied appetites sharpened by fatigue. Only one of them, Victor Marchand, was absent from the feast. After hesitating a long time he went into the hall where the proud Léganès family lay in distress, and looked sadly at the sight which the room presented. It was the room where, the previous evening, he had seen the heads of the two girls and the three young men whirl round in the waltz. He shuddered to think that very soon those heads would roll, cut off by the executioner's knife. Tied to their gilded chairs the father and mother, the three sons and the two daughters were completely motionless. Eight servants were standing with their hands tied behind their backs. These fifteen people looked at each other solemnly and their eyes betrayed little of the feelings in their hearts. A profound resignation and regret at having failed in their enterprise could be read in the faces of some of them. Motionless soldiers were guarding them, respecting the grief of these cruel enemies. An expression of curiosity lit up their faces when Victor appeared. He gave the order to untie the condemned family and with his own hands loosened the ropes which made Clara a prisoner on her chair. She smiled sadly. The officer could not help touching her arms lightly as he admired her dark hair and slender figure. She was a real Spaniard. She had a Spanish complexion, Spanish eyes with long curving eyelashes and pupils blacker than a raven's wing.

'Did you succeed?' she asked, giving him one of those melancholy smiles in which there still is something of a young girl's charm.

Victor could not suppress a groan. He looked in turn at the three brothers and at Clara. One of them, the eldest, was thirty. Although small and rather ill-favoured, he had a proud, disdainful bearing, was not without a certain nobility of manner and did not seem to lack that delicacy of feeling which made Spanish gallantry so famous in the past. His name was Juanito. The second son, Philippe, was about twenty. He looked like Clara. The youngest was eight. A painter would have seen in Manuel's features some of that Roman firmness which David has given to the children in his Republican pictures. The old marquis had a head of white hair which looked as if it had escaped from a Murillo painting. At the sight of the family, the young officer shook his head, having no hope of seeing the general's offer accepted by one of these four people. Nevertheless he had the courage to entrust it to Clara. The Spanish girl shuddered at first but she quickly resumed her calm expression and kneeled before her father.

'Oh,' she said, 'make Juanito swear that he will faithfully obey the orders that you will give him, and we shall be satisfied.'

The marchioness gave a start of hope, but when, leaning towards her husband, she heard Clara's horrible secret, the mother fainted. Juanito understood it all. He paced up and down like a lion in a cage. Victor took upon himself to dismiss the soldiers, after obtaining an assurance of absolute submission from the marquis. The servants were taken away and handed over to the executioner who hanged them. When only Victor was left on guard over the family, the old father got up.

'Juanito,' he said.

Juanito replied only with a movement of the head which was equivalent to a refusal, fell back on to his chair and dry-eyed gave his parents a terrible look. Clara came and sat on his knee and said cheerfully, as she put her arms round his neck and kissed his eyes. 'If you knew how sweet death would be to me if it were given by you. I would not have to endure the loathsome touch of the executioner's hands. You will cure me of the ills which were awaiting me, and ... my dear Juanito, you didn't want me to belong to any man, so ...'

Her soft eyes darted a fiery glance at Victor as if to arouse in Juanito's heart his horror of the French.

'Take courage,' said his brother Philippe, 'otherwise our almost royal line will become extinct.'

Suddenly Clara got up. The group which had formed around Juanito separated. And the son, quite justifiably rebellious, saw standing in front of him his old father, who cried solemnly, 'Juanito, I order you to do it.'

As the young count did not move, his father kneeled before him. Involuntarily, Clara, Manuel and Philippe imitated him. They all stretched out their arms to the one who was to save the family from oblivion and seemed to repeat the father's words. 'My son, do you lack Spanish energy and genuine feeling? Will you leave me kneeling for long and ought you to consider your own life and sufferings? Is he my son, Madame?' added the old man turning round to the marchioness.

'He agrees,' cried the mother in despair as she saw Juanito

move his eyebrows in a way that only she understood.

Mariquita, the second daughter, was kneeling and pressing her mother in her slender arms. And as she was weeping bitterly, her little brother Manuel came and scolded her. At that moment the castle chaplain came in. Immediately the whole family surrounded him and took him to Juanito.

Victor, unable to bear this scene any longer, signed to Clara and hurried away to make a last attempt to move the general. He found him in a good mood in the middle of the banquet and drinking with his officers who were beginning to crack jokes.

An hour later a hundred of the most important inhabitants of Menda came on to the terrace to witness the execution of the Léganès family according to the general's orders. A detachment of soldiers was stationed to see that the Spaniards remained in line under the gallows on which the marquis' servants had been hung. The townsfolk's heads almost touched the martyrs' feet. Thirty paces away from them a block had been erected and a scimitar was gleaming. The executioner was there in case Juanito refused. Soon, in the midst of the deepest silence, the Spaniards heard the steps of several people, the measured tread of a detachment of marching soldiers and the slight clatter of their guns. These different sounds were mingled with the gay voices of the officers' celebration just as, not long before, the dance-music of a ball had camouflaged the preparations for the blood-stained betrayal. All eyes turned towards the castle and the noble family could be seen walking forwards with an incredible assurance. All their faces were calm and serene. One single man, pale and drawn, was supported by the priest, who lavished all the consolations of religion on that man, the only one who was to live. Like everyone else the executioner understood that Juanito had accepted his position for one day. The old marquis and his wife, Clara, Mariquita and their two brothers came and knelt down several paces from the fatal spot. Juanito was led by the priest. When he reached the block, the executioner, taking him by the sleeve, drew him aside and presumably gave him some instructions. The confessor arranged the victims so that they could not see the execution. But they were true Spaniards and they held themselves erect without weakness.

Clara was the first to rush forward towards her brother. 'Juanito,' she said, 'take pity on my lack of courage! Begin with me!'

At that moment the hurried steps of a man could be heard. Victor arrived at the spot where this scene was taking place. Clara was already kneeling, already her white neck was exposed to the scimitar. The officer turned pale but he found the strength to hurry to her side.

'The general will spare your life if you will marry me,' he said in a low voice.

The Spanish girl looked at the officer with contemptuous pride.

'Go on, Juanito,' she said in a deep voice. Her head rolled at Victor's feet. The Marquise de Léganès started convulsively when she heard the sound. That was her only sign of grief.

'Am I in a good position, dear Juanito?' little Manuel asked his brother.

'Oh, you are crying, Mariquita,' Juanito said to his sister.

'Oh, yes,' the girl replied, 'I am thinking of you, my poor Juanito. You will be very unhappy without us.'

Soon the tall figure of the marquis appeared. He looked at his children's blood, turned towards the speechless and motionless spectators, stretched out his hands to Juanito and said in a strong voice, 'Spaniards, I give my son my paternal blessing. Now, *Marquis*, strike without fear, you are without reproach.'

But when Juanito saw his mother coming supported by the confessor, he cried, 'She nursed me.'

His words drew a shout of horror from the assembled company. The noise of the banquet and the happy laughter of the officers ceased at this terrible cry. The marchioness realized that Juanito's courage was exhausted. With a leap she hurled herself over the balustrade and split her head open on the rocks below. A cry of admiration arose. Juanito had collapsed in a faint.

'Marchand has just told me something about this execution,

sir. I wager that you didn't give orders for it,' a half-drunken officer said to the general.

'Do you forget, gentlemen,' exclaimed General G–t–r, 'that in a month's time five hundred French families will be in tears and that we are in Spain? Do you want to leave our bones here?'

After this short speech there was no one, not even a sub-lieutenant, who dared to empty his glass.

Despite the marks of respect with which he is surrounded, in spite of the title of *El Verdugo* (the executioner) which the King of Spain has given as a title of honour to the Marquis de Léganès, he is consumed with grief. He shuns society and rarely appears in public. Overwhelmed by the burden of his glorious crime, he seems to be waiting impatiently until the birth of a second son gives him the right to join the shades who never leave him.

1829

Domestic Peace

THE events related in this Scene[1] took place about the end of November, 1809, a time when Napoleon's ephemeral Empire had reached the height of its splendour. The fanfares of the victory of Wagram were still resounding in the heart of the Austrian monarchy. Peace was being signed between France and the Coalition. So kings and princes came, like stars, to perform their revolutions around Napoleon, who gave himself the pleasure of dragging all Europe in his train, a magnificent first exercise of the power which he later displayed at Dresden. Never, according to contemporary opinion, had Paris seen more splendid festivities than those which preceded and followed the marriage of this ruler to an Austrian archduchess. Never, in the greatest days of the old monarchy, had so many crowned heads thronged on the banks of the Seine and never had the French aristocracy been as rich and as brilliant as at that time. The diamonds lavishly displayed on the women's finery, the gold and silver embroidery of the uniforms were such a strong contrast to Republican austerity that the riches of the whole world seemed to be circulating in the salons of Paris. A general intoxication had, as it were, gripped this short-lived Empire. All the soldiers, not excepting their leader, were enjoying, like parvenus, the treasures conquered by a million men with woollen epaulettes, men whose demands were satisfied with a few yards of red ribbon. At that period, most women displayed the free and easy manners and the lax moral standards which had characterized the reign of Louis XV. Whether it was in imitation of the style of the collapsed monarchy, or because certain members of the imperial family had set the example, as the dissidents of the Faubourg Saint-Germain maintained, it is certain that men and

1. This story originally appeared in *Scenes of Private Life* in 1830.

women alike rushed into pleasure with an intrepidity which seemed to foretell the end of the world. But there was, then, another reason for this licence. The women's infatuation with the soldiers became a kind of madness and was too much in line with the Emperor's views for him to curb it. The frequent calls to arms, which made all the treaties concluded between Europe and Napoleon like armistice agreements, exposed love affairs to endings as sudden as the decisions of the supreme commander of these colbacks, dolmans and shoulder-knots, which were so attractive to the fair sex. So hearts, at this period, were nomadic like regiments. Between a first and a fifth bulletin of the Grand Army a woman could be, in succession, sweetheart, wife, mother and widow. Was it the prospect of impending widowhood, of a marriage settlement, or the hope of bearing a name which would go down in history, that made these military men so attractive? Were women drawn towards them by the certainty that the secret of their passions would be buried on the battlefields? Or should one look for the cause of this gentle fanaticism in the noble attraction of courage? Perhaps all these reasons (which the future historian of imperial manners will no doubt enjoy evaluating) counted for something in the speed and facility with which the women embarked on love affairs. However that may be, let us admit it here; at that time laurels covered up many failings. Women ardently sought out these bold adventurers who seemed to them real sources of honours, riches and pleasures, and in the eyes of the girls an epaulette, that symbol of the future, meant happiness and freedom. A feature of this period, which was characteristic of it and unique in our annals, was an unbridled passion for everything that glittered. Never were there so many firework displays, never did diamonds attain so high a value. The men were as greedy as the women for these white pebbles and like the women were decked out with them.

Perhaps the necessity of putting booty into the most easily transportable form gave jewels a place of honour in the army. A man was not as ridiculous as he would be today if his shirt-front or his fingers sported large diamonds. Murat, a man of

quite oriental tastes, set an example of absurd luxury amongst
the modern military.

The Comte de Gondreville, who was formerly called Citizen
Malin and who was made famous by being kidnapped, had
become one of the Luculluses of that Conservative Senate
which conserved nothing. He had postponed his celebrations
in honour of the peace for the sole purpose of paying court
to Napoleon more effectively, by trying to outshine the
flatterers who had preceded him. The ambassadors of all the
powers friendly to France pending the drawing up of treaties,
the most important people in the Empire, even some princes,
were at that moment gathered together in the opulent senator's salons. The dancers were flagging, everyone was waiting
for the Emperor whose presence had been promised by the
count. Napoleon would have kept his word but for the scene
which broke out that very evening between Joséphine and
himself, a scene which revealed the coming divorce of this
august husband and wife. The news of the incident, kept quite
secret at the time but recorded by history, did not reach the
courtiers' ears, and it affected the gaiety of the Comte de
Gondreville's party only because it was the cause of Napoleon's absence. The prettiest women in Paris, eager to go to
his house on the strength of hearsay, were at that moment
vying with each other in luxury, coquetry, dress and beauty.
Proud of its wealth, the Bank challenged these dazzling
generals and these high officers of the Empire, newly crammed
with crosses, titles and decorations. These large parties were
always opportunities grasped by rich families to show off their
heiresses to Napoleon's praetorians, in the crazy hope of exchanging their magnificent dowries for an uncertain favour.
Women who thought that their beauty alone was sufficient
came to try out its power. There, as elsewhere, pleasure was
only a mask. The serene, cheerful faces, the calm brows concealed odious calculations; the indications of friendship were
false and more than one person was less on his guard against
his enemies than against his friends. These remarks are necessary to explain the events of the little imbroglio, the subject
of this Scene, and the picture, however much it may be

softened, of the tone prevailing at that time in the salons of Paris.

'Turn your eyes a little towards that half-pillar with a candelabra on top. Do you see a young woman with a Chinese hairstyle? There, in the corner, on the left; she has blue bellflowers in the ringlets of chestnut hair which fall on each side of her head. Can't you see? She is so pale that you'd think she was unwell. She is dainty and quite small. Now she is turning her head towards us. Her blue, almond-shaped eyes are charmingly gentle and seem formed for the express purpose of weeping. But look! She's bending down to look at Madame de Vaudremont through that maze of continually moving heads whose tall hairstyles block her view.'

'Oh, I see her, my dear fellow. All you had to do was to describe her as the most white-skinned of all the women here, I should have recognized her. I have already had a good look at her. She has the most beautiful complexion I have ever admired. I bet you can't make out from here the pearls which separate each one of the sapphires of her necklace. But she must either have high principles or be a coquette, for the ruching of her bodice hardly allows one to suspect the beauty of her form. What shoulders! What lily-like whiteness!'

'Who is she?' asked the man who had spoken first.

'Oh, I don't know.'

'Aristocrat! So, Montcornet, you want to keep them all for yourself.'

'It well becomes you to make fun of me,' replied Montcornet with a smile. 'Do you think you have the right to insult a poor general like me because you are Soulanges' fortunate rival and cannot make a single pirouette without alarming Madame de Vaudremont? Or is it because I have been in the promised land for only a month? How insolent you are, you administrators who remain glued to your chairs while we are surrounded by shells! Come, come, Monsieur le Maître des Requêtes, let us glean in this field where one gets a precarious foothold only as one leaves it. What the deuce, everyone has to live! My friend, if you knew the German women, you would, I think, help me with the Parisian lady who attracts you.'

'General, since you have honoured with your attention this woman whom I see here for the first time, have the charity to tell me if you have seen her dancing.'

'Oh, my dear Martial, where have you been? If you are sent to an embassy, I prophesy you won't do well. Don't you see three rows of the most intrepid coquettes in Paris between her and the swarm of dancers who buzz under the chandelier, and didn't you need the help of your eye-glass to discover her in the angle formed by that pillar, where she seems buried in darkness in spite of the candles which shine above her head? Between her and us, so many diamonds and so many glances are flashing, so many feathers are streaming, so much lace, so many flowers and tresses are waving that it would be a real miracle if any dance-partner could notice her in the midst of these luminaries. What, Martial, haven't you guessed that she is the wife of some sub-prefect from La Lippe or La Dyle[2] who has come to try to turn her husband into a prefect?'

'Oh, he'll be that alright,' the Maître des Requêtes said eagerly.

'I doubt it,' said the colonel of the cuirassiers with a laugh. 'She seems as much a novice in intrigue as you are in diplomacy. I bet, Martial, that you don't know how she got there.'

The Maître des Requêtes gave the colonel of the cuirassiers of the Guard a look which revealed as much disdain as curiosity.

'Well,' continued Montcornet, 'she no doubt arrived punctually at nine o'clock, the first perhaps, and probably greatly embarrassed the Comtesse de Gondreville who can't string two ideas together. Rebuffed by the lady of the house, pushed back from chair to chair by each new arrival right into the shadows of that little corner, she has let herself be hemmed in there, a victim of the jealousy of these ladies, who wanted nothing better than to hide that dangerous face in this way. She hasn't had a man friend to encourage her to defend the front seat she must have occupied to start with; each one of

2. The department of La Lippe in Germany, with Münster as its capital, was not in fact created till 1810. The department of La Dyle, with Brussels as its capital, was created in 1794. Both were abolished in 1814.

these treacherous young women has ordered the men of her circle not to ask our poor friend to dance under pain of the most terrible punishments. That, my dear friend, is how these pretty faces, apparently so frank and affectionate, have formed their coalition against the stranger; and that without any of those women saying anything to each other but, "My dear, do you know that little lady in blue?" Well now, Martial, if you want to be overwhelmed in a quarter of an hour, by more looks and provocative questions than you will get perhaps in your whole life, try to penetrate the triple rampart which defends the Queen of La Dyle, La Lippe or La Charente. You will see if the most stupid of these women can't immediately invent a trick which would stop even the man most determined to bring our plaintive stranger into the limelight. Don't you think that she looks a little like an elegy?'

'Do you think so, Montcornet? So you think she's married?'

'Why shouldn't she be a widow?'

'She would be more active,' said the Maître des Requêtes with a laugh.

'Perhaps she's a widow whose husband is playing *bouillotte*,' replied the handsome cuirassier.

'Yes, indeed. Since the peace, a lot of women have become widows of that kind!' replied Martial. 'But my dear Montcornet, we are two idiots. That face still expresses too much ingenuousness, too much youth and freshness are still visible on the brow and the temples for her to be a married woman. What vivid flesh tints! There are no lines round the nose. The lips, the chin, everything in that face is as fresh as a white rosebud, although its expression is, as it were, veiled by the clouds of sadness. Who can be making that young woman cry?'

'Women cry for so little,' said the colonel.

'I don't know,' continued Martial. 'But she is not crying because she's stuck there without a dance-partner. Her grief doesn't date from today. You can see that she has made herself beautiful for this evening, of set purpose. She is in love already, I would bet.'

'Bah! Perhaps she's the daughter of some German princeling. No one is speaking to her,' said Montcornet.

'Oh, how unhappy a poor girl is,' resumed Martial.

'Could anyone have more grace and delicacy than our little stranger? Well, not one of those hags, who surround her and call themselves sensitive, will address a word to her. If she were to speak, we would see if her teeth are beautiful.'

'Oh, do you go off, then, like milk at the least rise in temperature?' cried the colonel, a little vexed to find his friend a rival so soon.

'What!' said the Maître des Requêtes, paying no attention to the general's question and looking through his eye-glass at all the people around them. 'What! Can no one here tell us the name of that exotic flower?'

'Oh, she's some lady's companion,' said Montcornet.

'Good! A lady's companion wearing sapphires fit for a queen and a Mechlin lace dress! Try something else, General. You won't be very good at diplomacy either, if in your judgements you go in one moment from a German princess to a lady's companion.'

General Montcornet caught the arm of a little fat man whose greying hair and witty eyes could be seen at all the corners of the room in turn and who mingled informally with the different groups where he was respectfully received.

'Gondreville, my dear fellow,' said Montcornet. 'Who is that charming little woman sitting over there under that enormous candelabra?'

'The candelabra? It is by Ravrio, old chap; it's from a design by Isabey.'

'Oh, I know your taste and magnificence in the matter of furniture; but the young woman?'

'Oh, I don't know her. She must be a friend of my wife's.'

'Or your mistress, you sly old fellow.'

'No, on my word of honour. The Comtesse de Gondreville is the only woman capable of inviting people whom nobody knows.'

In spite of this biting remark, the fat little man retained on his lips the smile of inner satisfaction aroused by the sugges-

tion of the colonel of the cuirassiers. The latter rejoined the
Maître des Requêtes who was then in a neighbouring group,
busy trying to obtain information about the stranger, but
without success. Montcornet seized his arm and whispered to
him, 'My dear Martial, watch out! Madame de Vaudremont
has been looking at you for some minutes with frantic attention. She is a woman capable of guessing just from the movement of your lips what you are saying to me. Our eyes have
already said far too much. She has clearly noticed and followed
their direction and I think that, at this moment, she is more
occupied than we are with the little lady in blue.'

'That's an old trick of war, my dear Montcornet. What does
it matter to me, anyway? I am like the Emperor. When I make
conquests, I keep them.'

'Martial, your conceit needs to be taught a lesson. What,
you, a civilian, you have the good fortune to be the prospec-
tive husband of Madame de Vaudremont, of a widow of
twenty-two, afflicted with an income of four thousand napoleons, of a woman who places on your finger diamonds as
handsome as that one,' he added, taking the left hand of the
Maître des Requêtes who obligingly let him do so, 'and you
still have the pretension to behave like Lovelace, as if you
were a colonel and obliged to uphold the reputation of the
military in garrisons! Fie upon you! But just think what you
may lose.'

'At least I shan't lose my liberty,' replied Martial with a
forced laugh.

He looked passionately at Madame de Vaudremont who replied only with an anxious smile, for she had seen the colonel
examining the Maître des Requêtes' ring.

'Listen, Martial,' resumed the colonel, 'if you hover around
my young stranger, I shall undertake the conquest of Madame
de Vaudremont.'

'You have my permission, my dear cuirassier, but you
won't get as much as that,' said the young Maître des Requêtes,
putting his polished thumbnail under one of his upper teeth
and so making a little jocular sound.

'Note that I am a bachelor,' continued the colonel, 'that

my sword is all my fortune and that to challenge me in this way is to seat Tantalus before a feast that he will devour.'

'Prrrl'

This mocking accumulation of consonants served as a reply to the general's provocation and his friend looked him up and down jokingly before leaving him. The fashion of that time required a man at a ball to wear white cashmere breeches and silk stockings. This attractive dress set off Montcornet's shapely legs. He was then thirty-five years old and attracted the eye by the great height required for cuirassiers of the Imperial Guard whose fine uniform enhanced his appearance still further; he still looked young in spite of the corpulence resulting from horse-riding. His black moustache added to the frank expression of a truly military face with a broad, open forehead, aquiline nose and bright red lips. Montcornet's manners, marked by a certain nobility due to the habit of command, might please a woman who had the intelligence not to want to make a slave of her husband. The colonel smiled as he looked at the Maître des Requêtes, one of his best friends whom he had known from their school days, whose slender, short figure forced Montcornet to lower his friendly glance a little in order to reply to his teasing.

Baron Martial de la Roche-Hugon was a young man from Provence whom Napoleon protected and who seemed destined for some splendid diplomatic post. He had charmed the Emperor by an Italian obligingness, by his skill at intrigue, by that drawing-room eloquence and *savoir-faire* which are such an easy substitute for the outstanding virtues of a man of solid worth. Although he was young and lively, his face already had the static gleam of tin, one of the qualities indispensable to diplomats and which allows them to hide their emotions, to conceal their feelings, assuming that this impassiveness does not reveal that they have no emotions and that their feelings are dead. The hearts of diplomats can be looked on as an insoluble problem, for the three most illustrious diplomats of the period distinguished themselves by the persistence of hatred and by romantic attachments. Nevertheless, Martial belonged to that class of men capable of calculating their future in the midst of their most ardent pleasures; he had already judged society and concealed his ambition beneath the foppishness of a ladies' man, disguising his talent in the livery of mediocrity after noticing the speed of the advancement of those who gave little offence to the master.

The two friends had to separate and they shook hands warmly as they did so. The *ritornello*, which gave notice to the ladies to form sets for a new square-dance, cleared the men from the large space where they were chatting in the middle of the salon. This rapid conversation, held in the interval which always separates the dances, took place in front of the fireplace of the large salon of the Gondreville mansion. The questions and answers of this gossip, common enough at balls, had been, as it were, whispered by the two participants to each other. Nevertheless, the chandeliers and fireplace lamps cast such a full light on the two friends that, in spite of their diplomatic discretion, their faces, too strongly illuminated, could not conceal from the subtle countess or from the guileless stranger the barely perceptible expression of their feelings. This spying out of thoughts is, perhaps, one of the pleasures which idlers find at social gatherings, while so many hoodwinked fools are bored at them, without daring to admit it.

So that you can fully appreciate the interest of this conversation, I must relate an incident which was going to link by invisible bonds the people of this little drama, who were then in different parts of the salons. At about eleven o'clock, just as the women dancers were resuming their places, the company at the Gondreville mansion had seen the most beautiful woman in Paris arrive. She was the queen of fashion, the only person missing from this splendid gathering. She made it a rule never to arrive until the moment when the salons were so full of animation and movement that the women could not keep for long the freshness of their faces or their ball dresses. That fleeting moment is like the springtime of a ball. An hour later, when the pleasure has passed, when fatigue has arrived, everything is faded. Madame de Vaudremont never committed the fault of staying at a party long enough to be seen there with drooping flowers, limp curls or crushed trimmings, or with a face like all those which, longing for sleep, don't always manage to resist it. She took care not to be seen, like her rivals, with her beauty out of action. She knew how to maintain skilfully her reputation for coquetry by always leaving a ball as dazzling as she had come into it. The women whispered to each other, enviously, that she laid out and put on as many ball-dresses as she had balls in an evening. This time, Madame de Vaudremont was not to be free to leave the salon when she chose, the salon where she was just then arriving in triumph. She stopped for a moment in the doorway and looked carefully, though swiftly, at the women, whose dresses she studied straight away so as to be sure that hers would eclipse them all. The celebrated coquette, escorted by one of the bravest colonels of the artillery of the Guard, one of the Emperor's favourites, the Comte de Soulanges, invited the admiration of the gathering. The chance, momentary union of these two people no doubt had something mysterious about it. When they heard Monsieur de Soulanges and the Comtesse de Vaudremont being announced, wallflowers got up and men, hurrying from the adjoining rooms, crowded at the doors of the main salon. One of those wits, who never fail to be at these crowded parties, said, as he saw the countess and her escort come in, that 'the ladies were just as curious to see a man faithful to his passion, as were the men to study a pretty woman who was difficult to settle'.

Although the Comte de Soulanges, a young man of about thirty-two, was gifted with that highly strung temperament which produces great qualities in a man, his delicate physique and pale complexion predisposed few people in his favour. His black eyes suggested that he was very lively, but in society he spoke little and nothing about him indicated one of the talented public speakers who were to shine on the Right in the legislative assemblies of the Restoration. The Comtesse de Vaudremont was a tall, slightly plump woman, with a dazzling white skin, who carried her little head well and possessed the enormous advantage of inspiring love by the graciousness of her manners; she was one of those creatures who fulfil all the

promises of their beauty. This couple, for some moments the
object of general attention, did not allow curiosity to be exercised about them for long. The colonel and the countess
seemed to understand perfectly that chance had just placed
them in an embarrassing situation. When he saw them come
into the room, Martial hurriedly joined the group of men who
were standing by the fireplace so that, across the heads which
formed a kind of rampart around her, he could watch Madame
de Vaudremont with the jealous attention inspired by the
first flame of passion. An inner voice seemed to tell him that
the success he was so proud of was perhaps precarious. But
the cold, polite smile with which the countess thanked Monsieur de Soulanges and the gesture with which she dismissed
him as she sat down beside Madame de Gondreville, relaxed
all the muscles of Martial's face which had been contracted
with jealousy. Nevertheless, as he noticed Soulanges standing
two paces from the couch where Madame de Vaudremont
was sitting and apparently not understanding the look with
which the young coquette had told him that they were both
making themselves ridiculous, the impetuous Provençal again
puckered the black eyebrows which shaded his blue eyes; he
stroked the curls of his brown hair to keep himself in countenance and, without betraying the emotion which made his
heart beat, he watched the face of the countess as well as that
of Monsieur de Soulanges, while at the same time joking with
his neighbours. He even shook the hand of the colonel who
had come up to renew acquaintance with him, but he was so
preoccupied that he listened to him without taking in what
he said. Soulanges was looking calmly at the four rows of
women who lined the senator's enormous salon, admiring
the border of diamonds, rubies, sheafs of gold and ornamented
heads, whose brilliance almost dimmed the flame of the candles, the crystal of the chandeliers and the gilt decorations.
His rival's carefree calm disconcerted the Maître des Requêtes.
Unable to control the secret impatience which was overcoming
him, Martial moved towards Madame de Vaudremont to
greet her. When the Provençal appeared, Soulanges gave
him a dull look and turned his head away impertinently.

A solemn silence prevailed in the room where curiosity was at its height.

On all the tensely expectant faces were the oddest expressions, everyone fearing, yet expecting, one of those outbursts which well-bred people take care to avoid. Suddenly the count's pale face became as red as the scarlet of the facings on his uniform and he looked down at the floor straight away, so that no one should guess the cause of his embarrassment. When he saw the unknown young woman sitting humbly at the base of the candelabra, he went sadly past the Maître des Requêtes and took refuge in one of the card-rooms. Martial and the assembled company thought that Soulanges was publicly giving way to him, through fear of the ridicule which always clings to dethroned lovers. The Maître des Requêtes raised his head proudly and looked at the unknown lady. Then, when he sat down confidently beside Madame de Vaudremont, he listened to her so absent-mindedly that he didn't hear these words which the coquette spoke behind her fan.

'Martial, you will oblige me by not wearing this evening the ring which you made me give you. I have my reasons and I shall explain them to you in a moment when we leave the ball. Give me your arm and we shall go to the Princesse de Wagram's.'

'But why did you take the colonel's hand?' asked the baron.

'I met him at the entrance porch,' she replied. 'But leave me; everyone is watching us.'

Martial rejoined the colonel of the cuirassiers. And so the little lady in blue became the bond between the anxieties which troubled, at the same time and in such different ways, the cuirassier, Soulanges, Martial and the Comtesse de Vaudremont. When the two friends separated, after ending their conversation with a challenge to each other, the Maître des Requêtes hurried to Madame de Vaudremont and managed to place her in the midst of the most brilliant quadrille. Profiting from the sort of intoxication aroused in a woman by the dancing and movement of a ball (where the men in their dress clothes are no less attractive than the women in their toilettes),

Martial thought he could abandon himself with impunity to the spell which drew him to the unknown lady. Although he succeeded in concealing from the countess's anxiously active eyes the first glances he cast at the lady in blue, he was soon caught in the act. And if he was pardoned an initial preoccupation, he did not justify the impertinent silence with which he replied later to the most seductive question a woman can address to a man: 'Do you love me, this evening?' The more absent-minded he was, the more teasingly pressing was the countess. While Martial was dancing, the colonel was going from group to group, seeking for information about the young stranger. After exhausting the indulgence of everyone, even the indifferent, he determined to profit from a moment when the Comtesse de Gondreville seemed free, to ask *her* the mysterious lady's name. But just then he noticed a slight space between the broken pillar which supported the candelabra and the two couches on either side of it. The colonel took advantage of the moment when, because of the dancing, a large number of the chairs, forming several rows of fortifications defended by mothers or middle-aged women, were left empty and he undertook to cross the fence covered with shawls and handkerchiefs. He began by paying compliments to the dowagers, then, going from woman to woman, from polite remark to polite remark, he finally reached the empty place by the stranger. At the risk of bumping into the gryphons and chimeras of the huge chandelier, he kept his position there under the flame and the wax of the candles, to Martial's great displeasure. Too shrewd to start talking suddenly to the little lady in blue who was on his right, the colonel began by saying to a tall, rather plain lady sitting on his left, 'What a lovely ball this is, Madame! What luxury, what animation! On my word of honour, all the women are pretty! If you are not dancing, it's presumably because you don't want to.'

The colonel's aim in starting this banal conversation was to make his right-hand neighbour talk. She, silent and preoccupied, did not pay the slightest attention to him. The officer had ready a host of phrases which were to end with, 'And

39

you, Madame?' on which he counted a great deal. But he was strangely surprised to see tears in the eyes of the unknown lady, who seemed entirely captivated by Madame de Vaudremont.

'You are no doubt married, Madame?' Colonel Montcornet finally asked hesitantly.

'Yes, Monsieur,' replied the stranger.

'Your husband is presumably here?'

'Yes, Monsieur.'

'Then why, Madame, do you stay in this place? Is it out of coquetry?'

The unhappy young woman smiled sadly.

'Grant me the honour, Madame, of being your partner for the next dance, and I shall certainly not bring you back here. I can see an empty sofa near the fireplace, let's go to it. When so many people are ready to lord it, and when royalty is the craze of the day, I don't see how you can refuse to accept the title of queen of the ball which seems appropriate to your beauty.'

'Monsieur, I shall not dance.'

The tone of the lady's short replies was so heartbreaking that the colonel saw himself forced to retreat. Martial, who guessed the colonel's last request and the refusal that he was experiencing, began to smile and stroked his chin, showing off the gleaming ring on his finger.

'What are you laughing at?' asked the Comtesse de Vaudremont.

'At the poor colonel's lack of success. He has just made a blunder.'

'I asked you to take off your ring,' interrupted the countess.

'I didn't hear you.'

'If you hear nothing this evening, you see everything, Monsieur le Baron,' replied Madame de Vaudremont acidly.

'That young man is showing off a very fine diamond,' the unknown lady then said to the colonel.

'Magnificent,' he replied. 'The young man is Baron Martial de la Roche-Hugon, one of my closest friends.'

40

'Thank you for telling me his name,' she continued. 'He looks very pleasant.'

'Yes, but he is a little frivolous.'

'It looks as if he is on good terms with the Comtesse de Vaudremont,' said the young lady with a questioning look at the colonel.

'On the best of terms!'

The unknown lady turned pale.

'Well, well,' thought the soldier, 'she is in love with that rascal Martial.'

'I thought that Madame de Vaudremont had been associated for a long time with Monsieur de Soulanges,' continued the young woman, having recovered a little from the painful emotion which had just affected the brightness of her complexion.

'The countess has been deceiving him for a week,' the colonel replied. 'But you must have seen poor Soulanges when he came in. He is still trying not to believe in his misfortune.'

'I saw him,' said the lady in blue. Then she added, 'Monsieur, thank you,' in a tone which was equivalent to a dismissal.

At this moment, the dance being nearly over, the colonel, disappointed, only had time to withdraw, saying to himself by way of consolation, 'She is married.'

'Well, brave cuirassier,' cried the baron, leading the colonel into a window bay to breathe the fresh air from the gardens, 'how did you get on?'

'She is married, my dear fellow.'

'What difference does that make?'

'The deuce! I am a moral man,' replied the colonel. 'I only want to court women whom I can marry. Besides, Martial, she firmly expressed the wish not to dance.'

'Colonel, let's bet your dapple-grey horse against a hundred napoleons that she will dance with me this evening.'

'I agree,' said the colonel shaking the smug fellow's hand. 'Meanwhile, I am going to see Soulanges. Perhaps he knows this lady who seemed to take an interest in him.'

'My good fellow, you have lost,' said Martial with a laugh. 'My eyes met hers and I'm a connoisseur in these matters.

My dear Colonel, you won't bear me a grudge if I dance with her after she has refused you?'

'No, no. He who laughs last laughs longest. Besides, Martial, I am a good sport and a good enemy. I warn you she likes diamonds.'

With these words, the two friends separated. General Montcornet went to the card-room where he saw the Comte de Soulanges sitting at a *bouillotte* table. Although between the two colonels there was only that commonplace friendship arising from the perils of war and service duties, the colonel of cuirassiers was very sorry to see the artillery colonel, whom he knew to be a sensible man, taking part in a game in which he might be ruined. The piles of coins and bank notes spread out on the fatal card table bore witness to the ferocity of the game. A circle of silent men surrounded the players at the table. At times a few words rang out like, 'Pass', 'Game', 'Hold', 'A thousand louis', 'Held', but if one looked at these five motionless people they seemed to talk only with their eyes. When the colonel, frightened by Soulanges' paleness, came up to him, the count was winning. The Maréchal Duc d'Isemberg and a well-known banker, Keller, got up from the table completely cleaned out of considerable sums. Soulanges became even gloomier as he gathered up a mass of coin and notes. He did not even count them. His lips were curled in bitter disdain. He seemed to threaten fortune instead of thanking her for her favours.

'Take courage, Soulanges!' said the colonel. Then, thinking he would render him a real service by dragging him away from the cards, he added, 'Come, I have some good news for you, but on one condition.'

'What is that?' asked Soulanges.

'Answer the question I'm going to ask you.'

The Comte de Soulanges got up quickly and wrapped his winnings carelessly in a handkerchief which he twisted convulsively, with an expression so fierce that it never occurred to any of the players to take it amiss that he gave them no opportunity to take their revenge. Their faces even seemed to relax when that miserable, ill-tempered countenance was no longer in the circle of light cast over the *bouillotte* table by the candlestick.

'These military fellows work together like thieves at a fair,' whispered a diplomat among the onlookers as he took the colonel's place.

One solitary, pale, weary figure turned towards the new player and, giving him a look which dazzled and expired like a diamond's sparkle, said, 'He who says military does not say civilian, Monsieur le Ministre.'

'My dear fellow,' Montcornet said to Soulanges, taking him into a corner, 'this morning the Emperor talked of you in terms of praise, and your promotion to marshal is not in doubt.'

'The chief doesn't like the artillery.'

'Yes but he adores the nobility, and you are a *ci-devant*,'[3] continued Montcornet. 'The chief has said that those who got married in Paris during the campaign oughtn't to be considered in disgrace. Well?'

The Comte de Soulanges did not seem to understand this speech.

'Well, now,' said the colonel, 'I hope you will tell me if you know a charming young woman sitting at the base of a candelabra . . .'

At these words the count's eyes lit up. With incredible violence he seized the colonel's hand.

'My dear Colonel,' he said in an obviously strained voice, 'if anyone but you had asked me that question, I would crack his skull with this bundle of gold. Leave me alone, I beg of you. This evening I want to blow my brains out more than to . . . I hate everything I see around me. So I am going to leave. This happiness, this music, these stupid laughing faces get on my nerves.'

'My poor friend, you are in a state!' said Montcornet gently, tapping Soulanges' hand in a friendly manner. 'What would you say then if I told you that Martial is thinking so little of Madame de Vaudremont that he has fallen in love with that little lady?'

3. *Ci-devant* was a name given to former members of the nobility during the French Revolution.

'If he speaks to her,' cried Soulanges stuttering with rage, 'I'll make him as flat as his wallet, even if the conceited puppy were to be in the Emperor's lap.'

And the count collapsed as if stunned into a settee where the colonel had led him. The latter withdrew slowly. He realized that Soulanges was a prey to an anger too violent to be calmed by witticisms or by the attentions of a superficial friendship. When Colonel Montcornet returned to the main ballroom, Madame de Vaudremont was the first person he set eyes on, and he noticed on her usually calm face traces of an ill-concealed agitation. There was a vacant chair beside her; the colonel came and sat down on it.

'You look upset!' he said.

'It's nothing, General. I should like to go. I have promised to be at the Grande-Duchesse de Berg's ball, and before that I have to go to see the Princesse de Wagram. Monsieur de la Roche-Hugon knows this but he is amusing himself saying sweet nothings to dowagers.'

'That's not the whole cause of your anxiety and I wager a hundred louis that you will stay here this evening.'

'You impertinent fellow!'

'So I have spoken the truth?'

'Well, what am I thinking of?' replied the countess giving the colonel's fingers a rap with her fan. 'I am capable of rewarding you if you guess.'

'I shan't accept the challenge. I have too many advantages.'

'What presumption!'

'You are afraid of seeing Martial at the feet of . . .'

'Of whom?' asked the countess, pretending to be surprised.

'Of that candelabra,' replied the colonel pointing to the beautiful unknown lady and looking at the countess with embarrassing attention.

'You have guessed correctly,' replied the coquette, hiding her face behind her fan and beginning to play with it. After a moment's silence she resumed, 'Old Madame de Lansac, who, you know, is as cunning as an old monkey, has just told me that Monsieur de la Roche-Hugon was taking risks in paying court to that unknown young woman who is here this evening

like a kill-joy. I would rather see death than that cruelly beautiful face, as pale as a ghost. She is my evil genius.' She uttered
a sigh of annoyance and continued, 'Madame de Lansac, who
goes to a ball only to see everything while she pretends to
sleep, has made me distressingly anxious. Martial will pay
dearly for the trick he is playing me. But, General, since he's
your friend, make him promise not to distress me.'

'I have just seen a man who proposes nothing less than
blowing Martial's brains out if he says a word to that
little lady. That man, Madame, is as good as his word. But
I know Martial. These dangers are so many incentives.
What's more, we have bet . . .' Here the colonel lowered his
voice.

'Is that true?' asked the countess.

'On my honour.'

'Thank you, General,' replied Madame de Vaudremont
giving him a very coy look.

'Wiil you do me the honour of dancing with me?'

'Yes, but the second dance. During this one, I want to
know how this intrigue will develop and who is that little
lady in blue. She looks intelligent.'

The colonel, seeing that Madame de Vaudremont wanted
to be alone, went away satisfied that he had begun his attack
so well.

At parties one comes across a few ladies like Madame de
Lansac, who are there like old mariners on the sea-shore busy
watching young sailors struggling with the storms. At that
moment, Madame de Lansac, who seemed interested in the
characters of this scene, could easily guess at the struggle
which was consuming the countess. In vain the young coquette
fanned herself graciously, smiled at young men who greeted
her and employed the tricks which a woman uses to hide her
emotion; the dowager, one of the most perspicacious and
malicious duchesses whom the eighteenth century has bequeathed to the nineteenth, could read her heart and her
thoughts. The old lady seemed to recognize the imperceptible
movements which reveal the affections of the heart. The
slightest crease which wrinkled this white, pure forehead, the

merest quiver of the cheekbones, the play of the eyebrows, the most imperceptible curve of the lips whose moving coral could not hide anything from her, all these were for the duchess like letters in a book. From the depths of her armchair, which was completely filled by her dress, the former coquette, as she chatted with a diplomat who sought her out so as to listen to the stories which she told so well, admired her past self in the young coquette. Seeing her hide her grief and the torments of her heart so well, she took a fancy to her. In fact Madame de Vaudremont felt as much grief as she feigned gaiety. She had thought that in Martial she had met a man of talent whose support she could count on to enrich her life with all the delights of power. At this moment she realized she had made an error as cruel for her reputation as for her vanity. In her, as in the other women of this period, the suddenness of the passions enhanced their keenness. Those who experience a lot quickly don't suffer any less than those who are consumed by one single affection. The countess's predilection for Martial was only very recent, it is true, but the most inexpert surgeon knows that the suffering caused by the amputation of a living limb is more painful than that of a diseased one. There was a future in Madame de Vaudremont's fancy for Martial, while her previous passion was without hope and was poisoned by Soulanges' remorse. The old duchess, who was watching for the opportune moment to speak to the countess, quickly dismissed her ambassador, for even with an old woman everything pales before the quarrels of lovers and their mistresses. As a start to the struggle, Madame de Lansac gave Madame de Vaudremont a sardonic look which made the young coquette fear that her fate was in the dowager's hands. There is something in these glances from woman to woman of the torches brought on at the end of a tragedy.

One had to know that duchess to appreciate the terror which the expressions of her face aroused in the countess. Madame de Lansac was tall; because of her features people said of her, 'That's a woman who must have been pretty!' She put so much rouge on her face that her wrinkles were hardly visible, but far from acquiring an artificial brilliance from this dark red, her eyes were only made more dull by it. She wore quantities of diamonds, and dressed with enough taste not to be ridiculous. Her pointed nose suggested skill at making epigrams. A well-fitting denture gave her face an ironic expression which recalled Voltaire's. However, the perfect courtesy of her manners softened the malicious bent of her thoughts so well that she could not be accused of ill-nature. The old lady's grey eyes lit up, and a triumphant look accompanied by a smile which said, 'That's just what I promised you!' crossed the salon and spread the crimson of hope on the pale cheeks of the young woman who was sighing at the foot of the candelabra. This alliance between Madame de Lansac and the stranger could not escape the practised eye of the Comtesse de Vaudremont, who sensed a secret and wanted to discover it. At this moment, the Baron de la Roche-Hugon, having finished questioning all the dowagers without being able to learn the name of the lady in blue, turned in despair to the Comtesse de Gondreville, and received only this unsatisfactory reply. 'She is a lady that the dowager Duchesse de Lansac introduced to me.'

Turning by chance towards the old lady's armchair, the Maître des Requêtes surprised the glance of complicity which she had cast at the stranger, and although he had been for some time on fairly bad terms with the duchess he decided to approach her.

Seeing the sprightly baron prowling round her chair, the old duchess gave a knowing, sardonic smile, and looked at Madame de Vaudremont in a way which made Colonel Montcornet laugh.

'If the old gipsy puts on a friendly manner she's probably going to play me some nasty trick,' thought the baron.

'Madame,' he said to her, 'I am told you have undertaken to watch over a very precious treasure.'

'Do you take me for a dragon?' asked the old lady. 'But whom are you speaking of?' she added in a gentle tone which restored Martial's hopes.

'Of that unknown little lady whom the jealousy of all these

coquettes has stuck over there. No doubt you know her family?'

'Yes,' said the duchess. 'But what's your concern with a provincial heiress, who has been married for some time, a girl of good family whom you society people don't know? She goes nowhere.'

'Why is she not dancing? She is so lovely! Are you willing to make a peace treaty with me? If you will deign to tell me everything I am concerned to know, I assure you that I shall strongly urge the Emperor to support a request for the restitution of the Navarreins woods by the Land Registration Office.'

The younger branch of the house of Navarreins quarters the Lansac arms which are azure with a lopped baton argent impaled on six lance heads and the old lady's liaison with Louis XV had obtained for her the title of *duchesse à brevet*; but as the Navarreins had not yet returned to the country, the young Maître des Requêtes was quite simply proposing an underhand action to the old lady, by suggesting that she should claim property belonging to the older branch.

'Monsieur,' replied the old lady with deceptive gravity, 'bring me the Comtesse de Vaudremont. I promise to reveal to her the secret which makes our unknown lady so interesting. Look, all the men at the ball have become as curious as you. Involuntarily all eyes are turning towards that candelabra where my protégée has modestly placed herself. She is receiving all the admiration that others wanted to steal from her. Fortunate is the man whom she will take as a partner!' With this, she paused and gazed at the Comtesse de Vaudremont with one of those looks which say so clearly, 'We are talking about you.' Then she added, 'I think you would rather learn the stranger's name from the lips of your beautiful countess than from mine.'

The duchess's demeanour was so tantalizing that Madame de Vaudremont got up, came across to her and sat down on the chair which Martial offered her. And paying no attention to him, she said with a laugh, 'I can guess, Madame, that you are talking about me. But I confess my inferiority; I don't know if it's for good or ill.'

48

Madame de Lansac pressed the young woman's pretty hand with her old, shrivelled one and whispered compassionately in reply, 'My poor dear!'

The two women looked at each other. Madame de Vaudremont realized that Martial was *de trop* and dismissed him, saying with a lordly air, 'Leave us alone.'

The Maître des Requêtes, not very pleased at seeing the countess under the spell of the dangerous sibyl who had summoned her, gave her one of those masculine looks which make a powerful impression on a heart blindly in love but which seem ridiculous to a woman when she is beginning to judge the man she is in love with.

'Are you trying to imitate the Emperor?' said Madame de Vaudremont, turning her head to glance ironically at the Maître des Requêtes.

Martial was too well-bred, too shrewd and calculating, to risk breaking with a woman in such good standing at court and whom the Emperor wanted to see married. Moreover, he counted on the jealousy that he was planning to arouse in her as the best means of discovering the secret of her coldness, and he went away all the more willingly as at that moment everyone was getting ready for a new dance. The baron looked as if he were giving way to the sets of dancers. He went and leaned against a marble table, crossed his arms on his chest and stood there absorbed in the two ladies' conversation. From time to time he followed the looks which both of them directed repeatedly at the stranger. Then, as he compared the countess with this new beauty, who was made so attractive by the mystery surrounding her, the baron indulged in the odious scheming usual with ladies' men. He hesitated between grasping at a fortune and satisfying a whim. The reflections of the lights made his gloomy, anxious face stand out so clearly against the white, watered-silk hangings, which were rumpled by his black hair, that he might have been compared to some evil genius. From the distance, more than one observer must probably have said to himself, 'There's yet another poor devil who seems to be having a good time!' With his right shoulder resting lightly on the frame of the door between the ballroom and the card-room, the colonel could laugh unnoticed behind his large moustache. He was enjoying the pleasure of watching the animation of the ball. He could see a hundred pretty heads whirling round according to the capricious movements of the dance. On some faces, as on those of the countess and his friend Martial, he could read secret agitation. Then, turning away his head, he wondered what was the connection between the gloomy expression of the Comte de Soulanges, who was still sitting on the settee, and the pathetic countenance of the unknown lady whose face showed in turn the joys of hope and the anguish of an involuntary fear. Montcornet stood there like the king of the party; in this animated scene he found a complete picture of the world, and he laughed at it as he received the self-interested smiles of a hundred brilliantly dressed women; a colonel of the Imperial Guard, a post which brought the rank of brigadier, was indeed one of the most eligible bachelors in the army. It was about midnight. The conversations, the cards, the dancing, the flirtation, the conflicting interests, the malicious remarks and the schemes, all were arriving at that degree of intensity which makes a young man exclaim, 'What a lovely ball!'

'My dear angel,' Madame de Lansac was saying to the countess, 'you are at an age when I made many mistakes. Seeing you a moment ago, suffering agonies, it occurred to me to give you some charitable advice. To make mistakes at the age of twenty-two, isn't that to spoil one's future, to tear the dress one's going to put on? My dear, we only learn very late in life how to wear it without crumpling it. Continue making skilful enemies and friends who don't know how to behave, and you will see, my love, what a nice little life you will lead one day.'

'Oh, Madame, it's very difficult for a woman to be happy, isn't it?' the countess exclaimed ingenuously.

'My dear, at your age you must know how to choose between the pleasures of life and happiness. You want to marry Martial, who is neither stupid enough to make a good husband nor passionate enough to be a lover. He has debts, my dear; he is a man who would devour your fortune. But that wouldn't matter if he made you happy. Don't you see how old he looks? That man must often have been ill; he is enjoying what remains to him of life. In three years, he will be a finished man. The ambitious side of him will start to work; perhaps he will succeed. I don't think so. What is he? An intriguer who may have an admirable business head and chatter pleasantly. But he is too conceited to have real worth. He won't go far. Besides, look at him! Can't you read in his face that, at this moment, it's not a pretty young woman he sees in you but the two millions that you own? He doesn't love you, my dear, he estimates your value as if you were a business proposition. If you want to marry take an older man who is well-esteemed and half-way up the ladder. A widow ought not to turn her marriage into a little love affair. Is a mouse caught twice in the same trap? Now, a new marriage contract ought to be a business speculation for you. In marrying again you must have at least the hope of hearing yourself called one day "Madame la Maréchale".'

At this moment the two women gazed naturally at the handsome figure of Colonel Montcornet.

'If you want to play the difficult role of a coquette and not marry,' the duchess continued good-naturedly, 'oh, my poor child, you, more than anyone else, will know how to accumulate the storm-clouds and then scatter them. But, I beg you, never make a pleasure of disturbing the peace of married couples, of destroying family unity and the happiness of contented women. I, my dear, have played that dangerous role. Alas, for the sake of a triumph of vanity, one often kills poor, virtuous creatures. For, my dear, virtuous women really exist and you create mortal enemies for yourself. I learned a little too late that, as the Duc d'Albe said, one salmon is worth more than a thousand frogs! To be sure, a genuine love affair gives a thousand times more happiness than the ephemeral passions one arouses. Well, I have come here to give you a sermon. Yes, you are the reason for my appearance in this salon which reeks of the plebs. Have I not just seen actors here? In the old days, my dear, we received them in our boudoirs, but in the drawing-room, unthinkable! Why do you look at me with such surprise? Listen to me. If you want to amuse yourself with men,' continued the old lady, 'disturb the hearts only of those who haven't a fixed way of life, of those who have no duties to fulfil. The others do not forgive us for the disorders which have made them happy. Profit from this wisdom which my long experience has taught me. That poor Soulanges, for instance, whose head you have turned and whom you have intoxicated for fifteen months, God knows how much – well, do you know who is affected by your blows ... on his whole life? He has been married for two and a half years. He is adored by a charming creature whom he loves and whom he deceives. She lives in tears and the bitterest silence. Soulanges has had moments of remorse more cruel than his pleasures were sweet. And you, artful girl, you have betrayed him! Well, come and look at your work.'

The old duchess took Madame de Vaudremont's hand and they got up.

'Look,' Madame de Lansac said, indicating with a glance the pale, unknown girl, trembling under the lights of the candelabra, 'that's my little great-niece, the Comtesse de Sou-langes. Today, at last, she gave in to my entreaties. She agreed to leave the sorrow-laden room where the sight of her child brought her only poor consolation. Do you see her? You think she's charming. Well, my dear, think what she was like when happiness and love spread their bloom on that now faded face.' The countess turned her head away silently and seemed a prey to serious thoughts. The duchess led her to the door of the card-room. Then, after looking in it as if she were searching for someone, she said to the coquette in a significant tone, 'And there is Soulanges.'

The countess shuddered when she saw, in the darkest corner of the room, the pale, anguished face of Soulanges who was leaning against the settee. His sagging limbs and expressionless face revealed the extent of his grief. The players came and went past him, paying him no more attention than if he were dead. The picture presented by the wife in tears and the hus-band sunk in dismal gloom, separated from each other in the midst of this party like the two halves of a tree struck by lightning, perhaps contained something prophetic for the countess. She was afraid of seeing in it a representation of the revenge which the future held in store for her. Her heart was not yet so hardened that feeling and kindness were entirely banished from it. She squeezed the duchess's hand and thanked her with one of those smiles which have a certain childish charm.

'My dear child,' the old lady whispered to her, 'from now on, think that we can repulse men's homage as well as attract it.'

'She is yours, if you aren't a fool.' Madame de Lansac whispered these last words in Colonel Montcornet's ear, while the beautiful countess gave herself up to the compassion inspired by Soulanges' appearance. For she still loved him sincerely enough to want to restore his happiness and she promised herself to use the irresistible power which her charms still exercised over him to send him back to his wife.

'Oh, what a sermon I'll preach to him!' she said to Madame de Lansac.

'Do nothing of the kind, my dear,' cried the duchess going back to her armchair. 'Choose a good husband and close your door to my nephew. Don't even offer him your friendship. Believe me, my child, a woman doesn't receive her husband's heart from another woman. She is a hundred times happier to think that she has reconquered him herself. By bringing my niece here, I think I have given her an excellent way of winning back her husband's affection. The only cooperation I ask from you is to tease the general.'

And when the duchess pointed to the Maître des Requêtes' friend, the countess smiled.

'Well, Madame, do you know that stranger's name at last?' the baron asked the countess in a vexed tone when she was left alone.

'Yes,' said Madame de Vaudremont, looking at the Maître des Requêtes.

Her face expressed shrewdness as well as gaiety. The smile animating her lips and cheeks, the moist glow in her eyes, were like the will o' the wisps which deceive the traveller.

Martial, who thought he was still loved, then assumed that flirtatious attitude in which a man so complacently lulls himself when he is with the woman he loves, and said pompously, 'And you won't bear me a grudge if I seem to set great store on knowing this name?'

'And you won't bear me a grudge,' replied Madame de Vaudremont, 'if, because of a remnant of love, I don't tell you and if I forbid you to make the slightest advance to that young lady? You would perhaps risk your life.'

'Madame, to lose your favour, isn't that to lose more than life?'

'Martial,' the countess said severely, 'it is Madame de Soulanges. The husband will blow your brains out, if you happen to have any.'

'Oh,' he replied with a foppish laugh, 'will the colonel let the man who has robbed him of your heart live in peace, and fight for his wife? What a reversal of principles! Do let me dance with that little lady. Thus you will be able to have proof of how little love that icy heart had for you, for if the colonel objects to my dancing with his wife, after having allowed that with you, I . . .'

'But she loves her husband.'

'An additional obstacle which I shall have the pleasure of overcoming.'

'But she is married.'

'That's an amusing objection!'

'Oh,' said the countess smiling bitterly, 'you punish us for our faults as much as for our repentance.'

'Don't get annoyed,' Martial said quickly. 'Oh, do please forgive me. Look, I'll think no more of Madame de Soulanges.'

'You deserve that I should send you over to her.'

'I am going,' said the baron with a laugh, 'and I'll come back more in love with you than ever. You will see that the prettiest woman in the world cannot capture a heart which belongs to you.'

'That is to say that you want to win the colonel's horse.'

'Oh, the traitor,' he replied laughing, shaking his finger threateningly at his friend who was smiling.

The colonel came up to them; the baron gave him his place beside the countess, saying sarcastically, 'Madame, here is a man who boasted of being able to win your favour in an evening.'

He went away congratulating himself on having stimulated the countess's vanity and done a disservice to Montcornet. But, in spite of his normal shrewdness, he had not appreciated the irony contained in Madame de Vaudremont's remarks and did not notice that without either of them knowing it, she had gone as far towards his friend as his friend had gone towards her. As the Maître des Requêtes, flitting from person to person, came near to the candelabra under which the pale, timorous Comtesse de Soulanges seemed to live only with her eyes, her husband reached the salon door, his eyes gleaming with rage. The old duchess, heedful of everything, rushed up to her nephew, asked him to give her his arm and to order her carriage so that she could go, pretending that she was bored to tears and flattering herself that in this way she was preventing an unfortunate outburst. Before leaving, she gave her niece a peculiar, significant look, indicating the enterprising young man who was about to speak to her; the look seemed to say, 'Here he is, take your revenge.'

Madame de Vaudremont intercepted the look exchanged by the aunt and the niece. She had a sudden illumination; she was afraid of being the dupe of that crafty, scheming old lady. 'That treacherous duchess has perhaps found it amusing to moralize to me, while playing me some nasty trick of her own,' she said to herself.

At this thought, Madame de Vaudremont's vanity was, perhaps, even more strongly concerned than her curiosity to unravel the thread of the intrigue. The inner preoccupation to which she was a prey prevented her from having complete control of herself. The colonel, interpreting to his own advantage the embarrassment in the countess's speech and behaviour, became, in consequence, more ardent and more pressing. The blasé old diplomats, who enjoyed watching the play of people's expressions, had never before met with so many intrigues to follow or to unravel. The passions which agitated the two couples were repeated in varying forms with different modifications on different faces at each step in these crowded rooms. The sight of so many keen emotions, all the lovers' quarrels, the sweet revenges, the cruel favours, the ardent looks, all this passionate life around them made them feel their own impotence only the more keenly.

At last the baron obtained a seat beside the Comtesse de Soulanges. His eyes wandered surreptitiously over a neck as fresh as dew, perfumed like a wild flower. He admired at close range charms which had amazed him from a distance. He saw a well-shod little foot, and measured with his eyes a supple and graceful figure. At that period, women tied the belts of their dresses just below the bust, in imitation of Greek statues; it was a pitiless fashion for those whose bust line was not perfect. Casting furtive glances at her bosom, Martial was charmed by the perfection of the countess's figure.

'You haven't danced once this evening, Madame,' he said in a gentle, unctuous voice. 'I imagine it's not for lack of a partner.'

'I don't go into society, no one knows me,' replied Madame de Soulanges coldly. She had not in the least understood the look by which her aunt had just suggested to her that she should charm the baron.

Then to keep himself in countenance Martial made play with the beautiful diamond which adorned his left hand. The gleaming stones seemed to cast a sudden light into the young countess's heart. She blushed and looked at the baron with an enigmatic expression.

'Do you like dancing?' the Provençal asked in an attempt to resume the conversation.

'Oh, very much, Monsieur.'

At this strange reply, their eyes met. The young man, surprised at the eager tone which awoke a vague hope in his heart, suddenly looked questioningly at the young woman.

'Well, Madame, is it too bold of me to suggest myself as your partner for the next dance?'

A naïve embarrassment turned the countess's white cheeks red.

'But, Monsieur, I have already refused one partner, a soldier . . .'

'Was it that tall cavalry colonel that you can see over there?'

'That's the one.'

'Oh, he's my friend. There's nothing to fear. Will you grant me the favour that I dare to hope for?'

'Yes, Monsieur.'

Her voice revealed an emotion, so deep and so unusual, that the Maître des Requêtes' blasé heart was moved by it. He was overcome by a schoolboy shyness and lost his self-assurance; his Southern temperament was aroused. He wanted to speak, but his phrases seemed to him devoid of charm compared to Madame de Soulanges' subtle, witty replies. Fortunately for him, the dance began. Standing beside his beautiful partner, he felt more at ease. For many men, dancing is a mode of behaviour. By using their physical graces, they think they can influence women's hearts more powerfully than by using their minds. Presumably the Provençal wanted at this moment to use all his powers of seduction, judging from the pretentiousness of all his movements and gestures. He had led his conquest to the set where the most brilliant women, attaching an illusory importance to it, preferred to dance. While the orchestra played the introduction to the first figure, the baron experienced an incredible feeling of satisfied pride. As he inspected the women dancers standing along the sides of this formidable square, he saw that Madame de Soulanges' dress could challenge even Madame de Vaudremont's.

By a chance which was perhaps contrived, the latter, together with the colonel, took their places opposite the baron and the lady in blue. For a moment all eyes were turned to Madame de Soulanges. A murmur of admiration revealed that she was the subject of conversation of every dancer with his partner. Such keen glances of admiration and envy were directed at her that the young woman, ashamed of a triumph which she seemed to reject, modestly lowered her eyes, blushed and became only the more charming. When she glanced up from under her blond eyelashes it was to look at her infatuated partner as if she wanted to give back to him the glory of this admiration and to tell him that she preferred his to all others. Her coquetry contained a kind of innocence, or rather she seemed to give herself up to that naïve admiration which is the beginning of love, with a sincerity which is found only amongst the young. When she danced, the onlookers could easily believe that she displayed her charms only for Martial, and although she was modest and inexperienced in the tricks of the salons, she was as able as the most skilful coquette to raise her eyes to him at the right moment and to lower them with a feigned modesty. When the figures of a new dance, invented by the dancer Trenis and named after him, brought Martial in front of the colonel, he said with a laugh, 'I have won your horse.'

'Yes, but you have lost an income of eighty thousand pounds,' replied the colonel indicating Madame de Vaudremont.

'What does that matter?' replied Martial. 'Madame de Soulanges is worth millions.'

At the end of this dance more than one whisper was murmured into more than one ear. The least pretty women made self-righteous remarks to their partners about the budding liaison between Martial and the Comtesse de Soulanges; the most beautiful were surprised at such an easy conquest. The men could not understand the good fortune of the little Maître des Requêtes, whom they did not think particularly seductive. Some good-natured women said that one must not judge the countess hastily; young women would be very unfortunate if an expressive look or a few gracefully performed dance steps were enough to compromise them. Martial alone knew the extent of his good fortune. At the last figure, when the ladies of the set had to form a *moulinet*,[4] his fingers pressed the countess's and through the fine, perfumed kid gloves he thought he could feel the young woman's fingers respond to his amorous appeal.

'Madame,' he said as the dance finished, 'don't go back to that horrid corner where up till now you have buried your face and your dress. Is admiration the only advantage you can

4. A dance figure in which two or four dancers join their right hands.

obtain from the diamonds which adorn your white neck and your beautifully arranged hair? Come and walk through the rooms and enjoy the party and your own appearance.'

Madame de Soulanges followed her would-be seducer, who thought that she would be more securely his if he managed to show her off. Together they then walked a little through the groups who crowded into the mansion's reception rooms. The Comtesse de Soulanges, full of anxiety, stopped a moment before going into each room and only went in after craning her neck to take a look at all the men. This fear, which delighted the little Maître des Requêtes, seemed calmed only when he had said to his trembling companion, 'Don't worry; *he* isn't there.'

In this way they reached an enormous picture gallery in a wing of the house, where they enjoyed an advance view of a magnificent cold collation prepared for three hundred people. As the meal was about to begin, Martial led the countess to an oval boudoir looking on to the gardens, where the rarest flowers and a few shrubs formed a scented arbour beneath gleaming blue hangings. The hum of the party died away there. The countess shuddered as she entered and obstinately refused to follow the young man. But after looking in a mirror, she no doubt saw that there were others there for she went and sat down on a couch with quite good grace.

'This room is delightful,' she said, admiring a sky-blue hanging ornamented with pearls.

'Everything here is love and pleasure,' said the young man, greatly moved.

In the mysterious light of the boudoir, he looked at the countess and was surprised to see on her gently agitated face a look of embarrassment, of modesty and of desire which delighted him. The young woman smiled and this smile seemed to put an end to the struggle of contradictory feelings in her heart. In the most charming way she took her admirer's left hand and removed the ring, on which her eyes had fallen, from his finger.

'What a beautiful diamond!' she cried with the naïve expression of a girl revealing the thrills of a first temptation.

Martial, moved by the involuntary but intoxicating caress which the countess had given him as she took off the jewel, looked at her with eyes as sparkling as the jewel.

'Wear it,' he said, 'as a souvenir of this hour and for love of . . .'

She looked at it with such ecstatic delight that he did not finish his sentence; he kissed her hand.

'You are giving it to me?' she asked in amazement.

'I should like to give you the whole world.'

'You are not joking?' she continued in a voice that was altered by too keen a satisfaction.

'Do you accept only my diamond?'

'You will never take it away from me?' she asked.

'Never.'

She put the ring on her finger. Martial, expecting soon to be made happy, made a move to put his arm round the countess's waist. But she got up suddenly and said clearly and calmly, 'Monsieur, I accept this diamond with all the less scruple, as it belongs to me.'

The Maître des Requêtes was quite taken aback.

'Monsieur de Soulanges took it recently from my dressing table and told me he'd lost it.'

'You are mistaken, Madame,' said Martial testily. 'I got it from Madame de Vaudremont.'

'Quite so,' she replied with a smile. 'My husband borrowed this ring from me, gave it to her and she presented it to you. My ring has travelled, that's all. Perhaps this ring will tell me everything I don't know, and will teach me the secret of being always attractive. Monsieur,' she continued, 'if it hadn't been mine, you can be sure that I wouldn't have risked paying so dearly for it. For they say, that near you, a young woman is in danger. But look,' she added, manipulating a spring hidden under the stone, 'Monsieur de Soulanges' hair is still there.'

She dashed into the reception rooms with such speed that it seemed useless to try to rejoin her. Moreover, Martial was so disconcerted that he did not feel in any mood to make the attempt. Madame de Soulanges' laugh had found an echo in the boudoir where the young fop caught sight of the colonel and Madame de Vaudremont between the shrubs; they were laughing heartily.

'Would you like my horse to run after your conquest?' asked the colonel.

The good grace with which the baron put up with Madame de Vaudremont's and Montcornet's extensive teasing earned him their discretion about the evening when his friend bartered his war horse for a rich, pretty young woman.

While the Comtesse de Soulanges was going from the Chaussée-d'Antin to the Faubourg Saint-Germain where she lived, her heart was a prey to the most acute anxiety. Before leaving the Gondreville mansion she had gone through all the rooms without finding her aunt or her husband, who had left without her. Terrible forebodings then tormented her ingenuous heart. She had been a discreet witness of the sufferings experienced by her husband from the day that Madame de Vaudremont had attached him to her chariot and she confidently hoped that repentance would soon bring her husband back to her. So it was with an extreme repugnance that she had consented to the plan made by her aunt, Madame de Lansac, and at this moment she was afraid she had made a mistake. The evening had saddened her guileless heart. Frightened at first by the Comte de Soulanges' ill and mournful appearance, she was still more so by her rival's beauty; and the corruption of society life had made her sick at heart. As she crossed the Pont-Royal she threw away the profaned hair from under the diamond which had formerly been given to her as a pledge of pure love. She wept as she recalled the acute suffering to which she had been prey for so long and shuddered more than once on reflecting that the duty of women who want domestic peace forces them to bury in the depths of their hearts and without complaint sufferings as cruel as her own.

'Alas,' she said to herself, 'how can women who are not in love manage? Where is the source of their kindness and understanding? I can't believe, as my aunt says, that reason is enough to support them in such devotion.' She was still sighing when her footman lowered the steps of her smart carriage and she rushed into the entrance hall of her house. She hurried upstairs and when she reached her room she gave a terrified start as she saw her husband sitting by the fireplace.

'Since when, my dear, have you been going to balls without me, without telling me?' he asked in a voice filled with emotion. 'You should know that, without her husband, a woman is always out of place. You compromised yourself strangely in the remote corner where you installed yourself.'

'Oh, my dear Léon,' she said in a caressing tone, 'I couldn't resist the happiness of seeing you without your seeing me. My aunt took me to the ball, and I was very happy there.'

This speech disarmed the count and his expression lost its feigned severity, for he had just been reproaching himself keenly and dreaded his wife's return. She had, no doubt, learned at the ball of an infidelity that he had hoped to conceal from her and, as guilty lovers are wont to do, he was trying to forestall the countess's only too justified anger by finding fault with her. He looked silently at his wife who, in her brilliant ball dress, seemed to him more beautiful than ever. Happy to see her husband smiling and to find him at this hour in a room which for some time now he had visited less frequently, the countess looked at him so tenderly that she blushed and lowered her eyes. Her forgiveness delighted Soulanges all the more in that this scene followed the tortures he had experienced during the ball. He grasped his wife's hand and kissed it in gratitude. Isn't gratitude often to be met with in love?

'Hortense, what have you on your finger which hurt my lips so much?' he asked smilingly.

'It's my diamond which you said was lost and which I have found again.'

General Montcornet did not marry Madame de Vaudremont, in spite of the good understanding that reigned between them for a short while. She was one of the victims of the terrible fire which made famous for ever the ball given by the Austrian ambassador on the occasion of the marriage of the Emperor Napoleon to the daughter of the Emperor Francis II.

1829

A Study in
Feminine Psychology

THE Marquise de Listomère is one of those young women reared in the spirit of the Restoration. She has principles, she eats no meat on Fridays, she goes to communion and, all dressed up, to balls, to the Bouffons and to the Opéra. Her spiritual director allows her to combine the sacred and the profane. Her duties both to the Church and to the world of society are always performed and she is thus a reflection of the present age which seems to have adopted the word *Legality*, for its motto. The behaviour of the marchioness contains exactly enough religious zeal to enable her, should there be a new Maintenon,[1] to attain to the gloomy piety of the last days of Louis XIV and enough worldliness to adopt equally well the gallant ways of the early years of that reign, if it were to return.

At the present time, she is virtuous by design, or perhaps by inclination. Having been married for seven years to the Marquis de Listomère (one of those deputies who is waiting for a peerage) she may also think that her behaviour furthers her family's ambition. Some women, before passing judgement on her, are waiting for the moment when M. de Listomère will be a peer of France and when she will be thirty-six years old. That is the time of life when most women realize that they are the dupes of the laws of society.

The marquis is a fairly insignificant man. He is well thought of at court. His good qualities, like his failings, are negative; the former can no more give him a reputation for virtue than the latter can give him the kind of notoriety gained by vice. In the Chamber of Deputies he never says a word but he votes

1. Madame de Maintenon, who was distinguished by her strict piety, married Louis XIV secretly in 1684 and exercised a considerable influence over him during the latter part of his life.

for the government. At home he behaves in the same way as he does in the Chamber. And so he has the reputation of being the best husband in France. He may not be capable of exalted passion, but he never scolds, unless he is kept waiting. His friends have dubbed him 'cloudy weather'. And, indeed, with him you never have either too bright a light or complete darkness. He is like all the ministers that have succeeded each other in France since the Charter.[2] For a woman of principle, it would be difficult to fall into better hands. Is it not a great deal for a virtuous woman to have married a man incapable of committing follies?

There have been dandies who were impertinent enough to press the marchioness's hand lightly as they danced with her. They received in reply only scornful looks and they were all treated with that insulting indifference which, like frost in spring, destroys the seed of the finest hopes. Handsome men, wits, fops, men who profess fine feelings and who earn their livings by the way they hold their walking-sticks, men with great names or of great renown, high or low fliers, with her they have all drawn a blank. She has earned the right to talk with men whom she finds witty for as long and as often as she wants to, without being put on the slanderer's list. Certain coquettes are capable of following this plan for seven years so that later on they can satisfy their fancies. But it would be a calumny on the Marquise de Listomère to suppose that she had this in mind.

I had the good fortune to see this phoenix of marchionesses; she talks well, I am a good listener, she liked me, I go to her parties. That was as far as my ambition went. Madame de Listomère is neither ugly nor pretty. She has white teeth, a dazzling complexion and very red lips. She is tall and has a good figure. She has a small, slender foot and she doesn't reveal it too much. Her eyes, far from being dull like those of most Parisians, have a gentle gleam which becomes fascinating if she happens to become animated. One can glimpse a soul behind that indecisive exterior. If she is interested in the con-

2. The French constitutional charter of 1814, granted by Louis XVIII, guaranteed certain liberties to the French people.

versation, she displays a graciousness which is buried beneath a cool guarded demeanour, and then she is charming. She is not out for success but she achieves it. One always finds what one is not looking for. This remark is true too often for it not to be turned into a proverb one day. That will be the moral of the tale, which I would not allow myself to tell if, at the moment, it were not all over the salons of Paris.

About a month ago the Marquise de Listomère danced with a young man as modest as he is scatterbrained. He is full of virtues but shows only his failings. He is passionate but makes fun of the passions. He has talent but he conceals it. When he is with aristocrats he behaves like a scholar but when he is with scholars he behaves like an aristocrat. Eugène de Rastignac is one of those very sensible young men who try everything and who seem to sound out people to find out what the future will bring. Not having yet reached the age when a man is ambitious, he makes fun of everything. He has charm and originality, two unusual virtues because they are mutually exclusive. Without thinking about making a good impression, he chatted for about half an hour with the Marquise de Listomère. While not taking seriously the vagaries of a conversation which, after beginning with the opera, *William Tell*, came on to the duties of women, he had more than once looked at the Marquise de Listomère in a way that embarrassed her. Then he left her and did not talk to her any more the whole evening. He danced, sat down to écarté, lost some money, and went home to bed. I have the honour to assure you that this is what happened. I add nothing, I omit nothing.

The next morning Rastignac woke late. He stayed in bed, where he doubtless indulged in some of those morning reveries in which a young man glides, like a sylph, under more than one silk, cashmere or cotton bed-curtain. In these moments, the heavier the body is with sleep, the more agile is the mind. At last Eugène got up, without yawning too much as so many ill-bred people do, rang for his valet, ordered some tea and drank an inordinate amount of it. This will not seem extraordinary to people who like tea, but to explain the matter to people who accept it only as a panacea for indigestion, I shall add that Eugène was writing. He was sitting comfortably with his feet more often on his fire-dogs than in his foot-muff. Oh, to have one's feet on the polished bar which joins the two griffons of a fender, to think of one's love affairs when one is getting up and in a dressing-gown, is something so delightful that I am extremely sorry to have neither mistress, nor fire-dogs, nor dressing-gown. When I have all that, I shall not make comments on them, I shall profit from them.

The first letter which Eugène wrote was finished in a quarter of an hour. He folded it, sealed it and let it lie in front of him without addressing it. The second letter which he began at eleven o'clock was not finished till midday. It filled four pages.

'That woman runs in my head,' he said, as he folded the second letter, which he left in front of him, meaning to address it after he had finished his involuntary reverie. He crossed the two ends of his flowered dressing-gown, placed his feet on a stool, slipped his hands into the pockets of his red cashmere trousers and leaned back in a delightful wing-chair whose seat and back described the comfortable angle of a hundred and twenty degrees. He drank no more tea and sat motionless, his eyes fixed on the gilded hand at the top of his shovel without seeing the hand or the shovel or the gilt. He did not even poke the fire. That was a tremendous mistake, for is not pottering about with the fire a very keen pleasure when one is thinking about a woman? Our wit gives a language to the little blue tongues of flame which suddenly leap out and chatter in the hearth. We can interpret the powerful, sharp language of a *bourguignon*.

Let us stop at this word and, for the sake of the ignorant, insert here an explanation provided by a very distinguished etymologist who wants to remain anonymous. *Bourguignon* is the popular, symbolic name which, since the reign of Charles VI, has been given to those noisy explosions which shoot out on to a carpet or a dress a little piece of coal, the slight cause of conflagration. They say that the fire releases an air bubble that a gnawing worm has left in the heart of the wood. *Inde amor, inde burgundus*. One trembles at seeing the piece of coal, that one had tried to place so carefully between the flaming logs, roll down like an avalanche. Oh, to poke the fire when one is in love, does that not naturally develop one's thoughts?

It was at this moment that I walked into Eugène's room. He gave a start and said, 'Oh, there you are, my dear Horace,[3] how long have you been there?'

'I have just come.'

'Oh!'

Eugène took the two letters, addressed them and rang for his servant.

'Take these to town.'

And Joseph went without comment. What an excellent servant!

We began to talk about the Morean expedition[4] in which I was looking for a job as a doctor. Eugène commented that I would lose a lot by leaving Paris and we spoke of indifferent matters. I don't think that anyone will bear me a grudge for not recording our conversation.

When the Marquise de Listomère got up about two o'clock in the afternoon, her maid, Caroline, handed her a letter. She read it while Caroline did her hair. (This is an imprudence which many young women commit.)

'*O dear angel of love, treasure of life and happiness!*'

At these words the marchioness was going to throw the letter into the fire, but there came into her head a whim that every virtuous woman will understand perfectly. She wanted to see how a man who began a letter in this way would finish it. She read on. When she had turned the fourth page, she let her arms fall as if she were tired.

'Caroline, go and find out who delivered this letter here.'

'Madame, I got it from Monsieur le Baron de Rastignac's servant.'

There was a long silence.

3. The narrator of this story is Horace Bianchon, who also narrates 'The Atheist's Mass' and 'La Grande Bretèche'.
4. An expedition of 1828 which drove the Turks from the Peloponnese.

'Do you wish to dress, Madame?' asked Caroline.

'No.'

'He must be very impertinent,' thought the marchioness.

I beg all women to imagine her commentary for themselves.

Madame de Listomère finished hers by firmly resolving to close her door to Monsieur Eugène and to treat him with more than disdain should she meet him in society, for his insolence could not be compared with any of those which the marchioness had, in the end, forgiven. At first she wanted to keep the letter, but on reflection she burnt it.

'Madame has just received a splendid declaration of love, and she read it!' Caroline said to the housekeeper.

'I would never have believed that of Madame,' the old woman replied, in amazement.

In the evening, the countess went to the Marquis de Beauséant's where Rastignac was probably to be found. It was a Saturday. Since the Marquis de Beauséant was distantly related to Monsieur Rastignac, that young man could not fail to come in the course of the evening. At two o'clock in the morning, Madame de Listomère, who had stayed only to crush Eugène with her coldness, had waited for him in vain. A man of wit, Stendhal, has had the strange idea of giving the name *crystallization* to the processes of the marchioness's thoughts before, during and after that evening.

Four days later, Eugène was scolding his servant.

'I shall be forced to dismiss you, Joseph my boy!'

'What are you saying, sir?'

'You are continually committing blunders. Where did you deliver the two letters which I gave you on Friday?'

Joseph was stunned with surprise. Like a statue in a cathedral porch, he remained motionless, entirely absorbed by the working of his imagination. Suddenly he smiled foolishly and said, 'Well, sir, one was for Madame la Marquise de Listomère, Rue Saint-Dominique, and the other for your lawyer . . .'

'Are you sure of what you are saying?'

Joseph was quite taken aback. I realized that I had better interfere, since I still happened to be there.

'Joseph is right,' I said. Eugène turned round towards me. 'I couldn't help reading the addresses and . . .'

'And,' Eugène said, interrupting me, 'wasn't one of the letters for Madame de Nucingen?'

'No, definitely not! So I thought, my dear fellow, that your heart had pirouetted from the Rue Saint Lazare to the Rue Saint-Dominique.'

Eugène clapped his hand to his brow and began to smile. Joseph realized that the fault was not his.

Now, here are the moral lessons that all young men should meditate on. *First fault*: Eugène thought it was amusing to make Madame de Listomère laugh at a mistake that had made her mistress of a love letter which was not for her. *Second fault*: He did not go to see Madame de Listomère till four days after the incident, thus allowing the thoughts of a virtuous young woman to crystallize. There were at least about ten other faults, of which I make no mention, so that I can give the ladies the pleasure of deducing them *ex professo* for those who cannot guess them. Eugène arrived at the marchioness's door, but when he wanted to go in, the porter stopped him and told him that Madame la Marquise had gone out. As he was getting into his carriage again, the marquis came in.

'Do come in, Eugène, my wife is at home.'

Oh, you must excuse the marquis. However good a husband may be, it is difficult for him to reach perfection. As he went upstairs, Rastignac then became aware of the ten faults of society logic which were in this chapter of the beautiful book of his life. When Madame de Listomère saw her husband come in with Eugène, she could not help blushing. The young baron noticed the sudden blush. If the most modest man still retains a little residue of vanity which he never discards, any more than a woman rids herself of her inevitable coquetry, who could blame Eugène for saying to himself then, 'What, this stronghold too?' And he straightened his tie. Although young men are not very stingy they all like adding a head to their collection of medals.

Monsieur de Listomère grabbed the *Gazette de France*,

which he caught sight of in a corner of the fireplace, and went to a window bay in order to acquire, with the journalist's help, a personal opinion on the state of France. A woman, even a prude, does not stay out of countenance for long, even in the most difficult situation in which she may find herself. It is as if she always has handy the fig leaf given to her by our Mother Eve. So when Eugène, interpreting in favour of his vanity the fact that he had been denied admission, greeted Madame de Listomère somewhat deliberately, she was clever enough to conceal her thoughts with one of those feminine smiles which are more enigmatic than a king's word.

'Are you unwell, Madame? You had me refused admittance.'

'No, Monsieur.'

'Perhaps you are about to go out?'

'Not at all.'

'You were expecting someone?'

'No one.'

'If my visit is indiscreet, it is the fault of Monsieur le Marquis. I was obeying your mysterious order when he himself led me into the sanctuary.'

'Monsieur de Listomère was not in my confidence. It's not always wise to let a husband into certain seerets . . .'

The firm, gentle tone in which the marchioness said these words and the imperious look she gave him made Rastignac think that he had been in too much of a hurry to straighten his tie.

'Madame, I understand you,' he said with a laugh. 'I must then doubly congratulate myself at having met Monsieur le Marquis. He has given me the opportunity to offer you an explanation which would be fraught with danger, were you not kindness itself.'

The marchioness looked at the young baron with some surprise, but she replied with dignity, 'Monsieur, silence will be your best excuse. As for me, I promise you to forget it all completely, a pardon which you scarcely deserve.'

'Madame,' said Eugène quickly, 'a pardon is unnecessary where there has been no offence. The letter which you received and which you must have thought so impertinent was not intended for you,' he added in a low voice.

The marchioness could not help smiling. She was determined to have been offended.

'Why tell a lie?' she replied, with a disdainfully playful air, but in quite a gentle voice. 'Now that I have scolded you, I shall gladly laugh at a stratagem which is not without subtlety. I know some poor women who would be caught by it. "Goodness, how much in love he is!" they would say.' The marchioness began a forced laugh and added indulgently, 'If we are to remain friends, let there be no more question of mistakes which cannot deceive me.'

'On my honour, Madame, you are deceived more than you think,' Eugène quickly replied.

'But what are you two talking about?' asked Monsieur de Listomère, who had been listening to the last moment of the conversation without being able to understand its obscurities.

'Oh, it won't interest you,' replied the marchioness.

Monsieur de Listomère calmly resumed reading his newspaper and said, 'Oh, Madame de Mortsauf has died; your poor brother is probably at Clochegourde.'

'Do you know, Monsieur,' continued the marchioness turning towards Eugène, 'that you have just uttered an impertinence?'

'If I didn't know the strictness of your principles,' he replied naïvely, 'I would think that you wanted either to give me ideas which I do not allow myself or to drag my secret from me. Or perhaps again you want to make fun of me.'

The marchioness smiled. This smile irritated Eugène.

'May you still believe, Madame, in an offence that I have not committed,' he said. 'And I ardently hope that chance will not lead you to discover in society the person who should have read that letter.'

'What, would it still be for Madame de Nucingen?' exclaimed Madame de Listomère, more inquisitive to penetrate a secret than to avenge herself for the young man's wisecracks.

Eugène blushed. One needs to be more than twenty-five years old not to blush at being reproached with the folly of a fidelity which women make fun of, so as not to show how much they are envious of it. Nevertheless he said, in a fairly detached way, 'Why not, Madame?'

These are the mistakes that one makes at twenty-five. This confidence produced a violent emotion in Madame de Listomère. But Eugène did not yet know how to analyse a woman's face by looking at it fleetingly or by giving a side glance. Only the marchioness's lips had turned pale. Madame de Listomère rang to ask for wood, and so Rastignac was forced to get up to go.

'If that is so,' said the marchioness, stopping Eugène with a cold, calm look, 'it would be difficult for you to explain to me, Monsieur, by what chance my name came to be written by your pen. An address written on a letter is not like a neighbour's opera hat that one might mistake for one's own, on leaving a ball.'

Eugène, abashed, looked at the marchioness with an expression that was both self-satisfied and stupid. He felt that he was becoming ridiculous, stammered out a schoolboy phrase of farewell and departed. Some days later the marchioness acquired irrefutable proofs of Eugène's veracity. She has not been anywhere for a fortnight.

The marquis tells everyone who asks him the reason for this change, 'My wife has gastritis.'

But I who am treating her and who know her secret, I know that she is only having a little attack of nerves which she is using as an excuse to stay at home.

1830

An Incident in the
Reign of Terror

ABOUT eight o'clock in the evening of 22 January 1793, in Paris, an old lady was going down the steep slope leading to the church of Saint-Laurent in the Faubourg Saint-Martin. It had snowed so much all day that her footsteps were barely audible. The streets were deserted. The terror under which France was groaning at that time added to the fear naturally aroused by the silence; so no one had yet crossed the old lady's path, and her sight, which had long been poor, was not good enough for her to discern in the distance, in the glimmer of the street-lamps, a few passers-by thinly dispersed like shadows in the wide road which runs through that quarter. Boldly she walked through the deserted streets, as if her age were a talisman which was bound to preserve her from any misfortune.

When she had passed the Rue des Morts, she thought she heard the heavy, firm step of a man walking behind her. It seemed to her that it was not the first time that she had noticed this sound. She was afraid that she had been followed and tried to hurry so as to reach a fairly well-lit shop, hoping to be able to see by its light if there were any justification for the suspicions which were frightening her. As soon as she was in the horizontal shaft of light which came from the shop, she turned her head sharply and caught sight of a human form in the gloom. This vague glimpse was enough to make her stagger for a moment, struck with terror, for by this time she was quite sure that the stranger had followed her from the first step she had taken outside her home, but the anxiety to escape from a spy gave her strength. She was incapable of thinking rationally and began to run, as if she could get away from a man who was bound to move more quickly than she could. After running for a few minutes, she reached a cake-shop, went in and almost fell on to a chair in front of the counter. At the rattle of the door-latch, a young woman busy embroidering looked up, recognized through the shop-window the old-fashioned violet silk cloak which enveloped the old lady, and hurriedly opened a drawer as if to take from it something which she had to hand over to her. The gesture and the expression of the young woman not only showed that she wanted to get rid of the visitor quickly, as if she were one of those people whom one doesn't enjoy seeing; she also let a gesture of impatience escape her when she found the drawer empty. Then, without looking at the lady, she hastily left the counter, went to the back part of the shop and called her husband, who suddenly appeared.

'Where did you put ...?' she asked him mysteriously, glancing at the old lady and leaving her sentence unfinished.

Although the pastry-cook could see only the visitor's head-gear, a huge silk bonnet trimmed with bows of violet ribbon, he disappeared after giving his wife a look which seemed to say:

'Do you think I would leave that under your counter?'

Surprised that the old lady sat so still and silent, the shop-keeper's wife went up to her again and looking at her, felt moved to pity and perhaps also to curiosity. Although the old woman's complexion was naturally very pale, like that of someone who had taken secret vows of austerity, it was easy to see that some recent shock had made it even paler than usual. Her bonnet was arranged so as to hide her hair, which was white, no doubt with age, for she obviously wore no powder, there being no sign of it on the collar of her dress. This absence of ornament gave her face a kind of religious severity. Her features wore a solemn and proud expression. Formerly the manners and habits of people of rank were so different from those of the other classes that it was easy to recognize a person of noble birth. And so the young woman was sure that the unknown lady was a *ci-devant*,[1] and that she had belonged to the Court.

'Madame?' she said involuntarily and respectfully forgetting that this title was prohibited.

1. *Ci-devant* was a name given to former members of the nobility during the French Revolution.

The old lady said nothing. She stared at the shop-window as if some terrifying object were outlined against it.

'What's the matter with you, *citoyenne*?'[2] asked the master of the house who reappeared at that moment.

The *citoyen*[2] pastry-cook roused the lady from her day-dream by handing her a little cardboard box covered with blue paper.

'Nothing, nothing, my friends,' she replied gently.

She looked up at the pastry-cook as if to thank him with a glance, but seeing a red cap on his head, she cried out,

'Ah! . . . You have betrayed me!'

In reply the young woman and her husband made a gesture of horror so that the visitor blushed, either with shame at having suspected them, or perhaps with relief.

'Forgive me,' she said sweetly like a child. Then, taking a louis d'or out of her pocket, she gave it to the pastry-cook: 'Here is the price we agreed,' she added.

There is a kind of poverty which the poor can recognize instinctively. The pastry-cook and his wife looked at each other, exchanging the same thought, as they glanced at the old lady. This was evidently her last louis d'or. The old lady's hands trembled as she held out the coin, looking at it sadly yet ungrudgingly; but she seemed to appreciate the full extent of her sacrifice. Fasting and poverty were as clearly marked on her face as fear and asceticism. Her clothes still bore traces of richness, threadbare silk, a neat, though faded cloak, carefully mended lace; in short, the rags of wealth! The shopkeepers, torn between pity and self-interest, first of all soothed their consciences with words.

'But, *citoyenne*, you look very frail.'

'Would Madame like some refreshment?' asked the wife, interrupting her husband.

'We have some very good soup,' said the pastry-cook.

'It is so cold, perhaps Madame got chilled while walking; but you can rest here and warm up a little.'

'We are not heartless devils,' exclaimed the pastry-cook.

Won over by the friendly tone of the charitable shop-

2. *Citoyen* (feminine *citoyenne*) was a form of address during the French Revolution, replacing *monsieur*, *madame* and *mademoiselle*.

keepers, the lady revealed that she had been followed by a man and that she was afraid to go home alone.

'Is that all that's worrying you?' replied the man with the red cap. 'Wait for me, *citoyenne*.'

He gave the louis to his wife. Then, moved by a kind of gratitude which steals into the heart of a shopkeeper when he receives an exorbitant price for goods of very little value, he went to equip himself in his National Guard's uniform, took up his hat, put on his sword and reappeared as an armed guard; but his wife had had time to reflect. As so often happens, Reflection closed the open hand of Benevolence. Anxious and afraid that her husband might become involved in some untoward incident, the pastry-cook's wife tried to stop him by pulling at his coat-tail; but the good fellow, obeying his charitable feeling, immediately offered to escort the old lady.

'It looks as if the man whom the *citoyenne* is afraid of is still prowling round the shop,' said the young woman sharply.

'I am afraid so,' frankly admitted the old lady.

'He might be a spy? It might be a plot? Don't go, and take the box back from her . . .'

These words, whispered by his wife into the pastry-cook's ear, froze his newly found courage.

'Oh! I'll go and say a word to him and get rid of him for you right away,' exclaimed the pastry-cook opening the door and rushing out.

The old lady, passive as a child and half dazed, sat down again on her chair. The honest shopkeeper was not long in reappearing; his face, naturally fairly red and flushed still more by the oven-heat, had suddenly become deathly pale. He was so overcome by terror that his legs were trembling and his eyes were like those of a drunken man.

'Do you want to have our heads cut off, wretched aristocrat?' he exclaimed in a fury. 'Clear out and don't show your face here again. And don't count on me to help you with your plots!'

As he finished saying these words, the pastry-cook tried to take back from the old lady the little box which she had put in one of her pockets. The visitor would rather brave the dangers of the road with no protector save God than lose what she had just bought, so that the moment the pastry-cook's impudent hands touched her clothes she regained the agility of her youth; she rushed to the door, quickly opened it and disappeared from the view of the husband and wife, leaving them amazed and trembling.

The moment the unknown lady was outside the shop, she began to walk quickly; but her strength soon failed her, for she heard the spy who was following her pitilessly, as his heavy step crunched the snow; she had to stop, he stopped too. She had not the courage to speak to him nor to look at him, either because of the fear which gripped her, or because she did not know what to do. She continued on her way, walking slowly; then the man slowed down, remaining at a distance from which he was able to keep an eye on her. The stranger seemed to be the very shadow of the old woman. Nine o'clock struck as the silent couple again went past the church of Saint-Laurent. In everyone, even in the most faint-hearted, it is natural for a period of calm to follow a violent emotion, for, even if our feelings are boundless, our physical organs are limited. And so as the unknown lady came to no harm at the hands of her apparent persecutor, she was inclined to look on him as a secret friend eager to protect her; she reviewed all the situations in which the stranger had appeared, as if to find plausible motives for this soothing opinion, and she then chose to think that his intentions were good rather than evil. So forgetting the fright that the man had just given the pastry-cook, she steadily walked on through the higher parts of the Faubourg Saint-Martin. After half-an-hour's walk, she came to a house standing where the road to the Barrière de Pantin forks off from the suburb's main street. This is still one of the most deserted places in all Paris. The north wind, blowing across the heights of Saint-Chaumont and Belleville, was whistling through the houses, or rather the hovels, scattered over this almost uninhabited valley where the dividing walls are made of mud and bones. This desolate spot seemed the natural refuge of poverty and despair. The implacable pursuer of the poor creature who was bold enough to go through these silent streets by night seemed impressed by the scene that lay before him. He stopped, thoughtful and hesitant, in the faint light of a street-lamp whose feeble glimmer barely penetrated the gloom. Fear sharpened the sight of the old woman who thought she could see something sinister in the stranger's features; she felt her terrors revive, and taking advantage of a kind of uncertainty which made the man pause, she slipped away in the darkness to the door of the solitary house, touched a spring and disappeared with fantastic speed. The man, without moving, stared at the house which, in a way, was typical of the squalid dwellings of the district. The tumble-down hovel, built of rubble, was covered with a layer of dirty yellow plaster, so cracked it looked as if the least puff of wind would blow it down. The brown tiled roof was overgrown with moss and was sagging in several places so that it seemed on the point of giving way under the heavy snow. Each storey had three windows whose frames were so rotted with damp and warped by the sun that the cold was bound to penetrate into the rooms. This isolated house was like an old tower which time had forgotten to destroy. A faint light lit up the windows irregularly placed in the attic at the top of the building, but the rest of the house was shrouded in complete darkness.

It was with difficulty that the old woman climbed up the rough awkward staircase whose only hand-rail was a rope. Furtively she knocked at the door of a flat in the attic and almost collapsed on to a chair which an old man pushed forward for her.

'Hide, hide!' she said. 'Although we hardly ever go out, our activities are known, our movements are spied on.'

'What's the latest?' asked another old woman sitting by the fire.

'The man who has been prowling round the house since yesterday followed me this evening.'

At these words, the three inhabitants of the garret looked at each other without trying to conceal the expressions of intense fear on their faces. The old man was the least upset of the three, perhaps because it was he who was in most danger. Under the weight of a great misfortune or under the yoke of persecution, a brave man straight away, as it were, sacrifices himself; he thinks of his days only as so many victories over fate. It was easy to see from the way the two women looked fixedly at the old man that he was the sole object of their intense concern.

'Why despair of God, my sisters?' he said in a hollow but solemn voice. 'We sang his praises in the midst of the shouts of the murderers and the cries of the dying at the Carmelite convent. If He decided to save me from that slaughter, it was surely to preserve me for a fate which I ought to accept without complaint. God protects His own, He can dispose of them according to His will. We must worry about you, and not about me.'

'No,' said one of the two old women, 'what are our lives worth in comparison with a priest's?'

'From the moment I was outside the Abbaye de Chelles I regarded myself as dead,' exclaimed the nun who had not been out.

'Look,' continued the one who had just come in, handing the little box to the priest, 'here are the wafers. But,' she exclaimed, 'I can hear someone coming up the stairs.'

At these words, all three began to listen. The sound stopped.

'Don't be afraid,' said the priest, 'if someone tries to make contact with you. Someone whose loyalty we can rely on was to arrange to cross the frontier; he will come for the letters which I have written to the Duc de Langeais and the Marquis de Beauséant asking them to consider how to rescue you from this terrible country, from the death or destitution which awaits you here.'

'So you won't follow us?' cried the two nuns softly with a kind of despair.

'My place is where there are victims,' said the priest simply.

The nuns were silent and gazed with admiration at their saintly guest.

'Sister Martha,' he said turning to the nun who had gone out for the wafers, 'this messenger ought to reply *Fiat voluntas* to the word *Hosanna*.'

'There is someone on the stairs!' cried the other nun, opening a hiding-place fitted into the roof.

This time, in the absolute silence, they could easily hear a man's footsteps resounding on the stairs, which were covered with hardened mud. The priest crawled with difficulty into a kind of wardrobe and the nun threw some clothes over him.

'You can shut the door, Sister Agatha,' he said in a muffled voice.

The priest had only just been hidden when three knocks at the door startled the two saintly women, who looked at each other questioningly without daring to utter a single word. They both looked about sixty years old. As they had had no contact with the world for forty years, they were like plants used to a hot-house atmosphere, which die if they are taken out of it. They were so accustomed to convent life that they could no longer imagine any other. One morning their convent gates had been broken down and they had shuddered at finding themselves free. It is not hard to imagine the kind of unnatural numbness which the events of the Revolution had produced in their innocent minds. Used as they were to convent ways, they were incapable of coping with the difficulties of life and they did not even understand their situation. They were like children who had once been taken care of and who, then deprived of the loving care of a mother, prayed instead of crying. And so they remained dumb and passive in face of the danger they foresaw at that moment, knowing no defence other than Christian resignation. The man who was knocking at the door interpreted this silence in his own way; he opened the door and suddenly appeared. The two nuns trembled as they recognized the person who, for some time, had been prowling round their house and obtaining information about them. They looked at him without moving, with an apprehensive curiosity like shy children who silently examine strangers. He was a tall, heavy man, but nothing in his step, his demeanour or his face suggested an ill-natured man. Like the nuns, he remained motionless and slowly looked round the room he had entered.

Two straw mats placed on the bare boards served as beds

for the nuns. There was only one table in the middle of the room and on it was a copper candlestick, some plates, three knives and a round loaf. A small fire burned in the grate. And a few pieces of wood, piled up in a corner, showed how poor the two recluses were. The walls were coated with a layer of very old paint, and brown streaks where the rain had come in indicated the bad condition of the roof. A relic, probably rescued when the Abbaye de Chelles was sacked, adorned the mantelpiece. Three chairs, two chests and a shabby chest of drawers completed the furniture of the room. A door beside the fireplace led one to suppose that there was a second room.

The person who had intruded, in such terrifying circumstances, into the intimacy of this household soon sized up all the contents of this little cell. An expression of pity came over his face; he cast a kindly glance at the two women and seemed just as ill-at-ease as they were. All three of them stood there in an uncanny silence, but this did not last long, for the stranger finally realized the helplessness and the inexperience of the two poor creatures, and he then said in a voice which he tried to make gentle, 'I don't come here as an enemy, *citoyennes* . . .' He stopped and then went on, 'My sisters, if any misfortune were to come upon you, believe me that it would not be because of me. I have a favour to ask of you . . .'

They still remained silent.

'If I disturb you, if . . . I am in your way, speak freely . . . I shall go away; but please understand I am completely devoted to you; that, if there is anything I can do for you, you can make use of me without fear and that I, alone, perhaps, am above the law, since we no longer have a King . . .'

These words had such a ring of truth that Sister Agatha, the nun who belonged to the Langeais family and whose manners suggested that in the past she had been familiar with the atmosphere and splendour of court society, quickly pointed to one of the chairs as if to ask their guest to sit down. The stranger, who understood the gesture, looked pleased yet sad, but waited till the two worthy ladies had sat down before sitting down himself.

'You have given refuge,' he continued, 'to a venerable non-juring priest, who escaped miraculously from the massacres of the Carmelites.'

'*Hosannal* . . .' said Sister Agatha interrupting the stranger and looking at him with anxious curiosity.

'I don't think that's his name,' he replied.

'But sir,' said Sister Martha eagerly, 'we have no priest here, and . . .'

'Then you ought to be more careful and prudent,' the stranger replied, gently stretching out his hand to the table and picking up a breviary. 'I don't think you know any Latin, and . . .'

He did not go on, for the extraordinary emotion expressed on the faces of the two poor nuns made him fear he had said too much; they were trembling and their eyes filled with tears.

'Calm down,' he said frankly. 'I know your guest's name and yours too, and three days ago I learned about your difficulties and about your devotion to the venerable abbé of . . .'

'Hush!' said Sister Agatha, innocently putting a finger to her lips.

'You see, my sisters, that if I had had the horrible intention of betraying you, I could already have done it more than once . . .'

When he heard these words, the priest emerged from his prison and came back into the middle of the room.

'I cannot believe, sir,' he said to the stranger, 'that you are one of our persecutors, and I trust you. What do you want of me?'

The trust of the saintly priest, the nobility of his whole countenance would have disarmed a murderer. The mysterious person who had brought excitement to this scene of poverty and resignation gazed for a moment at the group formed by these three people; then, in a confidential tone he said to the priest,

'Father, I came to beg you to celebrate a requiem mass for the repose of the soul of . . . of an anointed person whose body will never rest in consecrated ground.'

The priest shuddered involuntarily. The two nuns, not yet understanding whom the stranger was talking about, sat there, their faces turned eagerly towards the two speakers in an attitude of curiosity. The cleric looked carefully at the stranger: anxiety was clearly evident in his face, and his eyes expressed ardent supplication.

'Well,' replied the priest, 'come back tonight at midnight, and I shall be ready to celebrate the only funeral service we can offer in expiation of the crime you mention.'

The stranger gave a start, but a satisfaction that was both gentle and serious seemed to triumph over a secret grief. After bowing respectfully to the priest and the two pious women, he departed with an expression of dumb gratitude which these three generous hearts understood. About two hours later, the stranger returned, knocked quietly at the door of the attic, and was let in by Mademoiselle de Beauséant who took him into the second room of this modest dwelling, where everything had been prepared for the ceremony. The two nuns had pushed the old chest of drawers between two stove-pipes; its old-fashioned shape was hidden by a magnificent altar cloth of green watered silk. The eye could not help being attracted by a big crucifix, of wood and ivory, which was fixed on to the yellow wall, and made it look even more bare. Four slender little candles that the sisters had managed to fix on to this improvised altar with sealing-wax cast a pale glimmer, which was poorly reflected by the wall. This feeble light scarcely lit the rest of the room; but since it illuminated only the sacred objects, it was like a beam directed from heaven on to the simple altar. The floor was damp. An icy wind blew through cracks in the roof which, as is usual in attics, sloped steeply on both sides. Nothing could be less magnificent, yet nothing was perhaps more impressive than this mournful ceremony. Silence so profound that the faintest cry uttered on the Route d'Allemagne could have been heard, cast a kind of sombre majesty over the midnight scene. In short the grandeur of the deed contrasted so strongly with the poverty of the implements that it created a feeling of religious awe. On each side of the altar, the two aged nuns, kneeling on the tiled floor regardless of the fatal damp, prayed together with the priest. Dressed in his priestly robes, he set out a golden chalice adorned with precious stones, presumably a sacred vessel saved from the pillage of the Abbaye de Chelles. Beside this ciborium, the sole remains of regal splendour, stood two glasses, scarcely good enough for the most miserable inn, containing the water and wine for the holy sacrifice. Since there was no missal, the priest had placed his breviary on a corner of the altar. An ordinary dish had been put ready for washing these innocent and untainted hands. It was all immense, but small; poor, but noble; profane and sacred at the same time.

The stranger knelt devoutly between the two nuns. But when he saw black crêpe on the chalice and on the crucifix (for as there was nothing to indicate for whom this funeral mass was being said, the priest had put God Himself into mourning), he was suddenly overcome by a recollection so violent that drops of sweat formed on his high forehead. Without a word, the four actors in this scene then looked at each other mysteriously; then, as if influencing each other, they silently communicated their mutual feelings and were united in their religious pity. It was as if their thoughts had conjured up the martyr whose remains had been devoured by quick-lime, and as if his shade stood before them in all its royal majesty. They were celebrating an *obit* without the body of the deceased. Under these loose tiles and slats, four Christians were about to intercede with God for a King of France and attend his funeral without the coffin. It was an expression of the purest devotion, an astonishing act of fidelity performed with absolutely no ulterior motive. In the eyes of God, it was no doubt like the glass of water which counts in the scales as much as the greatest virtues. The whole Monarchy was there, in the prayers of a priest and two poor women; but perhaps the Revolution too was represented by the man whose face showed so much remorse that he was obviously fulfilling vows occasioned by profound repentance.

Instead of saying the Latin words: *Introibo ad altare Dei*, etc. the priest, as if with divine inspiration, looked at the three people there who represented Christian France, and to take their minds off the wretchedness of the garret, said, 'We are about to enter God's sanctuary!'

At these words, which were uttered with impressive fervour, the man and the two nuns were gripped with a religious awe. God would not have revealed Himself in greater majesty under the arches of Saint Peter's at Rome than he did then to the eyes of these Christians in this poverty-stricken refuge: for it is indeed true that between God and man no intermediary is needed, and God's greatness derives only from himself. The stranger's devotion was genuine, and so it was a unanimous feeling which united the prayers of these four servants of God and of the King. The sacred words rang out like heavenly music in the silence. At one moment the stranger was overcome with tears; it was at the *Pater noster*. The priest added to it a Latin prayer which no doubt the stranger understood: *Et remitte scelus regicidis sicut Ludovicus eis remisit semetipse* (And forgive the regicides as Louis XVI himself forgave them).

The two nuns saw two large tears roll down the stranger's manly cheeks and drop on to the floor. The service for the dead was recited. The *Domine salvum fac regem*, sung in a low voice, touched the hearts of these faithful royalists who realized that the boy-king, for whom they were at this moment beseeching the Most High, was a captive in the hands of his enemies. The stranger shuddered at the thought that a new crime might still be committed, a crime in which he would, no doubt, be forced to participate. When the funeral service was concluded, the priest made a sign to the two nuns, who left the room. As soon as he was alone with the stranger, he went up to him sadly yet gently and said in a fatherly tone, 'My son, if you have dipped your hands in the blood of the Martyr-King, confide in me. In the eyes of God, there is no fault which cannot be wiped out by repentance as touching and sincere as yours appears to be.'

At the first words uttered by the cleric, the stranger involuntarily shuddered with terror; but his face recovered its calm, and he looked confidently at the astonished priest. 'Father,' he said in a voice clearly touched with emotion, 'no one is more innocent than I of the blood which has been spilt.'

'I must believe you,' said the priest . . .

He paused while he examined his penitent a second time; then, persisting in the belief that he was one of those timid members of the Convention who had sacrificed a sacred and anointed head in order to preserve his own, the priest solemnly resumed, 'Reflect, my son, that to obtain absolution for this great crime it is not enough not to have had a hand in it. Those who were able to defend the King and yet left their swords in their sheaths will have a very heavy account to render to the King of Heaven. Oh! yes,' added the old priest shaking his head expressively to and fro, 'yes, very heavy! . . . for, by doing nothing, they became passive accomplices in that terrible crime . . .'

'You believe that even indirect participation will be punished,' asked the stranger, aghast. 'The soldier commanded to line the streets, is he then guilty?'

The priest hesitated. The stranger was glad to have embarrassed this puritan royalist by placing him between the dogma of passive obedience which, according to the partisans of the monarchy, was absolute in military law, and the equally important dogma which holds sacred the person of a King; he was thus quick to see in the priest's hesitation a favourable solution to doubts which appeared to torture him. Then, so as not to give the venerable Jansenist any more time for reflection, he said, 'I should blush to offer you any payment for the funeral service which you have just celebrated for the repose of the King's soul and for the relief of my conscience. One can pay for something priceless only with a gift which is also priceless. So deign to accept, sir, this gift of a holy relic . . . The day will perhaps come when you will understand its value.'

As he finished saying these words, the stranger presented the cleric with a little box which felt extremely light. The priest took it almost mechanically, for the man's solemn words, the tone in which he spoke, the respect with which he held the box, had profoundly astonished him. They then returned to the room where the two nuns were waiting.

'You are in a house,' the stranger said, 'whose owner, Mucius Scaevola, the plasterer who lives on the first floor, is

famous in the section for his patriotism; but secretly he is
attached to the Bourbons. He used to be huntsman to Monseigneur le Prince de Conti, and he owes his fortune to him.
As long as you don't go out of his house you are more safe
here than in any other place in France. Stay here. Devout
souls will take care of your needs and you will be able to wait
in safety for less evil times. At the end of a year, on the 21st
of January . . .' (he could not repress a shudder as he said
these last words) 'if you adopt this wretched place as your
refuge, I shall return to celebrate with you the atonement
mass . . .'

He did not finish his sentence. He bowed to the speechless
inhabitants of the attic, cast a final glance at the signs of their
poverty, and disappeared.

For the two innocent nuns, such an adventure had all the
interest of a romance; so, as soon as the venerable abbé had
told them about the mysterious gift which the man had so
solemnly presented to him, they put the box on the table, their
three anxious faces, faintly illuminated by the candle, express-
ing extreme curiosity. Mademoiselle de Langeais opened the
box, and found in it a very fine cambric handkerchief, soiled
with sweat. As they unfolded it, they saw stains on it.

'It is blood! . . .' said the priest.

'It is marked with the royal crown!' exclaimed the other
sister.

The two sisters, horrified, dropped the relic. For these two
simple souls the mystery surrounding the stranger became inexplicable. And as for the priest, from that day on he did not
even try to account for it.

The three prisoners soon noticed that, in spite of the Terror,
a powerful hand was stretched out over them. To begin with,
they received wood and provisions; then the two nuns guessed
that a woman was associated with their protector, for they
were sent linen and clothes so that they could go out without
being made conspicuous by the aristocratic style of the clothes
that they had been obliged to go on wearing; finally Mucius
Scaevola gave them two *cartes civiques*. Often information
necessary for the priest's safety reached him in roundabout

ways, and he realized that these counsels came at such opportune moments that they could only have been given by someone with inside knowledge of State secrets. In spite of the famine which oppressed Paris, the outlaws found, at the door of their hovel, rations of white bread which were brought there regularly by invisible hands; nevertheless they thought that they recognized in Mucius Scaevola the mysterious agent of these charitable deeds which were both ingeniously and intelligently performed. The noble inhabitants of the attic were in no doubt that their protector was the person who had come to ask them to celebrate the atonement mass during the night of 22 January, 1793. And so he became the object of a very special devotion for these three beings whose only hope he was and who lived only through him. They had added to their prayers special prayers for him; morning and evening these pious souls expressed wishes for his happiness, for his prosperity, for his safety; they besought God to keep all snares away from him, to deliver him from his enemies and to grant him a long and peaceful life. Their gratitude, which was, as it were, renewed from day to day, necessarily became linked with a feeling of curiosity which each day became more keen. The circumstances which had attended the stranger's appearance formed the subject of their conversations, they made thousands of conjectures about him and the distraction caused by thinking about him was a boon of another kind. They promised themselves not to let the stranger escape from their professions of friendship on the evening he was to return, according to his promise, to celebrate the sad anniversary of the death of Louis XVI. That night, so impatiently awaited, came at last. At midnight, the sound of the stranger's heavy footsteps was heard on the old wooden staircase. The room had been prepared to receive him, the altar was ready. This time, the sisters opened the door before he knocked and both of them hurried forward to light the staircase. Mademoiselle de Langeais even went down a few steps the sooner to see her benefactor.

'Come in,' she said in a voice filled with emotion, 'come in. We are waiting for you.'

The man raised his head, looked gloomily at the nun and did not reply. She felt as if a sheet of ice had fallen on her and said no more. Gratitude and curiosity were stilled at the sight of him. Perhaps in reality he was less cold, less taciturn, less terrible than he seemed to those excited hearts, longing for demonstrations of friendship. The three poor prisoners, realizing that this man wanted to remain a stranger to them, resigned themselves to the situation. The priest thought he noticed a quickly repressed smile on the stranger's lips when he saw the preparations which had been made to receive him. He heard mass and prayed, but having replied with a few polite words of refusal to Mademoiselle de Langeais' invitation to share the little supper they had prepared, he departed.

After 9 Thermidor, the nuns and the Abbé de Marolles were able to go out and about in Paris, without incurring any danger. The old priest's first outing was to a perfumery shop at the sign of the Reine des Fleurs, kept by *citoyen* and *citoyenne* Ragon, formerly perfumiers to the court. They had remained faithful to the royal family and the Vendéens[3] used them to correspond with the Princes and the royalist committee of Paris. The abbé, dressed as the times required, was on the doorstep of this shop, which was situated between Saint-Roch and the Rue des Frondeurs, when a crowd that filled the Rue Saint-Honoré prevented him from going out.

'What is it?' he asked Madame Ragon.

'It's nothing,' she replied, 'it's the tumbril and the executioner going to the Place Louis XV. Oh! We often saw it last year, but today, four days after the anniversary of the 21st of January, we can look at this dreadful procession without distress.'

'Why?' said the abbé. 'What you are saying isn't Christian.'

'Oh! It's the execution of Robespierre's accomplices; they defended themselves as long as they could; but now it's their turn to go where they sent so many innocent people.'

The crowd which was filling the Rue Saint-Honoré passed

3. The Vendéens, inhabitants of La Vendée (a remote region south of Brittany), were ardent royalists who organized risings against the French Revolution.

on like a flood. The Abbé de Marolles, overcome by a feeling of curiosity, looked up and saw, standing above the heads, the man who, three days previously, had listened to his mass . . .

'Who is that? . . .' he asked. 'The man who . . .'

'It's the executioner,' replied Monsieur Ragon, giving the *exécuteur des hautes œuvres* the title by which he was known under the monarchy.

'My dear! My dear!' cried Madame Ragon. 'Monsieur l'abbé is dying.'

And the old lady picked up a bottle of vinegar to revive the old priest, who had fainted.

'He must have given me,' said the priest, 'the handkerchief which the King used to wipe his brow as he went to his martyrdom . . . Poor man! The steel blade had a heart when all France had none! . . .'

The perfumiers thought that the poor priest was delirious.

1830

The Conscript

Sometimes they saw that, by a phenomenon of vision or movement, he could abolish space in its two aspects of Time and Distance, one of these being intellectual and the other physical.
Histoire Intellectuelle de Louis Lambert.

ONE evening in the month of November 1793, the most important people in Carentan were gathered together in the drawing-room of Madame de Dey, who received company every day. Certain circumstances, which would not have attracted attention in a large town but which were bound to arouse curiosity in a small one, gave an unwonted interest to this everyday gathering. Two days earlier, Madame de Dey had closed her doors to visitors, and she had not received any the previous day either, pretending that she was unwell. In normal times these two events would have had the same effect in Carentan as the closing of the theatres has in Paris. On such days existence is, in a way, incomplete. But in 1793 Madame de Dey's behaviour could have the most disastrous consequences. At that time if an aristocrat risked the least step, he was nearly always involved in a matter of life and death. To understand properly the eager curiosity and the narrow-minded cunning which, during that evening, were expressed on the faces of all these Norman worthies, but above all to appreciate the secret worries of Madame de Dey, the part she played at Carentan must be explained. As the critical position in which she was placed at that time was, no doubt, that of many people during the Revolution, the sympathies of more than one reader will give an emotional background to this narrative.

Madame de Dey, the widow of a lieutenant-general, a chevalier of several orders, had left the Court at the beginning of the emigration. As she owned a considerable amount of property in the Carentan region, she had taken refuge there, hoping that the influence of the Terror would be little felt in those parts. This calculation, founded on an accurate knowledge of the region, was correct. The Revolution wrought little havoc in Lower Normandy. Although, in the past, when Madame de Dey visited her property in Normandy, she associated only with the noble families of the district, she now made a policy of opening her doors to the principal townspeople and to the new authorities, trying to make them proud of having won her over, without arousing either their hatred or their jealousy. She was charming and kind, and gifted with that indescribable gentleness which enabled her to please without having to lower herself or ask favours. She had succeeded in winning general esteem thanks to her perfect tact which enabled her to keep wisely to a narrow path, satisfying the demands of that mixed society without humiliating the touchy *amour propre* of the parvenus, or upsetting the sensibilities of her old friends.

She was about thirty-eight years old, and she still retained, not the fresh, rounded good looks which distinguish the girls of Lower Normandy, but a slender, as it were aristocratic, type of beauty. Her features were neat and delicate; her figure was graceful and slender. When she spoke, her pale face seemed to light up and come to life. Her large black eyes were full of friendliness, but their calm, religious expression seemed to show that the mainspring of her existence was no longer within herself. In the prime of her youth she had been married to a jealous old soldier, and her false position at a flirtatious court no doubt helped to spread a veil of serious melancholy over a face which must once have shone with the charms and vivacity of love. Since, at an age when a woman still feels rather than reflects, she had always had to repress her instinctive feminine feelings and emotions, passion had remained unawakened in the depths of her heart. And so her principal attraction stemmed from this inner youthfulness which was, at times, revealed in her face and which gave her thoughts an expression of innocent desire. Her appearance commanded respect, but in her bearing and in her voice there was always the expectancy of an unknown future as with a young girl.

Soon after meeting her the least susceptible of men would find himself in love with her and yet retain a kind of respectful fear of her, inspired by her courteous, dignified manner. Her soul, naturally great but strengthened by cruel struggles, seemed far removed from ordinary humanity, and men recognized their inferiority. This soul needed a dominating passion. Madame de Dey's affections were thus concentrated in one single feeling, that of maternity. The happiness and the satisfactions of which she had been deprived as a wife, she found instead in the intense love she had for her son. She loved him not only with the pure and profound devotion of a mother, but with the coquetry of a mistress and the jealousy of a wife. She was unhappy when he was away, and, anxious during his absence, she could never see enough of him and lived only through and for him. To make the reader appreciate the strength of this feeling, it will suffice to add that this son was not only Madame de Dey's only child, but also her last surviving relative, the one being on whom she could fasten the fears, the hopes and the joys of her life. The late Comte de Dey was the last of his family and she was the sole heiress of hers. Material motives and interests thus combined with the noblest needs of the soul to intensify in the countess's heart a feeling which is already so strong in women. It was only by taking the greatest of care that she had managed to bring up her son and this had made him even more dear to her. Twenty times the doctors told her she would lose him, but confident in her own hopes and instincts, she had the inexpressible joy of seeing him safely overcome the perils of childhood, and of marvelling at the improvement in his health, in spite of the doctors' verdict.

Due to her constant care, this son had grown up and developed into such a charming young man that at the age of twenty he was regarded as one of the most accomplished young courtiers at Versailles. Above all, thanks to a good fortune which does not crown the efforts of every mother, she was adored by her son; they understood each other in fraternal sympathy. If they had not already been linked by the ties of nature, they would instinctively have felt for each other that mutual friendship which one meets so rarely in life. At the age of eighteen the young count had been appointed a sub-lieutenant of dragoons and in obedience to the code of honour of the period he had followed the princes when they emigrated.

Madame de Dey, noble, rich and the mother of an *émigré*, thus could not conceal from herself the dangers of her cruel situation. As her only wish was to preserve her large fortune for her son, she had denied herself the happiness of going with him, and when she read the strict laws under which the Republic was confiscating every day the property of *émigrés* at Carentan, she congratulated herself on this act of courage. Was she not watching over her son's wealth at the risk of her life? Then, when she heard of the terrible executions decreed by the Convention, she slept peacefully in the knowledge that her only treasure was in safety, far from the danger of the scaffold. She was happy in the belief that she had done what was best to save both her son and her fortune. To this private thought she made the concessions demanded by those unhappy times, without compromising her feminine dignity or her aristocratic convictions, but hiding her sorrows with a cold secrecy. She had understood the difficulties which awaited her at Carentan. To come there and occupy the first place, wasn't that a way of defying the scaffold every day? But, supported by the courage of a mother, she knew how to win the affection of the poor by relieving all kinds of distress without distinction, and made herself indispensable to the rich by ministering to their pleasures. She entertained at her house the *procureur*[1] of the commune, the mayor, the president of the district, the public prosecutor and even the judges of the revolutionary tribunal. The first four of these were unmarried and so they courted her, hoping to marry her either by making her afraid of the harm they could do her or by offering her their protection. The public prosecutor, who had been *procureur* at Caen and used to look after the countess's business interests, tried to make her love him, by behaving with devotion and

1. An official elected to represent the central government on local courts and administration.

generosity – a dangerous form of cunning! He was the most formidable of all the suitors. As she had formerly been a client of his, he was the only one who had an intimate knowledge of the state of her considerable fortune. His passion was reinforced by all the desires of avarice and supported by an immense power, the power of life and death throughout the district. This man, who was still young, behaved with such an appearance of magnanimity that Madame de Dey had not yet been able to form an opinion of him. But, despising the danger which lay in vying in cunning with Normans, she made use of the inventive craftiness with which Nature has endowed women to play off these rivals against each other. By gaining time, she hoped to survive safe and sound to the end of the revolutionary troubles. At that period, the royalists who had stayed in France deluded themselves each day that the next day would see the end of the Revolution, and this conviction caused the ruin of many of them.

In spite of these difficulties, the countess had very skilfully maintained her independence until the day on which, with unaccountable imprudence, she took it into her head to close her door. The interest she aroused was so deep and genuine that the people who had come to her house that evening became extremely anxious when they learned that it was impossible for her to receive them. Then, with that frank curiosity which is engrained in provincial manners, they made inquiries about the misfortune, the sorrow, or the illness which Madame de Dey must be suffering from. An old servant named Brigitte answered these questions saying that her mistress had shut herself up in her room and wouldn't see anyone, not even the members of her own household. The almost cloister-like existence led by the inhabitants of a small town forms in them the habit of analysing and explaining the actions of others. This habit is naturally so invincible that after pitying Madame de Dey, and without knowing whether she was really happy or sad, everyone began to look for the causes of her sudden retreat.

'If she were ill,' said the first inquirer, 'she would have sent for the doctor. But the doctor spent the whole day at my house playing chess. He said to me jokingly that nowadays there is only one illness ... and that unfortunately it is incurable.'

This jest was made with caution. Men and women, old men and girls then began to range over the vast field of conjectures. Each one thought he spied a secret, and this secret filled all their imaginations. The next day their suspicions had grown nastier. As life is lived in public in a small town, the women were the first to find out that Brigitte had bought more provisions than usual at the market. This fact could not be denied. Brigitte had been seen first thing in the morning in the market-square and – strange to relate – she had bought the only hare available. The whole town knew that Madame de Dey did not like game. The hare became a starting point for endless conjectures. As they took their daily walk, the old men noticed in the countess's house a kind of concentrated activity which was revealed by the very precautions taken by the servants to conceal it. The valet was beating a carpet in the garden. The previous day no one would have paid any attention to it, but this carpet became a piece of evidence in support of the fanciful tales which everyone was inventing. Each person had his own. The second day, when they heard that Madame de Dey said she was unwell, the leading inhabitants of Carentan gathered together in the evening at the mayor's brother's house. He was a retired merchant, married, honourable, generally respected, and the countess had a high regard for him. That evening all the suitors for the hand of the rich widow had a more or less probable tale to tell, and each one of them considered how to turn to his own profit the secret event which forced her to place herself in this compromising position. The public prosecutor imagined a whole drama in which Madame de Dey's son would be brought to her house at night. The mayor thought that a non-juring priest had arrived from La Vendée and sought asylum with her.[2] But the purchase of a hare on a Friday couldn't be explained by

2. The priests often helped the inhabitants of La Vendée in the west of France in their risings against the Revolution.

this story. The president of the district was convinced that she was hiding a chouan[3] or a Vendéen leader who was being hotly pursued. Others thought it was a noble who had escaped from the Paris prisons. In short, everyone suspected the countess of being guilty of one of those acts of generosity which the laws of that period called a crime and which could lead to the scaffold. The public prosecutor, however, whispered that they must be silent and try to save the unfortunate woman from the abyss towards which she was hastening.

'If you make this affair known,' he added, 'I shall be obliged to intervene, to search her house, and then! . . .' He said no more but everyone understood what he meant.

The countess's real friends were so alarmed for her that, on the morning of the third day, the *procureur-syndic*[4] of the commune got his wife to write her a note urging her to receive company that evening as usual. Bolder still, the retired merchant called at Madame de Dey's house during the morning. Very conscious of the service which he wanted to render her, he insisted on being allowed in to see her, and was amazed when he caught sight of her in the garden, busy cutting the last flowers from her borders to fill her vases.

'She must have given refuge to her lover,' the old man said to himself, as he was overcome with pity for this charming woman. The strange expression of the countess's face confirmed his suspicions. The merchant was deeply moved by this devotion which is so natural to women, but which men always find touching because they are all flattered by the sacrifices which a woman makes for a man; he told the countess about the rumours which were all over the town, and of the danger in which she was placed. 'For,' he said in conclusion, 'though some of our officials may be willing to forgive you for acting heroically to save a priest, nobody will pity you if they find out you are sacrificing yourself for the sake of a love affair.'

3. The chouans were royalist insurgents from Western France who engaged in guerilla warfare against the Revolution.
4. See note 1 above.

At these words, Madame de Dey looked at the old man with a distraught and crazy expression which made him shudder, despite his age.

'Come with me,' she said taking him by the hand and leading him into her room where, having first made sure that they were alone, she took a dirty crumpled letter from the bodice of her dress. 'Read that,' she cried pronouncing the words with great effort.

She collapsed into her chair, as if she were overcome. While the old merchant was looking for his glasses and cleaning them, she looked up at him, examined him for the first time with interest and said gently in a faltering voice, 'I can trust you.'

'Have I not come to share in your crime?' replied the worthy man simply.

She gave a start. For the first time in this little town, her soul felt sympathy with another's. The merchant understood at once both the dejection and the joy of the countess. Her son had taken part in the Granville expedition;[5] his letter to his mother was written from the depths of his prison, giving her one sad, yet joyful hope. He had no doubts about his means of escape, and he mentioned three days in the course of which he would come to her house, in disguise. The fatal letter contained heart-rending farewells in case he would not be at Carentan by the evening of the third day, and he begged his mother to give a fairly large sum of money to the messenger who, braving countless dangers, had undertaken to bring her this letter. The paper shook in the old man's hands.

'And this is the third day,' cried Madame de Dey as she got up quickly, took back the letter, and paced up and down the room.

'You have acted rashly,' said the merchant. 'Why did you have food bought in?'

'But he might arrive, dying with hunger, exhausted, and . . .' She said no more.

5. Granville is a small town, south-west of Carentan, on the other side of the Cotentin peninsula. In 1793 the Vendéens tried unsuccessfully to capture it for the royalists.

'I can count on my brother,' continued the old man, 'I will go and bring him over to your side.'

In this situation the merchant deployed again all the subtlety which he had formerly used in business and gave the countess prudent and wise advice. After they had agreed on what they both should say and do, the old man, on cleverly invented pretexts, went to the principal houses in Carentan. There he announced that he had just seen Madame de Dey, who would receive company that evening, although she was not very well. As he was a good match for the cunning Norman minds who, in every family, cross-examined him about the nature of the countess's illness, he managed to deceive nearly everybody who was interested in this mysterious affair. His first visit worked wonders. He told a gouty old lady that Madame de Dey had nearly died from an attack of stomach gout. The famous Doctor Tronchin had on a former, similar occasion advised her to lay on her chest the skin of a hare, which had been flayed alive, and to stay absolutely immobile in bed. The countess who, two days ago, had been in mortal danger, was now, after having punctiliously obeyed Tronchin's extraordinary instructions, well enough to receive visitors that evening. This tale had an enormous success, and the Carentan doctor, a secret royalist, added to the effect by the seriousness with which he discussed the remedy. Nevertheless, suspicions had taken root too strongly in the minds of some obstinate people, or of some doubters, to be entirely dissipated. So, that evening, Madame de Dey's visitors came eagerly, in good time, some to observe her face carefully, others out of friendship, most of them amazed at her recovery. They found the countess by the large fireplace in her drawing-room, which was almost as small as the other drawing-rooms in Carentan, for to avoid offending the narrow-minded ideas of her guests, she had denied herself the luxuries she had been used to and so had made no changes in her house. The floor of the reception room was not even polished. She left dingy old hangings on the walls, kept the local furniture, burnt tallow candles and followed the fashions of the place. She adopted provincial life, without shrinking from its most uncomfortable meannesses or its most disagreeable privations. But, as she knew that her guests would forgive her any lavishness conducive to their comfort, she left nothing undone which would minister to their personal pleasures. And so she always provided excellent dinners. She went as far as to feign meanness in order to please these calculating minds and she skilfully admitted to certain concessions to luxury, in order to give in gracefully. And so, about seven o'clock that evening, the best of Carentan's poor society was at Madame de Dey's house and formed a large circle around the hearth. The mistress of the house, supported in her trouble by the old merchant's sympathetic glances, endured with remarkable courage her guests' detailed questioning and their frivolous and stupid arguments. But at every knock on the door, and whenever there was a sound of footsteps in the street, she hid her violent emotion by raising questions of importance to the prosperity of the district. She started off lively discussions about the quality of the ciders and was so well supported by her confidant that the company almost forgot to spy on her, since the expression of her face was so natural and her self-possession so imperturbable. Nevertheless the public prosecutor and one of the judges of the revolutionary tribunal said little, watching carefully the least changes in her expression and, in spite of the noise, listening to every sound in the house. Every now and then they asked the countess awkward questions but she answered them with admirable presence of mind. A mother has so much courage! When Madame de Dey had arranged the card-players, and settled everyone at the tables to play boston or reversis or whist, she still lingered in quite a carefree manner to chat with some young people. She was playing her part like a consummate actress. She got someone to ask for lotto, pretended to be the only person who knew where the set was, and left the room.

'I feel stifled, my dear Brigitte,' she exclaimed as she wiped the tears springing from her eyes which shone with fever, grief and impatience. 'He is not coming,' she continued, as she went upstairs and looked round the bedroom. 'Here, I can breathe and live. Yet in a few more moments he will be here! For he is alive, of that I am sure. My heart tells me so. Don't you hear anything, Brigitte? Oh! I would give the rest of my life to know whether he is in prison or walking across the countryside. I wish I could stop thinking.'

She looked round the room again to see if everything was in order. A good fire was burning brightly in the grate, the shutters were tightly closed, the polished furniture was gleaming, the way the bed had been made showed that the countess had discussed the smallest details with Brigitte. Her hopes could be discerned in the fastidious care which had obviously been lavished on this room; in the scent of the flowers she had placed there could be sensed the gracious sweetness and the most chaste caresses of love. Only a mother could have anticipated a soldier's wants and made preparations which satisfied them so completely. A superb meal, choice wines, slippers, clean linen, in short everything that a weary traveller could need or desire was brought together so that he should lack for nothing, so that the delights of home should show him a mother's love.

'Brigitte,' cried the countess in a heart-rending voice as she went to place a chair at the table. It was as if she wanted to make her prayers come true, as if she wanted to add strength to her illusions.

'Ah, Madame, he will come. He is not far away – I am sure that he is alive and on his way. I put a key in the Bible and I kept it on my fingers while Cottin read the Gospel of St John . . . and, Madame, the key didn't turn.'

'Is that a reliable sign?' asked the countess.

'Oh, yes! Madame, it's well known. I would stake my soul he's still alive. God cannot be wrong.'

'I would love to see him, in spite of the danger he will be in when he gets here.'

'Poor Monsieur Auguste,' cried Brigitte, 'he must be on the way, on foot.'

'And there's the church clock striking eight,' exclaimed the countess in terror.

She was afraid that she had stayed longer than she should have done in this room where, as everything bore witness to her son's life, she could believe that he was still alive. She went downstairs but before going into the drawing-room, she paused for a moment under the pillars of the staircase, listening to hear if any sound disturbed the silent echoes of the town. She smiled at Brigitte's husband, who kept guard like a sentinel and seemed dazed with the effort of straining to hear the sounds of the night from the village square. She saw her son in everything and everywhere. She soon went back into the room, putting on an air of gaiety, and began to play lotto with some little girls. But every now and then she complained of not feeling well and sat down in her armchair by the fireplace.

That is how people and things were in Madame de Dey's house while on the road from Paris to Cherbourg a young man wearing a brown *carmagnole*, the obligatory dress of the period, was making his way to Carentan. When the conscription of August 1793 first came into force, there was little or no discipline. The needs of the moment were such that the Republic could not equip its soldiers immediately, and it was not uncommon to see the roads full of conscripts still wearing their civilian clothes. These young men reached their halting places ahead of their battalions, or lagged behind, for their progress depended on their ability to endure the fatigues of a long march. The traveller in question was some way ahead of a column of conscripts which was going to Cherbourg and which the mayor of Carentan was expecting from hour to hour, intending to billet the men on the inhabitants. The young man was marching with a heavy tread, but he was still walking steadily and his bearing suggested that he had long been familiar with the hardships of military life. Although the meadow-land around Carentan was lit up by the moon, he had noticed big white clouds threatening a snowfall over the countryside. The fear of being caught in a storm probably made him walk faster, for he was going at a pace ill-suited to his fatigue. On his back he had an almost empty rucksack, and in his hand was a boxwood stick cut from one of the high, thick hedges which this shrub forms around most of the estates of Lower Normandy. A moment after the solitary traveller had caught sight of the towers of Carentan silhouetted in the eerie moonlight, he entered the town. His step aroused the echoes of the silent, deserted streets and he had to ask a weaver who was still at work the way to the mayor's house. This official did not live far away and the conscript soon found himself in the shelter of the porch of the mayor's house. He applied for a billeting order and sat down on a stone seat to wait. But he had to appear before the mayor who had sent for him and he was subjected to a scrupulous cross-examination. The soldier was a young man of good appearance who seemed to belong to a good family. His demeanour indicated that he was of noble birth and his face expressed that intelligence which comes from a good education.

'What's your name?' asked the mayor looking at him knowingly.

'Julien Jussien,' replied the conscript.

'And where do you come from?' asked the official with an incredulous smile.

'From Paris.'

'Your comrades must be some distance away,' continued the Norman half jokingly.

'I am three miles ahead of the battalion.'

'Some special feeling attracts you to Carentan, no doubt, *citoyen réquisitionnaire*,'[6] said the mayor shrewdly.

'It is all right,' he added, as with a gesture he imposed silence on the young man who was about to speak. 'We know where to send you. There you are,' he added giving him his billeting order. 'Off you go, *citoyen Jussien*.'

There was a tinge of irony in the official's tone as he pronounced these last two words and handed out a billet order giving the address of Madame de Dey's house. The young man read the address with an air of curiosity.

'He knows quite well that he hasn't far to go. And once he's outside he'll soon be across the square,' exclaimed the

6. *Citoyen* was a form of address during the Revolution replacing *monsieur*. A decree passed by the National Convention in 1793 called for military service all men between eighteen and twenty-five. The conscripts were known as *réquisitionnaires*.

mayor talking to himself as the young man went out. He's got some nerve! May God guide him! He has an answer to everything. Yes, but if anyone but me had asked to see his papers, he would have been lost.'

At this moment, the Carentan clocks had just struck half past nine. The torches were being lit in Madame de Dey's ante-chamber; the servants were helping their masters and mistresses to put on their clogs, their overcoats or their capes; the card-players had settled their accounts and they were all leaving together, according to the established custom in all little towns.

'It looks as if the prosecutor wants to stay,' said a lady, who noticed that this important personage was missing when, having exhausted all the formulae of leave-taking, they separated in the square to go to their respective homes.

In fact that terrible magistrate was alone with the countess who was waiting, trembling, till he chose to go.

After a long and rather frightening silence, he said at last, 'I am here to see that the laws of the Republic are obeyed . . .'

Madame de Dey shuddered.

'Have you nothing to reveal to me?' he asked.

'Nothing,' she replied, amazed.

'Ah, Madame,' cried the prosecutor sitting down beside her and changing his tone, 'at this moment, one word could send you or me to the scaffold. I have observed your character, your feelings, your ways too closely to share the mistake into which you managed to lead your guests this evening. I have no doubt at all that you are expecting your son.'

The countess made a gesture of denial, but she had grown pale and the muscles of her face had contracted under the necessity of assuming a false air of calmness.

'Well, receive him,' continued the magistrate of the Revolution, 'but don't let him stay under your roof after seven o'clock in the morning. At daybreak, tomorrow, I shall come to your house armed with a denunciation which I shall have drawn up . . .'

She looked at him with a dazed expression which would have melted the heart of a tiger.

He went on gently, 'I shall demonstrate the falsity of the denunciation by a minute search, and by the nature of my report you will be protected from all further suspicion. I shall speak of your patriotic gifts, of your civic devotion, and we shall all be saved.'

Madame de Dey was afraid of a trap. She stood there motionless but her face was burning and her tongue was frozen. The sound of the door-knocker rang through the house.

'Ah,' cried the terrified mother, falling on her knees. 'Save him, save him!'

'Yes, let us save him!' replied the public prosecutor, looking at her passionately, 'even at the cost of *our* lives.'

'I am lost,' she cried as the prosecutor politely helped her to rise.

'Ah! Madame,' he replied with a fine oratorical gesture, 'I want to owe you to nothing . . . but yourself.'

'Madame, he's – ,' cried Brigitte thinking her mistress was alone.

At the sight of the public prosecutor, the old servant who had been flushed with joy, became pale and motionless.

'Who is it, Brigitte?' asked the magistrate gently, with a knowing expression.

'A conscript sent by the mayor to be put up here,' replied the servant showing the billet order.

'That's right,' said the prosecutor after reading the order. 'A battalion is due in the town tonight.' And he went out.

At that moment the countess needed so much to believe in the sincerity of her former lawyer that she could not entertain the slightest doubt of it. Quickly she went upstairs, though she scarcely had the strength to stand. Then she opened her bedroom door, saw her son, and fell half-dead into his arms. 'Oh, my child, my child,' she cried sobbing and covering him with wild kisses.

'Madame,' said the stranger.

'Oh! It's someone else,' she cried. She recoiled in horror and stood in front of the conscript, gazing at him with a haggard look.

'Oh, good God, what a strong resemblance!' said Brigitte.

There was silence for a moment and even the stranger shuddered at the sight of Madame de Dey.

She leaned for support on Brigitte's husband and felt the full extent of her grief; this first blow had almost killed her. 'Monsieur,' she said, 'I cannot bear to see you any longer; I hope you won't mind if my servants take my place and look after you.'

She went down to her own room half carried by Brigitte and her old manservant.

'What, Madame!' cried the housekeeper as she helped her mistress to sit down. 'Is that man going to sleep in Monsieur Auguste's bed, put on Monsieur Auguste's slippers and eat the *pâté* that I made for Monsieur Auguste? If I were to be sent to the guillotine, I . . .'

'Brigitte,' cried Madame de Dey.

Brigitte said no more.

'Be quiet, you chatterbox,' said her husband in a low voice. 'You'll be the death of Madame.'

At this moment, the conscript made a noise in his room as he sat down to table.

'I can't stay here,' exclaimed Madame de Dey. 'I shall go into the conservatory. From there I shall be able to hear better what's going on outside during the night.'

She was still wavering between the fear of having lost her son and the hope of seeing him come back. The silence of the night was horrible. When the conscript battalion came into town and each man had to seek out his lodgings, it was a terrible time for the countess. Her hopes were dashed at every footstep, at every sound; then soon the awful stillness of Nature returned. Towards morning, the countess had to go back to her own room. Brigitte, who was watching her mistress's movements, did not see her come out; she went into the room and there found the countess dead.

'She must have heard the conscript finishing dressing and walking about in Monsieur Auguste's room singing their damned *Marseillaise*, as if he were in a stable,' cried Brigitte. 'That will have killed her!'

The countess's death was caused by a more important feeling and, very likely, by a terrible vision. At the exact moment when Madame de Dey was dying in Carentan, her son was being shot in Le Morbihan. We can add this tragic fact to all the observations that have been made of sympathies which override the laws of space. Some learned recluses, in their curiosity, have collected this evidence in documents which will one day serve as a foundation for a new science – a science that has hitherto failed to produce its man of genius.

1831

The Red Inn

Introduction

SOME time ago, a Paris banker who had very extensive business connections in Germany, was entertaining one of those friends that businessmen make in different places by correspondence but whom, for many years, they don't know personally. This friend, the head of some important Nuremberg establishment, was a stout, good-natured German, a man of taste and learning, above all a pipe-smoker who had a broad, handsome Nuremberg face, with a square, open forehead embellished by a few meagre strands of blond hair. He was typical of the children of that pure and noble Germany, so rich in honourable characters, whose peaceful way of life has never faltered even after seven invasions. The foreigner laughed artlessly, listened carefully and drank extremely well, appearing to be perhaps as fond of champagne as of the straw-coloured Johannisberg wines. He was called Hermann, like all Germans put into books by authors. As a man who can do nothing by halves, he was comfortably seated at the banker's table, ate with that Teutonic appetite so renowned in Europe and said good-bye conscientiously to the dishes of the great Carême.[1]

To do honour to his guest, the master of the house had invited some intimate friends, bankers or merchants, and several charming pretty women whose pleasant chatter and easy-going manners were in keeping with Germanic cordiality. Indeed, if you had been able to see, as I had the pleasure of doing, that happy gathering of people who had drawn in their commercial claws to speculate on the pleasures of life, you would have found it difficult to hate exorbitant discount rates or to curse bankruptcies. Man cannot always do harm.

1. Carême was a celebrated cook and author of cookery books.

So even amongst pirates there must be some pleasant hours when, in their sinister vessel, you think you are, as it were, sitting in a swing.

'Before leaving us, I hope Monsieur Hermann will tell us yet another terrifying German story.'

These words were spoken at dessert by a pale, fair girl who had probably read the *Tales* of Hoffmann and the novels of Walter Scott. She was the banker's only daughter, a delightful young woman whose education was being completed at the Gymnase and who was crazy about the plays performed there. At that moment the guests were in the happy state of quiet lethargy which is induced by a superb meal when we have presumed too much on our digestive powers. Leaning back in his chair, his wrist resting lightly on the edge of the table, each guest toyed idly with the gilded blade of his knife. When a dinner reaches this moment of decline, some tease the pip of a pear, others roll a piece of bread between their finger and thumb; lovers make badly shaped letters with the fruit-peelings, misers count their plum-stones and arrange them on their plates as a dramatist places his subsidiary actors at the back of the stage. These are little gastronomic felicities which Brillat-Savarin has not mentioned in his book, that is otherwise so complete. The servants had disappeared. The dessert was like a fleet after a battle; everything was broken, pillaged, blighted. The dishes were scattered all over the table, in spite of the determination with which the mistress of the household tried to have them put back into place. A few people were looking at views of Switzerland hung symmetrically on the grey walls of the dining-room. None of the guests was bored. We don't know any man who has been depressed by the digestion of a good dinner. We like to stay then in an indefinable kind of calm, a sort of happy mean between the thinker's meditation and the satisfaction of ruminating animals which we ought to call the material melancholy of gastronomy. So the guests turned spontaneously towards the kindly German, all delighted to have a ballad to listen to, even if it was not interesting. During this blissful interval, the voice of a storyteller always seems delightful to our numbed senses:

it enhances their passive happiness. Being on the look out for pictures, I was admiring those faces lit up by a smile, illuminated by the candles and flushed with good fare; their different expressions produced striking effects through the candelabra, the porcelain dishes, the fruit and the glasses.

My imagination was suddenly gripped by the appearance of the guest who was sitting exactly opposite me. He was a man of average height, fairly grey and merry-looking, who had the manners and appearance of a stockbroker and who seemed to be gifted with only a very ordinary mind. I had not noticed him before. At that moment his face, no doubt darkened by the artificial light, seemed to me to have changed its character. It had become ashen; it was furrowed with purplish streaks. You would have said it was the corpse-like head of a dying man. Motionless, like the painted figures in a diorama, his staring eyes remained fixed on the gleaming facets of a cut-glass stopper. But he certainly was not counting them and seemed lost in some imaginary contemplation of the future or the past. When I had examined that equivocal face for a long time, it gave me these thoughts.

'Is he ill?' I said to myself. 'Has he drunk too much? Has he been ruined by the fall in value of government stock? Is he thinking of deceiving his creditors?'

'Look at him,' I said to my neighbour, indicating the stranger's face. 'Isn't he in the throes of a bankruptcy?'

'Oh,' she replied, 'if he were, he would be more cheerful.' Then with a charming movement of the head, she added, 'If *he* is ever ruined, I shall go and announce it in Peking! He owns a million in real estate! He used to be a contractor for the imperial armies, a good-natured, rather eccentric man. He remarried as a business speculation but nevertheless makes his wife extremely happy. He has a pretty daughter whom, for a long time, he was unwilling to acknowledge. But the death of his son, unfortunately killed in a duel, forced him to take her in, for he couldn't have any more children. Thus the poor girl has suddenly become one of the richest heiresses in Paris. The loss of his only son plunged the dear man into a grief which sometimes reappears.'

At that moment the contractor looked up at me. His look made me shudder, it was so gloomy and abstracted. Surely that glance epitomized a whole life. But suddenly his countenance became cheerful. He took the cut-glass stopper, put it mechanically in a carafe full of water that was in front of his plate and turned his head with a smile towards Monsieur Hermann. That man, in a state of beatitude after his gastronomic pleasures, probably did not have two ideas in his head and was thinking of nothing. So, in a way, I was ashamed to waste my divinatory skill *in anima vili* of a thick-headed financier. While I was making quite useless phrenological observations, the good German had stimulated his nose with a pinch of snuff and was beginning his story. It would be rather difficult for me to reproduce it in his own words, with his frequent interruptions and his wordy digressions. So I have written it in my own way, blaming the man from Nuremberg for its faults, and taking the credit for anything poetic or interesting there may be in it, with the frankness of those writers who forget to add to the titles of their books: '*Translated from the German*.'

1. The Thought and the Deed

'Towards the end of Vendémiaire of the year VII, a date of the Republican calendar which, in the present style, corresponds to 20 October 1799, two young men who had left Bonn early in the morning, had arrived, at the close of the day, at the outskirts of Andernach, a little town on the left bank of the Rhine, a few miles from Coblenz. At that time, the French army, commanded by General Augereau, was manoeuvring in sight of the Austrians who occupied the right bank of the river. The headquarters of the Republican division was at Coblenz and one of the half-brigades belonging to Augereau's forces was billeted at Andernach. The two travellers were French. At the sight of their blue and white uniforms with red velvet facings, of their sabres, and above all of their hats covered with green oil-cloth and decorated with red, white and blue plumes, even the German peasants would have recognized army doctors, men of learning and distinction, the majority of whom were loved not only in the army but also in the countries invaded by our troops. At that period, several sons of good families, who had been snatched away from their medical studies by General Jourdan's recent conscription law, had naturally preferred to continue their studies on the battlefield rather than be obliged to do military service, out of keeping with their early education and the peaceful careers for which they were destined. Knowledgeable, peace-loving and obliging, these young men did some good in the midst of so much misery and sympathized with the scientists of the different countries through which the cruel civilization of the Republic passed. The two young men, both provided with travel warrants and assistant-doctors' commissions signed by Coste and Bernadotte, were on their way to the half-brigade to which they were attached. Both belonged to middle-class families from Beauvais, but though these were of only moderate means, the gentle manners and the loyalty of the provinces were transmitted as a part of their heritage. Out of a curiosity very natural in young men, they had come to the theatre of war before they were due to take up their posts. They had travelled by coach as far as Strasbourg.

Although maternal prudence had let them take only a small sum of money with them, they thought themselves rich in possessing a few louis, a veritable treasure at a time when the *assignats*[2] had reached their lowest value and when gold was worth a lot of money. The two assistant-doctors, at most twenty years old, yielded to the poetry of their situation with all the enthusiasm of youth. Between Strasbourg and Bonn, they had visited the Electorate and the banks of the Rhine as artists, philosophers and observers. When we are destined for a scientific career, we are, at that age, truly multiple beings. Even when making love or travelling, an assistant-doctor must amass the rudiments of his fortune or his future glory. And so the two young men had abandoned themselves to the

2. Paper money issued during the French Revolution.

heartfelt admiration which grips educated men at the sight of the banks of the Rhine and the Swabian countryside, between Mainz and Cologne. Nature there is strong and rich, the high hills, full of feudal memories, covered with greenery but everywhere marked by the effects of fire and sword. Louis XIV and Turenne have cauterized this charming region. Here and there, ruins are a testimony to the pride or perhaps the foresight of the King of Versailles, who had destroyed the lovely castles which formerly adorned this part of Germany. At the sight of this marvellous land, covered with forests, and filled with ruins of the picturesque beauty of the Middle Ages, you can understand the German genius, its reveries and its mysticism. However, the two friends' stay in Bonn combined a scientific purpose with pleasure. The large hospital of the Gallo-Batavian army and of Augereau's division had been set up right in the Elector's palace. The newly commissioned assistant-doctors had thus gone there to see friends, to hand letters of recommendation to their chiefs and to become used to the initial requirements of their job. But there, and elsewhere, they got rid of some of the prejudices, to which we remain faithful for so long, in favour of the monuments and beauties of our native land. They were surprised at the appearance of the marble columns which decorate the Elector's palace and they came to admire the grandiose German buildings, finding at each step new treasures, both ancient and modern.

From time to time, the roads through which the two friends wandered on the way to Andernach brought them to the top of a granite mountain which was higher than the others. There, through a clearing in the forest, or a break in the rocks, they caught sight of a view of the Rhine framed in sandstone cliffs, or festooned by luxuriant vegetation. The valleys, the paths, the trees gave out that autumnal smell which inclines one to reverie. The treetops were beginning to turn golden, to take on the warm, brown colours which are signs of age. The leaves were falling but the sky was still a beautiful blue and the dry roads were traced like yellow lines in the countryside, then lit up by the sloping rays of the setting sun. They were half a mile from Andernach, and the silence was profound, giving no hint of the war that was devastating the beautiful countryside; the two friends followed a path made for goats across the high walls of blueish granite between which the Rhine seethes. Soon they came down by one of the slopes of the gorge at the bottom of which lies the little town, charmingly situated on the river bank and offering a pretty haven to boatmen.

"Germany is a very beautiful country," cried one of the two young men, called Prosper Magnan, as he caught sight of the painted houses of Andernach, lying close together like eggs in a basket, separated by trees, gardens and flowers. Then for a moment he admired the pointed roofs with projecting eaves, the wooden staircases, the balconies of a thousand peaceful dwellings and the boats rocked by the waves in the harbour.'

First Interruption

When Monsieur Hermann mentioned the name of Prosper Magnan, the contractor seized the carafe, poured some water into his glass and emptied it at one draught.

My attention was attracted by this movement and I thought I noticed a slight trembling of the capitalist's hands and moisture on his brow.

'What's the ex-contractor's name?' I asked my obliging neighbour.

'Taillefer,' she replied.

'Do you feel unwell?' I exclaimed, as I saw that strange individual turn pale.

'Not at all,' he said, thanking me with a courteous gesture. 'I am listening,' he added, nodding to the guests who all looked at him simultaneously.

'I have forgotten the other young man's name,' said Monsieur Hermann. 'Only Prosper Magnan's confidences informed me that his companion was dark, quite slim and with a merry temperament. If I may, I shall call him Wilhelm, so as to make the story clearer.'

The good German resumed his tale after thus baptizing the French assistant-doctor with a German name, regardless of Romanticism and local colour.

Continuation

'So when the two young men arrived at Andernach night had fallen. Assuming that they would waste a lot of time finding their officers, making themselves known and getting a military billet from them in a town already full of soldiers, they had decided to spend their last night of freedom in an inn about a hundred paces from Andernach. From the top of the cliffs they had admired its rich colours enhanced by the glow of the setting sun. This inn, which was painted red all over, stood out strikingly in the landscape, both through being detached from the general body of the town, and because of the contrasts formed by its broad, deep red expanse with the greenery of the different types of foliage and by its bright colours with the greyish tints of the water. The house owed its name to the external paintwork which had probably been prescribed for it since time immemorial by the whim of its founder. In accordance with an understandable commercial superstition the various owners of the house, which was well known to the Rhine boatmen, had carefully preserved its outer appearance.

As he heard the horses' steps the landlord of the Red Inn came to the door.

"My goodness, gentlemen," he cried, "a little later and you'd have had to sleep in the open air like most of your compatriots who are camping on the other side of Andernach. My house is full. If you are anxious to sleep in a good bed, I have only my own room to offer you. As for your horses, I'll have some litter put down for them in a corner of the yard. Today my stable is full of Christians."

"Do you come from France, gentlemen?" he continued after a slight pause.

"From Bonn," cried Prosper. "And what's more, we haven't eaten anything since this morning."

"Oh, as for food," said the innkeeper shaking his head,

"they come from ten miles around to have wedding parties at the Red Inn. You'll have a banquet fit for a prince, fish from the Rhine, no need to say more."

After entrusting their tired horses to the care of the landlord who called for his servants without much success, the assistant-doctors went into the public room of the inn. The thick, whitish clouds emitted by a large gathering of smokers prevented them at first from seeing the people with whom they were going to associate. But when they had sat down at a table, with the practical patience of philosophical travellers who have realized how useless it is to make a fuss, they made out through the tobacco fumes the inevitable furnishings of a German inn, the stove, the clock, the tables, the beer-mugs and the long pipes. Here and there were an assortment of faces, Jewish and German, and then the rough faces of a few boatmen. The epaulettes of several French officers glittered in the haze and the clatter of spurs and sabres on the floor could be heard continually. Some were playing cards, others were arguing, saying nothing, eating, drinking or walking about.

A plump little woman with a black velvet cap, a blue and silver stomacher, a pincushion, a bundle of keys, a silver clasp and plaited hair (the distinctive marks of all German land-ladies whose costume, moreover, is so precisely painted in a host of engravings that it is too well known to need description), the innkeeper's wife made the two friends be first patient and then impatient with remarkable skill. Imperceptibly the noise abated, the travellers retired and the cloud of smoke was dissipated. When the table was set for the two assistant-doctors, and the classic Rhine carp appeared on the table, eleven o'clock was striking and the room was empty. In the silence of the night there could be heard indistinctly the noise made by the horses as they ate their provender or pawed the ground, the murmuring of the waters of the Rhine and those indefinable sounds of a full inn when everyone is going to bed. The doors and windows were opening and shutting, voices were murmuring vague words and people were calling to each other from their rooms. At this moment of noise and silence, the two Frenchmen and the landlord, who was busy praising Andernach, the meal, his Rhine wine, the Republican army and his wife, listened with a certain interest to the hoarse shouts of boatmen and the rustling sounds of a boat approaching the harbour. The innkeeper, no doubt familiar with the guttural voices of the boatmen, left the room hurriedly. He soon came back bringing with him a fat little man behind whom walked two boatmen carrying a heavy case and some packages. When his parcels had been put down in the room, the little man took his case himself and kept it beside him; then he sat down opposite the two assistant-doctors.

"Go and sleep in your boat, since the inn is full," he said to the boatmen. "All things considered, that will be best."

"Monsieur," said the landlord to the new arrival, "here are all the provisions I have left." And he pointed to the supper he had served to the two Frenchmen. "I haven't a crust of bread, not a bone."

"No sauerkraut?"

"Not so much as would go in my wife's thimble! As I have had the honour of telling you, you cannot have a bed other than the chair you are sitting on and no room other than this one."

At these words, the little man gave the landlord, the room and the two Frenchmen a look which contained a mixture of prudence and terror.'

'Here, I must tell you,' said Monsieur Hermann interrupting his tale, 'that we never knew the real name or the story of this stranger. Only we learned from his papers that he came from Aix-la-Chapelle. He had taken the name of Walhenfer and owned a sizeable pin factory in the neighbourhood of Neuwied. Like all the manufacturers of that region, he wore an ordinary cloth frock-coat, dark green velvet breeches and waistcoat, boots and a large leather belt. His face was round, his manners frank and friendly, but that evening it was very difficult for him to conceal entirely some secret apprehensions or perhaps painful anxieties. The innkeeper's opinion has always been that this German businessman was fleeing from his own country. Later, I learned that his factory had been burned down by one of those accidents unfortunately so frequent in war time. In spite of his generally anxious expression, his countenance showed a great good nature. He had handsome features and above all a broad neck whose whiteness was so well set off by a black tie, that Wilhelm, in fun, pointed it out to Prosper . . .'

At this point, Monsieur Taillefer drank a glass of water.

'Prosper courteously invited the businessman to share their supper and Walhenfer accepted without ceremony, like a man who felt in a position to repay the courtesy. He placed his case on the ground, put his feet on it, took off his hat, settled himself at table, and laid aside his gloves and a pair of pistols which he had in his belt. The landlord, having quickly set a place, the three guests began to satisfy their appetites without saying much. The atmosphere of the room was so warm, and there were so many flies, that Prosper asked the landlord to open the window which gave on to the front door, in order to freshen the air. This window was secured by an iron bar whose two ends fitted in holes in the two corners of the window bay. For extra security, each of the shutters was fixed by two bolts. By chance, Prosper looked carefully at the way the landlord set about opening the window.'

'But since I am talking to you about the surroundings,' Monsieur Hermann said to us, 'I must describe the interior arrangement of the inn, for the interest of this story depends on a precise knowledge of the locality. The room, where the three people I am talking about were, had two exits. One opened on to the Andernach road which goes alongside the Rhine. In front of the inn there was naturally a little landing stage where the boat, hired by the businessman for his journey, was moored. The other door led into the inn yard. This yard was surrounded by very high walls and, for the moment, was filled with cattle and horses, since the stables were full of people. The big gate had just been so carefully barred that, for the sake of speed, the landlord had let in the businessman and the boatmen by the room door looking on to the street. After opening the window as Prosper Magnan had asked, he set about shutting this door, slid the bars into their sockets and tightened the bolt-screws. The landlord's room, where the two assistant-doctors were to sleep, was next door to the public room and was separated by a fairly thin wall from the kitchen where the landlady and her husband were probably to spend the night. The servant had just gone out to find a lodging in a manger, in the corner of an attic, or somewhere else. You can easily understand that the public room, the landlord's room and the kitchen were, in a way, isolated from the rest of the inn. In the yard there were two big dogs whose solemn barking showed that they were vigilant and easily aroused guardians.

"What silence and what a beautiful night," said Wilhelm looking at the sky when the landlord had finished shutting the door.

The lapping of the water was then the only sound to be heard.

"Gentlemen, allow me to offer you a bottle or two of wine to wash down your carp," said the businessman to the two Frenchmen. "We will refresh ourselves from the fatigues of the day by drinking. Judging from your appearance and the state of your clothes, I can see that, like me, you have come some distance today."

The two friends accepted and the landlord went out by the kitchen door to go to his cellar, situated presumably under that part of the building.

When five venerable bottles brought by the innkeeper were on the table, his wife finished serving the meal. She cast a hostess's glance on the room and the food; then, certain that she had seen to all the travellers' needs, she returned to the kitchen. The four table companions (for the landlord had been invited to drink) didn't hear her go to bed. But, later on, during the pauses in the drinkers' conversation, some very pronounced snores, which were made even more resonant by the hollow walls of the closet where she had tucked herself, made the friends, and particularly the landlord, smile. About midnight, when there remained on the table only biscuits, cheese, dried fruit and good wine, the table companions, principally the two young Frenchmen, became communicative. They talked of their country, of their studies and of the war. Finally, the conversation became animated. Prosper Magnan brought tears to the eyes of the fugitive businessman when, with Picard frankness and the naïveté of a kindly and affectionate nature, he imagined what his mother must be doing at that moment when *he* was on the banks of the Rhine.

"I can see her reading her evening prayer before going to bed," he said. "She certainly doesn't forget me and must be wondering, 'Where is my poor Prosper?' But if she has won a few sous at cards from her neighbour, your mother," he added nudging Wilhelm's elbow, "perhaps she will be putting them in the big, red earthenware jar in which she is collecting the sum she needs to buy thirty acres that cut into her little property at Lescheville. Those thirty acres are worth at least about sixty thousand francs. What good meadows they are! Oh, if I had them one day, I would live all my life at Lescheville, without ambition. How often my father wanted those thirty acres and the pretty stream that winds through those meadows. However, he died without being able to buy them. I have often played there."

"Monsieur Walhenfer, haven't you also your *hoc erat in votis*?" asked Wilhelm.

"Yes, Monsieur, yes. But it has all come to pass, and now . . ." The good fellow remained silent without finishing his sentence.

"As for me," said the landlord whose face had become slightly flushed, "last year I bought a vineyard that I had been wanting for ten years."

And so they chatted, as men whose tongues were loosened by wine, and conceived for each other that passing affection with which we are always lavish when we travel, with the result that when they went to bed Wilhelm offered his bed to the businessman.

"You can accept it the more readily," he said, "since I can sleep with Prosper. It certainly won't be the first or the last time. You are older than us; we must respect old age."

"Don't bother," said the landlord. "My wife's bed has several mattresses. Put one of them on the floor."

And he went to shut the window, a noisy operation.

"I accept," said the businessman. "I must confess," he added, lowering his voice and looking at the two friends, "that I would like that. My boatmen seem to me untrustworthy. For tonight I am not sorry to be in the company of two brave, good young men, two French soldiers. I have a hundred thousand francs in gold and diamonds in my case!"

The affectionate restraint with which this imprudent secret was received by the two young men reassured the good German. The landlord helped his travellers to undo one of the beds. Then, when everything was properly arranged, he bade them goodnight and went to bed. The businessman and the two assistant-doctors joked about the kind of pillows they had. Prosper was putting his and Wilhelm's instrument cases under his mattress in order to raise it and to substitute them for the missing bolster, just as Walhenfer, with an excess of caution, was putting his case under his pillow.

"We shall both sleep on our fortunes, you on your gold, me on my instrument case! It remains to be seen if my instruments will bring me as much gold as you have acquired."

"You can hope so," said the businessman. "Work and honesty achieve everything. But be patient."

Soon Walhenfer and Wilhelm fell asleep. Whether it was because his bed was too hard, or because his extreme fatigue caused insomnia, or because of an unfortunate frame of mind, Prosper Magnan remained awake. Imperceptibly his thoughts turned in an evil direction. He could think of nothing but the hundred thousand francs that the businessman was sleeping on. For him, a hundred thousand francs was an enormous fortune ready to hand. He began by using them in a thousand different ways, building castles in the air as we all so enjoy doing in the moment before sleep, when images arise confusedly in our minds and when often, in the silence of the night, thought acquires a magic power. He gratified his mother's wishes, he bought the thirty acres of meadow land, he married a young lady from Beauvais to whom he could not at that time aspire because of the disparity of their fortunes. With the money he organized a whole lifetime of enjoyment; he saw himself happy, the father of a family, rich, highly esteemed in his province and perhaps mayor of Beauvais. His Picard imagination took fire and he looked for ways of changing his fictions into reality.

With extraordinary ardour he thought out a theoretical crime. As he dreamed of the businessman's death, he could see distinctly the gold and the diamonds. His eyes were dazzled by them. His heart was throbbing. It was already a crime, no doubt, just to think about them. Fascinated by the heap of gold, he became morally intoxicated by reasoning in favour of murder. He asked himself if that poor German really needed to live and imagined that he had never existed. In short, he planned the crime in such a way that he could commit it with impunity. The other bank of the Rhine was occupied by the Austrians. Under the windows was a boat and boatmen. He could cut the man's throat, throw him into the Rhine, escape by the window with the case, offer gold to the boatmen, and cross to Austria. He went as far as calculating the degree of skill that he had been able to acquire in the use of his surgical instruments, so as to cut off his victim's head in such a way that he wouldn't utter a single cry . . .'

At this point, Monsieur Taillefer wiped his brow and drank yet another sip of water.

'Prosper got up slowly and without making any noise, certain that he hadn't woken anyone, he got dressed and went into the public room. Then with that intelligence which, inevitably, men suddenly find they possess, with the dexterity and will-power which prisoners and criminals never lack in the execution of their plans, he unscrewed the iron bars, took them out of their sockets without making the slightest sound, put them against the wall and opened the shutters, pressing heavily on the hinges so as to muffle their creaking. The moon cast its pale light on the scene so that he could faintly see the objects in the room where Wilhelm and Walhenfer were sleeping. At this point, he told me, he paused for a moment.

His heartbeats were so strong, so deep, so loud that he had been, as it were, frightened by them. Then he was afraid that he wouldn't be able to act with composure. His hands were trembling and the soles of his feet felt as if they were on coals of fire. But the execution of his plan was attended by so much good fortune that he saw a kind of predestination in this favour of fate. He opened the window, returned to the room, took up his case, and looked in it for the most suitable instrument with which to carry out his crime.

"When I got near the bed," he said to me, "I commended myself automatically to God."

Just as he was raising his arm, gathering all his strength, he heard, as it were, a voice within him and thought he saw a light. He threw the instrument onto his bed, fled into the other room, and went to the window. There he conceived the deepest horror of himself, and yet, feeling that his virtue was weak, still fearing that he might succumb to the fascination which possessed him, he jumped quickly onto the road and walked along by the Rhine, doing sentry duty, as it were, in front of the inn. Several times, he went as far as Andernach in his hurried walk, several times, too, his steps led him to the slope he had descended to reach the inn. But the silence of the night was so profound and he had such great faith in the watchdogs that, at times, he lost sight of the window which he had left open. His intention was to wear himself out so that he would sleep. Meanwhile, as he walked thus under a cloudless sky, admiring its beautiful stars, struck perhaps, too, by the pure night air and the melancholy plash of the water, he fell into a meditation which gradually brought him back to healthy moral ideas. In the end reason completely dissipated his momentary madness. The teachings of his upbringing, the precepts of religion and above all, he told me, the memories of the modest life that he had hitherto led under the paternal roof, triumphed over his evil thoughts. When he returned after abandoning himself to the charms of a long meditation on the bank of the Rhine, leaning his elbows on a large rock, he would have been able, so he told me, not to sleep but to stay awake beside a billion's worth of gold. As his honesty re-emerged proud and strong from this struggle, he knelt in a feeling of ecstasy and joy, thanked God and was happy, light-hearted and contented as on the day of his first communion, when he had thought himself worthy to be among the angels because he had spent the day without sinning in word, deed, or thought. He returned to the inn, shut the window without being afraid of making a noise and went to bed straight away. He was so weary morally and physically that he fell asleep without resistance. Shortly after putting his head on his mattress he fell into that first, fanciful drowsiness which always precedes a deep sleep. Then the senses become numbed and life gradually ebbs away; one's thoughts are incomplete and the final quivering of our senses imitates a kind of reverie.

"How heavy the air is," Prosper said to himself. "I feel as if I were breathing a damp mist."

He vaguely accounted for this effect of the atmosphere by the difference which was bound to exist between the temperature of the room and the pure air of the countryside. But soon he heard a recurrent sound rather like that made by drops of water falling from the tap of a fountain. Inspired by a terrified panic, he wanted to get up and call the landlord, to wake up the businessman or Wilhelm. But then, unfortunately for him, he remembered the wooden clock and thought he recognized the movement of the pendulum. With this indistinct and confused perception he fell asleep . . .'

Second Interruption

'Would you like some water, Monsieur Taillefer?' said the master of the house as he saw the contractor automatically pick up the carafe.

It was empty.

2. The Two Crimes

Monsieur Hermann continued his tale after the slight pause caused by the banker's remark.

'The next morning,' he said, 'Prosper Magnan was awakened by a great noise. He thought he had heard loud shouts and he felt that violent quivering of the nerves which we experience when, on awakening, we complete a painful sensation begun during our sleep. A physiological activity takes place within us, a start, to use the ordinary word, which has not yet been sufficiently observed although it contains curious phenomena of interest to science. This terrible tension, caused perhaps by too sudden a reunion of our two natures, almost always separated during sleep, does not usually last long. But with the assistant-doctor it persisted, even suddenly got worse and caused him the most terrible revulsion when he noticed a pool of blood between his mattress and Walhenfer's bed. The poor German's head was lying on the ground, his body had remained in the bed. All his blood had spurted from his neck. Seeing the eyes still open and staring, seeing the blood which had stained his sheets and even his hands and recognizing his surgical instrument on the bed, Prosper Magnan fainted and fell into Walhenfer's blood.

"That was already a punishment for my thoughts," he told me.

When he came to, he found himself in the public room. He was seated on a chair surrounded by French soldiers and facing an attentive and inquisitive crowd. He looked dazedly at a Republican officer busy collecting evidence from a few witnesses and presumably drawing up a report. He recognized the landlord and his wife, the two boatmen and the inn servant. The surgical instrument which the murderer had used . . .'

Third Interruption

At this point, Monsieur Taillefer coughed, took out his handkerchief to blow his nose and wiped his brow. I alone noticed these quite natural movements. All the guests had their eyes glued to Monsieur Hermann and were listening to him with a kind of avidity. The contractor rested his elbow on the table, leaned his head on his right hand and stared at Hermann. From that moment he showed no further sign of emotion or interest. But his face remained thoughtful and ashen as at the moment when he had played with the stopper of the carafe.

Continuation

'The surgical instrument which the murderer had used was on the table with Prosper's instrument case, wallet and papers. The company looked alternately at these incriminating objects and at the young man who seemed half-dead and whose dull eyes appeared to take nothing in. The confused noise which could be heard outside indicated the presence of the crowd, attracted in front of the inn by the news of the crime and perhaps also by the desire to see the murderer. The tread of the sentries posted outside the windows of the room, the noise of their guns dominated the hum of conversation among the crowd. But the inn was closed, the yard was empty and silent. Unable to endure the look of the officer who was drawing up the report, Prosper Magnan felt his hand being pressed by a man and raised his eyes to see who was his protector amongst this hostile crowd. From the uniform he recognized the army surgeon of the half-brigade stationed at Andernach. The man's glance was so searching and harsh that it made the poor young man shudder and he let his head fall on to the back of his chair. A soldier gave him vinegar to inhale and he immediately regained consciousness. However, his haggard eyes seemed so devoid of life and understanding that, after taking Prosper's pulse, the doctor said to the officer, "Captain, it is impossible to interrogate that man just now."

"Well, take him away," replied the captain, interrupting the doctor and addressing a corporal who was standing behind the assistant-doctor.

"You cursed coward," the soldier said in a low voice, "try at least to walk with a firm step in front of those German dogs in order to save the honour of the Republic."

This remark brought Prosper Magnan back to life. He got up and took a few steps. But when the door opened, when he felt the outdoor air strike him and when he saw the crowd come in, his strength left him, his knees gave way and he stumbled.

"That awful medical student deserves death twice over! For heaven's sake, walk!" said the two soldiers who were giving him their arms to hold him up.

"Oh! Coward! Coward! That's the man! That's the man! There he is! There he is!"

These words seemed to be spoken by a single voice, the noisy voice of the crowd which was walking along beside him, shouting insults and getting bigger at every step. During the walk from the inn to the prison, the noise made by the people and the soldiers as they walked, the hum of the different conversations, the sight of the sky and the coolness of the atmosphere, the view of Andernach and the rippling water of the Rhine, all these impressions were perceived by the assistant-doctor vaguely, confusedly and dully like all the sensations he had experienced since waking up. At times, so he told me, he thought he was no longer alive.'

'At that time I was in prison,' said Monsieur Hermann, interrupting his story. 'Enthusiastic as we all are at the age of twenty, I had wanted to defend my country and I commanded an independent company that I had organized in the neighbourhood of Andernach. Some days previously, during the night, I had fallen into the midst of a French detachment of eight hundred men. We were at most two hundred. My spies had betrayed me. I was thrown into Andernach prison. Then it was a question of shooting me, to make an example of me which would intimidate the district. The French also spoke of reprisals but the murder which the Republicans wanted to avenge by shooting me had not been committed in the Electorate. My father had obtained a three days' reprieve so that he could go and ask for my pardon from General Augereau; this was granted. So I saw Prosper Magnan just as he entered Andernach prison and he aroused in me the deepest pity. Although he was pale, dishevelled and bloodstained, his face expressed a candour and innocence which impressed me keenly. For me, the breath of Germany seemed to be in his long fair hair and blue eyes. A true picture of my country in difficulties, he seemed to me like a victim rather than a murderer. As he passed beneath my window he smiled, at what I don't know, with the melancholy and bitter expression of a madman who regains a fleeting glimpse of reason. That smile was certainly not a murderer's. When I saw the jailer, I questioned him about his new prisoner.'

"He hasn't spoken since he has been in his cell. He sat down, put his head in his hands and sleeps or thinks about his case. According to what the French say, he will be tried tomorrow morning and will be shot within the next twenty-four hours."

That evening, I stood under the prisoner's window during the short time that I was allowed to walk in the prison yard. We chatted together and he candidly told me his adventure, answering my different questions precisely enough. After this first conversation I no longer doubted his innocence. I asked and I obtained the favour of spending some hours with him. So I saw him several times and the poor boy took me frankly into his confidence. He believed himself to be both innocent and guilty. Remembering the horrible temptation that he had had the strength to resist, he was afraid that, during his sleep, in a fit of sleepwalking, he had committed the crime which he had imagined when he was awake.

"But your companion?" I asked.

"Oh," he exclaimed heatedly, "Wilhelm is incapable . . ." He didn't even finish his sentence.

At these warm-hearted words, full of youth and virtue, I shook his hand.

"When he woke up," Prosper continued, "he would have been terrified. He must have panicked and run away."

"Without waking you up," I said. "But then your defence will be easy, for Walhenfer's case won't have been stolen."

Suddenly he burst into tears.

"Oh yes, I am innocent," he cried. "I didn't kill anyone. I remember my dreams. I was playing rounders with my schoolfriends. I can't have cut off that man's head while dreaming that I was running."

But in spite of the gleams of hope which sometimes restored a little calm to him, he still felt overwhelmed by remorse. He had quite certainly raised his arms to cut off the businessman's head. He passed judgement on himself and did not find his heart pure, after committing the crime in his thoughts.

"And yet, I am a kind man," he exclaimed. "Oh, my poor mother! Perhaps at this moment she is cheerfully playing *impériale* with her neighbours in her little tapestried sitting-room. If she knew that I had as much as lifted a hand to murder a man . . . Oh, she would die! And I am in prison, accused of committing a crime. Even if I haven't killed that man, I shall certainly kill my mother."

At these words, he didn't weep. But with that keen, short-lived passion not unusual with men from Picardy, he dashed towards the wall and, if I had not held him back, he would have broken his head against it.

"Wait till you have been tried," I said. "You will be acquitted; you are innocent. And your mother . . ."

"My mother," he exclaimed passionately, "she will learn before anything else that I have been accused. That's how it is in small towns. It will make the poor woman die of grief. Besides, I am not innocent. Do you want to know the whole truth? I feel that I have lost the virginity of my conscience."

After this terrible speech, he sat down, folded his arms on his chest and looked gloomily at the ground. At that moment the warder came to ask me to return to my room. But upset at leaving my companion at a moment when his despair seemed to me so deep, I embraced him affectionately.

"Have patience," I said. "All will go well, perhaps. If an honest man's voice can silence your doubts, know that I esteem and love you. Accept my friendship and rest on my heart if you are not at peace with your own."

The next day a corporal and four fusiliers came for the assistant-doctor about nine o'clock. Hearing the noise made by the soldiers, I went to my window. When the young man crossed the yard, he glanced at me. I shall never forget that thoughtful look, laden with foreboding, with resignation and an indescribable, sad and melancholy charm. It was a kind of silent yet intelligible testament with which a friend bequeathed his lost life to his last friend. The night had no doubt been very hard and very lonely for him, but the paleness stamped on his face may also have indicated a stoicism derived from a newly acquired self-esteem. Perhaps he had been purified by remorse and believed that his grief and shame had washed away his fault. He walked with a firm step and first thing in the morning he had cleaned away the bloodstains with which he had been involuntarily soiled.

"My hands couldn't help dipping into it while I was asleep for my sleep is still very restless," he had said to me the day before, in a horrible tone of despair.

I learned that he was going to appear before a court-martial. The following day, the division was to advance and the commander of the half-brigade did not want to leave Andernach without punishing the crime at the very place where it had been committed . . . I remained in mortal anxiety while the court-martial was in session. Finally, towards mid-day, Prosper Magnan was brought back to prison. Just then I was taking my usual walk. He noticed me and flung himself into my arms.

"Lost," he said. "I am lost with no hope. Here, everyone will look on me as a murderer." He raised his head proudly. "This injustice has wholly restored my innocence. My life would always have been troubled, my death will be without reproach. But is there a future life?"

The whole of eighteenth-century philosophy lay in that sudden question. He remained thoughtful.

"But how did you answer?" I said. "What did they ask you? Didn't you tell them simply the facts as you told them to me?"

He stared at me for a moment; then, after that frightening pause, he replied, speaking with feverish excitement. "First they asked me, 'Did you leave the inn during the night?' I said 'Yes.' 'How did you get out?' I blushed and replied, 'By the window.' 'So you opened it?' 'Yes,' I said. 'You took great care. The innkeeper heard nothing.' I was flabbergasted. The boatmen said they saw me walking now to

Andernach, now towards the forest. They said I made several trips. I buried the gold and the diamonds. In short, the case has not been found! Then I was still in conflict with my remorse. When I wanted to speak, a pitiless voice cried out to me, 'You intended to commit a crime.' Everything was against me, even myself! ... They questioned me about my companion and I defended him entirely. Then they said, 'The culprit must be you, your friend, the innkeeper or his wife. That morning, all the windows and the doors were found shut.' At this remark," he continued, "I remained speechless, bereft of strength and feeling. More sure of my friend than of myself, I couldn't accuse him. I realized that we were both looked on as being equally accomplices in the murder and I was taken for the more stupid of the two. I wanted to explain the crime by sleepwalking and to exonerate my friend. Then I talked incoherently. I was lost. I read my condemnation in my judges' eyes. They exchanged smiles of incredulity. There is no more to be said. There is no doubt about it. Tomorrow I shall be shot. I am not thinking any more of myself," he added, "but of my poor mother!"

He stopped, looked up at the sky, but shed no tears. His eyes were dry but were moving convulsively.

"Frédéric!"'

Fourth Interruption

'Oh, the other one was called Frédéric, Frédéric! Yes, that was certainly the name!' cried Monsieur Hermann triumphantly.

My neighbour touched my foot and motioned to me to look at Monsieur Taillefer. The former contractor had carelessly put his hand over his eyes but between his fingers we thought we could see a menacing light in his eye.

'What do you think?' she whispered to me. 'What if he were called Frédéric?'

I replied by winking at her as if to say, 'Silence.'

Continuation

Hermann resumed thus:

'"Frédéric," cried the assistant-doctor, "Frédéric has deserted me like a coward. He must have been afraid. Perhaps he hid in the inn, for our two horses were still in the yard in the morning. What an incomprehensible mystery," he added after a moment's silence. "Sleepwalking, sleepwalking. I have had only one fit in my life and that was at the age of six. Shall I leave here," he said, tapping the ground with his foot, "taking away with me all that is left of friendship in the world? Shall I die twice through having doubts about a brotherly affection which began at the age of five and continued at school and University? Where is Frédéric?" He wept. So we care more for a feeling than for life.

"Let us go in," he said. "I would rather be in my cell. I wouldn't like to be seen crying. I shall go courageously to my death, but I cannot be heroic at the wrong moment and I confess that I regret my young life full of promise. Last night, I didn't sleep. I recalled the scenes of my childhood and saw myself running in those meadows whose memory has perhaps caused my ruin. I had a future," he said, interrupting himself. "Twelve men, a sub-lieutenant who will shout, 'To arms, aim, fire!' a roll of drums and dishonour, that is my future now. Oh, there is a God, or it would all be far too stupid."

Then he took me in his arms, and embraced me with all his strength.

"Oh, you are the last man to whom I shall have been able to pour out my heart. *You* will be free. You will see your mother. I don't know if you are rich or poor but what does it matter? You are the whole world for me. These fellows won't fight for ever. Well, when peace comes, go to Beauvais. If my mother survives the fatal news of my death, you will find her there. Say to her these comforting words. 'He was innocent!' She will believe you," he continued. "I am going to write to her, but you will take her my last look. You will tell her that you are the last man I embraced. Oh, how she will love you, poor woman! You, who will have been my last friend. Here," he said, after a moment's silence during which he stood as if overwhelmed by the weight of his memories, "the officers and soldiers are unknown to me and I inspire horror in them all. But for you, my innocence would be a secret between Heaven and me."

I swore to carry out his last wishes faithfully. My words, my expressions of affection touched him. Shortly afterwards, the soldiers returned to take him back before the court-martial. He was found guilty. I don't know the formal steps which had to follow or accompany this first judgement; I don't know if the young doctor defended his life in accordance with all the rules, but he expected to go to his doom the following morning and spent the night writing to his mother.

"We shall both be free," he said with a smile when I went to see him the next day. "I have heard that the general has signed your pardon."

I said nothing and looked at him so as to imprint his features deeply in my memory. Then his face took on an expression of disgust and he said, "I have been a miserable coward. All night I asked pardon of these walls." And he pointed to the walls of his cell. "Yes, yes," he continued, "I howled with despair, I rebelled, I endured the most terrible of moral death throes. I was alone. Now I think of what others will say ... Courage is like a disguise to be put on. I must go decently to death ... So ..." '

3. The Two Kinds of Justice

'Oh, don't finish,' cried the young lady who had asked for the story, suddenly interrupting the man from Nuremberg at that point. 'I want to remain in uncertainty and to believe that he was saved. If today I were to learn that he had been shot, I wouldn't sleep tonight. Tomorrow you will tell me the rest.'

We rose from the table. As she accepted Monsieur Hermann's arm, my neighbour said to him,

'He was shot, wasn't he?'

'Yes. I was present at the execution.'

'What, Monsieur!' she said. 'You were able to ...'

'He had wanted that, Madame. There is something very

terrible about following the funeral procession of a living man, of a man that one loves, of an innocent man. That poor young fellow didn't take his eyes off me. He seemed to be alive only through me. He said that he wanted me to take his last breath to his mother.'

'Well, did you see her?'

'After the peace of Amiens, I came to France to bring the mother these beautiful words, "He was innocent." I had religiously undertaken this pilgrimage. But Madame Magnan had died of consumption. It was not without a deep emotion that I burned the letter I was carrying. You may laugh at my Germanic emotionalism, but I saw a drama of sublime melancholy in the eternal secret which would bury these farewells exchanged by two graves, unknown to the rest of creation, like a cry uttered in the midst of the desert by the traveller surprised by a lion.'

'And if someone brought you face to face with one of the men who are in this room, saying to you, "There is the murderer!" would it not be another drama?' I asked him, interrupting. 'And what would you do?'

Monsieur Hermann took his hat and left.

'You are behaving like a youngster, and very thoughtlessly,' my neighbour said. 'Look at Taillefer! Look! Sitting in the armchair, there in the chimney corner. Mademoiselle Fanny is handing him a cup of coffee. He is smiling. Could a murderer who must have been in agony at the tale of this adventure remain so calm? Doesn't he look truly patriarchal?'

'Yes, but go and ask him if he took part in the war in Germany,' I cried.

'Why not?'

And with the boldness which women hardly ever lack when they are attracted by an undertaking or when their minds are dominated by curiosity, my neighbour went up to the contractor.

'Have you ever been to Germany?' she asked.

Taillefer almost dropped his saucer.

'Me! Madame, no, never!'

'What's that you're saying, Taillefer?' interrupted the

banker. 'Weren't you dealing with provisions in the Wagram campaign?'

'Oh, yes,' replied Monsieur Taillefer. 'I went there on that occasion.'

'You are making a mistake. He is a good man,' my neighbour said, returning to my side.

'Well,' I cried, 'before the end of the evening I shall chase the murderer out of the mud where he is hiding.'

Every day, before our eyes, there takes place a moral phenomenon of astonishing depth, yet too simple to be noticed. If, in a salon, two men meet, one of whom has good reason to despise or hate the other, either because he knows an intimate or hidden fact which is a stain upon the other man, or because of some secret situation, or even because of some vengeance which is due, these two men divine each other's secret feelings and have a presentiment of the abyss which separates them or is to separate them. They secretly watch each other, are preoccupied with each other. Their looks and gestures reveal an indefinable emanation of their thoughts; there is a magnet between them. I do not know which exercises the greatest attraction, vengeance or crime, hatred or insult. Like a priest who cannot consecrate the wafer in the presence of the evil spirit, they are both ill at ease, suspicious. The one is polite, the other gloomy, I don't know which; the one blushes or turns pale, the other trembles. Often the avenger is as cowardly as the victim. Few people have the courage to do harm, even though it is necessary, and many people remain silent or forgive because they hate making a fuss, or fear a tragic outcome. This intuition of our hearts and feelings established a mysterious struggle between the contractor and myself. Since the first remark that I had addressed to him during Monsieur Hermann's tale, he had avoided my glance. Perhaps he also avoided those of all the guests! He was chatting to the inexperienced Fanny, the banker's daughter, no doubt feeling the need, as all criminals do, to draw close to innocence, hoping to find peace beside it. But, although far away from him, I was listening to him and my piercing glance fascinated his.

When he thought he could spy on me with impunity, our

looks met and he lowered his eyes immediately. Tired of this ordeal, Taillefer eagerly tried to put an end to it by starting to play cards. I went to bet on his opponent's side, but wanting to lose my money. This wish was gratified. I replaced the departing player and found myself face to face with the murderer . . .

'Monsieur,' I said, while he dealt out the cards, 'would you be kind enough to change your counters?'

He fairly hurriedly passed his counters from right to left. My neighbour had come up beside me. I gave her a significant look.

'Are you, by any chance, Monsieur Frédéric Taillefer, whose family at Beauvais I knew well?' I asked, turning to the contractor.

'Yes, Monsieur,' he replied.

He dropped his cards, turned pale, put his head in his hands, asked one of the bystanders who was betting on him to take his hand, and got up.

'It's too warm here,' he cried, 'I am afraid . . .'

He did not finish his sentence. Suddenly his face took on an expression of horrible suffering, and he left abruptly. The master of the house followed Taillefer, apparently taking a lively interest in his condition. My neighbour and I looked at each other, but on her face I found an indescribable look of bitter sadness.

'Is your behaviour very compassionate?' she asked me, leading me into a window bay as I left the game after losing. 'Do you want the power of reading in all hearts? Why not leave human and divine justice to do their work? If we escape the one, we never avoid the other. Are the privileges of an assize court judge so much to be envied? You have almost performed the function of the executioner.'

'After sharing and stimulating my curiosity, you are preaching at me!'

'You have made me think,' she answered.

'So, peace to the scoundrels, let us make war on the unfortunate, and worship gold! But enough of that,' I added with a laugh. 'Do look at the young lady who is coming into the room at this moment.'

'Well?'

'I saw her three days ago at the Neapolitan Ambassador's ball. I have fallen passionately in love with her. For pity's sake, tell me her name. No one has been able to . . .'

'It's Mademoiselle Victorine Taillefer!'

I became dizzy.

'Her stepmother has recently withdrawn her from the convent where she has belatedly finished her education. For a long time her father refused to recognize her. This is her first appearance here. She is very beautiful and very rich,' said my neighbour in a voice I could hardly hear.

These words were accompanied by a sardonic smile. At that moment we heard violent but muffled shouts. They seemed to come from an adjoining room and echoed faintly in the gardens.

'Isn't that Monsieur Taillefer's voice?' I exclaimed.

We listened intently to the sounds, and terrible groans reached our ears. The banker's wife hurried towards us and shut the window.

'Let us avoid scenes,' she said. 'If Mademoiselle Taillefer were to hear her father, she might have an attack of hysterics.'

The banker came back into the drawing-room, sought out Victorine and said something to her in a low voice. Immediately the young woman uttered a cry, rushed to the door and disappeared. This incident produced a great sensation. The games stopped. Everyone questioned his neighbour. The hum of voices grew louder and people formed into groups.

'Could Monsieur Taillefer have . . .?' I asked.

'Killed himself?' exclaimed my mocking neighbour. 'You would cheerfully wear mourning for him, I think!'

'But what has happened to him?'

'The poor fellow is subject to an illness whose name I can't remember, although Monsieur Brousson has told it me often enough,' replied the mistress of the house, 'and he has just had an attack.'

'What kind of an illness is it?' an examining magistrate asked suddenly.

'Oh, it's a terrible illness, Monsieur,' she replied. 'The doctors don't know any cure for it. It seems that the pain is atrocious. One day, this unhappy Taillefer had an attack during a stay at my country house and I had to go to a neighbour's house so as not to hear him. He utters terrible cries, he wants to kill himself. On that occasion his daughter had to have him tied down on to his bed and put in a straitjacket. The poor man claims that he has animals in his head which gnaw at his brain; each nerve is stretched and pulled and, as it were, hacked with a saw. His head aches so terribly that he didn't feel the moxas that formerly they applied to try to relieve the pain. But Monsieur Brousson, whom he has taken as his doctor, has forbidden them, maintaining that it was a nervous affliction, an inflammation of the nerves, for which he had to have leeches at his neck and opium on his head. And indeed, the attacks have become less frequent and have only recurred once a year towards the end of the autumn. After he has recovered, Taillefer always says repeatedly that he would rather be broken on the wheel than experience such pain.'

'Then he appears to suffer a lot,' said a stockbroker, the wit of the salon.

'Oh,' she continued, 'last year he nearly died. He had gone alone to his country estate on urgent business. Perhaps because there was no one to help him, he remained flat out as if he were dead for twenty-two hours. He was saved only by a very hot bath.'

'Is it a kind of tetanus then?' asked the stockbroker.

'I don't know,' she answered. 'It's nearly thirty years now that he has been suffering from this illness which he contracted in the army. He says that he got a splinter of wood in his head through falling in a boat. But Brousson has hopes of curing him. They say that the English have found a way of treating the illness safely by means of Prussic acid.'

At that moment a scream more piercing than the others rang out in the house and froze us with horror.

'Well, that's what I heard continually,' went on the banker's wife. 'It made me start up on my chair and got on my nerves. But it's an extraordinary thing, this poor Taillefer, while suffering intolerable pain, is never in danger of dying. He eats and drinks as usual during the moments of respite which this dreadful torment leaves him. (Nature is very strange!) A German doctor told him that it was a kind of gout in the head. That would fit in well enough with Brousson's opinion.'

I left the group which had formed around the mistress of the house and went out with Mademoiselle Taillefer who had been sent for by a valet.

'Oh God, oh God!' she cried, weeping. 'What has my father done to Heaven to deserve to suffer thus? . . . He is such a good man!'

I went down the stairs with her and as I helped her to get into the carriage, I saw her father inside, bent double. Mademoiselle Taillefer tried to stifle her father's groans by covering his mouth with a handkerchief. Unfortunately he caught sight of me; his face seemed to become even more contorted, a convulsive cry rent the air, he gave me a horrible look and the carriage set off.

4. The Case of Conscience

That evening's dinner-party exercised a cruel influence on my life and on my feelings. I was in love with Mademoiselle Taillefer, perhaps precisely because honour and delicacy forbade me to ally myself to a murderer, however good a father and husband he might be. An extraordinary fate impelled me to have myself introduced into houses where I knew I could meet Victorine. Often, after giving myself my word of honour to give up seeing her, that very evening I would be at her side. My enjoyment was immense. My legitimate love, full of imaginary remorse, had the colour of a criminal passion. I despised myself for greeting Taillefer when he happened to be with his daughter, but I greeted him! To crown it all, Victorine is unfortunately not only a pretty girl; she is also well-informed, full of talent and charm, without the least touch of pedantry, without the slightest hint of conceit. She converses modestly and her character has an irresistible melancholy charm. She loves me, or at least she gives me grounds for believing so. She has a certain smile which she produces only for me and, for me, her voice becomes even more gentle. Oh, she loves me, but she adores her father. She lauds to me his kindness, his gentleness, his remarkable virtues. These praises are so many dagger-blows which she thrusts in my heart.

One day I found myself almost an accomplice in the crime on which the wealth of the Taillefer family is based; I wanted to ask for Victorine's hand in marriage. Then I fled, I travelled, I went to Germany, to Andernach. But I came back. I returned to find Victorine pale; she had gone thin. If only she had been in good health and happy when I saw her again, I would have been saved! My passion was rekindled with extraordinary violence. Fearing that my scruples would degenerate into monomania, I decided to summon a sanhedrin of men with pure consciences so as to cast some light on this serious ethical and philosophical problem. The question had become still more complicated since my return. So the day before yesterday, I assembled those of my friends who I think are the most upright and have the keenest sense of delicacy and honour. I had invited two Englishmen (a secretary of an embassy and a puritan), an ex-minister with mature political experience, young men still under the spell of innocence, a priest who was an old man, then my former guardian (an ingenuous man who gave me the finest guardianship account that the law courts can remember), a barrister, a solicitor, a magistrate, in short, representatives of all the views of society and of all the practical virtues.

We began by dining well, talking well and declaiming well. Then, at dessert, I told them my story simply and asked for some good advice, concealing the name of the young lady.

'Advise me, my friends,' I said in conclusion. 'Discuss the question at length as if it were a parliamentary Bill. The urn and the billiard-balls will be brought to you and you will vote for or against my marriage, with all the secrecy required by a ballot.'

Suddenly there was a profound silence. The solicitor declined to give an opinion.

'I have a contract to draw up,' he said.

The wine had reduced my former guardian to silence and we had to establish a guardianship over him so that no harm should come to him on his way home.

'I understand,' I cried. 'Not to give me an opinion is to tell me firmly what I ought to do.'

A stir went through the gathering.

A landowner who had contributed to an appeal for General Foy's children and for his tombstone, exclaimed,

'*Ainsi que la vertu, le crime a ses degrés!*'[3]

'Gasbag!' the former minister whispered to me nudging my elbow.

'Where's the difficulty?' asked a duke whose fortune consists of property confiscated from refractory Protestants at the time of the Revocation of the Edict of Nantes.

The barrister got up. 'In law, the case which has been submitted to us would not involve the slightest difficulty. The duke is right,' exclaimed the voice of the law. 'Hasn't the time limit been passed? Where would we all be if we had to investigate the origin of our fortunes? This is a matter of conscience. If you are determined to bring the case before a tribunal, go to the tribunal of penitence.'

The incarnation of the law said no more, sat down and drank a glass of champagne. The man whose duty it was to explain the Gospel, the good priest, got up.

'God has made us fragile,' he said firmly. 'If you love the heiress of the crime, marry her, but be satisfied with the money from her father's wife and give the father's possessions to the poor.'

'But,' cried one of those pitiless quibblers whom we meet so often in society, 'perhaps the father made such a wealthy marriage only because he had become rich. Hasn't the least of his good fortunes always been a result of the crime?'

'The discussion is in itself a judgement. There are things a man doesn't discuss,' cried my former guardian who thought he was enlightening the gathering by a drunken sally.

3. This is a quotation from Racine, *Phèdre*, Act IV, Scene 2. 'Crime, like virtue, has its degrees.'

'Yes,' said the embassy secretary.

'Yes,' cried the priest.

These two men didn't understand each other.

A doctrinaire[4] who had only lacked one hundred and fifty votes out of a hundred and fifty-five to be elected, got up.

'Gentlemen, this remarkable accident of intellectual nature is one of those which depart the most markedly from the normal conditions to which society is subjected,' he said. 'So the decision to be taken must be an extemporal fact of our conscience, a sudden concept, an instructive judgement, a fleeting subtlety of our private apprehension rather like the flashes which form judgements of taste. Let us vote.'

'Let us vote!' cried my guests.

I had two balls given to each of them, one white, the other red. The white one, a symbol of virginity, was to forbid the marriage and the red ball was to approve of it. I refrained from voting out of tact. My friends were seventeen in number, nine was an absolute majority. Each of them put his ball in the narrow-necked wicker basket in which the numbered balls are shaken up when players draw for turns at pool. We felt quite a keen curiosity, for this ballot about refinements of morals had something original about it. When the vote was examined, I found nine white balls! This result did not surprise me, but it occurred to me to count the young men of my own age whom I had placed among my judges. There were nine of these casuists. They had all had the same thought.

'Oh! Oh!' I said to myself. 'There is a secret unanimity for the marriage, and a unanimity in forbidding it to me! How shall I get out of the difficulty?'

'Where does the father-in-law live?' thoughtlessly asked one of my college friends who dissembled less well than the others.

'There is no longer a father-in-law,' I cried. 'My conscience spoke to me before, clearly enough to make your decision superfluous. And if today its voice is weakened, this is the explanation of my cowardice. Two months ago, I received this enticing letter.'

4. An adherent of a constitutionalist party which arose in France soon after 1815.

I showed them the following invitation which I pulled out of my wallet.

You are invited to be present at the funeral service and interment of M. JEAN-FRÉDÉRIC TAILLEFER, of the House of Taillefer and Company, former supplier of provisions, in his life time Chevalier of the Legion of Honour and of the Golden Spur, Captain of the First Company of Grenadiers in the Second Legion of the National Guard of Paris, died the first May at his home, Rue Joubert, and which will take place at . . . etc.

On behalf of . . . etc.

The Decision

'Now what shall I do?' I continued. 'I am going to ask the question in very broad terms. There is certainly a pool of blood in Mademoiselle Taillefer's property. Her father's legacy is a vast Aceldama.[5] I know that. But Prosper Magnan has left no heirs and I have found it impossible to trace the family of the pin-manufacturer murdered at Andernach. To whom should the fortune be returned? And ought one to return the whole fortune? Have I the right to betray a secret discovered accidentally, to add a severed head to the dowry of an innocent girl, to give her bad dreams, to take from her a lovely illusion, to kill her father a second time for her by saying to her, "All your money is tainted"? I have borrowed the *Dictionary of Cases of Conscience* from an old churchman and have found no solution to my doubts in it. Should I set up a religious foundation for the souls of Prosper Magnan, of Walhenfer, of Taillefer? But we are well into the nineteenth century. Shall I build an almshouse or set up a prize for virtue? The prize for virtue will be given to scoundrels! As for most of our almshouses they seem to me to have become nowadays protectors of vice. Besides, would these investments, which more or less gratify vanity, constitute reparations? And do I owe them? Then I am in love, passionately in love. My love is my life. If to a girl used to luxury, to elegance, to a life rich in

5. The name of the field near Jerusalem bought with blood-money received by Judas Iscariot, hence, figuratively, a sea of blood.

enjoyment of the arts, a girl who likes to listen languidly at the Bouffons to Rossini's music, if to such a girl I propose, without apparent motive, that she divest herself of fifteen hundred thousand francs in favour of stupid old men or chimerical down-and-outs, she will turn her back on me with a laugh, or her confidential maid will take me for a joker in bad taste. If, in an ecstasy of love, I extol the charms of a mediocre existence and my little house on the banks of the Loire, if I ask her to sacrifice her Parisian life in the name of our love, it will be, in the first place, a virtuous lie. Then I shall perhaps have a sad experience there and I shall lose the heart of that girl who is in love with balls, crazy about clothes and jewelry, and about me for the moment. She will be taken away from me by a spruce, slim officer with a well-curled moustache, who will play the piano, praise Lord Byron, and ride prettily. What shall I do? Gentlemen, have mercy, give me some advice . . .'

The honest man whom I have already mentioned – a kind of puritan rather like Jeanie Deans' father – and who up to this point had not said a word, shrugged his shoulders saying, 'You fool, why did you ask him if he came from Beauvais?'

1831

The Purse

THE hour when it is no longer day but night has not yet come is a delightful one for expansive temperaments. Then the glow of twilight casts its soft tints or its strange reflections over everything and encourages a reverie which blends vaguely with the play of light and shade. The silence which reigns nearly always at this moment endears it more especially to artists, who reflect, stand back from their work (which they can no longer continue) and pass judgement on it, intoxicating themselves with a theme whose inner meaning then suddenly flashes on the mind's eye of genius. Anyone who, lost in thought, has not lingered beside a friend during that moment of poetic reverie will find it difficult to understand its inexpressible benefits. In the half-light the physical tricks used by art to make things seem real disappear completely. If one is looking at a picture, the people represented seem both to speak and to walk; the shadow becomes real shadow, the daylight is real daylight, the flesh is alive, the eyes move, blood flows in the veins and fabrics glisten. The imagination helps every detail to appear natural and sees only the beauties of the work. At that hour illusion reigns supreme; perhaps it comes with the night? Is not illusion a kind of night for our thoughts, a night which we furnish with dreams? Illusion then spreads its wings, carries the soul away to the world of fantasies, a world rich in voluptuous and capricious desires, in which the artist forgets the real world, yesterday, tomorrow, and the future, even his troubles both good and bad.

At this magic hour, a talented young painter, who saw in art only art itself, was at the top of the double ladder that he was using to paint a large, high canvas, which was nearly completed. There, criticizing his work, admiring it in good faith, and following the drift of his thoughts, he was absorbed in one of those meditations which delight and exalt the soul, which charm and soothe it. His daydream must have lasted a long time. Night came. Whether he wanted to climb down the ladder or whether he made a false movement thinking he was on the floor, he could, in the circumstances, have no clear recollection of the causes of his accident. He fell, his head struck against a stool, he lost consciousness and lay motionless, for how long he did not know. A gentle voice roused him from the kind of daze in which he was sunk. When he opened his eyes the sight of a bright light made him shut them again quickly. But through the veil which shrouded his senses he heard two women whispering and felt two young, timid hands supporting his head. Soon he regained consciousness and, by the light of one of those old lamps with a double air-flow, he saw the most delightful girl's head that he had ever seen, one of those heads which are often taken for a fancy of the paintbrush. But for him this head suddenly made real the theories of ideal beauty which every artist creates for himself and which is the source of his talent. The unknown girl's face was of the fine-featured, delicate type, of the school of Proudhon's painting, as it were, and also had that poetic charm which Girodet gives to his imaginary faces. The smoothness of her brow, the regularity of her eyebrows, the purity of her features, the virginity clearly marked on her whole countenance, made of the girl a perfect creation. Her figure was lithe and slender, her curves were delicate. Her clothes, though simple and neat, indicated neither wealth nor poverty. As he returned to consciousness the painter expressed his admiration in a look of surprise, and stammered incoherent thanks. He found that his forehead was being pressed by a handkerchief and, in spite of the smell peculiar to studios, he recognized the strong smell of ether which must have been used to bring him round after his faint. Then, finally, he saw an old woman, who looked like a marchioness of the old régime, holding the lamp as she gave advice to the unknown girl.

'Monsieur,' replied the girl to one of the questions asked by the painter while his ideas were still in the state of confusion caused by the fall, 'my mother and I heard the noise of your fall on to the floor and we thought we could hear a groan.

The silence which followed the fall frightened us and we hurried upstairs. We found the key in the door, fortunately took the liberty of coming in and found you stretched out motionless on the ground. My mother went to get everything needed to make a compress and revive you. You are hurt on the forehead, there. Do you feel it?'

'Yes, now I can,' he said.

'Oh, it's not serious,' added the old mother. 'Fortunately your head hit this dummy.'

'I feel a lot better,' replied the painter. 'I only need a carriage to take me home. The porter will get one for me.'

He wanted to repeat his thanks to the two strangers, but at every sentence the old lady interrupted him, saying, 'Tomorrow, Monsieur, be sure you apply leeches or have yourself bled. Drink some glasses of cordial. Take care of yourself; falls are dangerous.'

The girl was looking furtively at the painter and at the pictures in the studio. Her expression and her glances were perfectly modest. Her curiosity seemed like absent-mindedness and her eyes appeared to express the interest which women, with gracious spontaneity, take in all our misfortunes. The two strangers seemed oblivious of the painter's works in the presence of the suffering artist. When he had reassured them about his condition, they left his room looking at him with a solicitude devoid of both exaggeration and familiarity; they asked no indiscreet questions and did not try to make him want to become acquainted with them. Their actions bore the mark of perfect simplicity and good taste. At first their noble, simple manners made little impression on the painter, but afterwards when he recalled all the circumstances of the accident, he was very much struck by them. As they came to the floor below the painter's studio, the old lady exclaimed gently, 'Adélaide, you left the door open.'

'That was to help me,' replied the painter with a grateful smile.

'Mother, you went downstairs just now,' replied the girl, blushing.

'Would you like us to go down with you?' the mother asked the painter. 'The staircase is dark.'

'No, thank you, Madame, I am much better.'

'Hold firmly on to the banisters!'

The two women stayed on the landing to give the young man a light, listening to the sound of his footsteps.

So that the reader can appreciate fully how piquant and unexpected this scene was for the painter, I must explain that he had only moved into his studio in the attic of this house a few days previously. The house was situated in the darkest and consequently the muddiest part of the Rue de Suresne, almost opposite the Madeleine church and two steps away from his flat in the Rue des Champs Elysées. As the fame which his talent had brought him had made him one of the most popular artists in France, he was beginning to be no longer in want, and, as he put it, he was enjoying his last days of poverty. Instead of going to work in one of the studios on the outskirts of the city whose reasonable rent was proportionate to the modesty of his earnings, he had satisfied a desire which used to be renewed each day, avoiding a long journey and loss of time, now more valuable to him than ever. No one would have aroused more interest than Hippolyte Schinner if he had been willing to make himself known, but he did not lightly confide the secrets of his life. He was the idol of a poor mother who had brought him up at the cost of the most severe privations. Mademoiselle Schinner, the daughter of an Alsatian farmer, had never been married. Her tender heart had formerly been cruelly hurt by a rich man who did not pride himself on being very scrupulous in love affairs. As a young girl in all the flower of her beauty, in all the radiance of her life, at the expense of her heart and of her beautiful illusions, she suffered that disenchantment which comes so slowly and yet so quickly, for we want to put off believing in evil as long as possible, and yet it always seems to come too soon. The day of her disenchantment was a whole century of reflections and it also was a day of religious thoughts and resignation. She refused the help of the man who had deceived her, withdrew from society, and turned her fault into a triumph. She gave herself up entirely to maternal love, asking from it all its joys in return for the pleasures of social life to which she bade farewell. She supported herself by her own work, laying up a treasure in her son. And so, later on, one day, one hour repaid her for the long drawn-out sacrifices of her poverty. At the last exhibition her son had received the Cross of the Legion of Honour. The newspapers, unanimously in favour of an unknown talent, were still loud in their sincere praise. The artists themselves acknowledged Schinner as a master and the dealers covered his pictures with gold. At the age of twenty-five Hippolyte Schinner, to whom his mother had transmitted her womanly feelings, appreciated more than ever her situation in society. He wanted to restore to his mother the pleasures of which society had so long deprived her and so he lived for her, hoping by dint of fame and fortune to see her one day happy, rich, respected, surrounded by famous men. Schinner had accordingly selected his friends from amongst the most honourable and distinguished men. Discriminating in the choice of his social contacts he wanted to raise even higher the position which his talent had made so high already. Work, to which he had been dedicated since his youth, in forcing him to live in solitude (always the mother of great thoughts) had left him that splendid faith which is the ornament of the early years of life. His adolescent soul was not unaware of any of the thousand traits of modesty that make a young man a being apart, with a heart full of joys, of poetry, of virgin hopes which seem trivial to sophisticated people but which are deep because they are simple. He had been gifted with those gentle, courteous manners which are so becoming and which attract even those who do not understand them. He was well built. His voice, which came from the heart, aroused noble feelings in others and, by a certain candour in its tone, indicated a genuine modesty. When you saw him you felt drawn towards him by one of those moral attractions which scientists fortunately cannot yet analyse. They would find in it some phenomenon of galvanism or the activity of some fluid or other and they would express our feelings in a formula of proportions of oxygen and electricity.

These details will perhaps enable self-assured people and well-dressed men to understand why, during the absence of the caretaker whom he had sent to the end of the Rue de la Madeleine to get a carriage, Hippolyte Schinner did not ask the porter's wife any questions about the two people whose kind hearts had been revealed to him. But although he replied with a 'yes' or a 'no' to the questions, quite natural in such a situation, which she asked him about his accident and the obliging intervention of the fourth-floor tenants, he could not prevent her from obeying her caretaker's instinct. She talked to him about the two strangers from her point of view and according to the below-stairs opinions of the porter's lodge.

'Oh,' she said, 'it must be Mademoiselle Leseigneur and her mother who have lived here for four years. We don't know yet what these ladies do. In the morning, only up to midday, an elderly half-deaf domestic help, who talks no more than a wall, comes to work for them. In the evenings, two or three old gentlemen, with decorations like yours, Monsieur, and one of them with a carriage, and servants and the reputation of having an income of sixty thousand livres, come to the ladies' flat and often stay very late. But they are very quiet tenants, like you, Monsieur. And they're economical too, they live on nothing; as soon as a bill comes, they pay it. It's odd, Monsieur. The mother has a different name from her daughter. Oh, when they go to the Tuileries, Mademoiselle is very splendid and she can't go out without being followed by young men. She very properly shuts the door in their faces. The landlord would never allow . . .'

The carriage had arrived, Hippolyte heard no more, and went home. His mother, to whom he told his adventure, dressed his injury again and did not allow him to go back to his studio the following day. The doctor was consulted, various remedies were ordered and Hippolyte stayed at home for three days. During this confinement his unoccupied imagination recalled vividly, as it were by fragments, the details of the scene which followed his fainting. The girl's profile stood out sharply from the haziness of his inner vision; he could see again the mother's worn face and still feel Adélaide's hands. He observed again a gesture which he had not noticed much at first but whose perfect grace was brought out by memory. Then an attitude or the sound of a melodious voice, made more beautiful by the distance of memory, suddenly reappeared like objects which come to the surface after being dropped to the bottom of a pond. So, on the day when he was able to start work again, he went back to his studio early. But the visit which he was undeniably entitled to make to his neighbours was the real cause of his eagerness; he was already forgetting the pictures he had begun. At the moment when a passion breaks through its swaddling clothes there is an inexplicable pleasure which those who have loved will understand. Thus some people will know why the painter slowly climbed the stairs leading to the fourth floor and will share the secret of his rapid heartbeats when he saw the brown door of Mademoiselle Leseigneur's modest dwelling. This girl, who did not have the same name as her mother, had aroused a thousand sympathies in the young painter. He liked to think that he and she were in similar positions and he endowed her with the misfortunes of his own origin. As he worked Hippolyte yielded himself completely to thoughts of love and made a lot of noise in order to oblige the two ladies to think of him just as he was thinking of them. He stayed very late at his studio and had dinner there. Then about seven o'clock he went downstairs to his neighbours' flat.

Perhaps out of delicacy, no painter of social manners has dared to let us into the secrets of the really strange homes of some Parisians, those dwellings from which emerge such smart, such elegant toilettes, women who are so dazzling and appear so rich, yet in whose homes can be seen everywhere the signs of a shaky fortune. If the picture here is too bluntly portrayed, if you find it wearisome, do not blame the description, which is, as it were, an integral part of the story; for the appearance of his neighbours' flat had a strong influence on the feelings and hopes of Hippolyte Schinner.

The house belonged to one of those landlords who have a deep, built-in horror of repairs and improvements, one of those men who consider their position of Parisian landlord as a profession. In the great chain of moral types, these people are half-way between the miser and the money-lender. They are all calculating optimists and faithful to the *status quo* of Austria. If you talk of altering a cupboard or a door, of making the most essential ventilator, their eyes flash, their anger is aroused, they shy like frightened horses. When the wind has blown a few tiles off their chimneys they are ill, and deny themselves a visit to the Gymnase or the Porte-Saint-Martin because of the repairs. Hippolyte had had the free performance of a comic scene with milord Molineux in connection with certain improvements to be made in his studio, and so he was not surprised at the dark, greasy colours, at the oily streaks, at the stains and other rather disagreeable accessories which adorned the woodwork. These marks of poverty are not, moreover, without poetry in the eyes of an artist.

Mademoiselle Leseigneur came herself to open the door. She recognized the young painter and greeted him. Then, at the same time, with the dexterity of a Parisian and the presence of mind which comes from pride, she turned round to shut the door of a glazed partition. Through this door Hippolyte might have glimpsed some washing hung on lines above the economical stove, an old trestle bed, embers, coal, irons, the household filter, dishes and all the utensils peculiar to small households. Fairly clean muslin curtains carefully concealed this *capharnaüm* (a word used colloquially to indicate this kind of laboratory), which was moreover badly lit by apertures looking on to a neighbouring courtyard. With the quick glance of an artist, Hippolyte saw the function, the furniture, the general state of this first divided room. The respectable part, which served both as ante-room and as dining-room, was papered with old, gold-coloured wallpaper with a velvet border, probably manufactured by Réveillon. Its holes and stains had been carefully concealed by wafers. Engravings by Lebrun representing Alexander's battles, but in frames with the gilt rubbed off, were hung symmetrically on the walls. In the middle of the room was a solid mahogany table of an old-fashioned shape and worn at the edges. A little stove, whose straight upright pipe was hardly visible, stood in front of the fireplace, and in the hearth was a cupboard. In strange contrast, the chairs showed traces of a past splendour; they were of carved mahogany. But the red leather of the seats, the gilded studs and the gold braid sported as many scars as the old sergeants of the Imperial Guard. The room served as a museum for certain things which are only found in this kind of ambiguous household, nameless objects partaking of both luxury and poverty. Amongst other curiosities Hippolyte noticed a magnificently decorated telescope hung above the little greenish mirror which adorned the chimney-piece. To match this strange furniture, there was, between the fireplace and the partition, a cheap sideboard painted to look like mahogany, of all woods the one that is the hardest to imitate. But the red, slippery tiled floor, the miserable little mats placed in front of the chairs, the furniture, everything shone with that polished cleanliness which lends a false lustre to old things by showing up even more their imperfections, their age and their long service. In the room there lingered an indefinable smell which came from the fumes of the *capharnaüm* mingled with the odours of the dining-room and the staircase, although the window was half open and the air from the street moved the cambric curtains. These were carefully draped so as to hide the recess where the previous tenants had left marks of their presence in several incrustations, like species of domestic frescoes. Adélaide quickly opened the door of the other room into which she showed the painter with a certain pleasure. Hippolyte who, in the past, had seen the same signs of poverty in his mother's home, noticed them with the peculiarly vivid impression which characterizes our earliest memories, and appreciated better than anyone else would have done the details of this existence. In recognizing the kind of things that he had known in his childhood, the good-hearted young man had neither scorn for this concealed misfortune nor pride in the luxury which he had just won for his mother.

'Well, Monsieur, I hope you no longer feel the effects of your fall,' said the old mother getting up from an old-fashioned easy chair in the chimney corner and offering him an armchair.

'No, Madame. I have come to thank you for the good care you gave me and especially to thank Mademoiselle who heard me fall.'

As he said these words, marked by the adorable stupidity
aroused in the mind by the first agitations of true love, Hippolyte looked at Adélaide. The girl was lighting the lamp with
the double air-flow, no doubt so that she could dispense with
a candle standing in a large, flat brass candlestick and decorated
with prominent ridges of wax because of excessive melting.
She gave a slight nod, went to put the candlestick in the ante-
room, and came back to put the lamp on the mantelpiece.
She sat down near her mother, a little behind the painter, so
that she could look at him comfortably while appearing to be
very busy getting the lamp going; its light, dimmed by the
damp of an unpolished chimney, was flickering as it struggled
with a black, badly trimmed wick. On seeing the large mirror
which decorated the chimney-piece, Hippolyte glanced at it
quickly so that he could admire Adélaide. The girl's little trick
thus served only to embarrass both of them. As he chatted
with Madame Leseigneur (for Hippolyte gave her that name
on the off-chance) he examined the sitting-room, but discreetly
and unobtrusively. The Egyptian faces of the iron fire-dogs
could hardly be seen in the ash-filled hearth, in which two
firebrands almost met in front of an artificial earthenware log
buried as carefully as a miser's treasure. An old Aubusson
carpet, well mended and much faded, threadbare as an old
soldier's coat, left bare some of the tiled floor, whose chill
could be felt. The walls were decorated with a reddish paper,
imitating a figured silk material with yellow designs. In the
middle of the wall opposite the windows the painter saw a
crack and the chinks made in the wallpaper by the doors of a
recess where presumably Madame Leseigneur slept and which
was ill-concealed by a couch placed in front of it. Opposite
the fireplace, above a mahogany chest decorated not without
richness and taste, hung the portrait of a high-ranking officer
which the painter could not see clearly in the dim light. But
the little that he saw made him think that this frightful daub
must have been painted in China. At the windows the red silk
curtains were faded, as was the suite, upholstered with red
and yellow tapestry, of this dual-purpose sitting-room. On
the marble top of the chest was a valuable malachite tray,

bearing a dozen magnificently painted coffee cups, probably made at Sèvres. On the mantelpiece was the ubiquitous Empire clock, a warrior guiding the four horses of a chariot with the number of an hour marked on each spoke of its wheel. The candles in the candelabra were yellowed with smoke and at each end of the mantelpiece could be seen a porcelain vase wreathed in artificial flowers, laden with dust and decorated with moss. In the middle of the room, Hippolyte noticed a card table set up and new cards. To an observer there was something indescribably sad in the sight of this poverty made up like an old woman who wants her face to belie her age. On seeing this room any sensible man would immediately have thought to himself: either these two women are the soul of honesty, or they live by scheming and gambling. But, looking at Adélaide, a young man as pure as Schinner was bound to believe in her perfect innocence and to ascribe to the most honourable causes the discrepancies of the furniture.

'Adélaide,' said the old lady to her daughter, 'I am cold. Make a little fire for us and give me my shawl.'

Adélaide went into a room next to the sitting-room, where presumably she slept, and came back bringing her mother a cashmere shawl which must have been very valuable when new (the patterns were Indian); but old, worn, and full of darns, it matched the furniture. Madame Leseigneur wrapped it round herself very artistically and with the skill of an old lady who wanted her words to be believed. The girl ran smartly to the *capharnaüm* and reappeared with a handful of sticks which she threw boldly on to the fire to relight it.

It would be quite difficult to reproduce the conversation which took place between these three people. Guided by the tact which nearly always comes from misfortunes experienced in childhood, Hippolyte did not dare to allow himself the slightest comment on his neighbours' circumstances as he saw around him the signs of such ill-concealed poverty. The simplest question would have been indiscreet and would have been permissible only in an old friend. Nevertheless, the painter was deeply affected by this concealed poverty, his generous soul was grieved by it. But as he knew how offensive any kind of pity, even the most friendly, can be, he was ill at ease because of the discrepancy between his thoughts and his words. The two ladies first of all talked about painting, for women are well aware of the hidden embarrassments occasioned by a first visit. Perhaps they experience these embarrassments themselves and their cast of mind provides a thousand ways of putting an end to them. As they asked the young man about the techniques of his art, about his studies, Adélaide and her mother skilfully encouraged him to talk. The indefinable nothings of their kindly conversation naturally led Hippolyte to utter remarks or reflections which revealed his ways and his nature.

Sorrows had prematurely aged the old lady's face which had no doubt once been beautiful. But she retained only the prominent features, the outlines, in short the framework of a countenance which, taken as a whole, indicated great delicacy; there remained, too, considerable graciousness in the play of the eyes in which lay the indefinable expression peculiar to ladies of the old court. These fine, delicate features could just as well indicate evil feelings, suggest feminine wiles to a high degree of perversity, as reveal the sensitivity of a beautiful soul. Indeed a woman's face presents a problem to ordinary observers, for the difference between openness and deceit, between the gift for intrigue and the gift for genuine feeling is imperceptible. A man endowed with penetrating insight can guess at the intangible shades of meaning indicated by a line more or less curved, by a dimple more or less deep, by a feature more or less rounded or prominent. This kind of interpretation is dependent entirely on intuition, which alone can discover what everyone is concerned to hide. The old lady's face was like the flat she lived in. It seemed as difficult to know if this poverty concealed vices or great integrity as it was to tell whether Adélaide's mother was a former coquette in the habit of weighing up everything, calculating everything, selling everything, or an affectionate woman full of nobility and lovable virtues. But at Schinner's age, the first impulse of the heart is to believe in the good. And so, as he studied Adélaide's noble and almost haughty forehead, and looked at her expressive, thoughtful eyes, he inhaled, as it were, the sweet, modest scents of virtue. In the middle of the conversation, he took the opportunity of talking of portraits in general so that he would have an excuse for examining the frightful pastel drawing which had all its colours faded and its bloom largely worn away.

'Presumably you are attached to this picture because it resembles someone, Mesdames, for it's horribly ill drawn,' he said looking at Adélaide.

'It was done in Calcutta, in a great hurry,' replied the mother in a voice filled with emotion.

She looked at the clumsy sketch with that deep concentration aroused by reawakened happy memories which fall on the heart like a beneficent dew in whose fresh traces one gladly lingers. But in the expression of the old lady's face there were also signs of eternal mourning. This, at any rate, is how the painter interpreted his neighbour's demeanour and expression. Then he came and sat down beside her.

'Madame,' he said, 'in a little while the colours of this pastel drawing will have disappeared. The portrait will exist only in your memory. Where you will see a beloved face, others won't be able to see anything. Will you allow me to transfer this likeness to canvas? It will be more firmly fixed there than it is on this piece of paper. Since we are neighbours, give me the pleasure of doing this service for you. There are times when an artist likes to take a rest from his important compositions by doing less serious work, and so it will be a relaxation for me to repaint that head.'

The old lady gave a start when she heard these words, and Adélaide gave the painter one of those thoughtful looks which seem to come straight from the heart. Hippolyte wanted to be linked with his neighbours by some kind of tie and to acquire the right to be part of their lives. His offer, which appealed to the keenest affections of their hearts, was the only one he could make. It satisfied his artist's pride and in no way offended the two ladies. Madame Leseigneur accepted the offer without being over-eager but with no reluctance, with the awareness of a fine soul that knows the extent of the bonds forged by such obligations and turns them into a token of great praise and esteem.

'Isn't that the uniform of a naval officer?' said the painter.

'Yes,' she said, 'it's the uniform of a ship's captain. Monsieur de Rouville, my husband, died in Batavia as the result of a wound received in a fight against an English ship which he encountered off the Asian coast. He commanded a frigate with fifty-six guns, and the *Revenge* was a ship with ninety-six. It was an unequal struggle but he defended himself so bravely that he fought till night came and he was able to escape. When I came back to France, Bonaparte wasn't yet in power and I was refused a pension. When, recently, I again asked for one the minister told me harshly that if Baron de Rouville had emigrated, he would still be alive, that he would probably have been a rear-admiral by now. Finally His Excellency ended by citing against me some law or other about the forfeiture of rights. I took this step, which friends urged me to take, only for the sake of my poor Adélaide. I have always disliked holding out my hand in the name of a grief which deprives a woman of her voice and her strength. I don't like this pecuniary evaluation of blood which has been irreparably spilt.'

'Mother, this topic of conversation always upsets you.'

At Adélaide's words, the Baronne Leseigneur de Rouville bowed her head and said no more.

'Monsieur,' said the girl to Hippolyte, 'I thought that painters' work didn't usually make a lot of noise?'

At this question, Schinner began to blush remembering the din he had made. Adélaide said no more and saved him from telling a lie by suddenly getting up at the sound of a carriage stopping at the door. She went into her room, from which she immediately returned with two gilded candlesticks containing half-used candles which she lit straight away. And without waiting for the ring at the bell, she opened the door of the first room where she left the lamp. The sound of a kiss being given and received went straight to Hippolyte's heart. The young man's impatience to see the person who was on such familiar terms with Adélaide was not satisfied immediately, for, speaking in low tones, the new arrivals had a conversation with her which he found very long. At last, Mademoiselle de Rouville reappeared followed by two men whose clothes, faces and appearance are in themselves a whole story.

The first one, aged about sixty, was wearing one of those jackets invented, I think, for Louis XVIII, who was then on the throne. By means of these jackets, a tailor, who ought to be immortalized, solved the most difficult sartorial problem. That artist certainly knew the art of compromise, an art which was the whole spirit of that politically mobile period. Is it not quite a rare merit to be able to judge one's own period? This coat, that the young men of today might take as legendary, was neither civilian nor military and could in turn pass for either. Embroidered fleurs-de-lis decorated the facings of the two coat-tails at the back. There were also fleurs-de-lis on the gilt buttons. On the shoulders two empty loops were crying out for useless epaulettes. These two military indications were there like a petition without a recommendation. In the buttonhole of the old man's royal blue cloth coat was a rosette made of several ribbons. He presumably always carried in his hand his three-cornered hat decorated with gold braid, for the snow-white tufts of his powdered hair showed no trace of pressure from the hat. He looked as if he was not more than fifty and seemed to enjoy robust health. While revealing the loyal, frank, character of the old *émigrés* his face also indicated the free-thinking, easy-going ways, the gay passions and light-heartedness of those musketeers who used to be so famous in the annals of gallantry. His gestures, his gait, his manners proclaimed that he was not willing to amend his royalism, his religion or his love affairs.

A truly fantastic figure followed this pretentious *voltigeur de Louis XIV* (that was the nickname given by the Bonapartists to these noble remnants of the monarchy). But to describe him properly I would need to make him the central figure of the picture where he is only an accessory. Imagine a thin, dried-up person, dressed like the first one, but as it were only his reflection, or if you like, his shadow. The one had a new coat, the other's was old and shabby. The hair powder of the second man seemed less white, the gold of the fleur-de-lis less brilliant, the epaulette loops more disconsolate and more crumpled, the intelligence weaker, the life more advanced towards its fatal ending than the first man's. In short he embodied Rivarol's remark about Champcenetz: 'He is my moonlight.' He was only the double of the other, a pale, poor double, for between them there was all the difference that exists between the first and last print of a lithograph. This silent old man was a mystery to the painter and always remained so. The chevalier (for he was a chevalier) did not speak and no one spoke to him. Was he a friend, a poor relation, a man who stayed with the old lady-killer like a paid companion with an old lady? Was he a cross between a dog, a parrot and a friend? Had he saved his benefactor's fortune or only his life? Was he the Trim of another Captain Toby? Elsewhere, just as at the Baronne de Rouville's, he always aroused curiosity without ever satisfying it. During the Restoration, who could remember the attachment which before the Revolution had bound this chevalier to his friend's wife, dead for twenty years?

The person who appeared to be the freshest of these two remnants went gallantly up to the Baronne de Rouville, kissed her hand, and sat down beside her. The other bowed and placed himself close to his model at two chairs' distance. Adélaide came and leaned her elbows on the back of the armchair occupied by the old nobleman, imitating, without realizing it, the pose which Guérin gave to Dido's sister in his famous painting. Although the familiarity with which the nobleman treated her was that of a father, for the moment his liberties seemed to displease the girl.

'Well, you are sulking!' he said. Then he gave Schinner one of those subtle, crafty side glances which diplomatically express the prudent concern, the polite curiosity of well-bred people who, on seeing a stranger, seem to ask, 'Is he one of us?'

'This is our neighbour,' the old lady said to him, indicating Hippolyte. 'Monsieur is a famous painter whose name you must know despite your lack of interest in the arts.'

The nobleman appreciated the old lady's trick in not mentioning the name and bowed to the young man.

'Indeed,' he said, 'I heard a lot about his pictures at the last Salon. Talent has great privileges, Monsieur,' he added looking at the artist's red ribbon. 'The distinction which we must earn at the cost of our blood and of long service, you artists obtain it young. But all men of renown are brothers,' he added touching his Saint-Louis Cross.

Hippolyte stammered a few words of thanks and then became silent again, content to admire with increasing enthusiasm the beautiful girl's head, which delighted him. He soon forgot himself as he gazed at her, thinking no more of the great poverty of the house. For him, Adélaide's face stood out against a halo of light. He replied briefly to the questions addressed to him; fortunately he heard them, thanks to our peculiar intellectual faculty of sometimes being able, in a way, to think of two things at once. Who has not been lost in a joyful or sad meditation and listened to its inner voice, and at the same time taken part in a conversation or attended to someone reading aloud? Admirable duality which often helps us to be patient with bores! Hope, smiling and full of promise, inspired him with a thousand thoughts of future happiness, and he no longer paid any attention to his surroundings. He was a trusting youth and felt that it was shameful to analyse a pleasure.

After a certain time he noticed that the old lady and her daughter were playing cards with the old nobleman. As for the latter's satellite, faithful to his role of shadow, he stood behind his friend, absorbed in his game, replying to the player's unspoken questions with little approving grimaces which reproduced the questioning movements of the other man's face.

'Du Halga, I always lose,' said the nobleman.

'You discard badly,' replied the Baronne de Rouville.

'For three months now I haven't been able to win a single game from you,' he continued.

'Have you the aces, Monsieur le Comte?' asked the old lady.

'Yes. One more doomed,' he said.

'Would you like my advice?' asked Adélaide.

'No, no, stay in front of me. The devil! It would be losing too much not to have you opposite me.'

At last the game ended. The nobleman took out his purse and, as he threw two louis on to the card table, he said, not without irritation, 'Forty francs, as right as gold. And deuce, it's eleven o'clock.'

'It's eleven o'clock,' repeated the silent character looking at the painter.

The young man, hearing these words a little more clearly than all the others, thought that it was time to take his leave. Then, coming back to the everyday world, he thought up some conventional words of conversation, bowed to the baroness, her daughter and the two strangers and left the room a prey to the first delights of true love, and without trying to analyse the unimportant events of the evening.

The next day the young painter felt a violent desire to see Adélaide again. If he had listened to his passion, he would have gone to visit his neighbours again at six o'clock in the morning on arriving at his studio. He had enough rationality, however, to wait until the afternoon. But as soon as he thought he could call on Madame de Rouville, he went downstairs and rang the bell, not without some wild beatings of the heart. Blushing like a girl, he shyly asked Mademoiselle Leseigneur, who had come to open the door, for the Baron de Rouville's portrait.

'Do come in,' said Adélaide who had no doubt heard him coming down from his studio.

The painter followed her. He was embarrassed, abashed, not knowing what to say, so stupid had happiness made him. To see Adélaide, to hear the rustle of her dress after having wanted for a whole morning to be near her, after having got up a hundred times, saying 'I am going downstairs!' and not to have gone downstairs, this for him was to live so fully that if these feelings had been prolonged for too long they would have worn out his soul. The heart has the strange power of setting an extraordinary value on trifles. What a delight it is for a traveller to pick a blade of grass or an unknown leaf if he has risked his life in looking for it! The trifles of love are like this.

The old lady was not in the sitting-room. Adélaide, finding herself alone with the painter, brought a chair so that she could reach the portrait. But when she saw that she could not take it down without standing on the chest, she turned to Hippolyte and said, blushing, 'I am not tall enough. Will you get it?'

A feeling of modesty, revealed in the expression of her face and the tone of her voice, was the true motive for her request, and the young man, appreciating this, gave her one of those understanding looks which are love's sweetest language. On seeing that the painter had guessed her thoughts, Adélaide lowered her eyes with a movement of virginal pride. Then, since he could think of nothing to say and was almost in awe of her, the painter took down the picture, examined it gravely in the light near the window and went away without saying anything to Mademoiselle Leseigneur but 'I'll bring it back soon.' During this fleeting moment both of them experienced one of those sharp emotional shocks whose effects on the soul can be likened to those produced by a stone thrown to the bottom of a lake. The sweetest thoughts arise in quick succession, indefinable, manifold, aimless, disturbing the heart like the rings which, starting from the spot where the stone fell, make ripples in the water for a long time. Hippolyte went back to his studio armed with the portrait. Already a canvas had been fixed on his easel, a palette had been filled with colours. The paint-brushes had been cleaned, and the position and lighting selected. And so till dinner time, he worked at the portrait with the ardour that artists devote to their whims. He returned the same evening to the Baronne de Rouville's and stayed there from nine o'clock till eleven. Apart from the different subjects of conversation, this evening was exactly like the previous one. The two old men came at the same time, they played the same game of piquet, the players made the same remarks, and Adélaide's admirer lost as large a sum of money as he had done the evening before. Only Hippolyte was a little bolder and dared to talk to Adélaide.

A week went by like this, a week in which the painter's and Adélaide's feelings underwent those delightful, slow changes which lead hearts to a complete understanding of each other. So, day by day, the look with which Adélaide greeted her friend became more intimate, more trusting, more gay and frank, her voice and manners became less restrained and more familiar. Schinner wanted to learn piquet. As he was ignorant and new to the game he naturally had to be taught again and again, and, like the old man, he lost nearly every game. Although they had not yet confided their love to each other the two lovers knew that they belonged to each other. Both of them laughed, chatted, exchanged their thoughts, and spoke about themselves with the naïveté of two children who, in the space of a day, have become as well acquainted as if they had known each other for three years. Hippolyte enjoyed exercising his power over his shy sweetheart. Adélaide made many concessions to him. Timid and devoted, she was taken in by those pretended sulks which the least skilful lover or the most naïve girl invents and makes use of continually, just as spoilt children take advantage of the power given them by their mother's love. So there was a sudden end to all intimacy between the old count and Adélaide. From the sharp tone of the few words Hippolyte uttered whenever the old man unceremoniously kissed her hands or neck, she understood the painter's distress and the thoughts concealed beneath his frowning brow. On her side Mademoiselle Leseigneur soon asked her lover for a strict account of his slightest actions. She was so unhappy, so anxious when Hippolyte did not come. She knew so well how to scold him for his absences that the painter had to give up seeing his friends and going into society. Adélaide showed a woman's natural jealousy when she learned that sometimes, on leaving Madame de Rouville's, the painter paid further visits and frequented the most brilliant salons of Paris. According to her, this kind of life was bad for the health. Then, with that deep conviction to which the voice, gesture and look of a loved one give so much weight, she claimed that 'a man who is obliged to lavish his time and the charms of his intelligence on several women at once could not be the object of a very keen affection'. So the painter was led as much by the tyranny of his passion as by the demands of a girl in love, to live only in this little flat where everything pleased him. In short, no love was ever more pure or ardent. On both sides, the same faith, the same delicacy made their passion grow without the help of the sacrifices with which many people seek to prove their love. There existed between them a continual interchange of such sweet feelings that they did not know which of the two gave or received more. An involuntary inclination made the union of their two hearts ever closer. The progress of this genuine feeling was so rapid that, two months after the accident to which the painter owed the happiness of knowing Adélaide, their lives had become one. First thing in the morning, as she heard the painter's step, the girl could say to herself, 'He is there!' When Hippolyte went home to his mother's at dinner time, he never failed to look in on his neighbours. And in the evening he hurried there at the usual time with the punctuality of a man in love. Thus the most tyrannical woman, the most ambitious in love, could not have made the slightest reproach to the young painter. Adélaide therefore enjoyed an unmixed and unlimited happiness as she saw the full realization of the ideal which it is so natural to dream of at her age. The old nobleman came less often. The jealous Hippolyte had replaced him in the evenings at the green card table, in his perpetual bad luck at cards. Yet, in the midst of his happiness, a troublesome idea struck him as he thought of Madame de Rouville's terrible situation, for he had had more than one proof of her poverty. Several times already he had said to himself as he went home, 'What, twenty francs every evening?' And he did not dare admit to himself horrible suspicions. He took two months to paint the portrait, and when it was finished, varnished, and framed he looked on it as one of his best works. The Baronne de Rouville had said nothing more to him about it. Was this because of lack of concern or pride? The painter did not try to explain her silence.

He conspired happily with Adélaide to put the portrait in its place in Madame de Rouville's absence. So one day, while her mother was taking her usual walk in the Tuileries gardens, Adélaide, for the first time, went upstairs alone to Hippolyte's studio, under the pretext of seeing the portrait in the favourable light in which it had been painted. She remained silent and motionless, a prey to a delightful meditation in which all her womanly feelings were fused into one. Were they not all summed up in admiration for the man she loved? When the painter, uneasy at this silence, turned to look at her, she held out her hand to him, unable to say a word. But two tears had fallen from her eyes. Hippolyte took her hand and covered it with kisses. For a moment they looked at each other in silence, both wanting to confess their love and not daring to. The painter kept Adélaïde's hand in his. The same warmth and the same agitation told them then that their hearts were beating equally strongly. Overcome with emotion, the girl gently drew away from Hippolyte and said, looking at him ingenuously, 'You will make my mother very happy.'

'What, only your mother?' he asked.

'Oh! I am too happy already.'

The painter bowed his head and said no more, frightened by the violence of the feelings which the tone of these words awoke in his heart. Then, as they both understood the danger of the situation, they went downstairs and hung the portrait in its place. For the first time, Hippolyte dined with the baroness who, in her emotion and all in tears, wanted to kiss him. In the evening, the old *émigré*, the former comrade of the Baron de Rouville, paid a visit to his two friends to inform them that he had just been appointed vice-admiral. His navigations by land across Germany and Russia had been counted in his favour as naval campaigns. At the sight of the portrait, he cordially shook the painter's hand and exclaimed, 'Faith! Although my old carcass isn't worth the trouble of preserving, I would gladly give five hundred pistoles to see as good a likeness of myself as my old friend Rouville's.'

At this suggestion, the baroness looked at her friend and smiled, while signs of a sudden gratitude lit up her face. Hippolyte had the impression that the old admiral wanted to give him the price of the two portraits in paying for his own. His artist's pride, perhaps, as much as his jealousy, took offence at this thought and he replied, 'Monsieur, if I were a portrait painter, I wouldn't have painted this one.'

The admiral bit his lips and began to play. The painter stayed beside Adélaide, who suggested six points at piquet. He accepted. As he played, he noticed that Madame de Rouville had a zeal for the game that surprised him. Never before had the old baroness shown such an ardent desire to win, nor such a keen pleasure as she handled the nobleman's gold coins. During the evening, evil suspicions disturbed Hippolyte's happiness and made him distrustful. Could it be that Madame de Rouville lived by gambling? Was she not playing just now in order to pay a debt, or egged on by some necessity? Perhaps she hadn't paid her rent? The old man seemed shrewd enough not to let his money be taken with impunity. What interest attracted him, a rich man, to this poor house? Why, when he had formerly been so familiar with Adélaide, had he given up the liberties he had acquired and which perhaps were due to him? These involuntary reflections stimulated him to look carefully at the old man and the baroness whose looks of mutual understanding and side glances at Adélaide and himself displeased him. 'Could it be that they are deceiving me?' was Hippolyte's final, horrible, degrading thought, in which he believed just enough to be tortured by it. He wanted to stay after the old man's departure so that he could confirm or refute his suspicions. He took out his purse to pay Adélaide. But, carried away by his agonizing thoughts, he put it on the table and fell into a reverie which did not last long. Then, ashamed of his silence, he got up, replied to a conventional question asked by Madame de Rouville and went up to her so that, as he talked, he could examine her old face more carefully. He left the house, a prey to a thousand doubts. After going down a few steps, he went back to pick up his forgotten purse.

'I left my purse with you,' he said to Adélaide.

'No,' she replied, blushing.

'I thought it was there,' he added pointing to the card table. He was ashamed for the baroness and for Adélaide that he did not see it there. He gave them a dazed look which made them laugh, turned pale and said as he felt his waistcoat, 'I've made a mistake, I've probably got it.'

In one of the compartments of that purse were fifteen louis and, in the other, some small change. The theft was so flagrant, so shamelessly denied, that Hippolyte no longer doubted his neighbours' immorality. He stopped on the stairs, and went down with difficulty. His legs were trembling, he was dizzy, he was perspiring, he was shivering and he found that he was not in a state to walk; he was struggling with the terrible emotion caused by the reversal of all his hopes. Then he dragged up from his memory a host of things he had noticed, apparently slight, but which corroborated his frightful suspicions and which, proving the reality of this final deed, opened his eyes to the character and way of life of these two women. Had they waited to steal the purse until the portrait had been delivered? Premeditated, the theft seemed even more loathsome. To add to his misery, the painter remembered that for two or three evenings, Adélaide, who, with the curiosity of a young girl, appeared to be examining the particular kind of needlework of the worn-out silk web, was probably checking the amount of money in the purse. She seemed to be teasing innocently as she did so, but her aim was probably to watch for the moment when the amount would be big enough to be worth stealing. 'Perhaps the old admiral has very good reasons for not marrying Adélaide, and then the baroness will have tried to . . .'

At this supposition, he stooped, not even finishing his thought which was contradicted by a very sensible reflection. 'If the baroness,' he thought, 'hopes to marry me to her daughter, they would not have robbed me.' Then, in order not to give up his illusions and his love, which was already so deeply rooted, he tried to explain his loss by blaming it on chance. 'My purse must have fallen on the floor,' he said to himself, 'it must have been left on my armchair. Perhaps I still have it, I am so absent-minded.' He searched himself quickly but did not find the accursed purse. His memory cruelly recalled the fatal truth, moment by moment. He could distinctly see his purse, lying on the top of the table but, since he had no more doubts about the theft, he then made excuses for Adélaïde, telling himself that one should not judge the unfortunate so hastily. There was no doubt some secret behind this deed which seemed so degrading. He did not want her proud and noble figure to prove false. Nevertheless the poverty-stricken flat seemed to him devoid of the poetry of love which beautifies everything. He saw it as dirty and shabby, and looked on it as the outward sign of an inner life which was ignoble, idle and vicious. Are not our feelings, as it were, inscribed on the things around us?

The next morning, he got up after a sleepless night. Heartache, that serious moral illness, had made enormous progress within him. To lose a happiness that had been dreamed of, to give up a whole future is a more acute suffering than that caused by the collapse of an experienced happiness, however complete it may have been. Is not hope better than memory? The meditations into which our minds suddenly fall are then like a sea without a shore, in whose depths we can swim for a moment but where our love must drown and perish. And it is a terrible death. Are not feelings the most brilliant part of our lives? In certain constitutions, delicate or strong, this partial death brings about the great ravages caused by disillusions, by unfulfilled hopes and passions. That was the case with the young painter. He left the house early and went for a walk in the cool shade of the Tuileries gardens, lost in his thoughts, forgetting everything in the world. There he happened to meet one of his closest friends, a school and studio companion with whom he had lived on better terms than one does with a brother.

'Well, Hippolyte, what's the matter?' asked François Souchet, a young sculptor who had just won the *grand prix* and was soon to go off to Italy.

'I am very unhappy,' replied Hippolyte seriously.

'Only an affair of the heart can upset you. Money, fame, esteem, you have everything.'

Gradually, the painter began to pour out his heart and confessed his love. As soon as he mentioned the Rue de Suresne and a young lady living on a fourth floor, Souchet cried cheerfully, 'Stop. She's a little girl whom I see every morning at the Assumption and whom I am courting. But, my dear fellow, we all know her. Her mother is a baroness. Do you believe in baronesses who live on the fourth floor? Brrr. Ah well, you are a man of the Golden Age. We see the old mother here, on this path, every day. But she's got a face, an appearance which tell the whole story. What, you haven't guessed what she is from the way she holds her bag?'

The two friends walked for a long time and were joined by several young men who knew Souchet or Schinner. The sculptor, thinking it not very serious, told them about the painter's experience.

'He's seen that little girl too,' he said.

There were comments and laughs and innocent teasing of the jocular kind usual with artists, but which made Hippolyte suffer terribly. A certain inner delicacy made him feel ill at ease at seeing his heart's secret treated so lightly, his passion rent apart and torn to shreds, and an unknown young girl whose face seemed so modest, subjected to true or false judgements made so thoughtlessly. He pretended to be moved by a spirit of contradiction. He seriously asked each of his companions for proofs of their assertions and the teasing started again.

'But, my dear fellow, have you seen the baroness's shawl?' asked Souchet.

'Have you followed the little girl when she trips along to the Assumption in the morning?' said Joseph Bridau, a young art student from Gros' studio.

'Oh, amongst other virtues, the mother has a certain grey dress which I regard as a model,' said Bixiou, the caricaturist.

'Listen, Hippolyte,' continued the sculptor, 'come here about four o'clock and just analyse the way the mother and daughter walk. If you still have doubts after that, well, we'll never be able to do anything with you. You will be capable of marrying your caretaker's daughter.'

A prey to the most conflicting feelings, the painter left his friends. It seemed to him that Adélaide and her mother must be above these accusations and in his innermost heart he felt remorse at having suspected the purity of this beautiful, unsophisticated girl. He went back to his studio, passed by the door of the flat where Adélaide lived and felt a pang which no man could mistake. He was so passionately in love with Mademoiselle de Rouville that, in spite of the theft of the purse, he still adored her. His love was like that of the Chevalier des Grieux who admired and purified his mistress even when she was on the cart which takes fallen women to prison. 'Why should not my love make her the purest of all women? Why abandon her to vice and evil without holding out a friendly hand?' He liked the idea of such a mission. Love turns everything to its advantage. Nothing attracts a young man more than to play the part of a good genius to a woman. There is something indescribably romantic about such an undertaking which suits passionate hearts. Is this not extreme devotion in its noblest and most gracious form? Is there not some greatness in knowing that you are so much in love that you still love when other people's love fades away and dies? Hippolyte sat down in his studio, looked at his picture without working at it, seeing the figures only through the tears which were swimming in his eyes, keeping his brush in his hand, and going up to the canvas as if to soften a colour, and not touching it. He was still in this state when night overtook him. The darkness aroused him from his meditation. He went downstairs, met the old admiral on the staircase, gave him a grim look as he greeted him and fled. He had meant to call on his neighbours, but the sight of Adélaide's protector froze his heart and made his resolution melt away. He wondered for the hundredth time what motive could bring the old lady-killer, a rich man with an income of eighty thousand livres, to this fourth floor where every evening he lost about forty francs; and he thought he could guess what that motive was. The next day and the following days, Hippolyte threw himself into his work and tried to fight against his passion with the enthusiasm of his ideas and the energy of his creative imagination. He half succeeded. Work consoled him, yet without managing to stifle the memories of so many affectionate hours spent with Adélaide.

One evening, as he left his studio, he found the door of the two ladies' flat half open. There was someone standing there in the window bay. Owing to the situation of the staircase and the door the painter could not pass by without seeing Adélaide. He bowed to her coldly giving her a glance loaded with indifference. But estimating the girl's sufferings by the extent of his own, he had an inner pang as he thought of the bitter grief which such a look and such coldness must arouse in a loving heart. To crown the sweetest joys that have ever delighted two pure hearts with a week's disdain and with the deepest and most utter contempt . . . what a frightful conclusion! Perhaps the purse had been found again, and perhaps Adélaide had waited every evening for her sweetheart. This simple, natural thought aroused further remorse in the lover. He asked himself if the affection which the girl had showed him, if the delightful conversations imbued with a love which had charmed him, did not deserve at least an inquiry, were not worth an attempt at justification. Ashamed at having resisted his heart's desires for a whole week, and considering that this struggle was almost criminal, he went that same evening to Madame de Rouville's. All his suspicions, all his evil thoughts vanished at the sight of Adélaide, who had turned pale and thin.

'My goodness, what's the matter with you?' he said after greeting the baroness.

Adélaide made no reply but gave him a look filled with melancholy, a sad, discouraged look which pained him.

'You have no doubt been working hard,' said the old lady. 'You have changed. It is because of us that you have shut yourself away. The portrait must have delayed some pictures which are important for your reputation.'

Hippolyte was happy to find such a good excuse for his discourtesy.

'Yes,' he said, 'I have been very busy, but I have suffered . . .'

At these words, Adélaide raised her head, looked at her lover and her anxious eyes ceased to reproach him.

'So you thought we were quite indifferent to what good or bad fortune might befall you?' asked the old lady.

'I was wrong,' he replied. 'Yet there are troubles that one can't confide to just anyone, even to friendships of longer standing than that with which you honour me.'

'The sincerity and strength of a friendship should not be measured according to time. I have seen old friends not shed a tear for each other in misfortune,' said the baroness shaking her head.

'But what's the matter?' the young man asked Adélaide.

'Oh, nothing,' the baroness replied. 'Adélaide has had some late nights finishing a piece of needlework and wouldn't listen to me when I told her that a day more or less mattered little.'

Hippolyte was not listening. When he saw these two calm, noble faces, he blushed at his suspicions, and attributed the loss of his purse to some unknown accident. The evening was delightful for him and perhaps for her too. There are secrets which young hearts understand so well. Adélaide guessed Hippolyte's thoughts. Without being willing to confess his errors, the painter acknowledged them. He returned to his mistress more loving, and more affectionate, trying in this way to buy himself a tacit pardon. Adélaide experienced such perfect, such sweet happiness, that she felt as if all the distress which had so cruelly hurt her was not too high a price to pay for it. Nevertheless, the genuine harmony of their hearts, this understanding full of a magic charm, was disturbed by a phrase of the Baronne de Rouville's.

'Shall we have our little game?' she asked; 'for my old friend Kergarouet is annoyed with me.'

This remark aroused all the young painter's fears. He blushed as he looked at Adélaide's mother, but he saw on her face only the expression of an honest good nature. No hidden thought destroyed its charm, its delicacy was not treacherous, its irony was gentle and no remorse disturbed its calm. So he sat down at the card table. Adélaide wanted to share the painter's hand, claiming that he didn't know piquet and needed a partner. During the game Madame de Rouville and her daughter exchanged signs of intelligence which made Hippolyte all the more uneasy as he was winning. But, in the end, a last trick made the two lovers the baroness's debtors. As he was looking for change in his pocket, the painter took his hands off the table, and then saw in front of him a purse which Adélaïde had slipped there, without his noticing it. The poor girl was holding the old one and to save face was looking in it for money to pay her mother. All Hippolyte's blood rushed so quickly to his heart that he nearly fainted. The new purse which had replaced his own and which contained his fifteen louis was embroidered with gold beads. The knots, the tassels, everything bore witness to Adélaïde's good taste. She had no doubt used all her savings to pay for the ornaments on this charming piece of work. It was impossible to say more delicately that the painter's gift could only be rewarded with a token of affection. When Hippolyte, overcome with joy, turned his eyes to Adélaïde and the baroness, he saw them trembling with pleasure, happy at this kindly trick. He felt petty, mean and foolish. He would have liked to be able to punish himself, to rend his heart. Tears came into his eyes, and, impelled by an irresistible feeling he got up, took Adélaïde in his arms, pressed her against his heart, kissed her and then, with an artist's directness, exclaimed looking at the baroness, 'I ask you for her hand in marriage.'

Adélaïde looked at the painter half angrily and Madame de Rouville, somewhat surprised, was thinking what to say in reply when the scene was interrupted by the sound of the doorbell. The old vice-admiral appeared followed by his shadow and Madame Schinner. Having guessed the reason for the sorrows which her son tried in vain to hide from her, Hippolyte's mother had made inquiries about Adélaïde from some of her friends. Rightly alarmed at the slanders which maligned the girl without the Comte de Kergarouet's knowledge, Madame Schinner (who had learned his name from the caretaker) had been to tell the vice-admiral about them. In his rage he said he wanted 'to cut off the brutes' ears'. Excited by his anger, the admiral had told Madame Schinner the secret of his voluntary losses at cards, since the baroness's pride allowed him only this ingenious method of helping her.

When Madame Schinner had greeted Madame de Rouville, the latter looked at the Comte de Kergarouet, the Chevalier du Halga (the former admirer of the late Comtesse de Kergarouet), Hippolyte and Adélaide, and said with the graciousness of true feeling, 'It seems that we are a family party this evening.'

1832

La Grande Bretèche

ABOUT a hundred yards from Vendôme on the banks of the Loir, there is an old, brown house with a very high roof; it is completely isolated for in the neighbourhood there exists neither a foul-smelling tannery nor a miserable inn such as you see on the outskirts of nearly all small towns. In front of this dwelling, stretching down to the river, is a garden where the box hedges, which line the paths and used to be clipped, now grow as they please. Willows with their roots in the Loir have grown quickly, like the boundary hedge, and half conceal the house. Plants which we call weeds adorn the sloping river bank with their beautiful vegetation. The fruit trees, neglected for ten years, produce no more fruit and their shoots form an undergrowth. The climbing plants look like hedgerows. The paths, formerly sanded, are full of purslane, but to tell the truth, not a trace of the paths is left. Looking as it from the top of the hill on which are perched the ruins of the old castle of the Dukes of Vendôme (the only spot from which the eye can penetrate this enclosure), one would say that, at some time which it is difficult to determine, this corner of the world was the delight of a country gentleman who busied himself with roses, with tulip trees, in short with horticulture, but above all who loved good fruit. One can see an arbour, or rather the remnants of an arbour, where there is still a table which time has not entirely consumed. At the sight of the remains of this garden which no longer exists, one can imagine the negative pleasures of the peaceful life enjoyed in the country, just as one can imagine the life of a good businessman on reading the epitaph on his tomb. To crown the sad yet pleasing thoughts which grip the heart, there is, on one of the walls, a sundial decorated with this bourgeois and Christian inscription: ULTIMAM COGITA! The roof of the house is horribly dilapidated, the shutters are always closed, the balconies are covered with swallows' nests, the doors are continually shut. Tall grasses have outlined in green the cracks in the doorsteps, and the ironwork is rusty. The moon, the sun, the winter, the summer, the snow have hollowed the woodwork, warped the timbers and eaten away the paint. The dismal silence which reigns there is disturbed only by birds, cats, weasels, rats and mice, free to trot to and fro, to fight and to eat each other. Everywhere an invisible hand has written the word *Mystery*. If, moved by curiosity, you were to go and look at the street side of the house, you would perceive a large door, rounded at the top, in which the children of the district have made numerous holes. I learned later that this door had been boarded up for ten years. Through these irregular gaps you would be able to see the perfect harmony that exists between the frontage on the garden side and that on the courtyard side. The same disorder reigns there. Clumps of grass surround the paving stones. Enormous cracks furrow the walls, whose blackened tops are festooned by a thousand garlands of pellitory. The front steps are loose, the bell rope is rotted, the gutters are broken. What fire from heaven has fallen this way? What court of law has given the order to scatter salt on this dwelling? Has God been insulted here? Has France been betrayed here? These are the questions you ask yourself. The snakes crawl about without giving you a reply. The empty deserted house is an immense riddle to which no one knows the answer. It used to be a little fief and bears the name of La Grande Bretèche. During my stay in Vendôme, where Desplein had left me to look after a rich patient,[1] the sight of this strange dwelling became one of my keenest pleasures. Was it not better than a ruin? Undeniably authentic memories are attached to a ruin, but this house, which was still standing, though gradually being demolished by an avenging hand, contained a secret, an unknown thought; it suggested at least a whim. More than once, in the evening, I got through the overgrown hedge protecting the enclosure. I braved scratches, I went into the garden without a master, into the estate which was no longer either public or private.

1. This story is related by the medical student, Horace Bianchon.

I stayed there for hours on end, looking at its disorder. I did not want to ask a single question of a loquacious inhabitant of Vendôme, even to reap the reward of learning the story of what had caused this strange sight. There, I made up delightful stories, I succumbed to charming little orgies of melancholy. If I had known the reason, perhaps very ordinary, for this desertion I would have lost the unpublished fictions with which I intoxicated myself. For me, this refuge represented the most varied images of human life, clouded by misfortunes. At times it had the atmosphere of a monastery without the monks, at times the peace of the cemetery without the dead who speak in their epitaphs. Today it is a leper house, tomorrow it will be the house of the Atridae. But, above all, it was provincial life with its meditations and its slow tempo. I have often wept there, I have never laughed there. More than once I have felt involuntary terror as I heard over my head the dull whirring of the wings of some hastening wood-pigeon. The ground there is damp. You have to watch out for lizards, vipers and frogs which disport themselves freely in the wildness of nature. Above all you must not be afraid of the cold, for in a few moments you can feel a cloak of ice being placed on your shoulders like the Commander's hand on Don Juan's neck. One evening I shivered there. The wind had turned an old rusty weathercock whose creaking was like a moan uttered by the house, just as I was finishing a pretty gruesome tale in explanation of this monument of grief. I came back to my hotel, a prey to melancholy ideas. When I had had my supper, the landlady came into my room with an air of secrecy and said, 'Monsieur, here is Monsieur Regnault.'

'What is Monsieur Regnault?'

'What, you don't know Monsieur Regnault? Oh, that's funny!' she said, leaving the room.

Suddenly there came in a tall, spare man dressed in black, holding his hat in his hand, who introduced himself like a ram ready to butt his rival. He had a receding brow, a little pointed head and a pale face rather like a glass of dirty water. You would have said he was like a minister's door-keeper. This stranger was wearing an old jacket very worn at the seams. But he had a diamond on his shirt ruff and gold rings in his ears.

'Monsieur, to whom have I the honour of speaking?' I asked.

He sat down on a chair, placed himself in front of my fire, put his hat on my table and answered me, rubbing his hands,

'Oh, it is very cold, Monsieur. I am Monsieur Regnault.'

I bowed, saying to myself, '*Il bondo cani!*[2] Seek further.'

'I am a lawyer at Vendôme,' he continued.

'I am delighted to hear it,' I exclaimed, 'but I am not in a position to make my will, for personal reasons.'

'One moment,' he replied, raising his hand as if to silence me. 'Allow me, Monsieur, allow me. I have heard that you sometimes go for a walk in the garden of La Grande Bretèche.'

'Yes, Monsieur.'

'One moment,' he said, repeating his gesture. 'That activity constitutes in fact a trespass. Monsieur, I come in the name of the late Comtesse de Merret and as executor of her will to request you to cease your visits. One moment! I am not a Turk and don't want to say you have committed a crime. Besides, you may well not know the circumstances which oblige me to let the most beautiful house in Vendôme fall into ruins. Nevertheless, Monsieur, you appear to be an educated man and ought to know that under pain of severe penalties, the law forbids entry into a closed estate. A hedge is as good as a wall. But the state the house is in may serve as an excuse for your curiosity. I would not ask for anything better than to leave you free to come and go in that house, but as I am obliged to carry out the terms of the will, I have the honour, Monsieur, to ask you not to enter the garden again. Since the will was opened I have not set foot in that house which, as I have had the honour to tell you, is part of the estate of Madame de Merret. We have only counted the number of doors and windows so as to ascertain the taxes, which I pay annually out of funds earmarked for this purpose by the late countess. Oh, my dear sir, her will created a great stir in Vendôme!'

2. *Il bondo cani* is the pseudonym of the disguised caliph in *The Caliph of Baghdad* (1800), a light opera by Boïeldieu.

At this point the worthy fellow stopped to blow his nose. I respected his loquacity, realizing perfectly that Madame de Merret's will was the most important event in his life, his whole reputation, his glory, his Restoration. I had to bid farewell to my beautiful daydreams, to my romances. So I had no objection to the pleasure of learning the truth officially.

'Monsieur,' I said, 'would it be indiscreet to ask you the reasons for this eccentricity?' At these words a look, which expressed all the pleasure felt by a man used to riding his hobby-horse, passed over the lawyer's face. He straightened his shirt collar with a kind of self-satisfaction, took out his snuff-box, opened it, offered me some snuff and, when I refused, took a substantial pinch. He was happy! A man without a hobby-horse does not know all the advantages that can be obtained from life. A hobby-horse is exactly half-way between a passion and a monomania. At that moment, I understood the full implication of Sterne's apt expression and I understood completely the joy with which Uncle Toby, helped by Trim, bestrode his war-horse.

'Monsieur,' said Monsieur Regnault, 'I was Monsieur Roguin's head clerk in Paris. It was an excellent practice that you may have heard of? No? Yet an unfortunate bankruptcy made it famous. Since I didn't have enough money to do business in Paris at the price to which practices rose in 1816, I came here and acquired my predecessor's. I had relatives in Vendôme, amongst others a very rich aunt who gave me her daughter in marriage. Monsieur,' he continued after a slight pause, 'three months after being admitted by Monseigneur the Keeper of the Seals, I was summoned one evening, just as I was going to bed (I wasn't yet married), by Madame la Comtesse de Merret to her country house of Merret. Her maid, a good girl who today works in this hotel, was at my door with Madame la Comtesse's carriage. Oh, one moment, I must tell you, Monsieur, that Monsieur le Comte de Merret had gone to Paris and died there two months before I came here. He perished there miserably having indulged in all kinds of excesses. You understand? The day of his departure, Madame la Comtesse had left La Grande Bretèche and taken away the furniture. Some people even claim that she burned the furniture, the hangings, in fact all the usual things which furnished the premises rented at present by the aforesaid party . . . (Goodness, what am I saying? Forgive me, I thought I was dictating a lease.) That she burned them,' he continued, 'in the meadow at Merret. Have you been to Merret, Monsieur? No,' he said, replying for me. 'Oh, it's a very beautiful spot. For about three months,' he said, continuing after a slight shake of the head, 'Monsieur le Comte and Madame la Comtesse had lived in a strange manner. They no longer received anyone. Madame lived on the ground floor and Monsieur on the first floor. When Madame la Comtesse was left alone, she was to be seen only at church. Later on, in her own home, at her own house, she refused to see the men and women friends who came to visit her. She was already very altered when she left La Grande Bretèche to go to Merret. That dear lady . . . (I say "dear" because she left me this diamond. And I only saw her once!) . . . well, this good lady was very ill. She had no doubt despaired of recovery for she died without allowing a doctor to be called. So many of our ladies thought that she was not in possession of her full reason. So, Monsieur, my curiosity was strangely excited when I learned that Madame de Merret needed my services. I wasn't the only one who took an interest in this story. That very evening, although it was late, the whole town knew that I was going to Merret. The maid replied rather vaguely to the questions that I put to her on the way. Nevertheless she told me that her mistress had received the last rites from the Merret curé during the day and that she seemed unlikely to survive the night. I arrived at the house about eleven o'clock. I went up the big staircase. After crossing large, high, dark rooms which were cold and devilishly damp, I reached the state bedroom where Madame la Comtesse was lying. Judging from the rumours which circulated about this lady (Monsieur, I would never finish if I were to repeat to you all the stories which have been told about her!) I imagined her to be a coquette. Can you conceive that I had great difficulty in finding her in the great bed where she was lying? It is true that to light this enormous bedroom with its friezes of the old régime, which were covered with so much dust that it made one sneeze only to look at them, she had one of those old Argant lamps. Oh, but you haven't been to Merret! Well, Monsieur, the bed is one of those old-fashioned ones with a high canopy decorated with flowered chintz. A little table was beside the bed and I saw on it an *Imitation of Christ*, which, by the way, I bought for my wife, as well as the lamp. There was also a large armchair for the confidential attendant and two chairs. What's more, there was no fire. That was all the furniture. It wouldn't have taken up ten lines in an inventory. Oh, my dear sir, if you had seen, as I did then, that enormous room draped with brown tapestries, you would have thought you had been transported into a veritable scene from a novel. It was icy, and worse than that, funereal,' he added, raising his arm with a theatrical gesture and pausing. 'By dint of looking as I came near to the bed, I finally saw Madame de Merret, thanks only to the glow of the lamp whose light shone on to the pillows. Her face was as yellow as wax and looked like two joined hands. Madame la Comtesse had a lace night-cap which revealed beautiful hair, but white as flax. She was sitting up and seemed to have great difficulty in remaining in that position. Her large black eyes, sunken by fever no doubt, and already half dead, scarcely moved under the bones. There,' he said, pointing to the arch of his brows. 'Her brow was damp. Her skeletal hands were like bones covered with a delicate skin. Her veins and muscles were clearly visible. She must have been very beautiful. But at the sight of her an indescribable feeling gripped me. According to those who prepared her for burial, no living creature had ever reached her state of thinness without dying. In short, it was terrible to see! Suffering had gnawed at this woman to such an extent that she was no more than a ghost. Her pale, purple lips seemed not to move when she spoke to me. Although my profession has made me familiar with these sights by sometimes taking me to the bedsides of the dying to record their last wishes, I confess that the families in tears and the deathbed scenes that I have witnessed were nothing compared to this lonely, silent woman in her vast country mansion. I could not hear the slightest sound, I could not see the movement which the sick woman's breathing should have given to the sheets which covered her, and I remained quite motionless, looking at her in a kind of daze. I feel as if I were still there. At last her large eyes moved. She tried to raise her right hand which fell back on the bed and these words issued from her mouth like a breath, for her voice was already no longer a voice: "I have been waiting for you very impatiently." Her cheeks suddenly acquired colour. It was an effort for her to speak, Monsieur. "Madame," I said to her. She signed to me to be silent. At that moment the old housekeeper got up and whispered to me, "Don't speak, Madame la Comtesse is not in a state to hear the slightest sound, and she might be upset by what you would say to her." I sat down. Some moments later, Madame de Merret gathered all the strength that remained to her, to move her right arm and put it, not without infinite difficulty, under her bolster. She paused for a brief moment. Then she made a final effort to withdraw her hand, and when she had picked up a sealed document, beads of sweat fell from her brow. "I entrust my will to you," she said, "Oh, God. Oh!" That was all. She grasped a crucifix which was on her bed, carried it swiftly to her lips and died. The expression of her staring eyes still makes me shudder when I think of it. She must have suffered a lot! There was joy in her final look, a feeling which remained imprinted on her closed eyes. I took away the will and, when it was opened, I saw that Madame de Merret had made me her executor. She left all her property to the Vendôme hospital except for some personal legacies. But these were her arrangements for La Grande Bretèche. She ordered me to leave that house for fifty full years in the state in which it would be at the time of her death. She forbade anyone at all to enter the rooms, she did not allow the slightest repairs to be made and she even earmarked money to pay guards, if necessary, to make sure that her intentions would be fully carried out. At the expiry of this term, if the desire expressed in the will has been fulfilled, the house is to belong to my heirs, for you know, Monsieur, that lawyers cannot accept legacies. Otherwise, La Grande Bretèche will revert to whoever is entitled to it, but on condition that he fulfills the stipulations contained in a codicil added to the will which is to be opened only at the end of the aforesaid fifty years. The will has not been disputed, so . . .' With this, and without finishing his sentence, the elongated lawyer looked at me triumphantly. I made him completely happy by paying him some compliments.

'Monsieur,' I said in conclusion, 'you have made such a great impression on me, that I can almost see that dying woman paler than her sheets. Her gleaming eyes frighten me and I shall dream of her tonight. But you must have made some conjectures about the arrangements contained in this strange will.'

'Monsieur,' he said with a comic reticence, 'I never allow myself to judge the behaviour of people who have honoured me with the gift of a diamond.'

I soon loosened the tongue of the scrupulous Vendôme lawyer who communicated to me, not without long digressions, the observations made by the profound politicians of both sexes whose word is law in Vendôme. But these observations were so contradictory and so diffuse, that I almost fell asleep in spite of the interest which I took in this true story. The heavy tone and the monotonous voice of the lawyer, no doubt used to listening to himself and to making his clients or his compatriots listen to him, got the better of my curiosity. Fortunately he went away.

'Oh, Monsieur,' he said on the staircase, 'many people would like to live forty-five years more; but, one moment,' and with a crafty look he placed the first finger of his right hand on his nose as if he wanted to say, 'Pay great attention to this!' 'To go as far as that, you must not be about sixty.'

I closed my door, after being awoken from my apathy by this last remark which the lawyer thought very witty. Then I sat down in my armchair, putting my feet on the two fire-dogs in my fireplace. I became absorbed in a Radcliffe-like novel, based on the legal information given by Monsieur Regnault, when my door, manipulated by a woman's light hand, turned on its hinges. I saw my landlady come in, a large, cheerful, good-humoured woman who had missed her vocation. She was a Fleming who should have been born in a Teniers picture.

'Well, sir', she said, 'Monsieur Regnault has no doubt been telling yet again his story of La Grande Bretèche.'

'Yes, my good Madame Lepas.'

'What did he tell you?'

I repeated in a few words the cold, gloomy story of Madame de Merret. At each sentence, my hostess craned forward, looking at me with the perspicacity of an innkeeper, a kind of cross between the instinct of a policeman, the wiliness of a spy, and the cunning of a shopkeeper.

'Madame Lepas, my good woman,' I added as I finished. 'You seem to know more about it, don't you? Otherwise, why did you come up to my room?'

'Oh, on my honour as an honest woman, and as truly as my name is Lepas . . .'

'Don't swear. Your eyes are laden with a secret. You knew Monsieur de Merret. What kind of a man was he?'

'Well you see, Monsieur de Merret was a handsome man who was so long that you never saw the end of him, a highly esteemed nobleman from Picardy who, as we say here, was quick to fly off the handle. He paid cash so that he would have no difficulties with anyone. But you see he was hot-tempered. The ladies here found him very agreeable.'

'Because he was hot-tempered?' I asked my landlady.

'Perhaps so,' she said. 'You can imagine, sir, that a man must have had good prospects, as they say, to marry Madame de Merret who, with no disrespect to others, was the richest and most beautiful young lady in Vendôme. She had an income of about twenty thousand livres. The whole town was at her wedding. The bride was sweet and charming, a real jewel of a girl. Oh, they made a handsome couple at that time.'

'Was it a happy marriage?'

'Well, yes and no, as far as one can tell, for, as you can imagine, people like us didn't live cheek by jowl with them. Madame de Merret was a good woman, very nice, who perhaps at times suffered a lot from her husband's bad tempers. But though he was a little proud, we liked him. Bah, that was his situation in life to be like that! When a man is a noble, you see . . .'

'But there must have been some catastrophe to make Monsieur and Madame de Merret separate so violently?'

'I didn't say there was a catastrophe, sir. I know nothing about it.'

'Good. I am sure now that you know the whole story.'

'Well sir, I'll tell you everything. When I saw Monsieur Regnault go upstairs to your room, I thought that he would certainly talk to you about Madame de Merret, about La Grande Bretèche. That gave me the idea of asking your advice, sir, for you seem to me a sensible man incapable of betraying a poor woman like me who never harmed anyone and yet is tortured by her conscience. Up till now I never dared unburden myself to the people around here. They are all chatterboxes with sharp tongues. In short, sir, I've never yet had a traveller who has stayed as long as you in my inn and to whom I could tell the story of the fifteen thousand francs . . .'

'My good Madame Lepas,' I replied, stopping the flow of her words, 'if your confidence is of a kind that would compromise me, I wouldn't want to be burdened with it for anything in the world.'

'There is nothing to be afraid of,' she said interrupting me, 'you will see.'

This eagerness made me think that I wasn't the only one to whom my good innkeeper had told the secret which I alone was to hear, and I listened.

'Well sir,' she said, 'when the Emperor sent Spanish or other prisoners of war here, I had to put up, at government expense, a young Spaniard who had been sent to Vendôme on parole. In spite of the parole, he went every day to report to the sub-prefect. He was a Spanish grandee! Excuse me a moment. He had a name ending in *os* and in *dia*, like Bagos de Feredia. I have his name on my register; you can read it if you want to. Oh, he was a handsome young man for a Spaniard – they are all said to be ugly. He was barely five feet

two or three inches tall, but he was well built. He had little
hands that he took great care of. Oh, you should have seen
him. He had as many brushes for his hands as a woman has
for all her beauty care! He had thick black hair, fiery eyes and
a rather copper-coloured complexion which I liked all the
same. He wore fine linen such as I've seen on no one else,
though I have put up princesses, and amongst others General
Bertránd, the Duke and Duchess of Abrantès, Monsieur De-
cazes and the King of Spain. He didn't eat much, but he had
such courteous, kindly manners that one couldn't hold it
against him. Oh, I liked him very much, though he didn't say
four words a day and it was impossible to have the slightest
conversation with him. If you spoke to him, he didn't reply.
That's a habit, a mania that they all have, so I'm told. He
read his breviary like a priest; he went to Mass and to all the
services regularly. Where did he sit in church? (We noticed
that later.) Two steps from Madame de Merret's chapel. As
he installed himself there the first time he came to church,
nobody imagined that he did so intentionally. Besides, he
never took his nose out of his prayer book, poor young man!
At that time, sir, in the evenings, he used to go for a walk in
the hills, in the castle ruins. That was the poor man's only
distraction; it reminded him of his own country. They say
that it's all mountains in Spain. From the very first days of
his detention here, he stayed out late. I was anxious at not
seeing him come back till the stroke of midnight. But we all
got used to his whim. He took the front-door key, and we
didn't wait up for him any more. He lodged in the house that
we have in the Rue des Casernes. Then one of our stable boys
told us that one evening, as he was taking the horses into the
water, he thought he saw the Spanish grandee swimming like
a fish far out in the river. When he came back I told him to
take care of the weeds. He seemed put out at having been
seen in the water.

Finally, sir, one day, or rather one morning, we couldn't
find him in his room. He hadn't come back. I rummaged
everywhere till I found in his table drawer a letter containing
fifty Spanish gold pieces that are called *portugaises* and are

worth about five thousand francs; then there were ten thousand francs' worth of diamonds in a little sealed box. His letter said that, in case he didn't return, he left us this money and these diamonds on condition that we founded Masses to thank God for his escape and to pray for his salvation. At that time, I still had my husband and he went off to look for the Spaniard. And here is the queer part of the story. He brought back the Spaniard's clothes which he found under a large stone among some piles on the river bank, on the castle side, almost opposite La Grande Bretèche. My husband had gone there so early in the morning that no one had seen him. He burned the clothes after reading the letter and, according to Count Feredia's wish, we declared that he had escaped. The sub-prefect set the whole police force on his trail. But, lor, they didn't catch him. Lepas thought the Spaniard had been drowned. But, sir, I don't think so. I believe, rather, that he had something to do with Madame de Merret, since Rosalie told me that the crucifix, to which her mistress was so attached that she had it buried with her, was made of ebony and silver. Now when Monsieur Feredia first came to stay here he had one of ebony and silver which I never saw in his possession again. Now, sir, isn't it true that I oughtn't to have any remorse about the Spaniard's fifteen thousand francs, and that they are really mine?'

'Certainly, but haven't you tried to question Rosalie?' I said.

'Oh, I certainly did, sir. But what could I do? That girl, she's like a wall. She knows something but it's impossible to get her to spill the beans.'

After chatting with me for a moment longer, my landlady left me a prey to vague, gloomy thoughts, to a romantic curiosity, to a religious terror rather like the deep feeling which grips us when, at night, we go into a dark church where we can see a faint, distant light under lofty arches; an indeterminate figure glides past, the rustle of a dress or a surplice can be heard . . . we have shuddered. La Grande Bretèche and its tall grasses, its condemned windows, its rusty ironwork, its closed doors, its deserted rooms, suddenly rose fantastically before me. I tried to penetrate the mystery of this dwelling as I searched for the clue of the solemn story, the drama that had killed three people. In my eyes Rosalie was the most interesting person in Vendôme. On looking at her carefully, I discovered the traces of a secret thought, despite the glowing health which beamed from her plump face. She had within her a source of remorse or of hope. Her demeanour suggested that she had a secret, like that of pious women who pray excessively, or of a girl guilty of infanticide who always hears her child's last cry. Yet her manner was ingenuous and uncouth. Her stupid smile had nothing criminal about it and you would have deemed her innocent at the mere sight of the big red and blue check handkerchief covering her strapping bust which was encased, squeezed, parcelled up in a white and purple-striped dress.

'No,' I thought, 'I shall not leave Vendôme without knowing the whole story of La Grande Bretèche. To achieve my aim, I shall become Rosalie's friend, if there is no other way.'

'Rosalie,' I said to her one evening.

'What is it, sir?'

'You are not married?'

She gave a slight start.

'Oh, I won't be short of men when the whim to be unhappy takes hold of me,' she said, with a laugh.

She recovered quickly from her embarrassment, for all women, from the great lady down to and including hotel maids, have a self-possession which is peculiar to them.

'You are young and attractive enough not to be short of lovers. But tell me, Rosalie, why did you become a hotel maid when you left Madame de Merret? Was it because she didn't leave you any income?'

'Oh yes, indeed she did. But, sir, my place is the best in the whole of Vendôme.'

This reply was one of those that judges and lawyers call 'dilatory'. Rosalie seemed to me to have a place in this romantic story like the square in the middle of a chess-board. She was in the very centre of the interest and of the truth. She seemed to me to be tied up in the web. It wasn't an ordinary seduction that I had to attempt. In this girl there was the last chapter of a novel. So, from that moment, Rosalie became the object of my predilection. Through studying this girl, I noticed that, like all women who preoccupy our thoughts, she had a host of good qualities. She was clean, and neat, she was beautiful, that goes without saying. Soon she had all the attractions that our desire lends to women in whatever situation they may be. A fortnight after the lawyer's visit, one evening, or rather, one morning, for it was very early, I said to Rosalie, 'Tell me everything you know about Madame de Merret.'

'Oh,' she replied terrified, 'don't ask me that, Monsieur Horace.' Her beautiful face clouded over, her lively, animated complexion turned pale, and her eyes lost their innocent, moist gleam.

'Well,' she continued, 'since you want me to, I shall tell you. But be sure and keep my secret.'

'Of course, my poor girl, I shall keep all your secrets with a thief's honesty. That's the most dependable there is.'

'If you don't mind,' she said, 'I prefer you to keep them with your own.'

With this, she rearranged her scarf and settled herself as if to tell a tale, for, indeed, a certain attitude of trust and security is necessary for the telling of a story. The best tales are told at a certain time, as now, when we are all here, at table.[3] No one has ever told a good story standing up, or when they are hungry. But if I had to reproduce word for word Rosalie's diffuse eloquence, a whole volume would scarcely be enough. Now, since the event of which she gave me a jumbled account is situated between the lawyer's and Madame Lepas' gossip as exactly as the middle terms of an arithmetical progression are between their two extremes, it only remains for me to tell it to you in a few words. So I abbreviate.

The room occupied by Madame de Merret at La Bretèche was on the ground floor. She used a little closet about four feet deep as her wardrobe. Three months before the evening whose events I am going to relate, Madame de Merret had

3. This story is one of three told at a supper-party.

been so seriously unwell that her husband left her alone in her room and he slept in a room on the first floor. By one of those chances which are impossible to foresee, that evening, he came back two hours later than usual from the club where he went to read the newspapers and talk politics with the inhabitants of the district. His wife thought that he had come home, gone to bed and fallen asleep. But the invasion of France had been the subject of a very lively discussion, the billiard game had become very keen and he had lost forty francs, an enormous sum at Vendôme where everybody amasses money, and where the style of life is kept within the limits of a praiseworthy modesty which perhaps becomes the source of a true happiness unknown to any Parisian. For some time Monsieur de Merret used to content himself with asking Rosalie if his wife was in bed. She always said 'yes' and, when he heard this, he immediately went to his own room with the complacency that comes from habit and confidence. That evening, when he came in, he took it into his head to go to Madame de Merret's room to tell her of his mishap, perhaps too to console himself for it. During dinner, he had thought that Madame de Merret was very elegantly dressed. As he returned home from the club, he said to himself that his wife was no longer unwell, that her convalescence had improved her looks and he noticed this, as husbands notice everything, a little late. Instead of calling Rosalie, who at that moment was busy in the kitchen watching the cook and the coachman playing a difficult game of bezique, Monsieur de Merret made his way to his wife's room by the light of the lantern that he had put down on the first step of the staircase. His easily recognizable step rang out under the arches of the corridor. Just as the nobleman turned the key of his wife's room, he thought he heard the door of the closet I have mentioned being shut, but when he came in, Madame de Merret was alone, standing in front of the fireplace. The husband thought naïvely that Rosalie was in the closet. However, a suspicion which rang in his ears like the sound of bells, put him on his guard. He looked at his wife and thought he saw an indefinable look of wild distress in her eyes.

'You are very late home,' she said.

Her voice which was usually so pure and gracious seemed to him slightly altered. Monsieur de Merret made no answer, for at this moment Rosalie came in. This was like a thunderbolt for him. He walked up and down the room, going from one window to the other with an even stride and his arms folded.

'Have you had some sad news, or are you not feeling well?' his wife asked apprehensively, while Rosalie undressed her.

He kept silent.

'You may go,' Madame de Merret said to her maid. 'I shall put in my curlers myself.'

She guessed something was wrong, just from the look of her husband's face, and wanted to be alone with him. When Rosalie had gone or when they thought she had gone, for she remained some moments in the corridor, Monsieur de Merret came and stood in front of his wife and said to her coldly, 'Madame, there is someone in your closet!'

She looked at her husband calmly and replied simply, 'No, Monsieur.'

This 'No' was heartbreaking to Monsieur de Merret. He did not believe it, yet his wife had never looked so pure and so devout as she seemed to be at that moment. He got up to go and open the closet. Madame de Merret took him by the hand, stopped him, looked at him sadly and said to him in a voice strangely filled with emotion. 'If you find no one there, you must reflect that everything will be over between us!'

The incredible dignity of his wife's attitude restored Monsieur de Merret's deep esteem for her and suggested to him one of those resolutions which only lack a wider setting to become immortal.

'No, Joséphine,' he said, 'I shan't go. In either case we would be separated for ever. Listen to me. I know how pure your soul is and I know that you lead a saintly life. You would not want to commit a mortal sin at the cost of your life.'

At these words, Madame de Merret looked at her husband with a drawn look on her face.

'Look, here is your crucifix,' he added. 'Swear to me before

God that there's no one there. I shall believe you. I shall not open that door.'

Madame de Merret took the crucifix and said, 'I swear.'

'Say it louder,' said her husband, 'and repeat, "I swear before God that there is no one in that closet." ' She repeated the words without embarrassment.

'Good,' Monsieur de Merret said coldly. Then, after a moment's silence, picking up the ebony crucifix inlaid with silver and very artistically carved, he said, 'You have a very beautiful object that I am not familiar with.'

'I found it at Duvivier's. When that group of prisoners passed through Vendôme last year, he bought it from a Spanish priest.'

'Oh,' said Monsieur de Merret, putting the crucifix back on its nail, and he rang the bell. Rosalie didn't keep him waiting. Monsieur de Merret went quickly to meet her, took her into the bay of the window which looks out on to the garden, and said to her in a low voice, 'I know that Gorenflot wants to marry you. Only poverty prevents you from setting up house together, and you have told him that you will not be his wife unless he finds a way of establishing himself as a master mason ... Well, go and find him and tell him to come here with his trowel and his tools. Do it in such a way that you don't wake up anyone in the house but him; his fortune will surpass your wishes. Above all, don't gossip when you leave here, otherwise . . .'

He frowned. Rosalie set off. He called her back. 'Here's my pass key,' he said. 'Take it.'

'Jean,' shouted Monsieur de Merret in a voice that thundered down the corridor. Jean, who was both his coachman and his man of confidence, left his game of bezique and came.

'Go to bed, all of you,' his master said to him, as he motioned to him to come nearer, and Monsieur de Merret added, but in a low voice, 'When they are all asleep, *asleep* you understand, you will come down and let me know.'

Monsieur de Merret, who had not lost sight of his wife as he gave orders, came back calmly beside her in front of the fire and began to tell her about the events of the billiard game and the discussions at the club. When Rosalie came back, she found Monsieur and Madame de Merret chatting in a friendly manner.

Monsieur de Merret had recently renewed the ceilings of all his reception rooms on the ground floor. Plaster is very scarce at Vendôme and transport adds considerably to the price; so Monsieur de Merret had ordered quite a large amount, knowing that he would always find purchasers for any that he had left over. This circumstance gave him the idea for the plan that he carried out.

'Monsieur, Gorenflot is here,' Rosalie said quietly.

'Tell him to come in,' replied the Picard nobleman out loud.

Madame de Merret turned slightly pale when she saw the mason.

'Gorenflot,' said her husband, 'go and get some bricks from under the coach house and bring enough to wall up that closet door; use the plaster that I have left over to plaster the wall.' Then drawing Rosalie and the workman aside, he said in a low voice, 'Now listen, Gorenflot, you will sleep here tonight. But, tomorrow morning, you will have a passport to go abroad to a town that I shall name. I shall give you six thousand francs for your journey. You will stay ten years in that town. If you are not happy there, you can settle in another provided that it is in the same country. You will go via Paris where you will wait for me. There, I shall guarantee you by contract six thousand francs more which will be paid to you on your return, if you have fulfilled the conditions of our bargain. For this reward, you will have to maintain absolute silence about what you have done here tonight. As for you, Rosalie, I shall give you ten thousand francs which will be paid to you only on your wedding-day and on condition that you marry Gorenflot. But in order to marry you must say nothing. Otherwise, there will be no dowry.'

'Rosalie,' said Madame de Merret, 'come and do my hair.'

Her husband calmly walked up and down keeping an eye on the door, the mason, and his wife, but without showing any insulting suspicion. Gorenflot could not help making a noise. Madame de Merret took advantage of a moment when

the workman was unloading bricks and when her husband
was at the other end of the room, to say to Rosalie, 'An income of a thousand francs for you, my dear, if you can tell
Gorenflot to leave a crack at the bottom.' Then, out loud, she
said to her composedly,

'Go and help him.'

Monsieur and Madame de Merret said nothing during the
whole time that Gorenflot took to wall up the door. The
husband's silence was intentional as he did not want to give
his wife an opportunity of making ambiguous remarks; she
was silent either out of caution or pride. When the wall was
half-built, the cunning mason took advantage of a moment
when the gentleman had his back turned, to break one of the
two glass panes of the door with his pick. This action made
Madame de Merret realize that Rosalie had spoken to Gorenflot. Then all three of them saw a gloomy, swarthy man's face,
black hair, and fiery eyes. Before her husband had turned
round, the poor woman had time to sign to the foreigner
with a movement of the head. For him this sign meant, 'Hope!'

At four o'clock, towards dawn, for it was September, the
construction was completed. The mason was put under the
guard of Jean, and Monsieur de Merret slept in his wife's
room. The next morning, as he got up he said carelessly, 'Oh,
what a nuisance, I must go to the town-hall for the passport.'

He put on his hat, took three steps towards the door, came
back and took the crucifix.

His wife gave a start of delight. 'He will go to Duvivier's,'
she thought.

As soon as Monsieur de Merret had gone out, Madame de
Merret rang for Rosalie; then she cried in a terrible voice,
'The pick, the pick. Set to work. I saw yesterday how Gorenflot set about it. We'll have time to make a hole and to fill it
up again.'

In the twinkling of an eye, Rosalie brought her mistress a
kind of axe. With indescribable energy she began to demolish
the wall. She had already dislodged some bricks when, as she
prepared to strike a blow even stronger than the others, she
saw Monsieur de Merret behind her. She fainted.

'Put Madame on her bed,' said Monsieur de Merret coldly. Foreseeing what would happen during his absence, he had set a trap for his wife. He had quite simply written to the mayor and sent for Duvivier. The jeweller arrived just as the disorder in the room had been tidied up.

'Duvivier,' asked Monsieur de Merret, 'did you buy some crucifixes from Spaniards who passed through the town?'

'No, sir.'

'Good, thank you,' said Monsieur de Merret giving his wife a ferocious look. 'Jean,' he added turning towards his confidential valet, 'have my meals served in Madame de Merret's room. She is ill and I shan't leave her till she is better.'

The cruel nobleman stayed at his wife's side for twenty days. At first, when there were some sounds in the walled-up closet and Joséphine wanted to beg his mercy for the dying stranger, he replied without letting her say a word, 'You swore on the cross that there was no one there.'

1832

A Tragedy by the Sea[1]

NEARLY all young people have a pair of compasses with which they like to measure the future. When their will-power matches the ambitious size of the angle which they make, the world is theirs. But this psychological phenomenon takes place only at a certain age. This age which, for all men, is between twenty-two and twenty-eight, is the time of great thoughts and new ideas, because it is the age of immense desires, the age when one has no doubts at all; he who doubts achieves nothing. After that age, which passes as quickly as the sowing season, comes the age of putting ideas into practice. In a way there are two youthful periods, one for growth and one for action. They often combine in men whom nature has favoured and who are like Caesar, Newton and Bonaparte, the greatest of the great.

I was working out how much time is needed to develop an idea. I was standing, compass in hand, on a rock a hundred fathoms above the ocean, where white horses were riding on the breakers, and I was mapping out my future, filling it with literary works, like a surveyor who plans fortresses and palaces on a piece of waste land. The sea was beautiful and I had just dressed after swimming. I was waiting for Pauline, my guardian angel, who was bathing in a granite pool lined with fine sand, a dainty bathtub designed by nature for sea nymphs. We were at the end of Le Croisic, a charming Breton peninsula; we were far away from the port, in a spot regarded by the tax authorities as so inaccessible that the customs officer hardly ever goes there. To swim in the air after swimming in the sea! Ah! Who wouldn't have wanted to swim in the

1. In Balzac's novel *Louis Lambert*, the hero, Louis Lambert, is driven mad by the excess of his philosophical genius. In this story, Lambert relates, in a letter to his uncle, an event which brought on a recurrence of his madness.

future? Why was I thinking? Why does a misfortune happen? Who knows? Ideas fall into your heart or head without consulting you. No courtesan is more temperamental or demanding than an Idea is for artists; it has to be gripped firmly by the hair, like Fortune, when she comes. Astride my thought like Astolphe on his hippogriff, I rode through the world, arranging everything as I pleased. I was looking about me for some omen favourable to the bold undertakings which my crazy imagination suggested to me, when a happy cry, the cry of a woman calling in the silence of a deserted spot, of a woman coming out of the water happy and invigorated by her bathe, rose above the splashing of the restless waves rising and falling on the indented coast-line. As I heard this heartfelt call, I thought I saw amongst the rocks an angel's foot; as he opened his wings, he had exclaimed, 'You will succeed!' I went down from the rock, radiant and light-hearted; I leapt down like a pebble thrown down a steep slope. When she saw me, she said, 'What's the matter?' I gave no answer, my eyes filled with tears. The previous evening, Pauline had understood my sorrows just as she now understood my joys with the magic sensitivity of a harp which responds to variations in the atmosphere. Human life has some wonderful moments! We walked along the shore in silence. The sky was cloudless, the sea was smooth. Others would have seen only two vast plains, one above the other. But we, we who understood each other without words, we saw these two sheets of infinity as a background to the illusions in which young people indulge; we grasped each other's hands at the least change which appeared either in the expanse of water or in the expanse of sky, for we interpreted these slight phenomena as material manifestations of our joint thoughts. Who, at moments of ssnsual pleasure, has not tasted that instant of boundless joy when the spirit seems to be freed from the bonds of the flesh and, as it were, returned to the world whence it came? Pleasure is not our only guide in these regions. Are there not times when feelings unite and soar away of their own accord just as two children often take each other by the hand and begin to run without knowing why? That is how it was with us. As the roofs of the town appeared in a greyish line on the horizon, we met a poor fisherman who was returning to Le Croisic. His feet were bare, his cotton trousers were in tatters at the bottom, in holes and badly patched; his shirt was made of sailcloth, he had old cloth braces and a ragged jacket. This poverty pained us, as if it were a discord in the midst of our harmony. We looked at each other to express our mutual regret at not having just then the power to draw on the treasures of Aboul-Casem. We noticed a superb lobster and a crab hooked on to a line which the fisherman was swinging in his right hand, while in the other he held his tackle and lobster-pots. We went up to him intending to buy his catch; the idea had occurred to both of us and Pauline expressed it in a smile to which I replied with a slight pressure on the arm I was holding and that I brought close to my heart. It is these nothings that memory later turns into poems when, as we sit by the fire, we recall the moment when this nothing moved us, the spot where it happened, and the illusion which we have not yet fully appreciated, but which often affects the objects around us when life is joyous and our hearts are full. The most beautiful landscapes are only what we make them. Is there a man with even a little of the poet in his make-up in whose memories a fragment of rock does not occupy more space than the most famous views of countries visited at great expense? Near this rock, what tumultuous thoughts he has had! Here a whole life's work was planned, there fears were dissipated, and there again rays of hope entered into his soul. Just then the sun, in sympathy with these thoughts of love and of the future, cast a shining gleam on the yellow sides of the rock, some mountain flowers caught my eye, the stillness and the silence made the rugged crag seem larger and, though in reality it was gloomy, my day-dreaming gave it colour. Then it looked beautiful with its sparse vegetation, its warm-tinted camomile and its downy maidenhair fern. It was like an extended fête, with magnificent decorations, a rapturous uplifting of the human spirit. Once before, the Lac de Bienne, seen from the Ile Saint-Pierre, had affected me in this way. Perhaps the rock at Le Croisic will be the last of these joys. But then, what will become of Pauline?

'You have had a fine catch this morning, my good fellow,' I said to the fisherman.

'Yes, sir,' he answered, stopping so that we could see his swarthy face, that of a man who is exposed for hours to the reflection of the sun on the water.

It was a face which bore the marks of long resignation, a fisherman's patience and a gentle disposition. The man had a voice which was not harsh and lips suggesting good nature. His look was devoid of ambition, and indefinably delicate and frail. We would not have wanted him to have any other kind of face.

'Where are you going to sell that?'

'In the town.'

'How much will you get for the lobster?'

'Fifteen sous.'

'And the crab?'

'Twenty sous.'

'Why is there so much difference between the lobster and the crab?'

'Well sir, the crab is much more delicate. Then it's as cunning as a monkey, and it's not often that I catch one.'

'Will you give us the two for a hundred sous?' said Pauline. The man was dumb with astonishment.

'You shan't have it,' I said laughing, 'I'll pay ten francs.' One must pay for emotions what they are worth.

'Well,' she answered, 'I *will* have it. I shall pay ten francs, two sous.'

'Ten sous.'

'Twelve francs.'

'Fifteen francs.'

'Fifteen francs, fifty centimes,' she said.

'One hundred francs.'

'One hundred and fifty.'

I gave in. At the time we weren't rich enough to push this auction up any further. Our poor fisherman didn't know if he should get angry at a practical joke or be delighted. We solved his problem by giving him our landlady's name and asking him to deliver the lobster and the crab at her house.

'Do you earn enough to live on?' I asked him trying to find out the cause of his poverty.

'With great difficulty and only at the cost of many hardships,' he said. 'When you have no boat or nets, and when you can only do it with traps or a fishing line, sea fishing is a chancy trade. You see, you have to wait for the fish or the shellfish to come, while the big fishermen go out to look for it in the open sea. It is so difficult to earn one's living in this way that I am the only man who fishes near the shore. I spend whole days without catching anything. For me to catch anything, a crab must have forgotten the tide and fallen asleep like this one, or a lobster must be careless enough to stay amongst the rocks. Sometimes after high tide, there are bass and then I grab them.'

'In all, with one thing and another, what do you earn a day?'

'Eleven to twelve sous. I would manage, if I were on my own but I have to support my father. The old man can't help me, he is blind.'

As he quietly made this statement, Pauline and I exchanged looks without saying a word.

'Have you a wife or a sweetheart?'

He gave us one of the most pitiable looks I have ever seen as he replied, 'If I had a wife, I would have to desert my father. I couldn't feed him and feed a wife and children as well.'

'Well, my poor fellow, why don't you try to earn more by carrying salt at the port or working in the salt marshes?'

'Oh, sir, I wouldn't be able to do that job for as long as three months. I am not strong enough and if I were to die, my father would have to go begging. I had to have a job which needed only a little skill and a lot of patience.'

'And how can two people live on twelve sous a day?'

'We eat buckwheat cakes and barnacles which I take off the rocks.'

'How old are you then?'

'Thirty-seven.'

'Have you ever been away from here?'

'I once went to Guérande to draw lots for military service, and I went to Savenay so that some gentlemen could see me and measure me. If I had been an inch taller I would have been a soldier. I would have died at the first test, and my poor father would today be asking for charity.'

I had imagined many moving situations; Pauline was used to deep emotions, since she was so close to me with my unstable temperament. Yet neither of us had ever heard more touching words than this fisherman's. We walked a little in silence, both appreciating the inarticulate depths of his obscure life, admiring his noble, unselfconscious devotion. The strength of his weakness amazed us; his uncomplicated generosity made us feel small. I could see this poor, instinctive creature bound to his rock, like a galley-slave to his chain and ball, watching the shellfish on it for twenty years in order to earn his living, his patience sustained by one single feeling. How many hours he must have spent on a small section of a shore! How many hopes dashed by a gust of wind, by a change of weather! He would remain hovering at the edge of a flat stone, his arm outstretched like an Indian fakir's, while his father, seated on a stool, silently and in darkness, would wait for the coarsest of shellfish and some bread, if the sea were willing.

'Do you ever drink wine?' I asked.

'Three or four times a year.'

'Well, you will drink some today, you and your father, and we shall send you a white loaf.'

'You are very kind, sir.'

'We shall give you dinner, if you will show us the way across the shore to Batz. We are going to see the tower that stands above the bay and the coast between Batz and Le Croisic.'

'With pleasure,' he said. 'Go straight ahead, following the path you are on. I shall come and find you after I have got rid of my tackle and my catch.'

We both nodded agreement and he set off happily for the town. This encounter did not alter our psychological state, but it diminished our gaiety.

'Poor man!' said Pauline in the tone which removes the hurtfulness of pity from a woman's compassion. 'Are we not ashamed to be happy when we see such poverty?'

'Nothing is worse than having desires which cannot be fulfilled,' I answered. 'Those two poor creatures, the father and the son, will no more know how much we feel for them than the world will know how beautiful their lives are, for they are piling up treasures in heaven.'

'What a poor countryside,' she said, pointing to cow-dung symmetrically laid out along a field surrounded by a dry-stone dyke. I asked what this was. A peasant woman, busy sticking pieces of dung together, answered that she was making wood. Just think, my friend, that when this dung is dry, these poor people collect it, stack it up and warm themselves with it. During the winter, it is sold like briquettes. I asked the peasant woman what she thought the most highly paid dress-maker earned. 'Five sous a day,' she said after thinking for a moment. 'But she gets her food.'

'Look,' I said to Pauline, 'the winds from the sea dry up or blow down everything. There are no trees. The remains of the disused boats are sold to the rich, for the cost of transport no doubt prevents them from using the firewood which is plentiful in Brittany. This land is beautiful only in the eyes of superior beings; insensitive people couldn't live here. It can be inhabited only by poets or barnacles. The salt depot had to be sited on this rock before anyone could live here. In one direction there is the sea, here there is the sand, above there is space.'

We had already passed the town and were in the desert-like area which separates Le Croisic from the town of Batz. Imagine, my dear uncle, two miles of waste land filled with gleaming seaside sand. Here and there rocks raised their heads, like gigantic animals lying in the dunes. Along by the sea we could see reefs with water splashing around them and making them look like big white roses floating on the expanse of liquid and coming to rest on the shore. I saw the quicksands bounded on the right by the ocean, and on the left by the great pool which the inrush of the sea forms between Le Croisic and the sandhills of Guérande; at their base lie the salt marshes where nothing grows. And then I looked at Pauline to ask her if she felt brave enough to face the burning sun and strong enough to walk in the sand.

'I have ankle-boots on, let's go,' she said, pointing to the Batz tower which blocked the view with an immense construction set down there like a pyramid. But it was a tapered, crenelated pyramid, one that was so poetically decorated that you could imagine it was the beginning of the ruins of a large Asiatic town. We walked forward a few steps so that we could sit on a part of the rock which was still in the shade. But it was eleven o'clock in the morning and the shade which only stretched as far as our feet was quickly disappearing.

'How beautiful the silence is,' she said, 'and how its depth is intensified by the rhythmical return of the quivering sea on the beach!'

'If you give yourself up to communion with the three vast-nesses which surround us, the water, the air, and the sand, and listen only to the repeated sound of the ebb and flow of the water,' I replied, 'you will not be able to endure their language; you will think you are discovering a thought which will overwhelm you. Yesterday, at sunset, I had that feeling; it was shattering.'

'Oh, yes,' she said, after a long pause. 'Let's talk about it. No orator is more terrible. I think I can discover the causes of the harmonies which surround us,' she continued. 'This landscape which has only three distinct colours, the brilliant yellow of the sand, the blue of the sky and the uniform green of the sea, is grand without being wild. It is vast without being a desert. It has only three elements and yet it is varied.'

'Only a woman can express her impressions so well,' I replied. 'You would be the despair of a poet, dear heart; I have understood your feelings so well.'

'The excessive midday heat casts one all-consuming colour over these three expressions of the infinite,' continued Pauline smiling. 'Here I can imagine the poetry and the passions of the East.'

'And *I* can understand despair.'

'Yes,' she said, 'this sand-dune is like a sublime cloister.'

We heard the hurrying step of our guide. He had put on his best clothes. We made a few insignificant remarks to him. He thought he noticed a change in our feelings towards him, and with the reserve which comes from misfortune, he kept silent. Although from time to time we pressed each other's hands to indicate our mutual feelings and impressions, we walked for half an hour in silence, either because we were overwhelmed by the brilliant waves of heat which rose up from the sand, or because our attention was concentrated on the difficulty of walking. We walked along holding hands like two children; we couldn't have walked twelve steps if we had gone arm in arm. There was no trodden path to the town of Batz. A gust of wind was enough to efface the footprints of horses or the marks of cartwheels. But the practised eye of our guide could tell the way from the scraps of cattle and sheep dung. It was a path which at times went down to the sea, and at times went up towards the fields, according to the lie of the land or to avoid rocks. By noon, we were only half-way.

'We'll have a rest up there,' I said pointing to a headland made of rocks, which were high enough to suggest that we would find a cave there.

When he heard me say this, the fisherman, who had looked in the direction I was pointing, shook his head, and said, 'There's someone there. Everyone who goes from Batz to Croisic, or from Croisic to Batz makes a detour so as not to go that way.'

The man spoke in a low voice suggestive of a mystery.

'Is he a thief or a murderer?'

Our guide replied only with a hollow exclamation which doubled our curiosity.

'But if we go that way, will something nasty happen to us?'

'Oh, no.'

'Will you go past there with us?'

'No, sir.'

'We'll go, then, if you assure us that there's no danger.'

'I don't say that,' the fisherman replied quickly. 'I only say that the man who is there won't speak to you and will do you no harm. Oh, Good Lord! He won't even budge from where he is sitting.'

'Who is it then?'

'A man!'

Never before had these two syllables been so tragically uttered. At this moment we were about twenty paces from the reef where the sea was coming and going. Our guide took the way round the rocks. We continued straight ahead, but Pauline took my arm. Our guide hastened his step so as to reach the spot where the two paths met at the same time as us. He presumably thought that, when we had seen the man, we would walk quickly. This aroused our curiosity which then became so keen that our hearts beat as if we had experienced a feeling of fear. In spite of the heat and a kind of fatigue caused by the walk along the sand, our hearts were still imbued with the inexpressible languor of an ecstatic harmony; they were filled with an unadulterated happiness which can only be described by comparing it to what one feels when listening to delightful music, such as Mozart's *Andiamo mio ben*. Two pure feelings which mingle, are they not like two beautiful voices which are singing? In order fully to appreciate the emotion which gripped us, you would have to share the half voluptuous state into which the morning's events had cast us. If for a long time you had been admiring a prettily coloured dove, perched on a curving branch, near a stream, you would utter a cry of distress at the sight of a kestrel pouncing on her, digging his steely claws right into her heart and carrying her off with the murderous speed of a bullet shot from a gun. We stepped forward into the space in front of the cave; it was a kind of esplanade a hundred feet above the ocean, protected from its fury by a series of steep rocks, and there we felt an electric shudder, rather like the start you get from a sudden noise in the middle of a silent night. We had seen, seated on a block of granite, a man who had looked at us. His glance, flaming like a gunflash, emerged from two bloodshot eyes, and his stoic immobility could only be compared to the unchanging shapes of the granite heaps which surrounded him. His eyes moved slowly, his body remaining rigid as if he had been turned into stone. Then, having given us this look which made such a violent impression on us, he turned his eyes again to the expanse of ocean; in spite of the light that flashed up from it he gazed at it without lowering his eyelids, just as eagles are said to gaze at the sun. He did not raise his eyes again. Try to recall, my dear uncle, one of those old oak trees, whose knotted trunk, lopped only the day before, rises in an uncanny shape on a lonely road, and you will have a true picture of this man. He had the remains of a herculean physique, a face like Jupiter of Olympus but ruined by age, by the rough work of a seaman, by grief, by coarse food, and as it were blackened by a thunderbolt. When I looked at his hairy, hard hands, I saw sinews like veins of iron. Everything about him, moreover, indicated a strong constitution. In a corner of the cave, I noticed a fairly large heap of moss and on a coarse slab, formed by chance in the face of the granite, an earthenware jug covered by half a round loaf. In imagining the deserts where the first anchorites of Christianity had lived, I had never pictured a face more grandly religious or more abjectly repentant than this man's. You who have experience of the confessional, my dear uncle, you have perhaps never seen such magnificent remorse; yet it was a remorse submerged under waves of prayer, the unceasing prayer of a dumb despair. This fisherman, this sailor, this rough Breton was rendered sublime, but I did not understand why. Had these eyes wept? Had this hand – a hand like that of a rough-hewn statue – struck a blow? This uncouth brow which was stamped with a fierce honesty and yet marked by strength with those traces of gentleness which are the prerogative of all true strength, this brow furrowed with wrinkles, was it in harmony with a great heart? Was this man in the granite? Why was the granite in this man? Which was man, which was granite? A whole world of thoughts came into our heads. As our guide had surmised, we passed by silently and quickly and when we met him again, he could see that we were filled with terror and astonishment. But he did not hold the truth of his predictions against us.

'You have seen him?' he asked.

'Who is this man?' I said.

'He is called the "Man-under-a-vow".'

You can imagine how our heads turned towards our fisherman at these words. He was a simple man. He understood our unspoken question, and this is what he told us in his own kind of speech. I shall try to retain its peasant flavour.

'Madame, the people of Le Croisic and of Batz think that this man is guilty of something and that he is doing the penance decreed by a well-known priest to whom he went to make confession beyond Nantes. Others think that Cambremer (that's his name) is under a spell which he passes on to anyone who passes him to leeward. So some people look which way the wind is blowing before going round his rock. If it is coming from the north-west,' he said pointing to the west, 'they wouldn't go on, even though they were on their way to look for a piece of the true cross. They go back, they are afraid. Others, the rich people of Le Croisic, say that Cambremer has made a vow. That's why he's called the Man-under-a-vow. He is there day and night and never leaves the cave. These rumours have a semblance of truth. Look,' he said, turning round to show us something we hadn't noticed. 'There, on the left he has put a wooden cross in the ground to show that he has placed himself under the protection of God, the holy Virgin and the saints. He wouldn't be inviolable like that but for the fright he gives everyone. He's as safe there as if he was guarded by the military. He hasn't said a word since he shut himself up in the open air. He lives on bread and water which his brother's daughter brings him every morning. She is a slip of a girl, twelve years old, to whom he has left all his possessions – and she's a pretty little thing, gentle as a lamb, a sweet charming youngster. She's got blue eyes, as big as that,' he said showing his thumb, 'and hair like an angel. When you ask her, "Pérotte, what does your uncle say to you?" – that's what we call Pierrette,' he said, interrupting himself. 'She is dedicated to Saint Pierre.

Cambremer is called Pierre and he was her godfather – "He says nothing," she replies, "nothing at all, nothing." "Well, what does he do to you?" "He kisses me on the forehead on Sundays." "Aren't you afraid of him?" "Oh well," she says, "he is my godfather. He wouldn't let anyone but me bring him his food." Pérotte maintains that he smiles when she comes, but you might as well talk of a ray of sunlight in drizzle. For they say that he is as gloomy as a fog.'

'But,' I said, 'you arouse our curiosity without satisfying it. Do you know what brought him to this? Was it grief, was it repentance, was it madness, was it a crime . . .?'

'Well, sir, my father and I are almost the only people who know the truth of the matter. My mother, who is now dead, was servant to a Justice of the Peace to whom Cambremer told everything. He was ordered to do so by a priest who gave him absolution only on that condition, according to what the people of the port say. My poor mother heard Cambremer unintentionally, because the Justice's kitchen was next door to his living room. She listened. Now she's dead. The judge who listened is also dead. My mother made us both promise, my father and me, to say nothing about it to the local people, but I can tell *you* that on the evening my mother told us this story, the hair on my head stood on end.'

'Well, tell us the story, my lad. We won't speak of it to anyone.'

The fisherman looked at us and continued as follows.

'Pierre Cambremer, whom you saw there, is the eldest of the Cambremers, who have been sailors from father to son. The sea has always given way to them; their name tells you that.[2] The one that you saw was a fisherman with his own craft. He had boats, fished for sardines and also for deep-sea fish for the dealers. He would have equipped a trawler and gone cod-fishing if he hadn't loved his wife so much. She was a beautiful woman, one of the Brouin family from Guérande, a magnificent, good-hearted girl. She was so much in love with Cambremer that she was never willing for her husband to leave her for longer than was necessary to go sardine-

2. In French *cambrer* means 'to bend', *la mer* means 'the sea'.

fishing. They lived over there, look!' said the fisherman, climbing on to a piece of rising ground to point out a small island in the little lagoon which lies between the dunes where we were walking and the salt marshes of Guérande. 'Do you see that house? That was his ... Jacquette Brouin and Cambremer had only one child, a boy whom they loved ... how can I express it? damme! as one loves an only child. They were crazy about him. Their little Jacques could have done something in the soup (if you'll pardon the expression) and they would have said it was as sweet as sugar. How many times we have seen them buying the prettiest trinkets for him at the fair! It was quite unreasonable, everyone told them so. Young Cambremer, seeing that he was allowed to do everything, became as vicious as a red donkey. Whenever you told old Cambremer, "Your son nearly killed little so-and-so," he would laugh and say, "Bah! he will be a fine sailor. He will command the King's navy." Or if someone else said, "Pierre Cambremer, do you know that your boy has given a black eye to the little Pougaud girl?" Pierre would say, "He will be fond of the girls!" The father found fault with nothing, So by the age of ten, the little wretch was beating up everyone and amusing himself by cutting the hens' throats and ripping up the pigs; in short he revelled in blood like a weasel. "He'll be a splendid soldier," Cambremer would say, "he has a taste for blood." You see, I remembered all that,' said the fisherman. 'And Cambremer did too,' he added, after a pause. 'By the time he was fifteen or sixteen, Jacques Cambremer was ... what shall I say? – a rotter. He would go to Guérande to have a good time, or run after the girls at Savenay. He needed cash. So he began to steal from his mother and she didn't dare say a word about it to her husband. Cambremer was such an honest man that he would walk twenty miles to give back two sous to someone who had overpaid him. At last, one day, the mother was denuded of everything. While his father was away fishing, the son carried off the dresser, the bread-bin, the sheets, the linen, leaving only the four walls. He had sold everything so that he could go on the binge at Nantes. The poor woman wept for days and nights. She would have to tell the father on his return and she was afraid of him, but not for herself, oh no! When Pierre Cambremer came home and saw his house furnished with things that had been lent to his wife, he said, "What's all this?" The poor woman was more dead than alive. She said, "We have been robbed." "But where is Jacques?" "Jacques, he is out drinking." Nobody knew where the rascal had gone. "He has too much of a good time," said Pierre. Six months later, the poor father learned that his son was going to be had up before the Justice at Nantes. He went on foot (it's quicker than going by sea), got hold of his son and brought him here. He didn't ask him, "What have you done!" He said to him, "If you don't behave yourself here for two years with your mother and me, going fishing and behaving like an honest man, you will have to reckon with me." The crazy fellow, counting on his parents' folly, made a face at him. At this Pierre gave him such a cuff on the ear that it laid Jacques up for six months. The poor mother was pining away with grief. One evening, she was sleeping peacefully beside her husband when she heard a noise. She got up and someone cut her in the arm. She cried out and her husband brought a light. Pierre Cambremer saw that his wife was hurt; he thought it was a thief, as if there were any in our part of the world, where you can carry ten thousand francs in gold from Le Croisic to Saint-Nazaire without anyone even asking you what you've got under your arm. Pierre looked for Jacques; he couldn't find his son. In the morning, the monster actually had the cheek to come back and say he had been to Batz. Now, I must tell you that his mother didn't know where to hide her money. Cambremer left *his* with Monsieur Dupotet at Le Croisic. Their son's escapades had eaten up hundred crown pieces, hundred franc pieces, louis d'or; they were as good as ruined and that was hard for people who used to have about twelve thousand livres, including their little island. No one knows how much Cambremer paid at Nantes to have his son back. Bad luck was ruining the family. Cambremer's brother had had misfortunes and needed help. To console him Pierre told him that Jacques and Pérotte (the younger Cambremer's daughter) would get married. Then, to enable

his brother to earn his living, Pierre employed him as a fishing
hand, for Joseph Cambremer was reduced to working for
others. His wife had died of fever – and Pérotte's wet nurse had
to be paid her monthly fee. Pierre Cambremer's wife owed a
hundred francs to different people for things for the little girl,
baby-linen, clothes, and two or three months' pay to la grande
Frelu who had a child by Simon Gaudry and was feeding
Pérotte. Cambremer's wife had sewn a Spanish gold piece into
the wool of her mattress, with "For Perotte" written on it.
She was well-educated, she could write like a lawyer's clerk.
She had taught her son to read and that's what ruined him.
No one knew how it happened, but that scoundrel Jacques
had sniffed out the gold, had taken it and gone boozing at Le
Croisic. By an unlucky coincidence, old Cambremer was just
then coming home with his boat. As he was landing he saw a
piece of paper floating on the water, picked it up and brought
it to his wife. She recognized her own writing and fell down
in a faint. Cambremer said nothing, went to Le Croisic and
there learned that his son was playing billiards. So then he
asked to see the good woman who kept the café and said to
her, "I had told Jacques not to use a gold piece that he will
pay you with. Give it back to me, I shall wait at the door and
give you silver instead." The good woman brought him the
coin. Cambremer took it, saying, "Good!" and went back
home. The whole town knew that part of the story. But here
is what *I* know and what other people only vaguely suspect.
He told his wife to tidy up their ground-floor room. He made
a fire in the grate, lit two candles, put two chairs on one side
of the hearth, and on the other side he put a stool. Then he
told his wife to get his wedding clothes ready and to smarten
up her own. He got dressed. When he was ready he went to
find his brother and told him to stand guard in front of the
house to warn him if he heard any noise on either of the two
shores, the one on this side and the one on the side of the
Guérande marshes. He went back into the house when he
thought his wife was dressed, loaded a gun and hid it in the
chimney corner. And now Jacques came home. He came home
late, he had been drinking and gambling till ten o'clock. He

had got someone to ferry him across at the Carnouf headland. His uncle heard him shout, went to fetch him at the shore by the marshes and rowed him across without saying a word. When he came in his father said, "Sit down there," and pointed to the stool. "You are, " he said, "in front of your father and mother whom you have wronged and who must now be your judges." Jacques began to howl because Cambremer's face was strangely contorted. The mother was as still as an oar. "If you shout, if you move, if you don't sit as straight as a mast on your stool," said Pierre aiming at him with his gun, "I shall kill you like a dog." The son became as silent as a fish, the mother said nothing. "Look here!" said Pierre to his son. "Here's a piece of paper which was wrapped round a Spanish gold coin. The gold coin was in your mother's bed; only your mother knew the place where she had put it. I found the paper on the water as I came in to land here. This evening you have just given that Spanish gold piece to mère Fleurant and your mother couldn't find her coin in her bed. Explain this." Jacques said he hadn't taken his mother's coin and that this one was left over from what he had had at Nantes. "So much the better," said Pierre. "How can you prove that to us?" "I had it." "You didn't take your mother's?" "No." "Can you swear by your eternal salvation that this is true?" He was going to swear but his mother looked up at him and said, "Jacques, my child, take care. Don't swear if it isn't true. You can amend your ways, you can repent. There is still time." And she wept. "You're no help," he said, "you have always wanted to down me." Cambremer turned pale and said, "What you have just said to your mother adds to your crimes. Let's go straight to the point. Are you going to swear?" "Yes." "Look," said Cambremer, "did your coin have on it this cross which the sardine merchant who gave it me had put on ours?" Jacques came to his senses and wept. "That's enough talk," said Pierre. "I am not going to say anything about what you did before that, but I don't want a Cambremer to be put to death on the square at Le Croisic. Say your prayers and let's get on with it. A priest will come to hear your confession." The mother had gone out so as not to hear the condemnation of her son. When she was out of the room, Cambremer, the uncle, came with the priest from Piriac; Jacques wouldn't say a word to him. He was cunning; he knew his father well enough to know that he wouldn't kill him before he had made confession. "Thank you, excuse us, sir," said Cambremer to the priest when he saw Jacques' obstinacy. "I wanted to give my son a lesson, then ask you to say nothing about it. As for you," he said to Jacques, "if you don't mend your ways, the first time you go wrong, that'll be the end. I'll finish you off without confession." He sent him to bed. The boy believed his father and imagined that he could make it up with him. Jacques fell asleep. His father stayed awake. When he saw that his son was fast asleep, he covered his mouth with rope, bound it up tightly with a piece of sailcloth, and then tied his hands and feet together. "He was in a fury, he wept blood," Cambremer told the Justice. What could he do? The mother threw herself at the father's feet. "He is judged," said Cambremer. "You must help me put him in the boat." She refused. Cambremer put his son in unaided, forced him down into the bottom of the boat and tied a stone round his neck. He rowed out of the bay and out to sea till he was abreast of the rock where he now sits. Then the poor mother, who had got her brother-in-law to take her out there, cried in vain for mercy – it was like showing a red rag to a bull. By the light of the moon, she saw the father throw into the water the son whom he still loved, and as there was no wind she heard a plop and then nothing, not a trace, not a bubble. The sea certainly keeps things safely. When he landed at the rock to soothe his sobbing wife, Cambremer found her half dead. The two brothers couldn't carry her. They had to put her in the boat which had just been used for her son and they took her home through the narrows at Croisic. Well, the beautiful Brouin girl, as they called her, didn't last a week. As she died, she asked her husband to burn the accursed boat. Oh! He did that, but he became all queer. He didn't know what he wanted. He staggered about as he walked, like a man who couldn't hold his liquor. Then he went away for ten days and when he came back he settled where you saw him. Since he has been there, he hasn't uttered a word.'

The fisherman didn't take long to tell us this story and told it even more simply than I have written it. Ordinary people make few reflections as they tell a story. They highlight the event that has struck them and portray it as they feel it. This story was as sharply impressive as an axe-blow.

'I shan't go to Batz,' said Pauline as we arrived at the upper shore of the bay. We came back to Le Croisic by the salt marshes, guided through the winding path by the fisherman who, like us, had become silent. Our mood had changed. We were both lost in melancholy thoughts, saddened by this tragedy which explained our sudden presentiment at the sight of Cambremer. We both had enough experience of the world to understand all the things that our guide had not told us about these three lives. We could imagine the misfortunes of these three beings as vividly as if we had seen them enacted in the scenes of a tragedy which culminated with the father's expiation of his necessary crime. We dared not look at the rock where the ill-fated man was sitting, a terror to a whole district. The sky was clouding over, mist was rising on the horizon, we were walking through the gloomiest countryside that I have ever come across. We were treading a ground that seemed sickly and unwholesome – salt marshes that one can rightly call the scrofula of the earth. On these marshes, the ground is divided into unequal squares, which are enclosed in great banks of grey earth and filled with brackish water, the salt rising to the top. These man-made ravines are divided internally into strips. The workers go along them carrying long rakes with which they skim off the brine and when the salt is ready to be heaped up in piles, they bring it on to round platforms erected at regular intervals. For two hours we walked along the edge of this dreary chess-board where vegetation is stifled by the abundance of salt and where we saw only a few *paludiers* (the name they give the salt workers) from time to time in the distance. These men, or rather this Breton clan, wear a special costume, a white jacket rather like a brewer's. They always marry among themselves. There is no case of a girl from this tribe marrying anyone but a *paludier*. The horrible appearance of these marshes with their symmetrically raked mud, and of this grey earth which is shunned by the Breton flowers, was in harmony with our melancholy feelings. When we reached the place where one crosses the channel formed by the irruption into this basin of the water which presumably feeds the salt marshes, we were glad to see the meagre vegetation growing by the beach. As we crossed the salt marshes, we saw in the middle of the bay the island where the Cambremers live. We turned our heads away.

When we got back to our hotel, we noticed a billiard table in a low room, and when we learned that it was the only public billiard table in Le Croisic, we got ready to leave during the night; the next day we were at Guérande. Pauline was still sad, and I was already feeling the beginnings of that inflammation which is consuming my brain. I was so cruelly tormented by my vision of those three lives that she said, 'Louis, write it down. You will divert this fever to a different channel.'

So, I have written you this adventure, my dear uncle. But it has already made me lose the peace of mind which I owe to my sea-bathing and to our stay here.

1834

The Atheist's Mass

A DOCTOR to whom science owes a fine physiological theory and who, while still young, achieved a place amongst the celebrities of the Paris school of medicine (that centre of enlightenment to which all the doctors of Europe pay homage), Doctor Bianchon, practised surgery for a long time before devoting himself to medicine. His early studies were directed by one of the greatest of French surgeons, by the celebrated Desplein who passed through the world of science like a meteor. Even his enemies admit that he took with him to the grave a method that could not be handed on to others. Like all men of genius he had no heirs; he carried his skill within him and he carried it away with him. A surgeon's fame is like an actor's. It exists only so long as he is alive and his talent can no longer be appreciated once he has gone. Actors and surgeons, great singers too, and virtuoso musicians who by their playing increase tenfold the power of music, are all heroes of the moment. Desplein's life is a proof of the resemblance between the destinies of these transitory geniuses. His name which was so famous yesterday is almost forgotten today. It will remain only in his own field without going beyond it. But extraordinary conditions are surely necessary for the name of a scholar to pass from the domain of Science into the general history of humanity. Did Desplein have that width of knowledge which makes a man the mouthpiece or the representative of an age? Desplein possessed a god-like glance; he understood the patient and his disease by means of a natural or acquired intuition which allowed him to appreciate the diagnosis appropriate to the individual, to decide the precise moment, the hour, the minute at which he should operate, taking into account atmospheric conditions and temperamental peculiarities. To be able to collaborate with Nature in this way, had he then studied the endless combination of beings and elemental substances contained in the atmosphere or provided by the earth for man, who absorbs them and uses them for a particular purpose? Did he use that power of deduction and analogy to which Cuvier owes his genius? However that may be, this man understood the secrets of the flesh; he understood its past as well as its future, by studying the present. But did he contain all science in his person as did Hippocrates, Galen, Aristotle? Did he lead a whole school towards new worlds? No. If it is impossible to refuse to this constant observer of human chemistry the ancient science of Magism, that is to say, the knowledge of the elements in fusion, of the causes of life, of life before life, of what it will be, judging from its antecedents before it exists, all this unfortunately was personal to him. In his life he was isolated by egoism, and today that egoism is the death of his fame. Over his tomb there is no statue proclaiming to the future, in ringing tones, the mysteries which Genius seeks out at its own expense. But perhaps Desplein's talent was in keeping with his beliefs, and consequently mortal. For him the terrestrial atmosphere was like a generative bag; he saw the earth as if it were an egg in its shell, and unable to know whether the egg or the hen came first, he denied both the fowl and the egg. He believed neither in the animal anterior to man nor in the spirit beyond him. Desplein was not in doubt, he affirmed his opinion. He was like many other scholars in his frank, unmixed atheism. They are the best people in the world but incorrigible atheists, atheists such as religious people don't believe exist. It was hardly possible for such a man to hold a different opinion, for from his youth he was used to dissecting the living being *par excellence*, before, during and after life, and to examining all its functions without finding the unique soul that is indispensable to religious theories. Desplein recognized a cerebral centre, a nervous centre and a circulatory centre, of which the first two do duty for each other so well that at the end of his life he was convinced that the sense of hearing was not absolutely necessary to hear, nor the sense of sight absolutely necessary to see, and that the solar plexus could replace them without anyone noticing it.

He thus found two souls in man and this fact confirmed his atheism, although it still tells us nothing about God. He died, they say, impenitent to the last, as unfortunately do many fine geniuses. May God forgive them!

This really great man's life exhibited many pettinesses, to use the expression of his enemies who in their jealousy wanted to diminish his fame, but it would be more appropriate to call them apparent contradictions. Envious or stupid people who do not know the reasons which explain the activities of superior minds immediately take advantage of a few super-ficial contradictions to make accusations on which they obtain a momentary judgement. If, later on, the plans which have been attacked are crowned with success, when the prepara-tions are correlated with the results, some of the calumnies which were made beforehand remain. Thus, in our own time, Napoleon was condemned by our contemporaries when he spread out the wings of his eagle over England: but we needed the events of 1822 to explain 1804 and the flat-bottomed boats at Boulogne.[1]

Since Desplein's fame and scientific knowledge were un-assailable, his enemies attacked his strange disposition and his character, while in fact he was simply what the English call eccentric. At times he dressed magnificently like the tragedian Crébillon, at times he seemed unusually indifferent to clothes. Sometimes he was to be seen in a carriage, sometimes on foot. He was now sharp-tempered, now kind, apparently hard and stingy, yet capable of offering his fortune to his exiled rulers who honoured him by accepting it for a few days. No man has inspired more contradictory judgements. Although, to obtain the Order of Saint Michael (which doctors are not sup-posed to solicit), he was capable of dropping a Book of Hours from his pocket at Court, you can be sure that inwardly he laughed at the whole thing. He had a profound contempt for

1. In 1804 Napoleon planned to invade England, using a fleet of flat-bottomed boats based on Boulogne. But he was unable to gain com-mand of the sea, and abandoned this plan in favour of the land conquest of Europe. In 1822 the French Government wanted to intervene in the civil conflict in Spain, in spite of the vigorous protest of Great Britain. Balzac's point is, however, unclear.

mankind, having studied them from above and from below, having surprised them without pretence, as they performed the most solemn as well as the pettiest acts of life. A great man's gifts often hang together. If one of these giants has more talent than wit, his wit is still greater than that of a man of whom one says simply, 'He is witty.' All genius presupposes moral insight. This insight may be applied to some speciality, but he who sees the flower must see the sun. The doctor who heard a diplomat whose life he had saved ask, 'How is the Emperor?', and who replied, 'The courtier is coming back to life, the man will follow!' was not only a surgeon or a physician, he was also extremely witty. Thus the close and patient observer of humanity will justify Desplein's exorbitant pretensions and will realize, as he himself realized, that he was capable of being as great a minister as he was a surgeon.

Among the riddles which Desplein's life reveals to his contemporaries we have chosen one of the most interesting, because the solution will be found at the end of this tale and will answer some of the foolish accusations which have been made against him.

Of all the pupils whom Desplein had at his hospital, Horace Bianchon was one of those to whom he became most warmly attached. Before doing his internship at the Hôtel Dieu,[2] Horace Bianchon was a medical student, living in a miserable boarding-house in the Latin Quarter, known by the name of La Maison Vauquer.[3] There this poor young man experienced that desperate poverty which is a kind of melting-pot whence great talents emerge pure and incorruptible, just as diamonds can be subjected to any kind of shock without breaking. In the violence of their unleashed passions, they acquire the most unshakeable honesty, and by dint of the constant labour with which they have contained their balked appetites, they become used to the struggles which are the lot of genius. Horace was an upright young man, incapable of double-

2. L'Hôtel-Dieu was one of the oldest and most important hospitals in Paris.

3. Life in La Maison Vauquer is depicted in Balzac's novel *Le Père Goriot*.

dealing in affairs of honour, going straight to the point without fuss, as capable of pawning his coat for his friends as of giving them his time and his night's rest. In short, Horace was one of those friends who are not worried about what they receive in exchange for what they give, certain as they are to receive in their turn more than they will give. Most of his friends had for him that inner respect which is inspired by unostentatious goodness, and several of them were afraid of his strictures. But Horace exercised these virtues without being prudish. He was neither a puritan nor a preacher; he swore quite readily when giving advice, and enjoyed a good meal in gay company when opportunity offered. He was good company, no more squeamish than a soldier, bluff and open, not like a sailor – for the sailor of today is a wily diplomatist – but like a fine young man who has nothing to hide in his life; he walked with his head high and his heart light. In a word, Horace was the Pylades of more than one Orestes, creditors being today the most real shape assumed by the ancient Furies. He wore his poverty with that gaiety which is perhaps one of the greatest elements of courage, and like all those who have nothing, he contracted few debts. Sober as a camel, brisk as a stag, he was unwavering both in his principles and in his behaviour. The happiness of Bianchon's life began on the day when the famous surgeon obtained evidence of the good qualities and failings which, the one as much as the other, made Doctor Horace Bianchon doubly precious to his friends. When a clinical chief adopts a young man, that young man has, as they say, his foot in the stirrup. Desplein always took Bianchon with him to act as his assistant in well-to-do homes, where some reward would nearly always find its way into the student's purse, and where little by little the mysteries of Parisian life were revealed to the young provincial. Desplein also kept him in his surgery during consultations and gave him work to do there. Sometimes he would send him to accompany a rich patient to a spa. In short, he was making a practice for him. The result of all this was that after a time the lord of surgery had a devoted slave. These two men, the one at the height of his fame and leader of his profession, enjoying an immense fortune and an immense reputation, the other, a modest Omega, having neither fortune nor fame, became intimate friends. The great Desplein told his assistant everything. He knew if a certain lady had sat down on a chair beside the master, or on the famous surgery couch where Desplein slept. Bianchon knew the mysteries of that temperament, both lion-like and bull-like, which in the end expanded and abnormally developed the great man's chest and caused his death from enlargement of the heart. The student studied the eccentricities of Desplein's very busy life, the plans made by his sordid avarice, the hopes of the politician concealed behind the scientist; he foresaw the disappointments in store for the only feeling hidden in that heart which was hardened rather than hard.

One day Bianchon told Desplein that a poor water-carrier from the Saint-Jacques quarter had a horrible illness caused by fatigue and poverty; this poor Auvergnat had eaten only potatoes during the severe winter of 1821. Desplein left all his patients. At the risk of working his horse to death, he rode as fast as he could, followed by Bianchon, to the poor man's house and himself had him carried to the nursing-home founded by the famous Dubois in the Faubourg Saint-Denis. Desplein attended the man, and when he had cured him, gave him the money to buy a horse and a water-cart. This Auvergnat was remarkable for one original characteristic. One of his friends fell ill; he took him straight away to Desplein and said to his benefactor, 'I would not have allowed him to go to another doctor.' Surly as he was, Desplein grasped the water-carrier's hand and said, 'Bring them all to me.' And he had the peasant from the Cantal admitted to the Hôtel Dieu, where he took the greatest care of him. Bianchon had already noticed several times that his chief had a predilection for Auvergnats, and especially for water-carriers. But as Desplein had a kind of pride in his treatments at the Hôtel Dieu, his pupil didn't see anything very strange in that.

One day, as Bianchon was crossing the Place Saint-Sulpice, he noticed his master going into the church about nine o'clock in the morning. Desplein, who at that period of his life never moved a step except by carriage, was on foot and slipping in by the door of the Rue du Petit-Lion, as if he had been going into a house of doubtful reputation. Bianchon's curiosity was naturally aroused, since he knew his master's opinions and that he was a 'devyl' of a Cabanist[4] (devyl with a y, which in Rabelais seems to suggest a superiority in devilry). Slipping into Saint-Sulpice, he was not a little astonished to see the great Desplein, that atheist without pity for the angels, who cannot be subjected to the surgeon's knife, who cannot have sinus or gastric trouble, that dauntless scoffer, kneeling humbly, and where? . . . in the chapel of the Virgin, where he listened to a Mass, paid for the cost of the service, gave alms for the poor, all as solemnly as if he had been performing an operation.

'He certainly didn't come to clear up questions about the Virgin birth,' said Bianchon in boundless astonishment. 'If I had seen him holding one of the tassels of the canopy on Corpus Christi day, I would have taken it as a joke; but at this hour, alone, with no one to see him, that certainly gives one food for thought!'

Bianchon did not want to look as if he was spying on the chief surgeon of the Hôtel Dieu and he went away. By chance Desplein invited him to dinner that very day, not at home but at a restaurant.

Between the fruit and the cheese, Bianchon managed skilfully to bring the conversation round to the subject of the Mass, calling it a masquerade and a farce.

'A farce,' said Desplein, 'which has cost Christendom more blood than all Napoleon's battles and all Broussais' leeches! The Mass is a papal invention which goes no further back than the sixth century and which is based on *Hoc est corpus*. What torrents of blood had to be spilt to establish Corpus Christi day! By the institution of this Feast the court of Rome intended to proclaim its victory in the matter of the Real Presence, a schism which troubled the Church for three centuries. The wars of the Counts of Toulouse and the Albigen-

4. Cabanis was the author of the *Traité du physique et du moral de l'homme*, an influential atheistic and materialistic work.

sians are the tail-end of this affair. The Vaudois and the Albigensians[5] refused to recognize this innovation.'

In short Desplein enjoyed himself, giving free rein to his atheistic wit, and pouring out a flood of Voltairean jokes, or, to be more precise, a horrible parody of the *Citateur*.[6]

'Well,' Bianchon said to himself, 'where is the pious man I saw this morning?'

He said nothing; he had doubts whether he really had seen his chief at Saint-Sulpice. Desplein would not have bothered to lie to Bianchon. They both knew each other too well; they had already exchanged ideas on subjects which were just as serious, and they had discussed systems *de natura rerum*, probing or dissecting them with the knives and the scalpel of incredulity. Three months went by. Bianchon did not follow up the incident, although it remained stamped on his memory. One day in the course of that year, one of the doctors at the Hôtel Dieu took Desplein by the arm, in Bianchon's presence, as if to ask him a question.

'What were you going to do at Saint-Sulpice, my dear chief?' he asked.

'I went to see a priest who had a diseased knee. Madame la Duchesse d'Angoulême did me the honour of recommending me,' said Desplein.

The doctor was satisfied with this excuse, but not so Bianchon.

'Oh! So he goes to see bad knees in church! He was going to hear Mass,' the student said to himself.

Bianchon determined to keep a watch on Desplein. He recalled the day and the time on which he had surprised him going in to Saint-Sulpice and he determined to go there the following year on the same day and at the same time, to find out if he would surprise him there again. If that happened, the regularity of his worship would justify a scientific investigation, for in such a man there should not be a direct contradiction between thought and deed. The following year, on the

5. The Vaudois and the Albigensians were twelfth-century heretical sects in the south of France.

6. *Le Citateur* was an anti-clerical pamphlet by Pigault-Lebrun.

day and at the hour in question, Bianchon, who was by this time no longer Desplein's assistant, saw the surgeon's carriage stop at the corner of the Rue de Tournon and the Rue du Petit-Lion. From there his friend crept stealthily along by the walls of Saint-Sulpice where he again heard Mass at the altar of the Virgin. It was certainly Desplein, the chief surgeon, the atheist *in petto*, the pious man on occasion. The plot became more involved. The famous scientist's persistence complicated everything. When Desplein had left the church, Bianchon went up to the sacristan who came to minister to the chapel, and asked him if the gentleman was a regular attendant.

'I have been here for twenty years,' said the sacristan, 'and for all that time Monsieur Desplein has been coming four times a year to hear this Mass; it was he who founded it.'

'*He* founded it!' said Bianchon as he walked away. 'This is as much a mystery as the Immaculate Conception, which of itself must make a doctor an unbeliever.'

Although Dr Bianchon was a friend of Desplein's, some time went by before he was in a position to speak to him about this strange circumstance of his life. If they met at a consultation or in society, it was difficult to find that moment of confidence and solitude when, with feet up on the fire-dogs and heads leaning against the backs of their chairs, two men tell each other their secrets. Finally, seven years later, after the 1830 Revolution, when the people stormed the Archbishopric, when, inspired by Republican sentiments, they destroyed the golden crosses which appeared, like flashes of lightning, in this vast sea of houses, when Disbelief and Violence swaggered together through the streets, Bianchon surprised Desplein going into Saint-Sulpice. The doctor followed him in and took a place near him without his friend making the least sign or showing the least surprise. Both of them heard the foundation Mass.

'Will you tell me, my friend,' Bianchon said to Desplein when they were outside the church, 'the reason for this display of piety? I have already caught you three times going to Mass, you! You must tell me the reason for this mysterious activity, and explain to me the flagrant discrepancy between your opinions and your behaviour. You don't believe in God, yet you go to Mass! My dear chief, you must answer me.'

'I am like many pious men, men who appear to be profoundly religious but are quite as atheistic as we are, you and I.'

And he let forth a torrent of epigrams about political personalities of whom the best known provides us in this century with a new edition of Molière's Tartuffe.

'That's not what I am talking about,' said Bianchon. 'I want to know the reason for what you have just been doing here. Why did you found this Mass?'

'Well, my dear friend,' said Desplein, 'since I am on the brink of the grave, there is no reason why I shouldn't speak to you about the beginning of my life.'

At this moment Bianchon and the great man happened to be in the Rue des Quatre-Vents, one of the most horrible streets in Paris. Desplein pointed to the sixth storey of one of those houses which are shaped like an obelisk and have a medium-sized door opening on to a passage. At the end of the passage is a spiral staircase lit by apertures called *jours de souffrance*. The house was a greenish colour; on the ground floor lived a furniture dealer; a different kind of poverty seemed to lodge on each floor. Raising his arm with an emphatic gesture, Desplein said to Bianchon, 'I lived up there for two years.'

'I know the place; d'Arthez lived there and I came here almost every day in my youth. At that time we called it the "jar of great men"! Well, what of it?'

'The Mass that I have just heard is linked to events which took place at the time when I lived in the attic where, so you tell me, d'Arthez lived. It is the one where a line of washing is dangling at the window above a pot of flowers. I had such a difficult time to start with, my dear Bianchon, that I can dispute the palm of the sufferings of Paris with anyone. I have put up with everything, hunger, thirst, lack of money, lack of clothes, of footwear, of linen, everything that is hardest about poverty. I have blown on my numbed fingers in that "jar of great men" which I should like to visit again with you. I worked during one winter, when I could see my own head steaming and a cloud of my own breath rising like horses' breath on a frosty day. I don't know what enables a man to stand up to such a life. I was alone, without help, without a farthing either to buy books or to pay the expenses of my medical education. I had no friends and my irritable, sensitive, restless temperament did me no good. No one could see that my bad temper was caused by the difficulties and the work of a man who, from his position at the bottom of the social ladder, was striving to reach the top. But I can tell *you*, you to whom I don't need to pretend, that I had that basis of good feeling and keen sensitivity which will always be the prerogative of men who, after having been stuck for a long time in the slough of poverty, are strong enough to climb to any kind of summit. I could get nothing from my family or my home beyond the inadequate allowance they made me. In short, at this period of my life, all I had to eat in the mornings was a roll which the baker in the Rue du Petit-Lion sold me more cheaply because it was yesterday's, or the day before yesterday's. I crumbled it up into some milk and so my morning meal cost me only two sous. I dined only every other day at a boarding-house where dinner cost sixteen sous. In this way I spent only nine sous a day. You know as well as I do the care I had to take of my clothes and my footwear. I don't think, later on in life, we are as much distressed by a colleague's disloyalty as you and I were when we saw the mocking grin of a shoe that was becoming unsewn, or heard the armhole of a frock-coat split. I drank only water; I had the greatest respect for cafés. Zoppi's seemed to me like a promised land which the Luculli of the Latin Quarter alone had the right to patronize. Sometimes I wondered whether I would ever be able to have a cup of white coffee there, or play a game of dominoes. In short, I transferred to my work the fury which poverty inspired in me. I tried to master scientific knowledge so that I should have an immense personal worth deserving of the place I would reach when I emerged from my obscurity. I consumed more oil than bread; the light which lit up those stubborn vigils cost me more than my food. The struggle was long, hard and unrelieved. I aroused no feelings of friendship in those around me. To make friends, you must mix with young people, have a few sous so that you can go and have a drink with them, go with them everywhere where students go. I had nothing. And no one in Paris realizes that "nothing" is "nothing". When there was any question of revealing my poverty I experienced that nervous contraction of the throat which makes our patients think that a ball is rising up from the gullet into the larynx. Later on I met people who, born rich and never having lacked for anything, don't know the problem of this rule of three: "A young man is to crime as a hundred sous piece is to X." These gilded fools say to me, "Why did you get into debt? Why did you take on such crushing obligations?" They remind me of the princess who, knowing that the people were dying of hunger, asked, "Why don't they buy cake?" I should very much like to see one of those rich people, who complains that I charge too much for operating on him, alone in Paris, without a penny, without a friend, without credit and forced to work with his two hands to live. What would he do? Where would he satisfy his hunger? Bianchon, if at times you have seen me bitter and hard, it was because I was super-imposing my early sufferings on the lack of feeling, the selfishness, of which I had thousands of examples in high places; or I was thinking of the obstacles which hatred, envy, jealousy, and calumny have placed between me and success. In Paris, when certain people see you ready to put your foot in the stirrup, some of them pull you back by the coat-tail, others loosen the buckle of the saddle-girth so that you'll fall and break your head; this one takes the shoes of your horse, that one steals your whip. The least treacherous is the one you see coming up to shoot you at point-blank range. You have enough talent, my dear fellow, soon to be acquainted with the horrible, unending battle which mediocrity wages against superiority. If one evening you lose twenty-five louis, the next day you will be accused of being a gambler and your best friends will say that the day before you lost twenty-five thousand francs. If you have a headache, you will be called a lunatic. If you have one outburst of temper, they will say you are a social misfit. If, in order to resist this army of pygmies, you muster your superior forces, your best friends will cry out that you want to eat up everything, that you claim to have the right to dominate and lord it over others. In short, your good qualities will become failings, your failings will become vices, and your virtues will be crimes. If you have saved a man, they'll say you have killed him; if your patient is in circulation again, they will affirm that you have sacrificed the future to the present; if he is not dead, he will die. Hesitate, and you will be lost! Invent anything at all, claim your just due, you will be regarded as a sly character, difficult to deal with, who is standing in the way of the young men. So, my dear fellow, if I don't believe in God, I believe still less in man. You recognize in me a Desplein very different from the Desplein everyone speaks ill of, don't you? But let's not rummage in this muck heap. Well, I used to live in this house; I was busy working to pass my first examination and I hadn't a sou. I had reached one of those extreme situations where, you know, a man says to himself, "I shall join the army." I had one last hope. I was expecting from home a trunk full of linen, a present from old aunts of the kind who, knowing nothing of Paris, think of your shirts and imagine that with thirty francs a month their nephew lives on caviar. The trunk arrived while I was at the school; the carriage cost forty francs. The porter, a German cobbler who lived in a garret, had paid the money and was keeping the trunk. I went for a walk in the Rue des Fossés-Saint-Germain-des-Prés and in the Rue de l'Ecole-de-Médecine, but I could not think up a plan which would deliver my trunk to me without my having to pay the forty francs; naturally I would have paid them after I had sold the linen. My stupidity made me realize that I was gifted for nothing but surgery. My dear fellow, sensitive souls whose gifts are deployed in a lofty sphere are lacking in that spirit of intrigue which is so resourceful in contriving schemes. *Their* genius lies in chance; they don't seek for things, they come on them by chance. Well, I returned at nightfall at the same time that my neighbour, a water-carrier named Bourgeat, a man from Saint-Flour, was going home. We knew each other in the way two tenants do who have rooms on the same landing, and who hear each other sleeping, coughing, and dressing, till in the end they get used to one another. My neighbour informed me that the landlord, to whom I owed three quarters' rent, had turned me out; I would have to clear out the next day. He himself had been given notice because of his calling. I spent the most unhappy night of my life. Where would I find a carrier to remove my poor household affairs and my books? How would I be able to pay the carrier and the porter? Where was I to go? I kept on asking myself these unanswerable questions through my tears, like a madman repeating a refrain. I fell asleep. Poverty has in its favour an exquisite sleep filled with beautiful dreams. The next morning, just as I was eating my bowlful of crumbled bread and milk, Bourgeat came in and said in his bad French, "*Monchieur l'étudiant*, I'm a poor man, a foundling from the Chain-Flour hospital. I've no father or mother and I'm not rich enough to get married. You haven't many relations either, or much in the way of hard cash. Now listen. I've got a hand-cart downstairs which I've hired for two *chous* an hour. It'll take all our things. If you're willing, we'll look for digs together since we're turned out of here. After all, this place isn't an earthly paradise."

' "I know that alright, Bourgeat, my good fellow," I replied. "But I'm in rather a jam. Downstairs I have a trunk containing linen worth a hundred crowns. With that I could pay the landlord and what I owe the porter, but I haven't got a hundred sous."

' "That doesn't matter, I've got some cash," Bourgeat replied cheerfully, showing me a filthy old leather purse. "Keep your linen."

'Bourgeat paid my three quarters' rent and his own and settled with the porter. Then he put our furniture and my linen on to his cart and dragged it through the streets, stopping in front of every house which had a "to let" sign hanging out. My job was to go up and see if the place to let would suit us. At midday we were still wandering about the Latin Quarter without having found anything. The price was a great difficulty. Bourgeat suggested that we should have lunch at a wine-shop; we left our cart at the door. Towards evening, I discovered in the Cour de Rohan, Passage du Commerce, two rooms, separated by the stair in the attic at the top of a house. The rent was sixty francs a year each. We were housed at last, my humble friend and I. We had dinner together. Bourgeat, who earned about fifty sous a day, had about a hundred crowns. He was soon going to be able to realize his ambition and buy a water-cart and a horse. When he learned about my situation (for he dragged my secrets out of me with a deep cunning and a good nature the memory of which still touches my heart), he gave up for some time his whole life's ambition. Bourgeat had been a street-merchant for twenty-two years; he sacrificed his hundred crowns to my future.'

Desplein gripped Bianchon's arm with emotion.

'He gave me the money I needed for my exams. My friend, that man realized that I had a mission, that the needs of my intelligence were more important than his own. He took care of me; he called me his child and lent me the money I needed to buy books. Sometimes he would come in very quietly to watch me working. Last but not least, he took care, as a mother might have done, to see that instead of the bad and insufficient food which I had been forced to put up with, I had a healthy and plentiful diet. Bourgeat, who was a man of about forty, had the face of a medieval burgess, a dome-like forehead and a head that a painter might have used as a model for Lycurgus. The poor man's heart was filled with affections which had no outlet. The only creature that had ever loved him was a poodle which had died a short time before. He talked to me continually about it and asked me if I thought that the Church would be willing to say Masses for the repose of its soul. His dog was, so he said, a true Christian and it had gone to church with him for twelve years, without ever barking there. It had listened to the organ without opening its mouth and squatted beside him with a look that made him think it was praying with him. This man transferred all his affections to me; he accepted me as a lonely and unhappy creature. He became for me the most attentive of mothers, the most tactful of benefactors, in short, the ideal of that virtue which delights in its own work. Whenever I met him in the street, he would glance at me with an understanding look filled with remarkable nobility; then he would pretend to walk as if he was carrying nothing. He seemed happy to see me in good health and well-dressed. In short, it was the devotion of a man of the people, the love of a working-girl transferred to a higher sphere. Bourgeat did my errands; he woke me up at night at the hours I asked him to. He cleaned my lamp and polished our landing. He was as good a servant as he was a father, and tidy as an English girl. He did the housework. Like Philopoemen he used to saw up our wood, doing everything with simplicity and dignity, for he seemed to realize that his objective added nobility to everything he did. When I left this good man to do my residence at the Hôtel Dieu, he felt an indescribable grief at the thought that he could no longer live with me. But he consoled himself with the prospect of saving up the money needed for the expenses of my thesis, and made me promise to come and see him on my days off. Bourgeat was proud of me; he loved me both for my sake and for his own. If you look up my thesis you will see that it was dedicated to him. During the last year of my internship, I had earned enough money to pay back everything I owed to this admirable Auvergnat, by buying him a horse and a water-cart. He was furious when he knew that I had been depriving myself of my money, and nevertheless he was delighted to see his wishes realized. He both laughed and scolded me. He looked at his cart and his horse, wiping a tear from his eyes as he said, "That's bad! Oh, what a splendid cart! You shouldn't have done it. The horse is as strong as an Auvergnat." I have never seen anything more moving than this scene. Bourgeat absolutely insisted on buying me that case of instruments mounted in silver which you have seen in my study, and which is for me the most valuable thing I have there. Although he was thrilled by my first successes, he never let slip the least word or gesture which implied, "That man's success is due to me." And yet, without him, poverty would have killed me. The poor man had dug his own grave to help me. He had eaten nothing but bread rubbed with garlic, so that I could have coffee to help me work at night. He fell ill. As you can imagine, I spent the nights at his bedside. I pulled him through the first time, but he had a relapse two years later, and in spite of the most constant care, in spite of the greatest efforts of medical science, his end had come. No king was ever as well cared for as he was. Yes, Bianchon, to snatch that life from death I made supreme efforts. I wanted to make him live long enough for me to show him the results of his work and realize all his hopes for me; I wanted to satisfy the only gratitude which has ever filled my heart and put out a fire which still burns me today.'

After a pause, Desplein, visibly moved, resumed his tale. 'Bourgeat, my second father, died in my arms leaving me everything he possessed in a will which he had had made by a public letter-writer and dated the year when we went to live in the Cour de Rohan. This man had the simple faith of a charcoal-burner. He loved the Blessed Virgin as he would have loved his wife. Although he was an ardent Catholic, he had never said a word to me about my lack of religion. When his life was in danger, he begged me to do everything possible to enable him to have the help of the Church. I had Mass said for him every day. Often, during the night, he would express fears for his future; he was afraid that he had not lived a sufficiently holy life. Poor man! He worked from morning to night. To whom then would Paradise belong – if there is a Paradise? He received the last rites like the saint he was and his death was worthy of his life. I was the only person to attend his funeral. When I had buried my only benefactor, I tried to think of a way of paying my debt to him. I realized that he had neither family nor friends, wife nor children. But he was a believer, he had a religious conviction. Had I any right to dispute it? He had spoken to me shyly about Masses said for the repose of the dead. He didn't want to impose this duty upon me, thinking that it would be like asking payment for his services. As soon as I could establish an endowment fund, I gave Saint-Sulpice the necessary amount to have four Masses said there a year. As the only thing I can give to Bourgeat is the satisfaction of his religious wishes, the day when this Mass is said at the beginning of each season, I say with the good faith of a doubter, "Oh God, if there is a sphere where, after their death, you place all those who have been perfect, think of good Bourgeat. And if there is anything for him to suffer, give me his sufferings so that he may enter more quickly into what is called Paradise." That, my dear fellow, is the most that a man with my opinions can allow himself. God must be a decent chap; he couldn't hold it against me. I swear to you, I would give my fortune to be a believer like Bourgeat.'

Bianchon, who looked after Desplein in his last illness, dares not affirm nowadays that the distinguished surgeon died an atheist. Believers will like to think that the humble Auvergnat will have opened the gate of heaven for him as, earlier, he had opened for him the gate of that earthly temple on whose doorway is written *Aux grands hommes la patrie reconnaissante*.[7]

7. These words (meaning 'To our great men from their grateful country') are inscribed above the doorway of the Panthéon in Paris where many of the great men of France are buried.

1836

Facino Cane

I was living at that time in a little street you probably don't know, the Rue de Lesdiguières: it starts at the Rue Saint-Antoine, opposite a fountain near the Place de la Bastille, and runs into the Rue de la Cerisaie.

For the love of knowledge I had gone to live in a garret, working by night and spending the day in a near-by library, the Bibliothèque de Monsieur. I lived frugally and I had accepted all the conditions of the monastic life which is essential for serious students. When the weather was fine, at best I took a walk on the Boulevard Bourdon. Only one passion could drag me away from my studious habits, but even that was a kind of study. I used to go and observe the people of the suburb, their characters and behaviour. Since I was as badly dressed as the working-men and did not bother about appearances, I did not arouse their hostility. I could mingle with them as they stood in groups, and watch them bargaining and arguing as they left their work.

I had already acquired a power of intuitive observation which penetrated to the soul without ignoring the body, or rather it grasped external details so well that it immediately went beyond them. This power of observation enabled me to live the life of the individual I was watching, allowing me to substitute myself for him, just like the dervish in the Arabian Nights who took on the body and soul of people over whom he pronounced certain words.

Sometimes, between eleven o'clock and midnight, as I passed a workman and his wife returning home together from the Ambigu-Comique, I would amuse myself by following them from the Boulevard du Pont-aux-Choux as far as the Boulevard Beaumarchais. These good folk would first of all talk about the play they had just seen; then gradually they would come to discuss their own affairs. The mother would

drag her child along by the hand, without paying any attention
to his complaints or demands. The husband and wife would
calculate the amount of money which was due to them the
following day and would think of twenty different ways of
spending it. Then came housekeeping details, complaints
about the terrible price of potatoes, or the length of the
winter, or the increased cost of fuel, and heated protests about
what they owed the baker. In the end the discussions would
grow acrimonious, and they would each reveal their characters
by the use of colourful language. As I listened to these people,
I was able to live their lives; I felt their rags on my back, and
walked with their worn-out shoes on my feet. Their wants,
their needs, all passed into my soul, or perhaps it was my soul
which passed into theirs. It was like the dream of a man who
is wide awake. I shared their indignation against tyrannical
foremen, or against bad customers who made them come back
several times without paying them. To discard my own habits,
to become someone other than myself by an exaltation of my
moral faculties, and to play this game at will, such was my
amusement. To what do I owe this gift? Is it a kind of second
sight? Is it one of those qualities which, if abused, could lead
to madness? I have never tried to explain this power; I possess
it and make use of it, that is all. All you need to know is that,
already, at that time, I had broken up into its elements the
heterogeneous mass called 'the people', and had analysed it in
such a way that I could appraise both its good and its bad
qualities. I already knew what use could be made of this district, this breeding-ground of revolutions which contains
heroes, inventors, technicians, rogues, scoundrels, virtues and
vices, all oppressed by poverty, stifled by want, soaked in
alcohol, worn out by strong drink. You cannot imagine how
many unrecorded adventures, how many forgotten dramas
there are in this town of suffering, how many horrible and
beautiful things. It would be impossible to imagine the truth
which is concealed in it and which no one can take steps to
reveal. You would have to dig too deep to discover these
wonderful scenes of tragedy and comedy, these masterpieces
produced by chance. I don't know how I have been able to

keep untold for so long the story I am about to tell you; it is one of those strange tales stored in the bag of memory and drawn out at random like numbers in a lottery. I know many more, as odd as this one and buried as deeply. But their turn will come, you may be sure.

One day my daily help, a workman's wife, came and asked me to honour her sister's wedding with my presence. So that you can appreciate what this wedding would be like, I must tell you that I paid forty francs a month to this poor creature who used to come every morning to make my bed, clean my shoes, brush my clothes, sweep the room and prepare my lunch. For the rest of the day she turned the handle of a machine, and at this nasty job she earned ten sous a day. Her husband, a cabinet-maker, earned four francs. But as the couple had three children, they could barely earn enough to live on. I have never met a more unshakeable honesty than this man's and this woman's. For five years after I had left the district mère Vaillant would come to congratulate me on my saint's day, bringing me flowers and oranges, even though she never had ten sous saved up. Poverty had brought us together. I could never give her more than ten francs, often borrowed for the occasion. This may explain my promise to go to the wedding. I hoped to forget my own worries in these poor folk's enjoyment.

The party, the dance, all took place on the first floor of a wine-merchant's in the Rue de Charenton. The large room was lit by lamps with tin reflectors and papered with filthy wallpaper up to the height of the tables; along the walls there were wooden benches. Eighty people, in their Sunday best, decked with flowers and ribbons, their faces flushed, all in carnival mood, were dancing as if the world were coming to an end. The bride and groom were kissing to everyone's satisfaction and there were facetious hee-hees and haw-haws which were really less vulgar than the timid ogling of so-called well-brought-up girls. The whole company expressed an animal happiness which was somehow infectious.

But neither the faces of the people at this gathering, nor the wedding, nor anyone of the company have anything to do with my story. The only thing to bear in mind is the unusual setting. Imagine the wretched, red-painted shop, smell the wine, listen to the shouts of joy, stay a while in this suburb, amongst these workers, these old men, these poor women who, for one night, have given themselves up to pleasure.

The orchestra was composed of three blind men from the Quinze-Vingts;[1] the first played the violin, the second the clarinet and the third the flageolet. They were paid a lump sum of seven francs for the night, between the three of them. Of course, for that price they didn't perform Rossini or Beethoven; they played what they wanted to or what they could. With charming tact no one complained! Their music assaulted my eardrums so violently that, after casting a glance at the company, I looked at the blind trio and was inclined to indulge as soon as I recognized their uniform. The musicians were sitting in a window bay, so that one had to be quite near them to see their faces clearly. I did not go up to them immediately, but when I did, in an unaccountable way, nothing else mattered. The wedding-party and its music ceased to exist; my curiosity was excited to the highest degree, for my soul passed into the body of the clarinet player. Both the violinist and the flageolet-player had quite ordinary faces, the usual faces of the blind, intense, attentive and serious, but the clarinettist's was one of those phenomena which arrest the attention of an artist or a philosopher.

Imagine Dante's death-mask lit up by the red glow of the lamp and crowned with a forest of silver-white hair. The bitter, sorrowful expression of this magnificent face was enhanced by blindness, for the power of thought gave a new life to the dead eyes. It was as if a burning gleam emanated from them, the effect of a single relentless desire which was vigorously marked on a high brow, furrowed with wrinkles like stone-courses in an old wall. The old man puffed away at random, without paying any attention to the time or the tune; his fingers went up and down touching the old keys mechanically. He did not worry about playing wrong notes, but neither

1. The Hospice des Quinze-Vingts was an institution for the blind founded by St Louis about 1254 for 300 knights blinded by the Saracens.

the dancers nor my Italian's two acolytes noticed them; for I was sure that he was an Italian and in fact I was right. There was something great and masterful about this old Homer who kept within himself an Odyssey doomed to oblivion. It was a greatness so real that it triumphed even over his abject condition, a masterfulness so strong that it dominated his poverty. Not one of the violent passions which can lead a man to good as well as to evil, make him a criminal or a hero, was absent from that nobly formed, sallow Italian face. It was a face with overhanging, greying eyebrows that cast their shade over the deep sockets below; I trembled lest I should see the light of thought reappear in them, just as I would be afraid to see robbers armed with torches and daggers come to the mouth of a cave. There was a lion in that cage of flesh and blood, a lion whose fury had been spent in vain against its iron bars. The conflagration of despair had expired in its ashes, the lava had grown cold. But the furrows, the devastation, a little smoke bore witness to the violence of the eruption, to the ravages of the fire. These thoughts aroused by the man's appearance were as burning in my soul as they were frozen on his face.

Between each dance, the violinist and the flageolet-player, busy in good earnest with their bottle and glass, hung their instruments on a button of their reddish-coloured coats; then they stretched out their hands to a little table placed in the window bay where their refreshments stood, and always handed the Italian a full glass which he could not take himself because the table was behind his chair. Each time, the clarinettist thanked them with a friendly nod. Their movements were carried out with that precision which is always so surprising in the blind from the Quinze-Vingts and which makes you think they can see. I approached the three blind men to listen to their conversation, but when I was close to them, they sized me up carefully, and, presumably not recognizing a workman's temperament, kept quiet.

'Where do you come from, you the clarinettist?'

'From Venice,' replied the blind man with a slight Italian accent.

'Were you born blind, or were you blinded by . . .'

'As the result of an accident,' he replied sharply, 'a cursed atrophy of the optic nerve.'

'Venice is a beautiful city; I have always had a longing to go there.'

The old man's face lit up, his wrinkles changed, he was deeply moved.

'If I went there with you, you would not be wasting your time,' he said.

'Don't talk to him about Venice,' said the violinist, 'or you'll set our Doge off; especially as he has already got two bottles inside him, that prince of ours!'

'Come on, get going, old Canard,' said the flageolet-player.

They all three began to play, but while they were playing the four dances, the Venetian was aware of me. He could feel the enormous interest which I took in him. His face lost its cold, sad expression. Some hope – I don't know what – enlivened all his features, slid into his wrinkles like a blue flame. He smiled and wiped his forehead, that bold, terrible forehead. Finally he brightened up like a man about to start on his hobby-horse.

'How old are you?' I asked him.

'Eighty-two!'

'How long have you been blind?'

'For nearly fifty years now,' he replied in a tone which showed that his regrets arose not only from the loss of his sight, but also from the loss of some great power of which he had been despoiled.

'Why do they call you "the Doge"?' I asked.

'Oh, they're just teasing,' he said, 'I am a patrician of Venice and I would have been Doge like the others.'

'Then, what's your name?'

'Here,' he said, 'they call me old Canet. They never could write my name in any other way on the registers. But, in Italian, it is Marco Facino Cane, principe de Varese.'

'What, you are descended from the famous condottiere, Facino Cane, whose conquests passed to the Dukes of Milan?'

'*È vero*,' he said. 'At that time, Cane's son took refuge in

Venice to escape being killed by the Visconti and had himself inscribed in the Golden Book. But now neither Cane nor the book exists any more.' And he made a terrible gesture which expressed his expired patriotism and his disgust for human affairs.

'But if you were a senator of Venice, you must have been rich: how did you come to lose your fortune?'

At this question he turned his head towards me, with a truly tragic movement as if to examine me and replied, 'In misfortunes.'

He no longer thought of drinking and, with a gesture, refused the glass of wine which the old flageolet-player was just at that moment handing to him; then he bowed his head. These details were not of a kind to dampen my curiosity. While these three machine-like musicians were playing the dance, I examined the old Venetian nobleman with the avid feelings of a twenty-year-old. I could see Venice and the Adriatic; I could see it in ruins on that ruined face. I walked in that town so beloved of its inhabitants. I went from the Rialto to the Grand Canal, from the Quai des Esclavons to the Lido; I went back to the cathedral, so distinctively sublime I looked at the windows of the Casa d'Oro, each of which is differently ornamented; I gazed at the old palaces with their wealth of marble, and, in short, at all those wonders which the scholar appreciates all the more in that he can colour them as he pleases and does not deprive his dreams of their poetry by the sight of reality. I reconstructed the life-history of this offspring of the greatest of the condottieri, trying to discover in it the traces of his misfortunes and the causes of that deep-seated physical and moral deterioration which made even more beautiful the newly revived sparks of greatness and nobility. His thoughts were no doubt the same as mine, for I think that blindness speeds up intellectual communication, by preventing the attention's being frittered away on external objects. I did not have long to wait for a proof of our fellow-feeling. Facino Cane stopped playing, rose from his chair, came up to me and said, 'Let's go.' The effect of his words on me was like an electric shock. I gave him my arm and we went out.

When we were in the street, he said, 'Will you take me to Venice, be my guide there? Will you have faith in me? You will be richer than the ten richest companies of Amsterdam or London, richer than the Rothschilds, in short, rich as the heroes of the *Arabian Nights*.'

I thought the man was mad, but there was a power in his voice which I obeyed. I let him lead me and he took me towards the moat of the Bastille as if he had had eyes. He sat down on a stone in a very lonely place where the bridge which connects the Saint-Martin canal to the Seine has since been built. I placed myself on another stone in front of the old man whose white hair gleamed like silver thread in the moonlight. The silence, barely disturbed by the bustling noise which reached us from the boulevards, the purity of the night, everything combined to make this a truly fantastic scene.

'You speak of millions to a young man, and you think that he would hesitate to endure a thousand ills in order to obtain them! Are you not making fun of me?'

'May I die without confession,' he said passionately, 'if what I tell you is not true. I was twenty years old, as you are at this moment. I was rich, handsome and noble. I began with the greatest of all follies, love. I loved as men no longer love, even to the extent of hiding in a chest and risking being stabbed there without having received anything but the promise of a kiss. To die for *her* seemed the most important thing in life. In 1760 I fell in love with a Vendramini, a woman of eighteen who was married to a Sagredo, one of the richest senators, a man of thirty who was crazy about his wife. My mistress and I were as innocent as two cherubim when *il sposo* surprised us talking of love. I was unarmed; his blow missed me; I leapt on him and strangled him with my two hands, wringing his neck like a chicken's. I wanted to go away with Bianca but she was unwilling to follow me. That's what women are like! I went away alone; I was found guilty and my possessions were confiscated in favour of my heirs. But I had taken away with me my diamonds, five rolled-up pictures by Titian, and all my gold. I went to Milan where I was left undisturbed. My case was of no interest to the State.'

'Just one little comment before I go on,' he said after a pause. 'Whether or not a woman's fancies influence her child while she is carrying him or when she conceives him, it is certain that, during her pregnancy, my mother had a passion for gold. I have a mania for gold which I feel such a need to satisfy that, whatever situation I have been in, I have never been without gold in my possession. I handle gold all the time. When I was young I always wore jewellery and I always had two or three hundred ducats on me.'

As he said these words, he pulled two ducats out of his pocket and showed them to me.

'I can sense gold. Although I am blind, I stop in front of jewellers' shops. This passion has ruined me. I became a gambler in order to play for gold. I was not a cheat and I was cheated and ruined. When my fortune was all gone, I was seized by a furious desire to see Bianca. I returned secretly to Venice, I found her again; for six months I was happy, hidden and kept by her. I thought with delight of ending my life in this way. She was courted by the Provedittore[2] who guessed he had a rival. In Italy they can sense these things. He spied on us and surprised us in bed, the coward! You can imagine how fiercely we fought. I didn't kill him but I wounded him severely. This adventure destroyed my happiness. Since that day, I have never found another Bianca. I have enjoyed great pleasures; I have lived at the court of Louis XV among the most celebrated women; nowhere have I found the virtues, the charms, the love of my adored Venetian. The Provedittore had his servants with him. He called them, they surrounded the palace and entered it. I defended myself so that I could die within sight of Bianca, who helped me to kill the Prove-dittore. She had earlier refused to escape with me, but after six months of happiness she wanted to die with me and was hit several times. I was wrapped in a large cloak that they flung round me, lifted into a gondola and taken away to an underground dungeon. I was twenty-two and I clung so tightly to the stump of my sword that to get it, they would have had to cut off my hand. By a strange chance, or rather

2. The Provedittore was an official of the Venetian Republic.

inspired by some instinct of self-preservation, I hid this iron object in a corner, as if it might be of some use to me. My wounds were dressed; none of them was mortal. At twenty-two one recovers from anything. I was to be beheaded; I pretended to be ill in order to gain time. I thought I was in a cell next to the canal; my plan was to escape by digging a hole under the wall and swimming across the canal, at the risk of being drowned. These were the calculations on which my hope was based. Every time the gaoler brought me food I read the signs written on the walls, such as "To the palace", "To the canal", "To the underground passage", and I finally discerned a plan, which did not worry me much, but which could be explained by the then unfinished state of the ducal palace. With the genius which the desire to recover one's liberty inspires, I managed, by feeling the surface of a stone with my finger tips, to decipher an Arabic inscription in which the man who had done the work informed his successors that he had dislodged two stones from the last row of masonry and dug eleven feet underground. To continue his work, one had to scatter the fragments of stone and mortar resulting from the excavation over the actual ground of the cell. Even if the gaolers and the inquisitors had not been reassured by the form of the building, which only needed to be guarded on the outside, the arrangement of the dungeons, to which you went down several steps, allowed the ground-level to be gradually raised, without the gaolers' noticing anything. This enormous labour had been wasted, at least for the unknown man who had undertaken it, for his failure to finish it proclaimed his death. If his efforts were not to be for ever wasted, a prisoner had to know Arabic, and I had studied oriental languages at the Armenian convent. A sentence written at the back of the stone told the fate of this unhappy man who had died a victim of his own immense wealth which Venice had coveted and seized. It took me a month's work to achieve anything. While I was working, and in the moments when I was overwhelmed by fatigue, I could hear the sound of gold, I could see gold in front of me, I was dazzled by diamonds. Now, I am coming to the point. One night, my blunted sword struck wood. I sharpened the stump and made a hole in this wood. In order to work, I crawled along on my belly like a snake, I stripped myself naked so that I could burrow like a mole with my hands in front, supporting myself on the rock itself. Two days before I was to appear before my judges, I determined to make one last effort during the night. I made a hole through the wood and my sword touched nothing on the other side. You can imagine how surprised I was when I put my eye to the hole. I was in the wooden panelling of a cellar where, by a dim light, I could see a pile of gold. The Doge and one of the ten were in this cellar; I could hear their voices. From their conversation I learned that here lay the secret treasure of the Republic, the gifts of the doges and the reserves of booty called "the pence of Venice", resulting from a tax on the spoils of expeditions. I was saved! When the gaoler came, I suggested to him that he should help me to escape and go away with me, taking with us as much as we could carry. It was a chance in a million; he accepted. A ship was about to set sail for the Levant, all precautions were taken and Bianca helped to organize the plan which I dictated to my accomplice. In order not to give the alarm, Bianca was to join us at Smyrna. In one night we enlarged the hole and we went down into the secret treasury of Venice. What a night it was! I saw four large casks full of gold. In the adjoining room silver was piled up in two equal piles; a path was left between them so that one could cross the room in which coins were banked up against the walls to a height of five feet. I thought the gaoler would go mad; he was singing, jumping, laughing, dancing about in the gold. I threatened to strangle him if he wasted time or made a noise. In his delight, he didn't at first see a table covered with diamonds. I pounced on it so skilfully that I filled my sailor's jacket and my trouser-pockets. My God! I didn't take a third of them. Under the table were gold ingots. I persuaded my companion to fill with gold as many sacks as we could carry, pointing out to him that it was the only way to avoid being discovered in a foreign country. "The pearls, the jewels, the diamonds would betray us," I told him. Despite our enormous greed, we could only take two thousand gold pounds, which required six journeys across the prison to the gondola. The sentinel at the water-gate had been bribed with a bag of ten gold pounds. As for the two gondoliers, they thought they were serving the Republic. At daybreak, we set off. When we were well out at sea and I recalled the night that had just passed, when I remembered the feelings I had experienced, and saw in my mind's eye that enormous treasure of which, according to my calculations, I was leaving behind thirty millions in silver and twenty millions in gold, several millions in diamonds, pearls and rubies. I became almost mad. I had gold-fever. We landed at Smyrna and re-embarked immediately for France. As we were boarding the French ship, God did me the favour of ridding me of my accomplice. At the time, I didn't think of all the consequences of this mishap; I rejoiced at it. We were so excited that we remained stunned, without saying a word to each other, waiting until we were in a place of safety to enjoy our riches at our ease. It is not surprising that the fellow went berserk. You will see how God has punished me. I didn't feel at ease until I had sold two thirds of my diamonds in London and Amsterdam, and turned my gold dust into commercial assets. For five years, I remained in hiding in Madrid. Then in 1770 I came to Paris, using a Spanish name, and lived in the most brilliant style. Bianca was dead. In the midst of my pleasures, when I was enjoying a fortune of six millions, I was struck with blindness. I have no doubt that this affliction was the result of my stay in prison and of my labours in the stone, unless my power of seeing gold constituted an abuse of the power of vision that predestined me to lose my sight. At the time, I was in love with a woman to whom I hoped to link my destiny. I had told her the secret of my name, she belonged to a powerful family and I had great hopes of the favour showed to me by Louis XV. I had put my trust in this woman who was a friend of Madame du Barry.[3] She advised me to consult a famous London oculist. But after a stay of some months in London, she deserted me in Hyde Park, having robbed me of all my fortune and leaving me without resources.

3. Madame du Barry was the favourite of Louis XV.

Since I was obliged to conceal my name which it would have exposed me to the vengeance of Venice, I could ask no one's help. I was afraid of Venice. Spies which this woman had attached to my person exploited my infirmity. I spare you the recital of adventures worthy of Gil Blas. Your Revolution came. I was forced to go into the Quinze-Vingts where this creature got me admitted after having had me detained for two years at Bicêtre as a madman. I have never been able to kill her; I couldn't see to do it and I was too poor to pay another to do it for me. If, before losing Benedetto Carpi, my gaoler, I had consulted him about the situation of my cell, I would have been able to find the treasure again and go back to Venice when the Republic was destroyed by Napoleon. However, in spite of my blindness, let us go to Venice! I shall find the door of the prison again. I shall see the gold through the walls, I shall sense it under the waters where it lies buried, for the events which overthrew the power of Venice were such that the secret of this treasure must have died with Vendramino, Bianca's brother. He was a doge who, I hoped, would have made my peace with the ten. I wrote to the First Consul, I proposed an agreement with the Emperor of Austria, they all dismissed me as a madman. Come, let us set off for Venice. We shall start out beggars, we shall come back millionaires. We shall buy back my property and you will be my heir, you will be Prince of Varese.'

I was staggered by this confidence, which in my imagination assumed the proportions of a poem, and looking at that white head in front of the black water of the moat of the Bastille, water as still as the canals of Venice, I made no reply. Facino Cane presumably thought that, like all the others, I judged him with a contemptuous pity. He expressed in a gesture the whole philosophy of despair. Perhaps this tale had taken him back to his happy days in Venice. He gripped his clarinet and played a melancholy Venetian song, a barcarolle, with all the talent he used to have when he was a nobleman in love. It was rather like the '*Super flumina Babylonis*'.[4] My eyes filled with

4. Psalm 137, 'By the waters of Babylon (we sat down and wept)', the lament of the Jews in exile in Babylon.

tears. If a few belated strollers happened to wander along the Boulevard Bourdon, they probably stopped to listen to this exile's last prayer, the last regret for a lost name, mingled with the memory of Bianca. But gold soon got the upper hand again, and the fatal passion quenched that glimmer of youth.

'That treasure,' he said, 'I can see it all the time, when I'm awake and in my dreams. I walk about amongst it; the diamonds gleam, I am not as blind as you think. The gold and the diamonds light up my darkness, the darkness of the last Facino Cane, for my title goes to the Memmi. Good God, the murderer's punishment has begun without delay! *Ave Maria.*'

He recited some prayers which I could not hear.

'We shall go to Venice,' I exclaimed as he got up.

'Then I have found a man, at last,' he cried, his face flushed with excitement.

I gave him my arm and led him back. He shook my hand at the door of the Quinze-Vingts, just as some of the people from the wedding were going home, shouting at the tops of their voices.

'Shall we set off tomorrow?' asked the old man.

'As soon as we have some money.'

'But we can go on foot. I shall ask for alms ... I am sturdy and when a man sees gold before him, he is young.'

Facino Cane died during the winter, having lingered for two months. The poor man had caught a chill.

1836

Pierre Grassou

EVERY time that you have gone, with serious intent, to the annual exhibition of painting and sculpture as it has been held since the 1830 Revolution, have you not been overcome by feelings of distress, boredom and sadness at the sight of the long, crowded galleries? There has been no real Salon since 1830. For a second time the Louvre has been taken by storm; this time by the crowd of artists who have maintained their position there. Formerly, by showing the very best works of art, the Salon carried off the greatest honours for the works which were shown there. Among the two hundred chosen pictures, the public would make a further choice; unknown hands would award a prize to a masterpiece. Passionate discussions would arise about a canvas. The insults lavished on Delacroix and Ingres served their fame no less well than the praise and the fanaticism of their partisans. Today neither the crowd nor professional art critics get excited about the products on show at this bazaar. They have to make the choice which formerly the examining jury used to make and their attention flags at the task. And by the time they have finished choosing, the Exhibition is about to close. Before 1817, the pictures accepted never occupied more space than the first two rows of the long gallery where the old masters are, but that year they filled the whole of that space, to the public's great astonishment. Historical painting, genre painting, easel painting, landscapes, flowers, animals, and water colours – these seven categories could not offer more than twenty pictures worthy of being looked at by the public who cannot take in a large number of works. As the number of artists got bigger and bigger the selection committee ought to have become more and more difficult to please. Once the Salon overflowed into the main gallery, everything was lost. The Salon ought to have remained a fixed, limited place, of inflexible proportions, in which every genre would have exhibited its masterpieces. Ten years' experience has shown how good the old system was. Instead of a tournament, you have a riot; instead of a magnificent exhibition, you have a rowdy bazaar; instead of selected pictures, you have everything. What is the result? The great artist is the loser. If Decamp's *Café Turc, Enfants à la fontaine, Supplice des crochets,* and *Joseph* had all four been exhibited in the big Salon alongside the hundred good pictures painted this year, they would have done his reputation more good than his twenty canvases lost amongst three thousand works, indiscriminately hung in six galleries. It is a strange fact that, since the door was opened to everyone, there has been much talk of unrecognized geniuses. When, twelve years earlier, Ingres' *La Courtisane* and that of Sigalon, Géricault's *Méduse,* Delacroix's *Le Massacre de Scio* and Eugène Deveria's *Baptême d'Henri IV* were admitted to the Salon by famous artists accused of jealousy, they showed the world, in spite of denials by the critics, that there existed young enthusiastic painters; then no one complained. Nowadays any dauber of canvas can send in his work and there is talk only of misunderstood painters. Where judgement is no longer exercised there is no longer any picture judged to be best. Whatever artists may do, they will come back to the scrutiny which recommends their paintings to the admiration of the multitude for whom they work. Without the Academy's choice the Salon will cease to exist, and without the Salon art may perish.

Since the catalogue became a fat book, there are many names in it which remain obscure, despite the ten or twelve pictures which are listed under them. Amongst these names, perhaps the least well-known is that of an artist called Pierre Grassou, who comes from Fougères and who, in the world of artists, is called Fougères for short. Today, he is very much in the limelight and has occasioned the bitter reflections with which this outline of his life begins – a life similar to that of some other members of the Tribe of Artists. In 1832, Fougères lived in the Rue de Navarin, on the fourth floor of one of those narrow, tall houses which look like the Luxor obelisk, have a passage-way, a dark, dangerous, winding staircase and not more than three windows on each floor; within they have a courtyard, or to be more precise, a square well. Above the three or four rooms of the flat occupied by Grassou de Fougères was his studio, which looked out on to Montmartre. The studio was painted brick colour, the polished floor was carefully stained brown, each chair had a little bordered mat and the couch, though simple, was as neat as if it were in the bedroom of a grocer's wife. The whole place indicated the meticulous way of life of a small-minded man and the carefulness of a poor one. There was a chest of drawers in which to put away the studio materials, a dining table, a sideboard, a desk and, finally, the tools which a painter needs all tidily arranged. The stove fitted appropriately into this system of Dutch carefulness which could be seen all the more clearly as the pure, unchanging light from the north filled the enormous room with its clear, cold brightness. Fougères, a simple genre painter, doesn't need those enormous appliances which ruin historical painters. He never thought himself gifted enough to tackle a large mural and restricted himself to work on an easel.

In the month of December, the Parisian bourgeois conceive the strange idea of immortalizing their faces (though there is already a bit too much of them). In the beginning of December of the year in question, Pierre Grassou, having got up early, was preparing his palette, lighting his stove, eating a roll dipped in milk, and waiting for the frost on his window panes to thaw so that the light could come through and he could start work. It was a fine, dry day. The artist was eating, with that patient and resigned look which reveals so much, when he recognized the step of a man who had influenced his life in the way in which this kind of person influences the lives of nearly all artists. It was Elias Magus, an art-dealer and speculator in canvases. He took the painter by surprise, just as he was going to start work in his clean and tidy studio.

'How are you, you old rogue?' asked the painter.

Fougères had been made a Chevalier of the Legion of Honour and as Elias used to buy his pictures for two or three hundred francs, he put on airs of being very much the artist.

'Business is bad,' answered Elias. 'You all ask for so much. Nowadays you talk of two hundred francs as soon as you have put six sous worth of paint on a canvas . . . But you are a good fellow, you are! You are a well-organized man and I have come to bring you a good deal.'

'*Timeo Danaos et dona ferentes*,' said Fougères. 'Do you know Latin?'

'No.'

'Well, that means that the Greeks don't make good business suggestions to the Trojans without making something out of it themselves. In the past, they used to say, "Take my horse," today we say, "Take my bear . . ." What do you want, Ulysses-Langeingeole-Elias Magus?'[1]

These words show the gentleness and wit with which Fougères used what the painters call the studio approach.

'I am not saying that you won't do two pictures for me for nothing.'

'Oh! Oh!'

'I leave you to decide; I am not asking for them. You are an honest artist.'

'Come to the point!'

'Well, I am going to bring you a father, a mother and an only daughter.'

'Each one is an only!'

'Certainly, yes! . . . and all with portraits to be painted. These bourgeois are crazy about the arts, and they have never dared venture into a studio. The girl has a dowry of a hundred thousand francs. You might well paint these people. For you perhaps they will be family portraits.'

The old German wood-carving who passes for a man and is called Elias Magus, interrupted himself with a dry laugh which frightened the painter. It was as if Mephistopheles was suggesting marriage.

1. In *L'Ours et le Pacha*, a play of 1820 by Scribe and Xavier, Marécot tries to replace the pasha's lost white bear. Laringeole (Balzac misremembers the name as Langeingeole) immediately offers him a black one, saying, 'Take my bear!'

'The portraits will be paid five hundred francs each. You can do three pictures for me.'

'Sure!' said Fougères laughingly.

'And if you marry the girl, you won't forget me.'

'Me, get married!' exclaimed Pierre Grassou. '*I* am used to going to bed quite alone, and to getting up early. *I* have my life all organized . . .'

'A hundred thousand francs,' said Magus, 'and a sweet girl with hair full of gold tints like a real Titian.'

'What do these people do?'

'They used to be business people. For the moment, they love the arts, have a country house at Ville d'Avray, and an income of ten or twelve thousand livres a year.'

'What was their business?'

'Bottles.'

'Don't say that. It makes me think I can hear corks being cut and my teeth are set on edge.'

'Shall I bring them?'

'Three portraits. I'll exhibit them in the Salon. I shall be able to make a career in portraits. All right, yes . . .'

Old Elias went downstairs to fetch the Vervelle family. In order to appreciate how this proposal was going to influence the painter and what impression my lord and lady Vervelle accompanied by their only daughter were to make on him, we must glance back at the past life of Pierre Grassou de Fougères.

As a pupil, Fougères had studied drawing in the studio of Servin who, in the academic world, was considered to be a great draughtsman. After that, he went to Schinner to discover the secrets of the powerful, magnificent colouring which is the mark of that master painter. Both the master and his pupils had been discreet. Pierre had found out nothing there. From there, Fougères had gone on to Sommervieux's studio, to acquaint himself with that branch of his art called Composition. But Composition was shy and did not reveal herself to him. Then he had tried to grasp the mysteries of the light and shade of their Interiors from Granet and Drolling. These two masters gave away nothing. Finally, Fougères had finished his education with Duval Lecamus. During these studies in these different environments, Fougères lived in a quiet and orderly manner which was laughed at in the different studios where he worked, but everywhere his fellow-students were disarmed by his modesty, and by his lamb-like patience and gentleness. The master-painters had no sympathy for this worthy fellow. The masters like the brilliant pupils, the unusual minds, or the witty, the passionate, the gloomy and deeply thoughtful ones who show signs of future talent. Everything about Fougères proclaimed his mediocrity. His surname of Fougères (that of the painter in d'Eglantine's play) occasioned many insulting remarks. But, by the force of circumstances, he accepted the name of the town where he had first seen the light.

Grassou de Fougères looked like his name. Plump (*gras-souillet*) and of medium build, he had an insipid complexion, brown eyes, black hair, a turned-up nose, a fairly wide mouth and long ears. These main features of his healthy, but inexpressive, countenance were not enhanced by his gentle, passive and resigned look. He was obviously not tormented by that superabundant vitality, by that violent intellectual activity, nor by that comic verve which is the mark of the great artist. This young man, born to be a virtuous bourgeois, had come from his province to be a clerk at a shop, selling painters' materials. He came from Mayenne, was a distant relative of the d'Orgemont, and it was Breton obstinacy that made him set himself up as a painter. What he suffered, how he lived during his student days, God alone knows. He suffered as much as great men suffer when they are harassed by poverty and hunted like wild beasts by the pack of mediocrities and the troop of Vanities, thirsting for vengeance. As soon as he thought he was strong enough to fly with his own wings, Fougères took a studio at the top of the Rue des Martyrs where he began to slog away. He made his debut in 1819. The first picture that he offered to the Selection Committee for the Louvre Exhibition represented a village wedding and it was quite painstakingly copied from Greuze's picture. The canvas was refused. When Fougères learned of the fateful decision, he did not fall into one of those rages, or one of those epileptic fits of *amour propre* to which vainglorious spirits are prone and which sometimes end with the sending of a challenge to the director or the secretary of the art gallery or with threats of murder. Fougères quietly picked up his canvas, wrapped it in his handkerchief, and took it back to his studio, vowing to himself that he would become a great painter. He put his canvas on his easel and went to his old teacher Schinner, a man of enormous talent, a gentle and patient artist who had been completely successful at the last Salon. Grassou asked him to come and criticize the rejected work. The great painter left everything and came. Poor Fougères set him in front of the work and, after the first glance, Schinner shook Fougères' hand.

'You are a good fellow, you have a heart of gold, I must not deceive you. You have turned out exactly according to the promise you showed at the studio. When that's the sort of thing that comes off your brush, my good Fougères, you would do better to leave your paints at Brullon's shop and not make off with canvas that can be used by others. Go home early, put on a night-cap, go to bed at nine o'clock. In the morning, at ten o'clock go to an office and ask for a job, and leave the Arts.'

'My good friend,' said Fougères, 'my canvas has already been condemned and it is not a judgement that I am asking for but the reasons for it.'

'Well, you make it grey and dark; you see Nature through a mourning veil. Your draughtsmanship is heavy and slovenly. Your composition is a copy of Greuze who made up for his faults only by the virtues which you lack.'

As he indicated the picture's faults, Schinner saw such a profound expression of sadness on Fougères' face that he took him off to dinner and tried to console him. The next day, from teven in the morning, Fougères was at his easel, working over the condemned picture. He heightened the colour; he made the corrections suggested by Schinner; he put more paint on the faces. Then, having had enough of patching up, he took the picture to Elias Magus. Elias Magus, a kind of Dutch-Belgian-Fleming, had three reasons for becoming a miser, and a rich one at that. Originally from Bordeaux, he was at that time setting up business in Paris, dealt in second-hand pictures and lived on the Boulevard Bonne-Nouvelle. Fougères, who needed the proceeds of his palette to enable him to go to the baker's, dauntlessly ate bread and nuts, or bread and milk, or bread and cherries, or bread and cheese, according to the season. Elias Magus, to whom Pierre offered his first canvas, looked it over for a long time; he gave him fifteen francs for it.

'With receipts of fifteen francs a year and expenses of a thousand francs,' said Fougères smiling, 'one can get on fast and go far.'

Elias Magus raised his arms and bit his thumbs, thinking that he might have had the picture for a hundred sous. For some days, Fougères went down the Rue des Martyrs every morning, hid in the crowd on the boulevard opposite where Magus' shop was, and directed his gaze at his picture which did not attract the attention of the passers-by. Towards the end of the week the picture disappeared. Fougères went back up the boulevard and made his way to the second-hand dealer's shop; he looked as if he were out for a stroll. The Jew was at his door.

'Well, have you sold my picture?'

'Here it is,' said Magus. 'I am putting a frame on it so that I can offer it to someone who thinks he knows something about painting.'

Fougères didn't dare to go back to the boulevard again. He set to work on a new picture. He spent two months at it, eating like a mouse and working like a galley-slave.

One evening he went as far as the boulevard. His feet took him inevitably right up to Magus' shop. He could not see his picture anywhere.

'I have sold your picture,' the dealer said to the artist.

'For how much?'

'I have got back what I spent on it with a little interest. Paint interiors for me, an anatomy lesson, a landscape; I'll pay for them,' said Elias.

Fougères could have hugged Magus; he looked on him as

a father. He went home delighted. So the great painter Schinner was wrong! In the huge town of Paris, there were hearts which beat in time with Grassou's; his talent was understood and appreciated. The poor fellow at the age of twenty-seven was as innocent as a boy of sixteen. Another man, one of those suspicious, aggressive artists, would have noticed Elias Magus' diabolical expression; he would have observed the twitching of the hairs of his beard, the ironic curve of his moustache, the movement of his shoulders which revealed the satisfaction of Walter Scott's Jew tricking a Christian. Fougères went for a walk on the boulevards bathed in a happiness which gave a proud expression to his face. He looked like a schoolboy who is going with a girl. He met Joseph Bridau, one of his fellow-artists, one of those eccentric talents destined for fame and misfortune. Joseph Bridau, who, as he put it, had a few sous in his pocket, took Fougères to the Opéra. Fougères didn't see the ballet, he didn't hear the music; he was having ideas for pictures, he was painting. He left Joseph in the middle of the evening; he ran home to make sketches by lamp-light. He thought up thirty pictures based on memories of paintings; he believed he was a genius. The very next day, he bought paints and canvases of various sizes. He put bread and cheese on his table, he put water in a jug, he got in wood for his store. Then, as they say in the studios, he slogged away at his pictures. He had a few models and Magus lent him materials. After two months of seclusion, the Breton had completed four pictures. He again asked Schinner's advice, and Joseph Bridau's as well. The two painters saw in these canvases a servile imitation of Dutch landscapes and of Metzu's interiors; in the fourth they saw a copy of Rembrandt's *Anatomy Lesson*.

'Still imitations,' said Schinner. 'Fougères finds it difficult to be original.'

'You ought to do something other than painting,' said Bridau.

'What?' asked Fougères.

'Throw yourself into literature.'

Fougères bent his head like a sheep when it rains. Then he

asked for and received useful advice, and touched up his pictures before taking them to Elias. Elias paid twenty-five francs for each canvas. At this price, Fougères made no profit, but he lost nothing, since he lived so abstemiously. He went for a few walks to see what had become of his pictures and had a strange hallucination. His canvases, which had been painted so clearly and which had the firmness of sheet-iron and the gleam of paintings on porcelain, were, as it were, covered with a fog; they looked like old pictures. Elias had just gone out. Fougères could get no information about this pheno-menon. He thought that he hadn't seen properly. The painter went back to his studio to make some new, old canvases. After seven years of steady work Fougères succeeded in com-posing and painting tolerable pictures. He did as well as most second-rate artists. Elias bought and sold all the pictures of the poor Breton who earned laboriously about a hundred louis a year and didn't spend more than twelve hundred francs.

At the Exhibition of 1829, Léon de Lora, Schinner and Bridau, who all three occupied important positions and were in the van of progress in the Arts, were filled with pity for the persistence and poverty of their old friend and so they had a picture by Fougères admitted to the Exhibition in the big Salon. This picture, on a powerful theme, resembled Vigneron in its feeling and was like the early work of Dubufe in its execution. It represented a young man in prison whose hair was being shaved at the nape of his neck. On one side was a priest, on the other an old woman and a young woman in tears. A clerk was reading an official document. On a rickety table could be seen a meal which no one had touched. The daylight came through the bars of a high window. The theme was enough to make the bourgeois tremble and the bourgeois trembled. Fougères had quite plainly been inspired by Gérard Dow's masterpiece; he had turned the group of the *Dropsical Woman* towards the window instead of showing its front view. He had put the condemned man in the place of the dying woman; there was the same pallor, the same look, the same appeal to God. Instead of the Flemish doctor he had painted the cold official figure of the clerk clothed in black, but he had put an old woman beside Gérard Dow's young girl. And, finally, the cruelly good-natured face of the executioner dominated the group. This cleverly disguised plagiarism was not recognized.

The catalogue contained the following:

510. GRASSOU DE FOUGÈRES (Pierre), rue de Navarin, 2. *The Toilette of a Chouan,*[2] *Condemned to Death in 1809.*

Although it was not very good, this picture had an enormous success for it reminded people of the affair of the *chauffeurs de Mortagne.*[3] Every day a crowd formed in front of the fashionable canvas and Charles X stopped in front of it. MADAME,[4] who had heard about the poor Breton's patient existence, became enthusiastic about him. The Duke of Orleans discussed the price of the canvas. The clergy told Madame la Dauphine that the subject was full of the right kind of thoughts; it had indeed a satisfactorily religious atmosphere. Monseigneur le Dauphin admired the dust on the window-panes – a very serious mistake, for Fougères had painted here and there greenish tints which showed there was damp at the foot of the walls. MADAME bought the picture for a thousand francs and the Dauphin ordered another. Charles X gave the Cross to the peasant's son who had fought for the royal cause in 1799. Joseph Bridau, the great painter, did not receive a decoration. The Minister of the Interior ordered two church pictures from Fougères. This Salon was for Pierre his whole fortune, his reputation, his future, his life. To invent anything is to want to die a slow death; to copy is to live. Having at last discovered a gold-mine, Grassou de Fougères adhered to the party of that cruel maxim, to which society owes the

2. A chouan was a royalist insurgent from Western France who engaged in guerilla warfare against the Revolution.

3. The name *chauffeurs* was given to royalist rebels in the west of France who burned the soles of their victims' feet to make them reveal the whereabouts of their money. In *L'Envers de l'histoire contemporaine*, Balzac tells the story of a group of royalist rebels, who in 1809, seized a large sum of government money at Mortagne and were then betrayed to the police by one of their number.

4. MADAME was the title given to the Duchesse de Berry, daughter-in-law of Charles X.

terrible mediocrities that, today, are supposed to elect the superior people in all social classes but who, naturally, elect each other and wage a bitter war against the real men of talent. The election principle when applied to everything is false; France will think better of it. But the modesty, simplicity and surprise of the kind, gentle Fougères silenced envy and recriminations. Moreover, he had on his side the successful Grassous who made common cause with the Grassous who had their way to make. Some people, touched by the persistence of a man whom nothing had discouraged, spoke of Domenichino and said, 'Determination in the Arts must be rewarded. Grassou hasn't stolen his success. He's been slogging away for ten years, poor fellow.' This exclamation of 'poor fellow!' constituted half of the statements of support and congratulations which the painter received. Pity raises up as many mediocrities as envy drags down great artists. The newspapers had not spared their criticisms but Fougères, Chevalier of the Legion of Honour, swallowed them, as he had swallowed his friends' advice, with an angelic patience. Now that he was rich with about fifteen thousand hard-earned francs, he furnished his flat and studio in the Rue de Navarin. There he painted the picture which Monseigneur le Dauphin had asked for and the two church pictures ordered by the Minister. He delivered them on the appointed day with an exactitude quite disconcerting for the Minister's finance department which was used to other ways. But marvel at the good fortune of orderly people! If he had delayed, Grassou would have been caught by the July Revolution and would not have been paid. By the time he was thirty-seven Fougères had manufactured for Elias Magus about two hundred pictures which remained completely unknown but which had helped him to reach that satisfying style, that peak of execution which makes the artist shrug his shoulders and which the bourgeoisie loves. Fougères was beloved by his friends for his uprightness, his reliability, his constant readiness to oblige, and his great loyalty. If they had no esteem for his palette, they loved the man who held it. 'What a pity that Fougères has the vice of painting,' his friends said to each other. Nevertheless, he could give excellent advice, like those journalists who are incapable of writing a book yet know very well what is wrong with books. But there was a difference between Fougères and the literary critics; he was fully aware of the beauties of a painting, he recognized them and his advice bore the stamp of a feeling for justice which made people acknowledge the aptness of his comments. After the July Revolution, Fougères submitted about ten pictures to every exhibition; of these the Committee accepted four or five. He lived with the strictest economy and his only servant was a cleaning woman. His only amusements were visiting friends, and going to see works of art, though he allowed himself a few little expeditions in France and planned a journey to Switzerland in search of inspiration. This execrable artist was an excellent citizen. He did his duty in the National Guard, went to the military reviews, and paid his rent and his bills as punctiliously as any bourgeois. Living as he had done, working hard and in poverty, he had never had the time to be in love. Until then he had been a bachelor and poor and wasn't inclined to complicate his very simple existence. As he couldn't think up a way of increasing his fortune, he took his savings and his earnings every quarter to his lawyer, Cardot. When the lawyer had a thousand crowns of Grassou's, he invested them in a mortgage with entitlement to reimbursement in preference to the borrower's wife (if the borrower were married) or in preference to other creditors, if the borrower had to complete a purchase. The lawyer himself received the interest and added it to the investments made by Grassou de Fougères. The painter was waiting for the happy moment when his mortgages would bring him an income of the imposing figure of two thousand francs so that he would have the *otium cum dignitate* of the artist and paint pictures, oh but pictures! real pictures at last! absolutely dandy, super, completed pictures. His future, his dreams of happiness, his ultimate hopes, do you want to know what they were? They were to become a member of the Institute, and to have the rosette of the Officers of the Legion of Honour. They were to sit beside Schinner and Léon de Lora, to reach the Academy before Bridau, to have a

rosette in his button-hole! What a dream! It is only mediocrities who think of everything.

When he heard the sound of several footsteps on the stair,
Fougères straightened his hair, fastened his bottle-green jacket
and was not a little surprised to see coming in a face of the
kind that in artists' studios is colloquially called a *melon*. This
fruit was mounted on a pumpkin, clad in blue cloth decorated
with a bundle of tinkling watch-seals. The melon was puffing
like a porpoise, the pumpkin was walking on turnips, im-
properly called legs. A real artist would have caricatured the
little bottle merchant in this way and would have immediately
shown him the door, saying that he didn't paint vegetables.
Fougères looked at the customer without laughing, for Monsieur Vervelle sported on his shirt a diamond worth a thousand
crowns.

Fougères looked at Magus and said: 'That's a juicy morsel,'
using a slang expression, then fashionable in the studios.

When he heard these words, Monsieur Vervelle frowned.
The bourgeois brought in his train another mixture of vegetables in the persons of his wife and daughter. The wife looked
as if her face was covered with mahogany stain; she was like
a coconut with a head on top and a belt round the middle. She
swivelled round on her feet and she wore a black-striped,
yellow dress. On her podgy hands she proudly displayed enormous gloves like the gauntlets on a shop-sign. Feathers like
those on horses at a first-class funeral waved on her over-
flowing hat. Her shoulders, decorated with lace, were as
rounded behind as they were in front, and so the spherical
shape of the coconut was perfect. Her feet, of the kind painters
call *abatis*, were embellished by half-inch rolls of fat above the
polished leather of her shoes. How did her feet get into them?
No one knows.

There followed a young asparagus in a green and yellow
dress. She had a little head surmounted by hair parted in the
middle, and of a carroty-yellow that a Roman would have loved,
skinny arms, freckles on quite a white skin, large innocent
eyes with white eyelashes, not much eyebrow, an Italian straw
hat with two passable satin bows edged in white, an innocent

girl's red hands and her mother's feet. As they looked at the studio, these three beings had a happy look which proclaimed a respectable enthusiasm for the arts.

'And it's you, Monsieur, who are going to print our likenesses?' said the father putting on a rather jaunty manner.

'Yes, Monsieur,' replied Grassou.

'Vervelle, he has been decorated with the Cross of the Legion of Honour,' said the wife under her breath to her husband, while the painter had his back turned.

'Would I have had our portraits painted by an artist who had not been given a decoration?' said the former bottle-cork dealer.

Elias Magus bowed to the Vervelle family and went out; Grassou went with him as far as the landing.

'Only *you* would fish up heads like that.'

'A dowry of one hundred thousand francs!'

'Yes, but what a family!'

'Three hundred thousand francs to look forward to, a house in the Rue Boucherat and a country house at Ville d'Avray.'

'Boucherat, bottles, bottle corks, bottles corked, bottles uncorked,' said the painter.

'You will be safe from want for the rest of your days,' said Elias.

This idea entered Pierre Grassou's head, as the morning light had irrupted into his attic. As he arranged the young lady's father, he thought his appearance was good and he admired the strong colours of the face. The mother and daughter hovered around the painter, marvelling at all his preparations. He seemed like a god to them. Fougères liked this obvious adoration. The golden calf cast its dazzling reflections on the whole family.

'I expect you earn bags of money, and spend it as you earn it,' said the mother.

'No, Madame,' replied the painter. 'I don't spend it. I can't afford entertainments. My lawyer invests my money. He knows how much I have. Once he has the money, I think no more about it.'

'*I* was told,' exclaimed the father, 'that artists are all spend-thrifts.'

'Who is your lawyer, if you don't mind my asking?' asked Madame Vervelle.

'A good fellow, very reliable, Cardot.'

'Well, well, isn't that funny!' said Vervelle. 'Cardot is our lawyer, too.'

'Keep still!' said the painter.

'Don't move, Anténor,' said his wife. 'You'll make Monsieur go wrong; if you saw him working you would understand . . .'

'Oh dear, why didn't you teach me Art?' said Mademoiselle Vervelle to her parents.

'Virginie,' said her mother, 'there are some things a young girl ought not to learn. When you are married . . . oh well, but till then, don't be inquisitive.'

During this first sitting the Vervelle family almost ceased to stand on ceremony with the honest artist. They were to come back two days later. As they left, the parents told Virginie to go on in front of them, but in spite of the distance she heard these words whose meaning was bound to arouse her curiosity.

'A man with a decoration . . . thirty-seven years old . . . an artist whose order-book is full, who invests his money with our lawyer. Shall we consult Cardot? Fancy being called Madame de Fougères! . . . He doesn't look a bad fellow! . . . What would you say to a businessman? . . . But until a businessman has retired you don't know what will become of your daughter, while an economical artist . . . and then we like the Arts . . . That settles it! . . .'

While the Vervelle family was thinking about him, Pierre Grassou was thinking about the Vervelle family. He found it impossible to stay quietly in his studio. He went for a walk on the boulevard and looked at the red-haired women who passed by. He reasoned in the strangest way: gold was the most beautiful of the metals, the colour yellow represented gold, the Romans liked red-headed women and he had become a Roman, etc. After two years of marriage, what man bothers about his wife's colouring? Beauty passes ... but ugliness remains! Money is half of happiness. In the evening when he went to bed, the painter already thought Virginie Vervelle charming.

When the three Vervelles came in on the day of the second sitting, the artist welcomed them with a friendly smile. The rascal had trimmed his beard and he had put on a white shirt. He had arranged his hair becomingly and he had chosen a pair of trousers which made the best of his figure and red slippers with turned-up ends. The family replied with a smile which was as flattering as the artist's, while Virginie turned as red as her hair, lowered her eyes and turned her head away as she looked at the sketches. Pierre Grassou thought these simpering little ways charming. Virginie was graceful. Fortunately she took after neither her father nor her mother. But whom did she take after?

'Ah, I've got it,' he said to himself. 'The mother will have been affected by the sight of gold as she conducted her business.'

During the sitting, there were skirmishes between the family and the painter, who boldly declared that Père Vervelle was witty. Thanks to this flattery, the family galloped into the artist's heart; he gave one of his drawings to Virginie and a sketch to her mother.

'For nothing?' they asked.

Pierre Grassou could not repress a smile.

'You mustn't give away your pictures like this, they're worth money,' said Vervelle.

At the third sitting, Père Vervelle talked of a fine picture gallery which he had in his country house at Ville d'Avray. It contained Rubens, Gérard Dows, Mieris, Terburgs, Rembrandts, a Titian, Paul Potters, etc.

'Monsieur Vervelle has been wildly extravagant,' said Madame Vervelle ostentatiously. 'He has a hundred thousand francs worth of pictures.'

'I like the Arts,' added the former bottle merchant.

By the time Madame Vervelle's portrait had been begun, her husband's was almost finished and the family's enthusiasm knew no bounds. The lawyer had been full of praise for the painter. In his eyes, Pierre Grassou was the most honest lad under the sun, one of the most orderly of artists who had, moreover, saved up thirty-six thousand francs. His days of poverty were over, he was increasing his savings by ten thousand francs a year, adding the interest to the capital, and finally, he was incapable of making a woman unhappy. This last opinion weighed enormously in the balance. The Vervelles' friends heard talk of nothing but the famous Fougères. The day Fougères started on Virginie's portrait, he was already *in petto* the Vervelle family's son-in-law. The three Vervelles flourished in this studio which they got used to thinking of as one of their residences. There was an inexplicable attraction for them in this clean, tidy, pleasant place belonging to an artist. *Abyssus Abyssum*, bourgeois attracts bourgeois. Towards the end of the sitting, there was a noise on the staircase, the door was roughly thrown open and, lo and behold, Joseph Bridau! He was in a great state, his hair flying, his large face distraught. His glances flashed all over the studio, he walked right round it and came abruptly back to Grassou, gathering his frock-coat over his gastric regions and trying, without success, to button it up, for the button had escaped from its cloth covering.

'Wood is dear,' he said to Grassou.

'Oh!'

'The bailiffs are after me. What, you paint those things?'

'Be quiet!'

'Oh, yes!'

The Vervelle family, extremely shocked by this strange apparition, turned from its ordinary red to the cherry red of a violent flame.

'That brings in the goods!' replied Joseph. 'Have you any cash on you?'

'Do you need much?'

'A five hundred franc note . . . I've got one of those shop-keepers like a bulldog after me – the kind that, once they have their teeth into you, never let go till they've got you. What a tribe!'

'I'll give you a note for my lawyer.'

'So you've got a lawyer?'

'Yes.'

'That explains then why you still paint pink cheeks; they are excellent for advertisements for cosmetics!'

Grassou could not suppress a blush. Virginie was sitting for him.

'Tackle Nature as it is,' continued the great painter. 'Mademoiselle is a red-head. Well, is that a mortal sin? In painting everything is magnificent. Put some vermilion on your palette, warm up those cheeks, dot in their little brown marks, lay it on! Do you want to do better than Nature?'

'Look here,' said Fougères, 'take my place while I go and write a note.'

Vervelle rolled up to the table and whispered in Grassou's ear.

'But that yokel will spoil it all,' he said.

'If he were willing to paint your Virginie's portrait, it would be worth a thousand times more than mine,' replied Fougères indignantly.

When he heard this, the bourgeois gently retreated to his wife who was struck dumb by the wild animal's intrusion and was very little reassured by seeing him cooperate in painting her daughter's portrait.

'Here you are, continue on these lines,' said Bridau giving back the palette and taking the note. 'I don't say thank you! Now I can go back to d'Arthez' country house where I am doing paintings for his dining-room and Léon de Lora is doing masterpieces for the overdoors. Come and see us!'

He went away without a farewell bow; he had had more than enough of looking at Virginie.

'Who is that man?' asked Madame Vervelle.

'A great artist,' replied Grassou.

There was a moment's silence.

'Are you quite sure that he hasn't spoiled my portrait?' said Virginie. 'He frightened me.'

'He has done it nothing but good,' replied Grassou.

'If he is a great artist, I prefer a great artist who is like you,' said Madame Vervelle.

'Oh, Mamma, Monsieur is a much greater painter. He will paint me full length,' remarked Virginie.

The ways of Genius had scared these tidy-minded bourgeois.

The phase of autumn, so pleasantly known as Saint Martin's summer, was just beginning. It was with the timidity of a neophyte in the presence of a genius that Vervelle took the bold step of inviting Grassou to come to his country house the following Sunday. He knew how few attractions a bourgeois family could offer an artist.

'You artists,' he said, 'you want excitement, wonderful sights and witty company. But there will be good wines and I am counting on my picture gallery to compensate you for the boredom which an artist like you might feel in the company of business people.'

This hero-worship, which flattered nothing but his vanity, won the heart of Pierre Grassou, who was little used to such compliments. The honest artist, this unspeakable mediocrity, this heart of gold, this loyal soul, this stupid draughtsman, this good fellow decorated with the royal Order of the Legion of Honour, dressed himself in battle array to go and enjoy the last fine hours of the year at Ville d'Avray. The painter travelled modestly by public transport and could not but admire the bottle merchant's beautiful country house placed in the middle of a five-acre park, at the top of Ville d'Avray where the view was at its best. To marry Virginie would be to own this beautiful house one day! He was received by the Vervelles with an enthusiasm, a joy, a good-nature an honest bourgeois obtuseness, which staggered him. It was a day of triumph. The future husband was shown round the sand-coloured garden paths which had been raked as if for a great man's visit. Even the trees looked as if they had been carefully combed and the lawns had been mowed. The pure country air wafted absolutely delightful smells from the kitchen. Indoors, everyone was saying, 'We have a great artist visiting.' Little Père Vervelle rolled about his big garden like an apple, the daughter undulated like an eel, and the mother brought up the rear with a noble and stately step. For seven hours

these three beings clung on to Grassou. After the dinner,
which was as sumptuous as it was long, Monsieur and Madame
Vervelle came to their great surprise; they opened the picture
gallery which was lit by lamps with special lighting effects.
Three neighbours, retired shopkeepers, an uncle with money
to leave who had been invited to do honour to the great artist,
a maiden aunt of the Vervelle family and all the dinner guests
followed Grassou into the gallery, eager to have his opinion
on little Père Vervelle's picture gallery, for he continually
wearied them with the enormous value of his pictures. It
looked as if the bottle merchant had wanted to rival Louis-
Philippe's redecoration of Versailles. The magnificently framed
pictures were labelled in black letters on a gold background:

RUBENS
Dance of Nymphs and Fauns

REMBRANDT
Interior of a Dissecting Room:
Doctor Tromp Demonstrating to his Pupils.

There were one hundred and fifty pictures, all polished and
dusted. Some were covered with green curtains which were
not opened in the presence of young ladies.

The artist stood there, stunned, open-mouthed and speech-
less as he recognized half of his own pictures in the gallery.
He was Rubens, Paul Potter, Mieris, Metzu, Gérard Dow!
He, all by himself, was twenty great masters.

'What's wrong? You are turning pale!'

'Fetch a glass of water, Virginie,' exclaimed Mère Vervelle.

The painter button-holed Père Vervelle and took him into
a corner, under the pretext of looking at a Murillo. Spanish
paintings were fashionable at the time.

'Did you buy your pictures from Elias Magus?'

'Yes. They are all originals.'

'Tell me in confidence how much you paid for the ones
that I am going to point out.'

They went round the gallery together. The guests were
amazed at the artist's gravity as, accompanied by his host, he
proceeded to examine the masterpieces.

'Three thousand francs!' said Vervelle in a low voice as they came to the last one. 'But I say it's worth forty thousand francs!'

'Forty thousand francs for a Titian?' the artist replied aloud. 'But that would be a gift.'

'Didn't I tell you I had a hundred thousand crowns' worth of pictures?' exclaimed Vervelle.

'I painted all those pictures,' Pierre Grassou whispered to him, 'I sold the whole lot for less than ten thousand francs.'

'If you can prove that,' said the bottle merchant, 'I shall double my daughter's dowry. For, in that case, you are Rubens Rembrandt, Terburg and Titian!'

'And Magus is a clever art dealer!' said the painter who now understood why his pictures were made to look old and the reason for the subjects the dealer had asked for.

Far from losing his admirer's high opinion of him, Monsieur de Fougères (for that's the name the family insisted on giving to Pierre Grassou) rose so much in Monsieur Vervelle's esteem, that the painter charged nothing for the family portraits and naturally gave them as gifts to his father-in-law, his mother-in-law, and his wife.

Today, Pierre Grassou, who doesn't miss a single art exhibition, is considered, in bourgeois society, to be a good portrait painter. He earns about twelve thousand francs a year and ruins about five hundred francs' worth of canvas. His wife's dowry amounted to an income of six thousand francs and he lives with his parents-in-law. The Vervelles and the Grassous, who get on splendidly together, own a carriage and are the happiest people in the world. Pierre Grassou mixes only in bourgeois circles where he is considered one of the greatest artists of the period. From the Barrière du Trône to the Rue du Temple no family portrait is painted by anyone other than this great artist, and at a fee of at least five hundred francs. The bourgeois' compelling argument for using this painter runs as follows: 'Say what you like, he gives his lawyer twenty thousand francs a year to invest for him!' As Grassou gave a good account of himself in the riots of 12 May, he has been made an Officer of the Legion of Honour. He is head of a battalion in the National Guard. The Versailles art gallery could not but commission a battle-scene from so excellent a citizen; he went about everywhere in Paris so that he could meet his old friends and say to them in an off-hand way, 'The King has asked me to paint a battle-scene!'

Madame de Fougères worships her husband to whom she has given two children. Yet this painter, who is a good father and a good husband, cannot rid himself of one distressing thought; the artists make fun of him, his name is a term of contempt in the studios, the journals ignore his works. But he goes on working, he is a candidate for the Academy and he will be elected. And then (a method of getting his own back which swells his heart with joy!) he buys pictures from famous painters when they are short of money and he replaces the rubbish of the Ville d'Avray gallery with real masterpieces which he did not paint.

There are more irritating and ill-natured mediocrities than Pierre Grassou. Moreover, he does good deeds without saying a word about them and is always ready to oblige.

1840